"Magical, grotesque, funny, tragic, a story and a world that leads you on, ever further and deeper. A masterpiece of the cohabiting familiar and bizarre."
Adrian Tchaikovsky, author of *Children of Time*

"Marvellous stuff: a great flowing river of a novel, endlessly inventive, gorgeously written, pungent and haunting and gripping. This is the kind of world that, in all its strangeness, feels very real: you inhabit it rather than read about it. The dragon Faynr: chef's kiss! Can't wait for the next volume."
Adam Roberts, BSFA award-winning author of *Jack Glass*

"Beard and Noon have created a fascinating place where bits of technology, like a crystal-powered radio, exist alongside supernatural elements. Fans of Scott Lynch's Gentleman Bastard books will love the skullduggery and potential treachery of this world as well as Cady's bravado."
Booklist

"It's a beautiful, strange, and occasionally nightmarish adventure story given a sense of vitality, urgency, and vast history by its authors."
Ancillary Review of Books

"Perfectly balanced, funny, charming, and dark; an unforgettable trip downriver... Each chapter is punchy and compelling, sometimes dropping you unexpectedly into hilarious scenes with no prior warning. Like everything else in this novel, it is carefully crafted for your consumption."
Karl Forshaw, SFF Insiders

Jeff Noon & Steve Beard

LUDLUDA

A SECOND CHRONICLE OF LUDWICH

ANGRY ROBOT

ANGRY ROBOT
An imprint of Watkins Media Ltd

Unit 11, Shepperton House
89-93 Shepperton Road
London N1 3DF
UK

angryrobotbooks.com
twitter.com/angryrobotbooks
A final blossoming

An Angry Robot paperback original, 2024

Edited by Simon Spanton Walker
Cover by Ian McQue and Alice Claire Coleman
Set in Meridien

ISBN 978 1 91599 831 6
Ebook ISBN 978 1 91599 832 3

Printed and bound in the United Kingdom by CPI Group (UK) Ltd, Croydon CR0 4YY.

9 8 7 6 5 4 3 2 1

PART ONE
Chasing The Beetle

Card No. 12. Medlock Hospital. Located on an island in the River Nysis, this grand sanatorium was built to confine the Faynr-afflicted of the Alkhym nobility, those princelings and maiden-waifs most likely to stir up trouble in the realm. Since then it has opened its doors to house the capering flower-hatted harlequins of the Wodwo and the mad prophets of the Azeel. Its most notorious occupant is Thrawl Zum, who tried to set fire to the House of Witan during the Frenzy, and now writes out the Oath of Fealty countless times each day and night.

Monocle Cigarette Cards – The Haunted River

First Blood

Cady Meade was squatting on a tin bucket, trying her best to squeeze out a shit. She grunted, held her breath, clenched, relaxed, clenched again, gasped, banged her fist against a bulkhead and cried out in pain and despair. All she managed was a thin squirt of greenish brown gloop, Lud knows what it was: didn't even smell bad, which was disappointing, because Cady was the kind of person who liked to revel in her own functions. She plopped back down onto the bucket and contemplated the bowel movements of the dragon Haakenur, imagining the great piles of excrement that must have littered the plains of Kethra in the Age of the Giant Lizards. But even such thoughts failed to get her moving. She was bunged up, good and proper. One by one her fingers searched out the seven buds that sprouted on her flesh, hard kernels of tightly folded petals – on her forearms, her thigh, her stomach, her shoulder. One of them, on the back of her left hand, was dead, the petals turned to dust. This saddened her greatly, for she thought of the buds as her babies in waiting.

She stood up and wiped her bottom with the front page of the *Ludwich Telegram*, two years old: *ARMY IN FINAL PUSH AT*

YONA HEIGHTS. Pulling up her bell-bottoms she felt a sudden fainting fit come upon her, and she swayed as the boat swayed, as the river moved on the tide, and her stomach gurgled. Oh Lud! Not again. She threw up, managing to get half of it in the bucket. The rest she wiped up with the sports section. Bollocking arseholes! How long was this going to go on for?

The hold was dark and dank and foggy with various aromas and gases. Shuffling aftwards she reached the large glass aquarium that housed the rare and strange creature known as Mr Carmichael. Some said he was older than Cady herself, which was very, very old indeed. One legend had him swimming around in the pools of ancient time. Certainly, he looked like a living fossil, with his scaly skin and his long thin body encrusted from head to tail with many fragments of crystal, which gave his species its commonly known name: the crystalback. Fully uncoiled he would reach at least six feet in length, an overgrown electric eel, perhaps, crossed with an axolotl and a boa constrictor, oh yes, and a television receiver. A single tap on the glass was enough; Mr Carmichael switched himself on in a burst of noise and colour. Cady was hoping for another message from Lord Pettifer, but instead the tank's water quivered with images drawn from local news broadcasts and the live entertainment circuits: footage of the preparations for the Hesting Festival, quips from the wireless comedy show *Much Wittering in the Murk*, snippets from private telephone calls – *Ooh, Ethel, you should have heard him!* – all mixed in with the Prime Minister's address to the nation, and even glimpses of the stage shows of Tolley Hoo – wherever a crystal sent out a message in the city, Mr Carmichael picked it up and amplified it, and swam about within it, his own crystals sparkling and crackling as they received the incoming signals.

Cady sat down on a three-legged stool and watched the display idly. The sound of the boat's propeller lulled her as it always did, especially at this slow steady speed, until her whole body was in rhythm with the vessel. And she started to drift away. Only the six remaining buds remained as areas of irritation, and once noticed, they started to itch like glory. Lud damn you! Unfurl your colours, why don't you, blossom forth and maybe attract a nice butterfly or two. *I have to get myself pollinated, and soon!* But such thoughts only made her more frustrated. She stood up and balanced herself on the stool somewhat precariously and threw a handful of dried shrimp into the tank. Mr Carmichael snapped them up. Seen from above, the surface of the water appeared as a ruffled screen of different colours, shapes, images. The sounds of a ruby-voiced newscaster rose from the water: *The festival is all set to start, in little more than an hour…* Electric flashes arced across from one side of the tank to the other. Cady was fascinated. Her buds seemed to be moving under their hard calyxes, perhaps stirred by the proximity of the electrical charge. Before she even knew what she was doing, her hands, both of them, had entered the water, down to the elbows. Yes, that was good! Maybe what she needed was a shock to the system to get herself flowering, like a spark plug firing up a motor vehicle's engine. Mr Carmichael's body writhed around her forearms, his sleek flesh giving way to the sharp crystals on his back, each sensation alternating, rough and smooth. The tank's imagery played around her fingers. She was dipping her hands into the very fabric of the city, grabbing the mystical telephone wires and the radio signals and the television waves and feeding off them. The itchiness had vanished in the haze of the messages. No more pain, no more queasiness, no more effing bloody palpitations of the never-you-minds!

Arcadia Watchwoman Meade was far too old to be brooding for offspring. So it was a lovely feeling, to be free of all needs, comforted by the flow of sounds and pictures that Mr Carmichael shared with her. But her mood changed as the water turned black, jet black, and all the projected pictures vanished, and the voices fell silent. Cady was standing on tippy-toes on the rickety stool. She reached down further into the filthy water, seeking comfort. The water turned thick and treacly and it clutched at her arms, perhaps to pull her under. Always one to follow an impulse, Cady bent over at the waist and lowered her head into the liquid, keeping her eyes open, even as the weeds and bits of shrimp got into them. She'd been given the crystalback as a present, what was it now, seven, eight years ago, yes, before the war, certainly. But this was the first time she'd looked into the water, *really* looked, face submerged. Mr Carmichael lay at the bottom of the tank. His crystallised skin shone a darker blue than was normal, and the signals he gave off slowly formed themselves into the head and face of Haakenur, the great dragon of legend. The beast's maw opened and the curved fangs glittered darkly. A breath of fire shot forward, boiling the water.

In her panic Cady slipped backwards, losing her footing on the stool. She fell on the curved decking of the hold with a bump, wetting the arse of her tartan trousers in the bilge water. She yelped and cursed to high heaven, and wiped her face with a sleeve. But the glass tank had returned to normal, the water coloured only by the scenes of Ludwich, and the various programmes on offer. The crystalback swam about placidly, as though nothing untoward had happened. But how on earth had such a vision been teletransported, and from where? Perhaps a crystal-show history drama, or a children's programme? Mr Carmichael must have chosen it for her, on purpose. But why? Cady squeezed water out of her sailor's pigtail, which reached halfway down her back. She blew sludgy black snot from her nostrils, each in turn, and banged on her ears to dislodge any water beetles. Satisfied that all was well, she made her way up top, climbing through the hatch and stepping out onto the foredeck of the *Juniper*.

Thrawl Lek was standing at the helm. Despite his various dents, scratches and breakages, he was still operational, expertly steering the boat along the River Nysis, negotiating other vessels as they emerged from the rolling banks of ghost fog. Like all of his make and model, Lek was a quick and sure pupil; once learned, nothing was lost. Despite this, Cady wondered how much life he had left in him.

The air was thick and murky, the colour of a day-old wound, cloying to the lungs. There was a stench about it of rotting fish and vinegar and sodden fruit. The going was slow; weeds grabbed at the propeller blades. Blood vapours coloured the clouds of fog. But already the mechanical pumps could be heard from up ahead. The atmosphere was changing. Cady was excited to see the city in its new guise. It seemed that already she could breathe a little easier. Speckles of bright glittering liquid were hitting the mist banks from left and right, each droplet exploding into colour on contact – red, yellow, sapphire blue. The *Juniper*'s prow parted the ghost's body, creating a rippling effect that shook along the boat's wake. The final curtain of mist pulled back and the great vistas of the river and the city were clearly seen.

Cady's green heart sang with the joy of it. She was back! Returned to the city of her first seeding, her growth in the earth, her plucking, and – who knows? – her final blossoming.

Ludwich, my Ludwich! Her body responded with a sudden urge to leap over the side and partake of the waters. Of course, she refused herself. This was no Alkhym spa, no fountain spring; the water was scummy, scabbed with litter and patches of oil, inhabited by mutated rats, blunt-headed fish, a dead dog or two. Signs of Faynr's sickness still lay upon the surface, most obviously in the coagulated crusts of brown sludge-muck that bubbled and popped with noxious gases. But the air above was cleaner, at least. The reason for this healing was soon apparent, in the form of two heavy-duty firefighting boats, one to port, the other towards the starboard bank. Cady had seen such vessels hard at work many times during the war, doing their best to tackle the fires that raged along the docklands, and around the financial district, after an Enakor bombing raid. But the boats had now been repurposed, no longer used to fight the flames, but to push back the effects of Faynr's sickness, or at least to dilute the effect; Cady had no idea how it worked. The hosepipes fixed to the decks swung back and forth under the control of the purification workers, each sweep leaving the ghost a little brighter looking, and clearer. Of course they were fighting the symptoms, not the cause of the sickness. But Cady was glad of the work done. Her leaving of Ludwich eighteen months ago was in large part caused by the smothering choking darkness of the Faynr Fog, so it was lovely indeed to view the churches, warehouses, streets and bridges in their former glory. She breathed in deeply, sticking out her tongue to taste the spindrift. Oh, it was glorious! She danced a hornpipe, her boot heels click-clacking on the deck.

Other purifiers were seen on the riversides, single operatives with canisters strapped to their backs, faces hidden behind protective masks. They walked the banks, down where the water met the pebbles and sand, often wading into the river to better go about their task. There were Nebulim among them, and Ephreme, and Azeels, and Wodwo, young and old. It was a dirty but necessary job; a joint effort from all the various tribes and religions.

"Oi, yah, eh, yaaar!"

The shouts came from the cabin's roof. Brin Halsegger was up there, in her favourite position behind the boat's spotlight. The kid was dancing in celebration, just like Cady but more briskly, swinging her arms high and low like some demented bat. Her legs skipped and kicked, and she spun around on one foot to face the same way as when she set off, and each spin ended in a shout of joy: "Ya, yahoo!" It was a big day for the girl. The last Friday in May was a bank holiday, the start of the Hesting, a rite of passage that all Alkhym children had to undergo in their tenth year.

Cady's eyes narrowed against the sunlight. The girl's figure blurred, disappeared, and then leapt into view again as she jumped down from the roof, landing nimbly on the deck. Cady's heart skipped a beat. "I do wish you wouldn't do that." She'd only known Brin, and her guardian Lek, for three and a bit days now, but yesterday's journey upriver from the estuary had bonded them into a crew. And then Lord Pettifer's warning came back to her, and she shivered. Her hands were jittery, sweat dripped down her neck. She watched as Brin hurried to the prow, where she stood next to the figurehead of the boat, looking ahead at the unfolding river, the rotunda of Saint Lupus, and the crumbling mass of the Fortress. Other boats were joining the Nysis from side canals, wharfs, and tributaries, forming a procession. Whistles blew, carrying greetings and warnings from one vessel to another. Skirls wheeled and hovered above the river's surface, hoping to catch any morsels thrown their way. Purification vessels were moored at various places along the banks. The air sparkled.

A brightly coloured beetle landed on Cady's hand. She brushed it away and felt in the pocket of her smock for her penknife. The vision of Haakenur came back to her, as conjured up by Mr Carmichael. Was it a message? And if so, what might it mean? Cady Meade was the type to be plagued by messages, portents, riddles, and various indecipherable signs. In this case, perhaps the crystalback was telling her not to give up the fight, the ongoing fight to protect the dragon's spirit? If so, she needed to make sure of one thing, and that was little Brin's true purpose in life.

She walked forward and listened; the girl was chattering away happily to Pok Pok, the crystal spirit who lived inside the figurehead, talking of her excitement at the upcoming festival, and how at the very same time she was a little scared of what might happen. Brin wore a smart polka-dotted top and a pair of blue trousers cut high on the ankles, and plimsolls. A pretty picture! She must have kept this outfit clean and folded in her suitcase, just for this special day. Cady saw that she was holding something in her hand, a shiny object. It was a gold coin, the Ludluda coin, as Brin called it, with the head of King Lud on one side, and that of Queen Luda on the other. It had become Brin's special talisman, ever since they had found it on yesterday's travels. But its sparkle irritated Cady. Carefully hiding her actions from Thrawl Lek, she opened the blade of her knife. Without a word of warning she pressed the tip against the nape of the girl's neck just above the right shoulder, and pressed forward until a droplet of blood appeared.

"Ow! What did you do?"

Brin turned in a hurry, a surprised look on her face. She reached round to rub at her shoulder, smearing the blood. And again she asked, "What did you do? Was that you, Mrs Meade?" She could not believe what had happened.

Speaking calmly, indeed coldly, Cady said, "Ah, it's just a little scratch, Brin."

"A scratch?"

"I wanted to see what colour your blood was."

"It's red. Red! See! What else did you expect? You think Alkhyms have blue blood? How ridiculous you are!"

"I wasn't sure. After all, my blood is green."

"Because you're a plant lady. But me... me, I'm just a..." She looked confused.

"Don't you know what you are?"

The girl's mouth opened and closed. She looked to Lek, but obviously decided against calling for his help. Too much pride! The boat's figurehead was making little mewling sounds, as though in speechless sympathy.

"Actually," Cady said, "I think it's time for your first tattoo." She displayed the penknife with its reddened tip. "After all, I was younger than you when I got my first ink. Eight years old, barely out of the soil. They carved a rune in my arm, here, see? It's the Hiza rune, meaning *root* in the first tongue. That from which I sprang, and which will always bind me, no matter how far I travel." Her face hardened. "And I have travelled, believe me. I have travelled so many fuckin' miles, to get to this place, at this time, standing here next to you."

The girl said in a mocking tone, "Must you swear, Mrs Meade?"

Cady merely smiled at this remark. "So then, what shall we decorate you with, eh?" She came to the crux of the matter.

"Shall we depict Faynr, the dragon's purest spirit? Or rather, shall we scratch deep a portrait of Gogmagog, the evil twin, the Night Serpent?"

Brin seemed bolder now. "Neither of them. Leave me alone."

"Oh, but you must choose, little girl. Good, or bad?"

The two of them stared at each other a while longer. Defiance came back to Brin's eyes.

The experiment was over.

Cady licked the blood off the blade, hoping for a deeper reading. Nothing, no clue; the girl's true substance remained unknown. She walked to the port beam, where she stood in contemplation. Colourful bunting fluttered from the rails of a large river cruiser. The decks were crowded with sightseers, as were the bankside pathways. Sunlight flashed across the water. How would this day end? A first cut had been made, that was all. First blood. But what had she been expecting, truly? For smoke to pour out of the girl's wound? Stupid! She looked at the little knife in her hand. It was a pitiful weapon. Would the blade be long enough, sharp enough? Hardly. Maybe her long thorny fingers would do the deed, pricking and closing around the young girl's throat until the final breaths were squeezed out. Or perhaps best to throw her overboard and follow her down to the river's bed, and hold her there? Yes, let the sacred waters do the work, that would be appropriate. But no matter the method, Cady would do the job, if necessary, if the warnings were correct, and young Brin Halsegger needed to die.

The duties of a watchwoman were often painful.

The Hesting Pools

The *Juniper* was a hardy little steam launch with more than five decades of service on the river, in her heyday ferrying a dozen passengers from Ludwich to the sea, and then making the return journey the next day, in all kinds of weather. But lately she had been demoted, acting as a ferryboat across the sea estuary. So this was her first journey into the city in more than a year and a half. She was nimble and sharp enough to easily nudge her way between the larger, sturdier vessels that now crowded the waters. The many smaller boats converged together, often so close to each other they made a kind of floating, if somewhat fragile, village. Cady chatted with captains and sailor men and riverwomen. A number of them knew her from her former days, and were all surprised to see her again in Ludwich.

A first one shouted to her, "I thought you'd retired, Cady, you old bird."

"Oh I have, I have."

Another: "I heard you were the May Queen of Pinchbeck Isle."

"Ha ha. Not quite that."

And a third, with a snarl in his voice: "A lighterman told stories of your drunken self, pissing on the prom at Anglestume, of all places. Is that true?"

"Probably, yes, very likely."

One more: "Cady, I heard you were married. To a downed Enakor pilot, no less."

"Never! Go and get stuffed."

Back and forth one after another the tales were told and accepted or refuted. Spirits were high and rowdy as the mass of boats approached the Beating Heart of Faynr. Cady took over from Lek at the helm. Her hands were sure and steady on the wheel as the air coagulated into thick mucus-like strands and globules of red and blue material, very like the kind of stuff village mediums spat out at their seances: ectoplasm. It pressed against Cady's face with a cold clammy touch and left her hair frizzled and her mouth dry and her eyes full of tears. Every sight was a remembrance. By now the *Juniper* was decked out in ghost blood stern to prow, some parts forming into bubbles, others into long snakelike veins and arteries that whipped to and fro across the deck and cabin. The blood of Faynr flowed to its own mysterious tides. Xilliths darted around the masts and radio aerials of the collected vessels as the boat pressed forward. The massive heart of the ghost pulsed and throbbed to a slow regular beat, loud enough now to be heard. It sounded inside Cady's skull, and in her chest.

The long arching span of Killigrew Bridge housed the very centre of the heart's presence. It truly was a magnificent sight. In a long-ago lifetime Cady had perused Dr John Dee's first sketches and formulae: "A Proposal for a National Circulatory System". Then, in a later life she had witnessed the first foundations of the apparatus being built on each side of the river, and then the giant cantilevered gantries and pillars. Within each of Cady's resurrections more and more devices and mechanisms were added, under one monarch's rule, then another, overseen by a series of engineers down the years, the decades, the centuries. The project never ended! Now it vaulted the river like a steel colossus, a wonder of the world. Beneath the latticework curve sat the throbbing heart of the ghost dragon.

Blood flowed in, blood flowed out, in a never-ending cycle.

Here, Faynr was at her strongest. Her body pulsed with vibrant life, too much life in fact. And this overabundance of spectral material blessed the country. Suction tubes gathered portions of the enriched material, transporting it along iron pipes to bankside pumping stations, to be distributed from there to specially built canals and culverts – wherever water flowed, there flowed Faynr, in her ever-diminishing array, until at the limits of her power she drifted away into the air. And so the National Veins went about their task, bringing energy to the cities and towns of Kethra. The land was nourished.

The *Juniper* entered the skin of the organ, alongside the other vessels; it was likened by poets through the ages to entering a cloud of desire, to meeting with a god's inner fire, to dreaming as the city dreams, to falling in love, to floating along on the winged breaths of Queen Lud herself, the one true daughter of the dragon. Oh, the poets went mad to outdo each other! Cady didn't know much about any of that, but my Lud, it felt grand to be enveloped by the veins and arteries of Faynr once more, so warm, so tender in the touch, so shivery in the loins.

The air was blue and red completely, the plasma tubes knotted about each other, the globules of blood bouncing gently against the skin and hair, painting the deck and cabin in their colours as the boat pushed gently forward. The city, seen through this airy gauze, was blue and red also. Lek stood to attention on the foredeck like a butler welcoming a very special guest to the house, while Brin swayed at the prow, one hand on Pok Pok's shoulder, the other raised high. Xilliths capered about, a great profusion of them, crackling and sparking, some of them gathering around the girl's head like a halo. Cady saw that the blood of the ghost was drawn to the tiny cut high on the girl's neck, the cut Cady herself had made: the two bloods mixing together, perhaps? Surely, this had to mean that Faynr welcomed the girl. Surely to goodness! One of the larger bubbles of blood entered Cady's chest, seeping through the skin like a stage-effect in a crystal horror-show. She pictured it travelling the fibres and vines of her body, seeking out the six remaining buds, stimulating them, tickling them.

But she remained closed up, cut off from blossoming.

Damn it!

Now the *Juniper* was nearing the very centre of the heart, where the veins were thickest and most entangled. Cady opened the throttle to give the screw some extra power. The continual *drum drum drum* of the heartbeat was overwhelming.

On occasions such as Hesting Friday, or Crown the Fool Day, or Mother in the Green Root Tuesday, the heart enacted a magical effect upon people who entered its central domain. To feel this effect was to be blessed by Faynr, and by the spirit of Queen Luda. The first sign was the raucous singing from the next vessel along, a family barge – husband, wife, and teenage son, all carolling praises to Haakenur. On another boat the skipper was prancing about in the most ridiculous fashion. Everywhere Cady looked, crewmen and passengers fell into sudden passionate embraces. One young couple were already hard at it on the upper deck of a pleasure cruiser. Nobody cared. All petty rules were banished. A pistol shot startled the skirls who flitted amid the veins; hopefully the shot went into the air, and not into the flesh of a fellow. Such things happened! A rugged bargeman ran half-naked along the deck of a lighter, calling for his dear dead mother. Joyous shouts, angry cries, songs of love and lust, all rang out. Tears were shed, faces were punched, revellers rattled their rattles, and the haphazard flag of mischief was raised high. Even Lek was dancing, after a fashion, jittering like a wind-up doll.

Cady had immersed herself in Faynr's love many the time, more often than any person alive. She even remembered the occasion of the Great Royal Orgy, and her own part in it. So rather than give in to her base feelings, she kept her nerve, raising her arms to expose the buds fully, hoping against hope. Her entire body yearned for release. Flower me! Flower me! The blood of the dragon pressed at her face, painting her red and blue in sticky streaks that mixed on her cheeks and chin and brow. Her eyes clouded over and she could hear Gogmagog in the empurpled mist, calling to her, mocking her with his voice of smoky whisperings.

You'll never catch me, Cady.
You'll never trap me, not ever again.
I will gain entrance to the city.
I will poison you, and all your friends and lovers.
I will feed off you.

Even here, you bastard! Even here in the midst of paradise?
No! Faynr's heart was meant to bring out the joy in people,
not the cares and woe. The voice was her own mind at
play, tormenting her. Bad blood! In a half-crazed attempt
to escape her fears she spun the wheel hard over, ramming
into the neighbouring barge. Other boats were caught in a
domino effect and before long the river was a chaos of traffic
as vessels fought to regain control. Cady wrenched the
wheel back, only to scrape against a schooner on the port
beam; the *Juniper* came off the worse from that collision,
losing a fender. One more wound for the collection.
Whistles and klaxons blared out. In return Cady laughed
wildly, she couldn't help herself. Gogmagog had vanished.
Faynr was inside her. Through the blood vision she saw Mr
Lek running from beam to beam, boathook in hand, using
it to push other boats away. Pok Pok howled and screeched
and yelped. A riot of noise enveloped everything. The
giant pistons of the pumping stations added a bass hum to
the rough melodious songs of the navvies working on the
girders of the bridge. And the blood of the ghost dragon
dripped down and burbled and bubbled about and floated
along, surging through skin and wood and metal and sail
canvas alike, passing through flags and ensigns, through
cargo holds and cabins and poop decks and cockpits. The
heart's beating was at its loudest. People were still singing
and shouting, but the drumming beat ruled, forcing all into
one rhythm. The boats found their own good channels,
guided by this same force, and the raggle-taggle fleet made
its way forward.

The *Juniper* sailed under the bridge's span. Cady held
the spokes of the wheel lightly. Her eyes were on Brin,
who stood at the prow as before, perfectly still, completely

unaffected by the antic behaviour all around her. She was the still point in the bedlam. And she was coated in ghost blood from head to foot like a cape. Cady stared and stared at her, piercing the red and blue strands of vapour with her sight, willing a sign to appear: to prove the girl was on the side of good.

And then Brin turned round.

It was a deliberate and very slow movement.

Lek lowered the boathook. He stepped forward a little, and then hesitated.

Brin's eyes were two circles of stark white in a red mask. She smiled.

There was a cruelty to it, Cady was sure. It unnerved her.

And then the *Juniper* left the heavy drag of the dragon's heart. The blood mist pulled away from the boat in a sweeping gesture, each bubble and strand breaking, each threadlike web of veins returning to the heart's core, until the boat was in clear waters again, the other craft alongside her. And so they passed out of the shadow of the bridge. Everyone looked aghast at their own behaviour and were highly embarrassed, as they always were, freed of the heart's influence. Apologies were made, trousers pulled up, skirts rearranged, hair combed into place. Brin was cleansed of the blood. The girl was still smiling, but nicely now, her manner all sweetness and light. Lek went to her, and she allowed herself to be comforted. Cady thought it all an act; legend claimed that Faynr's heart revealed the truth – *in cardio veritas*. But Cady needed proof, and not from her own fears and suppositions, and not from hallucinations brought on by the ghost's bloody release. No. She still had a difficult decision to make.

One good thing, though: the revelry had loosened her bowels. She gave the helm to Lek and rushed down into the hold, where she relieved herself mightily into the bucket. Ah, bliss. Another of those pesky semaphore beetles was crawling across the hull towards her. These brightly coloured insects had plagued her all morning, from the moment she woke up in her sister Nabs' house. She was tempted to squash this one under her heel just for the sake of it. Or maybe catch it and feed it to Mr Carmichael. But she remained seated, taking out her knife to dig scum from under her nails, and thinking all the time of the girl. Lud's bollocks! Is this my life from now on, she thought, to never make up my mind? To sit complacently within my own stench; or else to act, to leap forth, to dance, to kiss, to kill!

Noises from above roused her from the spell. Lek's growl of concern, Brin's laughter, another man's voice. Cady didn't even have time to move from her seat when a masked head appeared at the hatchway, staring down at her from behind a pair of black goggles.

"What the bleeding heckin' fuck!" She struggled to pull up her bloomers.

The young man laughed and then vanished from sight. Cady was up after him as fast as she could, her bell-bottoms nearer her knees than her hips.

"Blimey, Mrs, you'll give the skirls a fright, you will."

The youth had removed his mask and goggles. He was a purification operative, a mere lanky strip of a lad, an Ephreme with a broad East Ludwich accent. He wore a leather harness and a pair of metal canisters on his back, connected by a rubber pipe to the nozzle he held at the ready. His hair was spiked up more from dirt and grease than any kind of style. There was a crooked smile on his lips. Cady made to answer him back, but struggled to hitch up her trousers.

"You need a hand, madam?"

"No, I do not! And get that nozzle out of my face!"

"The nozzle goes where the nozzle must, that's our motto. No exceptions. Very strict they are, down the council, aye, we have to make sure every vessel is spick and span, every last inch."

In demonstration he raised the hose and squirted Cady, all over, head to foot.

This brought more giggles from Brin, a guffaw from Lek, and a hacking cough from Cady.

"Give me that! Give it to me–"

"Hey, hey, municipal property, this is. Hands off."

Cady grunted. She wiped her face with a sleeve, and licked her lips. "What's in that stuff, it tastes… it tastes sweet… like, like honey."

"That'll be the honey in it."

"The what?"

"The honey, like you said. And straight from the royal hives, I kid you not, by order of King Herald himself. No messing."

Lek shook his head. "I can't believe that, not for a second."

"It's true, I tell you." The boy studied the Thrawl. "Crikey. They don't make your kind these days. You should be in Ludwich Museum, on show for all to see. Here, he's not going to blow up on me, is he? Or attack me? Only, the council ain't paying me danger money."

Lek frowned at this, his expression flickering into place.

Brin explained, "Mr Lek is safe."

The young purifier rapped on the Thrawl's chest. "That's a nice bit of metal you've got there. I know a geezer, friend of mine, he runs a scrap-metal merchants, down Wickerchurch way, lovely chap, he could get a nice price for someone of your calibre."

"I am not for sale."

"Oh no, of course not, I'm just saying like, very nice price. Now, where was I? Oh yes, the ingredients of the purification fluid. Well, I shouldn't be telling you this, it being a secret recipe and all, but seeing as you're all so nice and welcoming, I can give a hint or two." By now they were all looking at the youth. He had them entranced. "You'll have heard of the syqod creature?"

"I have!" Brin offered. "We wore them as masks, yesterday, on the river."

"On the river, eh? East from here?"

"Far east."

"A tough journey, was it?"

"Oh yes. We started out from Anglestu–"

Cady grabbed Brin. "He doesn't need to know all of our story."

"Oh, I can see you've come a long way. Anglestume, eh? I went there once, when I was a nipper. Day trip. They do a lovely stick of rock."

He gave the boat an extended spray from his canister, covering the cabin walls inside and out, and then Lek and Brin, making them glisten.

"Course, this is only a temporary job for me, on account of the festival. Extra staff required. Those Alkhym toffs like Faynr to be nice and tidy for their little darlings." He smiled at Brin. "I have dreams beyond this, believe me." Then he walked through the cabin to the afterdeck.

Cady and the girl followed, leaving Lek at the wheel. The nozzle went about its work.

"What were you saying," Brin asked him, "about syqods?"

"Well, they're well known for their abilities at sieving out all the nasties from the dragon's ghost, her being sick and suffering as she is, poor beastie."

Brin nodded eagerly.

"So they catch a whole big batch of the little squirmers, and grind them down into a kind of mush, syqod soup we call it."

"Urgh!"

"Needs must, princess. And that's added to the mix. That will be the squidy smell beneath the honey. And then… Hang on, missed a bit. There we go. Job done." He turned off the hose. "Mavis!" Now he was yelling over the side of the *Juniper* at another vessel, a small and much battered motor cruiser, captained by a Wodwo woman. "Mavis, we've got a bit of a problem here. I'll need to do a respray. Catch you upriver, when I can." He waved as the cruiser jetted away. "Hey oh, that's got rid of her."

"How long does it last for, this spraying malarkey?" Cady asked.

"A good two hours. Three if you're lucky. Then the sickness creeps back, taking over your boat again. But listen, I can give you a double spray, if you like. Cash in hand, special offer just for you."

Cady refused this. "Not effin' likely, I know your sort."

The purifier shrugged. He unwound himself from his harness and hosepipe contraption and lowered the metal canisters off his back. Then he sat down on the bench and gave them a big smile. The dragon ensign fluttered in the breeze above his head. "Oh that's better. Plays merry havoc with my wings something terrible, it does, lugging that thing around all the day long." He shifted in his seat to show off the two stunted wings that popped out through a pair of vents in his bomber jacket. They were rather lacking in feathers. "Look at them." He fluttered them ineffectually. "No use to man nor pigeon."

Brin wanted to know everything: "Honey, syqod soup. What else?"

"Well. Let's see now."

Cady jumped in. "He's making it up, Brin."

The youth ignored her, keeping his attention on the girl. "You'll have heard of Holiph?"

"Of course. It's one of the Five Great Trees."

"There you go. Spot on. There are Five Great Trees of Kethra. Holiph Oak, Catholo, Yallax of the Shadow Woods, and then there's Fotheringall, that one's easy, and what's the last one, I can never remember it…"

Brin shook her head. Cady felt the lad knew the answer all along; he was just playing Brin for all he could get. So she was about to answer herself, when he beat her to it:

"Well knock me down with Haakenur's tail. Of course! Number five is the Bitterbark. How could I forget? Four centuries growing, out in Pennydrop Park."

"But what's all this got to do with your canisters?"

"Well that's what I'm saying, see, princess, we takes the holy sap from the great tree Holiph, and we… When I say *we*, mind, I mean the council, or the makers, the brewers. Anyways, they take this sap and add that to the mix. Oh it's all worked out, scientific like. Lord Olan Pettifer himself came up with the recipe."

Brin's eyes lit up. "You know Lord Pettifer?" Cady put her hands on the girl's shoulders, and squeezed tightly: *Don't say too much, girlie.*

"Not personally, no," the purifier went on. "But he's a clever gentleman, why, it's common knowledge. Helped us in the war with lots of snazzy gadgets and codebreaking, and the like. You know, I reckon I'll be a member of parliament one day, at the very least. Look at that now, what a sight, eh?"

They were passing the House of Witan, with its clock tower and its balustrades and pinnacles and crenelations and flying buttresses. Many of the surrounding offices, churches and minor palaces had taken bomb damage and were still in disrepair: the missing pieces of the Ludwich puzzle. But the House and the tower stood untouched.

The Old Bell of Bleary rang out twelve deep tolls that made the surface of the river vibrate. Cady could feel it through the *Juniper*'s hull.

Brin started to hop about. "It's noon, already! The festival has started, Mrs Meade."

"Don't worry, we'll get you there."

The youth took the girl's hands in his. "Ah, there's plenty of time yet, princess. Three whole days they have of it, the Alkhym folk, dancing, imbibing, carousing something rotten, worse than a Witherhithe pub on a Saturday night." He banged his heel on the deck and looked at Cady. "Nice little boat you've got here. She's taken a beating, though, from the looks of it."

"She'll survive."

"What is she, fifteen foot?"

"Sixteen, prow to stern."

"Six across?"

"And a half, if you don't mind."

"Shallow draft? Of course she is. Nipping about nice and easy, just like me, eh, slipping and sliding, doing what I may, when I may, making my way in the world."

"You know boats, do you?"

"My granddaddy, bless him, he ran a similar vessel, a river taxi."

"Is that right?"

"That is right, me old dear. I helped him, as a boy."

"Well, you're still a boy."

"Fifteen, I am, and already skilful. I know my signals, I know my knots, I know engines."

But Cady was suspicious. "What was your granddaddy's name?"

There was no hesitation. "Jebediah, same as me. I was named after him. But people call me Jeb, and you is people, ain't you?"

"We is people, we *is* people." Brin loved this little phrase. "We is people!"

"Jebediah Yeomanson."

"Never heard of him," Caddy said. "And I've been up and down the Nysis more times than anyone."

"Well maybe that's because you did the run down to the sea and back."

"What if I did?"

"Old Granddaddy Jeb sailed the westward river. Out from Ludwich to all those little ditsy towns where the well-to-do used to live, before the Fret took over that part of the world."

"That's not proper sailing, fresh water, no tide, all those fancy marinas, and the blasted canoes getting under your bows every minute. And neither mind the bowels of the ghost."

"Well there's no canoes there now, that's for sure. Could you imagine?" Jeb laughed. He nodded to Brin. "Now see, I can't help surmising that you're on your way to the Hesting. It's your year, is it? What's your name?"

"Brin. Yes, I'm ten now."

"Smashing. Now here's the thing, see, Brin. When you get up near the hesting pools, there's going to be a lot of river traffic, and all the official mooring places and docks will be filled up, you see what I'm saying?"

Brin nodded, a worried look on her face.

The youth carried straight on: "But it just so happens I know a chap, I do, he works a little backwater wharf, tucked away nice and secret, for those in the know. One of whom, of *whom*, I say, is none other than your very own, Jeb Yeomanson, true-hearted Ephreme, and weekend purifier of some renown." He stood up to make a bow at the waist. "For a special price I can get you moored up nice and snug, what do you say?"

Brin clapped with delight. "Please, Mrs Meade. Please!"

Cady was taken aback, both by Jeb's personality, and more so by the girl's complete reversal: the side of her uncovered by the passage through Faynr's Heart had vanished clean away. But which was the truth, which the mask?

Either way, the deal was done. Thrawl Lek paid Jeb Yeomanson a small fee and they sailed on, along the Nysis, past the Witan, past the Gallows, the Reckoning Hall, past the Nun's Lodge and the Garden of Mirrors, past the Blood Exchange and the broken spire of St Bartholme in the Mire and the remains of the Oaken Palace at Kingsmead. Every mile or so a fire-boat reinforced the purification process. The bankside walkways were packed with crowds of people. The river police were out in force. Officials stood on the foredecks of boats, using megaphones and hand signals and flags to channel oncoming vessels into side harbours and wharfs, hoping to ease the logjam. But Jeb had spoken truly, all of the places were taken; boats were banging and clattering into each other whichever way they turned. He guided them further on until he pointed to a thick curtain of vines hanging down the bankside wall. The prow of the boat parted the vines, entering a tunnel. It was a narrow unlit passage. Even at dead slow ahead the smoke from the boat's funnel proved a nuisance. Cady held the wheel steady as Lek used the boathook on each side, as needed, to nudge the *Juniper* away from the walls. The spotlight, under Brin's control, passed slowly over the water. Jeb stood at the prow, his mask on his face for protection from the smoke. He put up a hand and made a gesture to starboard. The tunnel spilt in two at this point. They followed the purifier's direction into a wider channel, where the smoke could escape through a series of flues. The water was brown and dirty, alive with insects, littered with tin cans and bottles. Viscous fluids came sloshing from inlet ducts on the walls. Faynr's body turned murky as she squeezed a blue-black tendril through the tunnel, forever clinging to her chosen medium, the River Nysis.

Lek came up to Cady at the helm. He said, "I believe we've entered a sewage system."

"What's wrong? I didn't think you had a sense of smell?"

"Actually, I–"

"Me, I quite like the stench." In demonstration, she took a great sniff of the rancid air. "Cleans out your passages. Mind you, we should keep an eye out for Gogmagog. You know how he loves to wallow in the shit."

Jeb Yeomanson had taken over boathook duties. Lek studied him for a moment. "I'm not sure about the lad. He might be a spy."

"A what?"

"He might lead us straight into Pettifer's arms."

"Ah, I know Jeb's kind. He's a one-and-sixer, nothing more."

Lek nodded. *"One-and-Sixer. Noun. Wodwo slang. A taker of risks, especially for their own ends. A scheming opportunist.* Is that meant to make me feel better?"

"Did you just look that up?"

"I retrieved it, if that's what you mean?"

"From where?"

"From the dictionary in my library, in the Crystal Palace."

"Right. And this... this Crystal Palace, it's inside your head, is it?"

"Yes, of course." He spoke in a matter-of-fact way. "Every Thrawl has a Crystal Palace."

"Fits right in your noggin? Can't be very big, for a palace, like."

A prideful took over his face. "I could walk its corridors for a year and never reach the limits. I did try mapping it once, but I kept getting lost."

Cady smiled at the image. Then she said, "I'm interested in a story Jeb told: that Lord Pettifer invented the purification fluid. Doesn't that mean that Pettifer's on the side of good?"

Lek's *somewhat-taken-aback* expression clicked into place.

Cady knew the look well from the last few days. She explained: "He's trying to heal Faynr. If Pettifer was truly in league with Gogmagog, he'd do the opposite, surely? Let Faynr suffer, and weaken. The weaker Faynr is, the more of a foothold Gogmagog has on our world."

Lek scowled. "I know Pettifer. I know him! I worked with him at Blinnings, I've seen him in action. How he used, and misused Brin's powers. I can't trust him."

Cady nodded. She let it go for now. But her own doubts remained, fighting each other inside her head: Brin is bad, Brin is good, Brin is bad, Brin is good, on and on it went. She had to take a breath. But something in her talk had set Lek going. He looked nervous.

"What's wrong?" she asked.

He spoke in a whisper. "I'm scared, Cady." His hands tightened on the boat's compass. "I'm afraid that when Brin hests, I'll lose her. She'll return to Alkhym society."

Cady was surprised, and she felt for him. "Don't worry. Her family is overseas, remember, in disgrace."

"Someone will take her in. She's too precious to pass by."

"Maybe you could go back with her? Eh? The loyal servant and all that."

"No. The days of the Thrawls are over." He touched the bullet lodged in the side of his skull, damage taken in an earlier battle to protect Brin. "The walls of crystal are crumbling, more and more every day. Sometimes I go to find a book or to look at an image in my Gallery of Expressions, and the item is missing. An empty shelf, a blank frame on the wall. No face to copy. If this carries on, Cady, how will I know how to express myself?" He paused. Then: "How am I supposed to look after Brin, in this state? Tell me."

"Oh, you poor bugger." It was all she could manage.

Lek turned to look at her. During the travails of yesterday's journey he had lost his rubber mask, so that his workings were on view through the translucent resin of his skull. The blue crystal perched at the centre of his head shone dully; around it a small portion of Faynr floated. Working together, crystal and Faynr processed Lek's thoughts. No wonder he was so messed up! His face was scarred and pitted and dented, including one nasty prang that Cady herself had given him with a pint-pot. His left eye socket was twitching. Only a few years before he had been the head of staff at a fancy Alkhym mansion, and personal valet to Lord Halsegger. Cady knew how much he desired control at all times, so this must be extra maddening for him.

Brin shouted down to them. "Listen, Mrs Meade! A train's coming!"

She was right: a trundling noise was heard, getting louder. Cady brought the *Juniper* to a slow as they drew near a huge cylinder of flesh that emerged from the rock-face supported on a grid of wooden beams and iron girders. This was just one of the many tentacles of the burrowing creature known as Psephekarnidraxapor, a vast entity born from the body of Faynr, and made up of hundreds of tubular organs and limbs. He had hidden himself away for a thousand years, until the excavations of the industrial age brought his body into view. The creature was thought to be as large as the city itself, stretching far and wide, and was these days used as a transportation system: the Tubular. The skin of Psephekarnidraxapor was milky white, pulsating, and semi-transparent, so that the hollow interior of each tentacle could be seen. The train was now in sight, a small-gauge pneumatic locomotive pulling a line of carriages. It came to a juddering halt, probably for a *stop* signal up ahead. Cady knew that West Bridal Street station was close by, if her bearings were good. The carriage windows were lit up and travellers' faces could be seen through the creature's skin. A small boy caught Cady's eye and stuck his tongue out at her. She gave him the same in return. Then the train went on its way, gathering speed. The *Juniper* sailed on alone.

Excitement over, Brin danced a few more steps and then fell down prone to the cabin roof, her upper body dangling down into the wheelhouse. A few Xilliths had stayed with her, attached to her fingertips. These crackles of energy were the nerve structure of the dragon's ghost, and she used them now to draw fanciful shapes in the air.

Lek called out, "Get down from there, Miss Brin, you're getting your clothes dirty. Don't you want to look your best?"

The girl laughed at this and then dropped to the deck with an easy grace. She sauntered over to the prow and started to talk to Jeb.

After a moment Cady said to Lek, "Maybe then, after what you've said, it's not such a good idea to have Brin hest." She spoke quietly.

"What? Of course she will. She has to!" His voice sounded like two off-kilter cogs grinding together.

"I'm sure. But what if I told you… that I'd received a message?"

"From whom?"

"Never mind that. But maybe we should wait awhile, that's all."

"No! No, Cady Meade. No. Despite my misgivings, I have come too far, I have struggled for too long. Brin will hest. I will deliver her to her moment of glory."

"You still think she's a child of the dragon's blood?"

"Yes, that's correct. I know what I'm doing."

But Cady could not afford to be hesitant: her role as the city's watchwoman won out. Perhaps she could even use the Thrawl's personal fears? "The thing is, Lek… Listen to me. Look at me! Brin might also be a child of Gogmagog. Have you thought of that? A sprog of the Night Serpent–"

He made a noise, a metallic growl formed deep down in his engine. Cady saw the full horror that dwelled inside his head as a series of tiny explosions of blue and red lights. She felt his skull might break apart at any moment. His eyes were crimson. His mouth moved but no words came forth. A line of rust-coloured liquid dribbled from his lips. And when he did speak it was to utter a twisted version of the Oath of Fealty that all newly made Thrawls had to take before the effigy of their creator, the late Jane Polter.

"I promise… I promise on my faith… on my… that I will… ah… I will always be always always always always be helpful to creatures of flesh and blood… ah! To never cause them *harm*!"

This last word came out as a yelp.

"Oh fuck, you're not going to switch yourself off, are you?"

But this was worse than a shut-down; it was a total malfunction. He shuddered violently. The growl grew louder. Brin heard this and she ran to his side. Lek pushed her calming hands away. He was losing control of his motor systems, his limbs now spasming, his back bending over. Then he shot back upright, and over, hunching down, his eyes flaming with bright red beams that burned two smouldering grooves in the *Juniper*'s decking, reaching almost as far as the figurehead, which made Pok Pok cry out in distress. Lek's voice rose in pitch.

"I promise to look after my charge. I promise to look after and protect the child!"

Cady shouted, "Get him under control, Brin. Come on!"

Some hidden switch was flipped from bad to worse. Lek spun about. He crashed into the helm and the wheel spun in Cady's hands. The boat's port beam scraped against the wall of the tunnel, adding to the noise and mayhem.

Jeb took in Lek's behaviour. "I know a bit about Thrawl mechanics." The young lad was still holding the boathook in his hands.

"You?" Cady screamed at him. "This is no time for—"

"Do something!" Brin cried.

Thwack! The boathook connected with the Thrawl's head, full impact. Lek stumbled into the cabin door, knocking it open. He fell through, landing half across the table. Teacups rattled and dropped to the floor, Cady's prized set of Maguire & Hill river charts were scattered. Brin ran to Lek. Jeb threw the boathook to the deck.

"What's he doing now?" Cady asked, as she brought the boat back into the midstream.

Jeb looked through. "He's doing fine, just fine. I knocked the crackle out of him."

Brin responded, "Thank you, Jeb. Thank you!"

"Jebediah to the rescue, as always."

Lek moaned from where he lay, now taking comfort from Brin's gentle care.

Cady wiped her brow with a rag, leaving oil stains on her face. "I swear, this is a ship of fools, a floating asylum. And myself chief among the inmates!"

Soon after they emerged into the sunlight again, at a wharf in Maidensford Basin. In the main it acted as a loading dock for the nearby Grey Angel Hospital. Porters in flat caps and brown coats were unloading cargos of food and medical supplies from small vessels. An ambulance boat carried patients into a canal system. The hospital's outbuildings loomed over the wharf on three sides; the fourth had been bombed out. It was from the depths of this ruin that the *Juniper* emerged. Jeb spoke with his contact there, the head porter, and following a rather steep payment the *Juniper* was given a mooring place. Cady stepped onto dry land and felt a sense of trepidation; what would this day bring? She noted that Lek had adopted one face and one face only, a cold determined emotionless straight-mouthed frown. *Grit No. 9*, he might have called it, in his catalogue of expressions. He was more machine than man, at this moment. Good, she liked that. Anything to keep him from blowing his top and strewing shards of crystal everywhere.

They joined a throng of people making their way along a lane to the hesting pools. Jeb came along with them. "You're like a barnacle, you are," Cady said to him. "Only, instead of clamping yourself to the bottom of the hull, you're eating at the captain's table!"

"Just want to make sure you get through, that's all, then I'll be gone."

The cries of the street merchants mingled with the general hubbub of excited children and worried parents. *Jellied eels, balloons, lollipops, champion pies! Get them here!* Wodwo urchins crept among the toffs, spinning football rattles and letting off penny bangers. Policemen chased the culprits away. A group of religious fanatics shouted out their warnings: *Faynr is sick for a purpose, good people. We have brought this on ourselves with our sinful ways. Repent, repent! That the dragon's ghost may yet be cured!* These strident voices competed with those of the many cocoon sellers, who chanted from every corner and alcove: *Finest cocoons, special offer, just for today, healthiest specimens!* Despite their boasts, the sellers' carts held only undersized brittle examples: it had been a poor harvest, the worst since the years of the Blight, so long ago. This fact of life served to make the massed attendees more predatory, more anxious. The crowds closed in, jamming the narrow walkways. Lek's presence helped a little; Thrawls were scarce in this part of the city, and were still viewed with a low-lying fear. Many people chose to back away from him, and he took full advantage, pushing Brin into the gaps. Cady was painfully aware of the lack of young men on view, so many killed in action, or injured, blinded, driven mad by the shriek and terror of battle. Even the well-off Alkhym had suffered, having given their older sons to the officer classes. It was all in contrast to the celebrations she remembered from the previous century: the men in their top hats and frock coats, the women in feathered bonnets and ruffled skirts. Now, in the main it was mothers, aunts and sisters who led the children along. This would be the first proper Hesting since the war, last year's festival having been a tawdry affair due to the sickness of Faynr, taking place not in public, but in the private gardens of the Alkhym. But now, with the ghost's purification in process, the populace was rushing towards this great event in a sort of desperate wonder: at last, we are back to normal, we are returned!

Cady didn't believe it for a moment: she knew too much, possessed too many scars.

Lek was keen that Brin hested at the main pool, with the High Priestess in attendance, and the huge spire of All Flowers Abbey towering above. But it became apparent that this was too popular a venue and they were pushed hither and about by the crush of people, all jostling to press their sons and daughters closer to the waters. Jeb swung into action, using his nozzle and canisters almost like a knight's lance.

"Coming through, make way! Municipal business, make way! Infection alert!"

Most people stepped aside for him. He gave a quick purification to any belligerents. And so the party made their way forward, deeper into the crowd. You could smell the sweetened air of the hesting pools by now, the hormones given off by the newly hatched myridi flies.

And then Lek bent close to Cady. "I see him!"

"Who? Pettifer?"

"Yes, he's here. I feared this. He wants to steal Brin back, to further his work."

Cady followed Lek's direction, but could see no sign of Lord Pettifer, only a trio of drunken ageing priests in white-powder masks and sunglasses. They looked comically sinister.

"Where is he?" she asked. "I can't see–"

"Come on. This way, quickly!"

He grabbed Brin by the hand and pulled her back, away from the main pool, forcing a path through the crowds by sheer force. There was no stopping him. Cady followed along, looking over her shoulder: faces, faces, so many of them, but no sign of Pettifer. But she had to keep up with Lek, otherwise be lost herself.

Jeb had disappeared, perhaps already latching on to some other, more lucrative target.

There was now some distance between herself and the Thrawl, but she could make him out thanks to his height and the impressive dome of his head. She ran on. "Lek! Wait for me, you cuss-bucket!" She was out of breath and red in the face by the time she found him at one of the numerous side pools, where a smaller throng of people stood in a queue. Brin was holding onto his hand. They were waiting patiently, but Lek's one fixed expression had started to flicker and roll like a picture on a cheap television set with a broken crystal. Glimpses of some other face could be seen, *Primal Anger No. 4*, something like that. Brin asked about Jeb.

"I lost him. Or he chose to leave. One or the other."

"It doesn't matter," Lek said. "We're here now. Do you have the cocoons?"

Brin showed him the metal box, her most prized possession. Other ten year-olds were holding similar containers, some simply made, others elaborate and overly decorative.

The queue moved along slowly. Cady could glimpse the priest at work near the water's edge. The ritual process only took ten minutes or so and every so often a family walked back along the line, shepherding their newly hested child, a smiling boy or girl whose temples now shone with blue light, and whose eyes, flecked with violet, were softly, deeply focused. The air was filled with the *ping ping ping* of telepathic promise. Cady scratched at her buds, having forgotten about them in all the commotion. Now the itch was back, worse than ever. She drew a little blood, so long were her nails, so vigorous the endeavour.

There was a hurly-burly down the line where two families were fighting each other, actually coming to fisticuffs. The Alkhym always had the politest of riots. But tensions were rising. Lek's face matched the mood, extreme anger and frustration breaking through to full exposure on his skull. He stormed forward to break up the scuffle, throwing both culprits to the side. He actually got a cheer for this. *I say, good show. Jolly good.* His butler mode kicked in, and he bowed elegantly at the waist to the crowd of onlookers. Cady laughed. Silly buggers! What did they think, that the old ways were back in place, the old manners? Bollocks to all that.

Lek took charge and steered Brin forward. People stepped aside to let her through. They had seen the Xilliths dancing

at the girl's fingertips and in the tangles of her hair. Some
of them were scared of this, seeing her as a freak of nature,
something to be avoided. Cady noted the looks of distaste
on their faces. But she also heard whispers of the *dragon's
blood*, and knew that legends persisted, and that people were
always hungry for salvation. Either way, little Brin held her
head high. They were soon at the water's edge. Contained
within Horseferry Yard – a circular courtyard of red-brick
walls – the hesting pool was some twelve feet across, fed by
a culvert direct from the Nysis. Strands of Faynr clung to the
surface, pink and white in colour. The water was motionless
and black and polished like a mirror. The sun was hiding
behind a cloud, giving the scene a purplish tinge. A number
of myridi flies hovered over the pool, evidence that some
of the earlier children had been refused: a terrible fate,
both physically and socially. The air seemed to hum with
potential life. Far off a brass band played a ballad of youth
and hope; the soundtrack to a crystal dream.

There was a sudden hush as everyone present stopped
talking all at once.

It was uncanny. Cady couldn't work out what was going
on. She'd witnessed a few hestings in her time, but never
before with such a strange atmosphere.

The officiating priest was a young man, untouched by
much of life. He was dressed in a blue robe and a matching
tricorn hat, the robe short enough to show his calves and
feet, which were bare. A pendant hung from his neck, a
myridi fly fashioned from precious metal. He asked Brin her
name and she answered in the full Alkhym fashion:

"Sabrina Clementine Far-Sight Abigail Maid-Of-The-
Vale Xiomara Delphine Poppy-Moth Mina-Moth Marion
Hollenbeck Halsegger the Third."

The surname drew gasps from the other supplicants. As well it might, for the Halseggers were a family of old repute, but more ill than good of late, ever since their behaviour at the start of the war. Most of Ludwich would have called them traitors, but here in the Alkhym enclave, close to the ancient sources of power, their name still carried some weight.

Brin handed the metal box to the priest and he opened it and inspected the contents. He picked up the first of the two cocoons and held it to his ear. He gave it a shake, and then licked at it with his tongue. He frowned. And then he crushed the cocoon in his fist, letting the dry flakes fall into the water at the pool's edge. He spoke in a reverent tone: "Dead." That single word.

Brin gasped. The crowd echoed her.

Lek grabbed Cady's hand in an involuntary gesture, squeezing tightly.

The priest took up the second and final cocoon from the box. He made the same movements as before, checking for life within the tightly wound skeins of silk. This time he nodded approval. It was good. Lek released his grip. And feeling this lack of pressure, Cady had a sudden panic. With painful clarity she recalled Lord Olan Pettifer's warning to her, broadcast through the medium of Mr Carmichael's crystal waves.

If that girl undergoes the hesting, she will have the power to open the doorway completely. Gogmagog will come through in all his might and glory, and he will destroy Faynr, he will destroy Ludwich, and all the people who live within–

His message had cut off at that point. It brought doubt to the forefront of Cady's mind, and the urge to step forward to stop the ritual was strong within her; but she held herself back. All she could do now was trust to the ghost, in the certain knowledge that Faynr knew for the best.

The priest was chanting in the old Alkhym language, the words flowing in a long undulating stream of vowels. He bent down and held the cocoon in the waters, allowing the loving strands of Faynr to fold over the precious object. It took a few seconds only. Then he straightened up and held the cocoon near to Brin's face. Again he intoned a chant. Not even Cady with her long endless years could understand the words. The cocoon trembled and then began to split open, to peel and fray as the insect within struggled to emerge into the daylight. It was free! The glittering wings flashed as it tested them, sitting on the priest's palm. Cady moved in for a closer look. The fly's large pulpy iridescent body glinted in yellow and green as it shifted about. Its antennae flicked back and forth rapidly. It had a white triangle on the back of its thorax; a unique marking.

The entire congregation kept their silence: not a breath was heard. They knew on some deeply rooted level that something special was happening. Cady looked to Brin. The girl stood perfectly at rest. The only sound was the electric crackle of Xillith sparks at her fingertips and brow. The myridi fly had crawled onto her face. Its feelers touched at her lips, and the girl's mouth opened willingly.

It was creeping inside. Her lips began to close.

A sudden scream broke the moment into pieces. Brin dropped to the flagstones that lined the pool and then rolled sideways, landing in the water. It was shallow and she floundered, rocking back and forth like a baby.

Cady could not move. What had happened? She couldn't work it out.

Lek splashed into the pool, bending down to Brin, wrapping his arms around her. The scream continued. The other families looked on, some people smiling, others in surprised concern or even shock, depending on how they felt about the Halseggers. The priest was at a loss, he backed away. Brin's reaction was too violent, too overpowering.

Now Cady knelt down next to Lek, where he held Brin at the pool's edge. The girl was quiet at last, but still distraught. Her temples were bleeding at the hesting points.

"What happened to her? I couldn't see."

The Thrawl looked at Cady. "She was refused."

"The myridi? It flew away?"

He nodded. "Poor Brin. Oh my poor child." He wiped at the blood.

Cady stood up, only to feel faint. She flopped down on a stone bench and let her head lower into her arms. She groaned to herself. A refusal meant one thing: that the ritual was over, and done with. A failure. *Oh Lud, help me now. By my wishes I have brought pain upon your people, upon a child!* And then she spotted the nasty little insect in question. It was resting on the bench, happily stroking its feelers with its forelegs, one after the other. The white triangle on its back seemed to glow like a single point of pain in Cady's head. An Alkhym boy knelt down and lowered his face towards the myridi. He smiled mischievously and made a cooing sound. The insect crawled into his mouth. The boy's lips closed over it tightly and he swallowed the little creature in a single gulp.

The sparkles of a faraway star were already in his eyes.

The Witch Of Threadbare Street

Thrawl Lek stood alone in the middle of a stretch of wasteland. This was the very edge of Alkhym territory, where it bled into the old Ephreme boroughs. A block of flats had taken a battering from a Molokoi, an Enakor flying robot, and was now a half tower of broken masonry. Living rooms and bedrooms were on view, many still furnished; a series of dust-covered stage sets. The clearances were still taking place, slow backbreaking work. Cady made her way gingerly over the rubble and nasty looking chunks of reinforced concrete. She was in a right old state, tired and breathless from the long run away from the pools, chasing after Lek who was chasing after Brin, the running girl, mad and screaming as she went, causing a ruckus in the crowds of celebrants. More than once Cady had tripped and fell. Her bell-bottoms were scuffed with dirt and mud. And on top of which, it was now raining. Not a heavy downpour but the soft drizzle. The rain brought mugginess with it, so that Cady was sweating in profusion, and her armpits squelched.

She stopped for a breather and looked to see what Lek was up to. He was standing near a squat brick-built structure, making repeated jerking movements with his right arm, swinging it back and forth, bent at the elbow. What in Lud's good name was he doing? There was no sign of Brin. Besodden and miserable and pissed off at the world, Cady walked on until she stood before the Thrawl. His arm was at rest now, but still bent into its angled shape. The structure, she now saw, was the entrance to a bomb shelter, its roof damaged and its walls decorated with moss and graffiti: *Pelham Rovers Rule*; *Scuttlers Forever*; *Raise your Wings!*

"Where is she? Where's the girl?"

Lek nodded to the open doorway of the bunker, which showed only darkness within. "She won't come out. She won't listen to me. She..." He could hardly articulate the feelings. "She... she howled at me, to stay away."

His face was stricken with pain, the expression seeping into his features from within and not quite taking hold, fragmenting under the strain. Other expressions kept cutting in – smiles, laughter, indignation, and so on, one after the other, and yet the pain always returning. It was a grotesque show, barely watchable. His eyes were black, void of any good concept of life, mechanical or otherwise. His fists were scuffed and cracked, and Cady saw the dents in the brick wall of the bunker where, she could only imagine, he'd been pummelling, over and over.

"We should have gone to the main pool with the priestess, it would have been alright then, everything would be good, and Brin would be... Miss Brin would have..."

"Lek, you ran from there, you took us away."

He stared at her wildly. "I know, I know."

"You saw Pettifer."

"I thought I did." His teeth ground together, producing sparks. "The man I saw possessed a seventy-two-per-cent match for Pettifer's features."

"So you weren't even sure?"

"No."

The admittance increased the brittleness of his features. His eyes found some colour, blinking red, then yellow, red, yellow, and Cady feared he meant himself harm.

"Come on, put a stopper in it." She had a firm grip of his arm, and could feel every tremble of him. "Let's not have another Frenzy, eh?"

His eyes settled into a steady ice blue, whatever that might mean. It looked better, anyway. But the feeling of calm soon passed as he spat out, "You must be happy now, Cady Meade."

"Me? No, of course I'm not. What makes you–"

"You did not want Brin to hest."

"I'm just saying, that's all…"

"What are you saying, precisely?"

"That maybe, maybe Faynr doesn't want her to. After all, this is the second refusal."

"Yesterday was not a refusal. There was a disturbance. A river quake."

"Caused by the voor, a creature born of Faynr–"

"No, no, no. NO!"

And his fist went back to its work, punching the same spot on the wall again and again. Cady let him do it, standing back a little as the brick shards came flying and grey-and-red dust rose in a cloud. Ruddy heck, he'll be knocking the shelter down at this rate, better than any bomb! Then she realised something quite alarming: every time the Thrawl's fist made contact with the bricks, the pained expression on his face was fixed, just for a second. So. Punch, punch, punch

– pain, pain, pain! He was keeping his goddamn expression in place through the act of violence. It was crazy! But at last his actions stopped and he seemed to just collapse, to fold up into a weightless bag of components.

"I'll have a word with her, shall I? You stay here, that's right. That's best."

Stone steps led down into the bunker's interior. Cady made her way carefully, feeling for each step with her booted heel. At the bottom she turned a corner and peered through the gloom. The stench of rotten weeds rose up to meet her, and damp, and mildew. And yes, rat droppings, and a dead mouse. Cady was very good on smells. At least down here the rain was kept off, only a little of it finding its way through the ragged hole in the roof. That hole also let in a slanted beam of light, illuminating two upturned tea-chests with a pack of playing cards, a few empty bottles of beer, and a pile of magazines resting on them. And just beyond this patch of light was the darkened form of Brin, sitting slouched down against the wall, all bundled up inside her own legs and arms.

Cady waited a moment before speaking.

"Brin. Brin darling–"

"Keep away from me. Keep away!"

"Come on petal, let's have a chat shall we, old bag to young beauty, like we used to, eh, on the *Juniper* yesterday. Do you remember, the lovely chats we had–"

"Keep away, Mrs Meade. I'm ugly. Ugly!"

"Now, now."

The truth was, Cady was a bit stuck. She didn't know what to say. Idly she scratched at the buds on her forearms, first the right, then the two on the left. The rain seemed to have loosened them a little, the *sense* of the rain even through her clothing.

Her voice echoed in the stony hollow. "Girlie, it's like this: life will throw a whole pile of horse dung your way, piss-poor horse dung at that, not the good horse dung, no, this stuff is not going to make your garden grow, so you might as well get used to it."

"You don't understand." The girl was still all scrunched up and her voice was muffled through a tangle of limbs. "You're not an Alkhym."

"That I am not, and glad for it. But really–"

"Shut up."

Cady did so. She waited. The bunker was cold and the floor was covered in puddles of water. There were patches of mould on the walls, and a string of electrical wiring dangled down from a ripped-out lamp bracket. Cobwebs everywhere. In such places the people had huddled as the bombs fell on home and factory and church and docks. She remembered the shiver and shake of Psephekarnidraxapor when she and thousands more had taken nightly refuge in the monster's tubular guts. It all seemed so long ago.

She stepped a little closer, speaking softly this time. "I know you're upset. I know that when the myridi refuses you, that's it, you have to wait a year before trying again. And even then... well, every year late it becomes more difficult, doesn't it? Less and less viable. Yes, from what I've heard, and witnessed."

Nothing. No response. This was proving difficult.

"I mean, look at me, I've been waiting more than a thousand years to have a proper flowering, and now I'm going to have six of them all at once, look, look at my arms, Brin, do you see, look at the little blighters waiting to bloom, if only they would. Ooh, they're painful! I need to put some of that good horse dung on them, rub it well in."

Was that a snort of laughter from the curled-up shape?

Cady sat down on a tea-chest, happy to rest her legs and take the weight off her corns. Some true believer had scrawled a message on the wall: *Beware of False Gods*. She picked up a magazine, a tatty copy of *Health & Vitality*, and with some interest flicked through the pages studying the black-and-white photographs of tennis-playing nudists. The magazine was so old it even had images of naked Thrawls serving lemonade and tiffin to the sun worshippers.

"Brin, did I ever tell you the story of when I slept with an Enakor fighter pilot?"

There was a pause. Then the girl's quiet voice: "No."

"Would you like to hear that story?"

Another pause. "Yes." The word drawn out with a little squeak at the end.

"Oric was his name. Oric Thosk. He was shot down in the first year of the war in the Battle of Kethra, and he spent the next five years in a prisoner-of-war camp on Pinchbeck Island, west of the salt flats, a couple of miles outside Anglestume. Anyway, a few months after the war ended they processed the POWs and released them. Most went home, sheepish like. But a few stayed on, and Oric was one of them."

Cady took out her pipe and contemplated making up a bowlful, but it remained an idea only.

"Oric came into the pub one night, my local, the Westward Oh. I got chatting with him. Now, understandably, not everyone was best pleased with the enemy in their midst, even though the war was done and over with. Too many friends, lovers, sons and husbands killed. But me, I got on with him well enough. He was a handsome devil, a wizard on the pub's piano, and the worst player of dominoes I ever did meet." She laughed a little, but then turned serious. "One time he told me that he had lost his faith in Enakorian politics, and did not want to return to that country, not ever."

Memories played in Cady's eyes, good and bad.

"Late one night he was beaten up by a gang of dockers. So he came round to my rooms, and I cleaned his wounds for him and gave him a tot or two of rum."

Brin was very quiet during all this; her breathing was steady.

"Oric was a warrior of the old school, very well-mannered and upright, with a strict code of honour. He was young, but this was already his third war, because you know those Enakors love to cause trouble. He told me once that aerial combat was like a sword fight, like an old-fashioned duel – swish, swish, lunge! One-on-one in the open skies and may the best man win."

The girl spoke up: "I want to know about when you slept with him."

"Oh that."

"Yes."

Cady smiled to herself. "It was too late for him to go home, and he was as drunk as a coot, and maybe the gang was still prowling about outside. So we lay next to each other on the same bed, side by side, me with my nightie on, and nothing but, imagine… and him fully dressed. Oh my. And Oric, not yet thirty!" She grinned impishly. "He-he, it was like a scene out of one of my steamy books. Except that, well… nothing much happened."

"No kissing?"

"Neither peck nor nibble. No, I kept myself to myself. More's the pity!" She turned suddenly wistful. "Ah, when I think back."

Brin shuffled about a little, loosening her tangles.

"The sad fact remains, that was the last time I ever shared a bed with a man. But I live in hope that my greatest love awaits me, perhaps upon this very day."

"Who, Mrs Meade?"

"Why, King Lud himself, by means of his flower of infinite promise, the Lud flower. Which exists somewhere hidden within this fine city of ours, a single precious bloom."

"Only one?"

"One and one only. A very old Haegra man told me this. You remember, when we were on Ludforsakenland?"

"Yes."

"You see, only the Lud flower can pollinate me, in this special kingly manner. And if that doesn't happen then I fear these little blossoms of mine will dry up and fall away. Look, I've lost one already. And if that happens, well then I do believe I am ready to leave this good world behind and to take my final resting place in the Garden of Dark Earth."

Brin unfolded herself, allowing her face to enter the light. It was a frightful mask, dabbled all over with blood and dirt, but Cady quelled the desire to say as such, instead murmuring sweet little nothings. Far worse than the face though was the trembling of the girl's body, her hands especially affected, a blur of movement, and her head nearly as bad, a softer blur. Cady grabbed the girl at the wrists and tried to calm her. The flesh was hot and damp, very hot, very damp. Three days ago, Lek and Brin had turned up at Cady's home by the sea asking for passage upriver to Ludwich, and the girl then had suffered the same afflictions, only not nearly as bad as now. The failed hesting had pushed back all the improvements of the river voyage, and now Brin was a quivering wreck. It was just too harrowing to see a youngster like this, in so much despair.

The girl was mumbling to herself.

"What is it, speak up."

"It's too late, next year, too late. I'm ill, Mrs Meade. Very ill. Far worse than Lek thinks."

"I know."

Something odd happened to the old sailor then, as she took in the young girl's face. She could either love this child, or hate this child, or even fear this child. And all these things might happen at the same time, one inside the other. As such, Cady felt in painful detail the exact complexity of her own bi-rooted nature; of flesh and flower was she made, and mostly they worked together but now and then they did not, they fought each other; such was this moment. Not only was she a woman of seventy-eight years, she was also a Haegra of many centuries' duration, bound to and victim of various portents and riddles. And being a Haegra meant she was also a watchwoman, committed by ancient Wodwo creed to protect the nation against villains of ghostly or demonic nature. And this wee damaged girl might well be a part of a demonic force; it was yet to be decided.

So then, Cady thought; let us sharpen the blade.

"Brin. I want to ask you some questions. And I want you to answer them truthfully. Do you understand me?"

The girl nodded. "Yes, Mrs Meade."

"Are you an agent of Gogmagog, the Night Serpent?"

"No, Mrs Meade."

"Are you possessed in any way by the evil spirit of Gogmagog, the poisonous twin of good Faynr?"

"No, Mrs Meade."

"Brin, are you Gogmagog in disguise?"

"No, Mrs Meade, no, I swear!"

Cady stared deep into the girl's eyes, seeking one speck of darkness, one tiny little drift of smoke, any evidence at all of the monster. But there was nothing.

"Wipe your face. You look terrible."

Brin did as she was told, using the sleeve of her jacket. It only made the effect worse. Cady leaned in close and said in an undertone, "If you're lying to me… Listen… If you're lying, Miss Fancy, I will spike you good and nasty, and not with some little penknife like I did this morning, no, but with my thorns, with the longest sharpest thorns that ever did grow from the outer fields."

She showed off the fields in question, the palms of her hands, left and right, from which spiky plants grew under her command. The revealed thorns pressed at Brin's shoulders.

"I shall prick thee to the bare bone."

"You're scaring me, Mrs Meade." Brin's eyes were wide. "I only want… I only want to hest. Please, let me hest! Please!"

"Up you get, come on. Let's go and see Mr Lek and then we can decide what to do."

She more or less grabbed the girl's collar and dragged her up the steps. The rain had stopped, and the ground outside was dark and muddy.

"We have a visitor," Lek said. "Yonder."

Cady looked to a part of the waste ground where a gang of workers were knocking down a half-demolished house. A figure could be seen in the brick dust that hung in the air, a young man with wings. Some avenging angel, perhaps? No. As he stepped forward Cady saw it was Jeb, still strapped into his purification apparatus, still smiling. He stood some feet away and said, "I see you're having a bit of bother."

"Have you been following us?" Cady asked.

"Keeping an eye on my new friends, is all. I saw what happened at the pools. The poor kid." He nodded at Brin, who was very subdued and distant, caught up within her own thoughts. He went on, "It just so happens that I know a lady who might be of assistance, for a modest fee, with the failed hesting. A relative of mine, she is, an auntie. Queenie is her name."

"What is she?" Lek asked. "A priestess?"

"Not as such."

"A doctor?"

"Absolutely not."

"What then?"

"A witch."

Cady groaned. But Lek perked up on hearing this. "She can really help Brin?"

"Seen it with my own two eyes, last year and the year before, the truth. I helped her out, as well, each time. Queenie can make the myridi have a second go."

The Thrawl looked to Brin. She stared ahead, sightlessly. He looked to Cady, who answered quickly, "Lek, he's having you on, there's no such thing as a *second go*, not in the same year, it doesn't work like that and you know it!"

"It might work."

"No, no. Have you ever heard of such a thing, tell me that?"

"No, but–"

"There you are then. Holy fuck. And you with your head full of knowledge, the Crystal Palace or whatnot, all those books in your noggin and you've never heard of such a thing, how can that be?"

Lek replied with surety, "The Ephreme, as you well know, Cady, do not write their knowledge down on paper, for fear the world will contaminate it. They use instead *sigils*, highly secretive symbols that contain entire *realms* of knowledge. They are not easily decoded."

"He's right there," added Jeb. "Most of what the elders write down is gobbledegook to me, and I'm of the tribe, born and bred."

"Also, a lot of their books were burned in the Holy Conflagration."

"Aye, dreadful that was, dreadful."

Cady broke in on their discussion: "When you two have quite finished."

"Well then, what do you say?" Lek asked. "Cady, shall we proceed?"

She held a breath and then answered, "The seeds are in the wind. Let them fall where they may."

Lek was gleeful and his face shone with it. "Young man, we accept your very kind offer."

"Jebediah Yeomanson at your service."

They set off across the bomb site, deeper into Pelham, an Ephreme estate built at the turn of the last century. It was a far longer walk than expected and Cady's feet ached something terrible. "When will I see my lovely *Juniper* again?" Nobody answered her. Brin did not speak a single word the whole journey. Eventually they came to a little village of prefabricated bungalows, all of them painted a lovely fresh pink. There was even a corner shop of the same design.

Jeb explained, "The entire area was bombed out in the war, knocked down and these beauties brought in on the backs of lorries. They're calling it Ibraxus Estate."

Cady piffled at this: "Naming it after King Lud's mighty sword, the dragon-slayer? Pah! It looks more like a doll town."

"Well, my auntie's very pleased to have no more of the old terraces."

"They kept the old street names, I see. Threadbare Street? Very *moderne*."

Jeb led them to the door of number 17. He rang the bell. "Queenie! It's me. It's Jeb. Open up, there's a dear, I've got a job for you." There was a noise from within, the sound of something falling over and then a curse. And finally the door opened wide. A woman stood on view. Cady knew two things straight away. One: from the state of her make-up-streaked face, the woman had recently been crying, bawling her eyes out. And two: the woman was completely and utterly sozzled.

They followed her inside, into the living room. The space was jam-packed with bric-a-brac arranged haphazardly on shelves, bookcases, tallboys, glass cabinets and cubbyholes: marble statuettes, glass animals, pottery shepherds, plaster ballerinas, far too many music boxes. It looked like Jebediah's aunt had stuffed the entire contents of her old two-up two-down into this single-storey structure. There was a television set perched in the corner of the room, its crystal abuzz and its miniscule screen displaying a bank holiday afternoon melodrama. Lengths of cotton dangled down from the ceiling, many of them, each one ending in a piece of card printed with an Ephremic sigil. The witch known as Queenie moved through this assemblage of objects, banging into things, knocking knick-knacks off shelves. "Jeb, put the kettle on, will you. The best cups." She gazed at Brin with bleary eyes. "And there are some custard creams in the tin." She paused long enough to light a cigarette, to cough profusely, and then to dab at her cheeks while examining herself in a wall mirror. Her reflection disturbed her and she turned quickly away. "It's all gone wrong, I suppose? A botched hesting?" Lek started to speak but Queenie shushed him impatiently. "Where did I put my bag? I can never find anything. Oh darn it!" A pile of magazines and pamphlets slid off a chair. She rubbed at her woollen stockings where she'd banged her knee against a table leg. "The milk's powdered, but you don't mind that, do you pet?" This last was aimed at Brin, who made no response beyond a constant shaking of her upper body and arms. This curious movement caught Queenie's attention. She bent down and studied the child, touching at the girl's hesting points, which were still seeping blood but at a much slower rate. "Is it hurting?" Brin nodded. "I have something for that. Jeb! Jeb, fetch me my bag, will you! Oh, where is that boy when you need him?"

"He's getting the tea," Cady reminded her.

"Right, yes, so he is." She hiccupped.

There was an awkward silence. Lek put on his best butler act, politely coughing into his hand and then saying, "I can't help observing your features, madam. They show evidence of recent lacrimation?"

"Madam. Oh *madam*, is it? Oh, I like this one! Madam indeed!" She wiped vigorously at her face. "As it happens, yes I have been… *crying*, as people might put it, crying on account of my Bertram, see, my dearly departed, gone from this world."

"I am very sorry to hear that."

"We were having a nice little chat, and everything was going fine, but then… Then he goes and tells me… Oh… Bertie…" She screwed her eyes shut to keep the sobs inside.

"You were chatting with your husband?" Lek was confused. "But I thought you said…"

"She's a medium," Cady explained. "Spirits are in the air."

Lek did a quick scan of the room, his eye-beams a very gentle sky-blue in colour, but not gentle enough to hold Queenie off from crying out.

"Don't do that! Don't! Oh see now, you're scared them away, oh my poor dears."

The lengths of cotton all fluttered madly in chaotic sequence and the printed sigils spun and spun, flashing their secretive knowledge.

"All departed, every last spirit, even my Bertie. Come back soon, my sweet!"

She collapsed into an armchair which exuded a cloud of dust under her weight.

Queenie was in her forties, tightly bound into a matching tweed skirt and jacket, a tightness relieved only by the twin darts at the shoulder blades that allowed her little wings to sprout forth; she had decorated the feathers with glitter and colourful beads and bits of tinsel. Her cheeks were quite plump under the streaked powder, and her nose had the pitted look of a long-time serious drinker. In contrast her hair was vibrant and fluffed up and proud and jet black – a wig to Cady's eye, an observation confirmed by the sight of a bare mannequin's head sitting on a shelf.

Now the Witch of Threadbare Street puffed on her cigarette and spoke with a gruff croaking voice: "It was your fault, actually." She was gazing at Lek.

He put on *Puzzlement No. 1*, perhaps one of the few faces he still had total control over. "My fault? I'm afraid I don't understand."

"Your fault. You killed him!"

"You mean a Thrawl killed your husband?"

She stubbed out her cigarette. "That's right, oh yes. In the Frenzy. Just crossing the Old Duck Road he was, my Bertie, on his way to the betting shop, when this black cab came careening out a side street, driven by a Thrawl, a mad Thrawl, a *maddened* Thrawl, and bang, straight into him, knocking my Bertie over stone dead, he never knew what hit him. But I did! Oh, I did. Ooh, the crystals were full of it, all these stories of incidents, accidents, acts of violence! And all of them happening at the exact same time. Terrible, terrible." Queenie rummaged around in a drinks cabinet beside her chair and found a bottle of sherry. The bottle clinked against the rim of a glass. "Poor sweet man, taken from me in his prime." She snuffled and wiped her nose on a handkerchief she kept stuffed up her sleeve.

Lek's face was a picture of pure discomfort. "Perhaps we should take our leave?"

"What? No, no! What's wrong with you?" She struggled out of her seat. "Ah, here's the boy. Right then, Jeb, you be mother. And find me my bag."

"It's right beside you, auntie, on the shelf." He placed a tray down on a side table.

"Oh yes, there it is, hiding away."

She opened the leather bag, the kind favoured by doctors, and searched inside until she found what she was looking for, a tiny jar of mint-green ointment. "Come here, child," she said. "That's right, nice and close. What's your name?"

"Brin."

"A pretty name. Now then Brin, I'm going to put a little of this salve on your sores, to relieve your discomfort. But first of all, it pains me to say... I'll need to be paid. Complete and up front, and no refunds if it goes wrong."

"It often goes wrong, does it?" Cady asked.

Queenie just glared at her.

Jeb's earlier promise of a *modest* fee turned out to be a fib. Cady had to wonder how much money Lek had remaining, stashed about in the various drawers and cubbyholes of his body. But this transaction sorted, Queenie proceeded to rub the ointment on Brin's temples.

"That's it, just so. There, does that feel better?"

"Yes, thank you."

"Oh, you are polite aren't you. Lovely. Now go and have a look in that tank. I have my beetle collection in there, seven different species from all around the world."

Brin walked over to a large dusty terrarium in the corner of the room. The glass tank was lit with a soft green light and filled with twigs and stones, over which the various beetles scuttled and crept, occasionally using their wings to fly onto the glass sides or a higher branch. Cady felt her skin crawling and looked down at her hand to see her very own accompanying species had found her out, even perhaps followed her here. She held her hand out for Queenie's inspection.

"Is this one of yours?"

"No, of course not, I don't let them wander free. That's a semaphore beetle."

"Yes, I know. I'm a sailor, as it happens. We use these out at sea, to send signals from ship to ship. On top of which, my sister Nabs uses them, to collect gossip."

"She chases the beetle, does she, this Nabs?"

"I just said she did."

"A nasty habit, if you don't mind my saying."

The beetle changed the colours on its thorax and abdomen a few times, red to yellow to blue to green. Queenie watched this display. "You've haven't led anyone to me, I hope."

"Why do you say that?"

"What I do here, with the refused children, well it's not exactly legal, if you get my drift. And nosey parkers use semaphore beetles to gather knowledge, to spy upon people. Oh yes, mark my words, someone is prying upon you!"

"Probably just my sister, keeping her eye on me."

But in fact Cady was worried now. Perhaps it was more than Nabs' nasty nosey habit; maybe it was Lord Pettifer? Was he the secret onlooker? Irritated by her own fears, Cady flicked the beetle into flight and said, "Can we begin please." Then she took a custard cream and dunked it in the cup of strong tea Jeb had given her.

"Of course, of course." Queenie turned to Brin. "Child, come to me, that's right. Do you see, I have a number of cocoons in this drawer. Not so many this year, but still, we only need one for a good hesting. Which of them would you prefer? That one? Very good. Now, do you know about the birds and the bees?"

Brin nodded. She was holding a nice fat looking cocoon in her cupped hands. Cady saw that the trembling had stilled itself to a mild but ceaseless shiver.

"So you'll know that there are male myridi, and female. And the two must join together."

Another nod.

"Now where does the female myridi live?"

Brin pointed to her own chest, at the sternum. She said proudly, "All Alkhym boys and girls are born with the myridi egg inside them."

Queenie smiled at the girl's knowledge. "And so it has been ever since the myridi first rose from the swamps of Faynr in their swarms and descended upon a chosen portion of the Wodwo, thereby creating the Alkhym."

Brin seemed pleased with the lesson. "The female hatches in our ninth or tenth year. She lives inside us, waiting for the hesting."

Queenie nodded. "Someone's been teaching you well. And where does the male fly live?"

"In the world."

"That's right, in the reed beds that grow alongside the river, wherever Faynr provides shelter for them. Now the male fly loves the female dearly and would like to pay her a visit, to woo her. But sometimes, just sometimes the male might seem to be a little… *reluctant*, shall we say. Or the lady insect might be sending out the wrong signals, *hormones*, as we call them. They're a kind of perfume. Oh it's all very complicated! But don't you worry, Queenie will make it work."

"What exactly is the method?" Lek asked. "Only, I can't allow Miss Brin to be harmed."

"The method is simple enough: we invigorate the male's desire."

"And how is that achieved?"

Queenie now had them all as an attentive audience: she was holding court in her little single-storey palace.

"You will know that the cocoon must always be held within Faynr before hatching. This is the key: Faynr's activation is essential to the myridi's vigour. So all we need to do is make sure the cocoon is steeped in the most powerful, most potent version of Faynr that we can find."

Cady had a bad feeling, hearing this; an inkling of what the witch's method might entail.

Queenie led Brin over to a shelf. "Now here, you see, this is where I keep my wigs."

The bare mannequin head sat at one end of the shelf alongside other similar head-like shapes, each one hidden under a red velvet cloth. She pulled off the first cloth. "Shopping Expeditions." The second cloth. "Ballroom Dancing at the Ritz." The third. "Tuesday Night Down the Bingo With Dot and Joan." Each revealed head sported a different style and colour of hairpiece. "And this one, ta da! My Hesting Special!" She pulled off the final cloth with a flourish and her laughter was wild as she did so; Queenie dearly loved her theatrical effects.

Cady heard Lek's squeak of shock. She didn't need to look round to know how his face would be coping with its several opposing expressions.

Sitting at the end of the shelf was a disembodied Thrawl's head. It was covered in scratches and indentations, containing a crystal that seemed to be on its last blue flicker, while a brown sludgy mist of Faynr floated around the lower half of the skull. It truly was a disgusting object, of little use to anyone. Yet Queenie was proud of her possession. "He might not be handsome, but I can assure you, Mr Hod here has served me well over the years, and has given hope of a good and proper life to many an Alkhym boy and girl. What do you say, eh? Pretty snazzy."

"Hod?" Lek said. "He's a D model."

"Vintage year! Vintage! Ooh, they knew how to make Thrawls back in those days. I reckon we would never have had the Frenzy if they'd stuck to the D models, and my Bertram, my Bert..." Her eyes were once again watering. "My Bertie would still be alive!"

Lek had a quaver in his voice. "Is this some kind of revenge?"

"What? No, no, of course not. Well, a little, perhaps. But after all, the method has been passed down through the decades, in whispers, first invented by the most illustrious witch, Theodora of the Silver Wings, one of my ancestors, as it happens. Isn't that right, Jeb?"

"Honest to goodness, the truth, I swear."

Cady still couldn't believe what she was hearing. "You're going to hatch the cocoon inside this Thrawl's head, in the Faynr, this dirty scummy Faynr? It looks like treacle! Mixed with shit!"

Queenie nodded eagerly. "Shall we proceed?"

But Brin suddenly stepped forward. She had something to say. "It's not good enough."

"I can assure you, Miss, I've performed many a–"

"It looks nasty." The girl wrinkled her nose. "I'll bet it smells inside of there. I don't think my cocoon will like it. And neither would I."

"And what would you like, your highness, if I dare ask?"

A prim but knowing smile came to Brin's lips. "If a newer head were presented to me, a more up-to-date Thrawl's head with a cleaner, nicer supply of Faynr, and a brighter more tantalising crystal... well then, I imagine my chances of hesting would be much improved, don't you think so, Mr Lek?"

Without a moment's hesitation Lek spoke up: "I believe such would be the case, Miss."

"Very well, then."

Brin gave him her loveliest smile. He could respond in one way only, by slowly nodding his head. He spoke softly: "I will do as you ask."

Queenie looked doubtful. "Well, I'm not so sure. I'm used to my tried and trusted methods."

"I think Miss Brin is right," Lek added. "I am the best Thrawl in the room."

Oh that look of *No. 5 Pride* on his face! The girl was playing a merry trick, and Cady knew it. "Now wait," she said. "Just wait a minute, Lek. Have a good think about it."

"I have *thought*. I have expended five thousand, two hundred and twenty-four thoughts upon it. And all of them point to the same conclusion."

Queenie snapped her fingers. "Child, to me. Quickly now!"

Brin presented herself, all politeness and dancing steps.

Cady groaned inwardly. She knew that a very dangerous and very *physical* event was about to take place, the outcome of which was uncertain not only in terms of the child's well-being, but also regarding the possibility of the demon Gogmagog's full emergence. Her heart was beating and her blood was up and charged with rich green life drawn from the Deep Root as her body channelled every last ounce of watchwomanly power. A Haegra stands alone against the dark!

Of course, in fifteen minutes they might all be having another cup of tea and nibbling on biscuits and even a bit of cake, who knows, and having a jolly good laugh together.

So then: she would keep her eyes peeled.

Jeb and Queenie worked in tandem, each to their different tasks, quickly and efficiently. The witch's drunkenness seemed only to enable her, not to hinder her, once the spell was under way. Curtains were drawn, shaded lamps lit, the television set left on but turned to silence, and suitable music found on the crystal wireless, a piece for solo cello with a sweeping Saliscanian feel to it. Queenie took a sip of sweet sherry and stood before the terrarium, bowing at the waist to some king or queen of the beetles. Meanwhile, Jeb attended to Lek, seating him in a wooden chair, folding down the Thrawl's collar at the back to reveal a small keyhole at the base of the neck. Cady had never noticed this before, but she had seen him work on Pok Pok's head, so knew it was certainly possible to gain access. But what in Lud's Heaven would it do to him, to have his workings messed with? What if it all went wrong?

Brin stood in the centre of the room, waiting quietly throughout these preparations. Queenie took a keyring from a drawer and approached the Thrawl. She said, "Now don't you worry, Mr Thrawl, I'm not going to unscrew your whole head. Too difficult that way, to persuade the fly to stay inside. No, I'm going to access your little plughole here, where an engineer might release your exhaust gases every few years or so. Do you understand?" Lek nodded. "Very good. Now let's see." The first key didn't quite fit, nor the second, but the third with a little jiggling turned well enough and a small aperture appeared in the Thrawl's neck. It was circular, less than an inch across. A stream of orange Faynr began to escape, but Jeb placed the pad of his thumb over the hole, sealing it. Now Queenie took the chosen cocoon from Brin, at the same time giving the girl's shoulder a reassuring squeeze. They were ready.

Cady's whole body had tensed up. This would be the third hesting she had witnessed in two days: the first a passionate but amateur affair on board a ship; the second earlier today by an official of the Alkhym Church, a liturgical ritual complete with chanting; and now this one – madcap, inventive, possibly fake, performed for cash at the shivering hands of a drunken witch in a dingy sitting room surrounded by hundreds of knick-knacks and trinkets. No words were spoken this time; rather Queenie made a series of random whistles, purrs, tongue-clicks and chuckles. It was absurd.

She was actually pushing the cocoon into the hole in Lek's head, squeezing it through the small aperture. The Thrawl was just sitting there, letting it happen. Cady shifted a little so she could see his face clearly: his eyes were blank and beamless, his face devoid of all expression. He had closed himself down for the duration, or else the turning of the key had deactivated him.

The job was done.

Jeb quickly replaced his thumb over the hole, trapping the cocoon inside the skull.

"What now?" Cady asked. For some reason she was whispering.

"Now we wait."

"And what happens to the cocoon afterwards?"

"It stays inside, and crumbles away. It does no harm. Now, please… Be silent!"

The witch raised her hands. Both Jeb and Cady leaned in for a better look. Something was moving around inside Lek's head, vaguely seen through the cloudy material of his skin.

"The cocoon has opened. Oh my!" Queenie sounded genuinely excited.

Suddenly a dark shape landed on the interior wall of Lek's upper skull. It fluttered madly. It gave Cady a fright and she took a step backwards. It was like seeing a moth trapped inside a light bulb. The Thrawl's crystal was burning more brightly than she'd ever seen, flickering in a rapid light blue, dark blue pattern. Surely the insect was going to get burned up!

"Quickly, Jeb, quickly now my boy!"

The aperture was exposed once more and Queenie bent her face close, making little cooing noises, the same as the young boy had done at the hesting pools. But these sounds were deeper, and scarier, drawn from ancient magic, perhaps from that mythological age when the Ephreme had proper full-grown wings and took to the air in glory. The witch was licking at the opening in the skull, hoping to coax the insect from its new home. Her tongue was long and pink, rather like a cat's. It made a rasping sound.

"Come to me, my beauty. Come on. Come to Queenie."

Cady looked on in fascination. The myridi fly was struggling, squeezing itself through the aperture, folding its wings tightly to do so. Its antennae twitched. It was halfway through. Queenie spoke to it in some unknown insect language, using tiny finger gestures to urge the creature on its way. Now the bulbous abdomen followed the thorax and it was free, flying around the room in a mad panicky fashion. Queenie's own wings fluttered in symphony. Immediately Jeb moved to insert the key back into Lek's head, turning it, sealing the skull once more. The Thrawl remained in his seat, still caught in his trance-like state. Meanwhile, the myridi had landed on top of the television set, drawn to the crystal aerial. Queenie moved quickly, placing a glass tumbler over its quivering form. But there was a worried look on her face.

"Do your job, witchwoman," Cady said. "Let the girl have her due, as promised, as bloody well paid for!"

Queenie shook her head. "I cannot. Not yet."

Cady's anger swelled and broke. "You cheating little squirmer. You lopsided scallywig. Why, you're nothing but a drunken bawd!"

"Something's wrong–"

"You're wrong! You are wrong!"

"Listen to me, old woman. We are not alone."

"What?"

"Someone is in the room with us. Some spirit, someone unknown, a stranger to me."

Cady's first thought was: *Gogmagog*.

She drew in a sharp breath and held it there. Her eyes darted about, seeking out every corner and cubbyhole expecting to see a creature of smoke and ash of some kind. There was nothing, but her skin was prickling. Waves of icy cold air passed over her face and shoulders. The lice in her hair started to lay their eggs all at once. Her mouth was dry. The thorns of the Outer Fields poked through her palms, ready for action.

"I can sense it," the witch said. "They are close, an intruder. See!"

The lengths of string were twisting and turning, their sigil cards spinning around and around at speed. Fear settled on Queenie's face, and was quickly transferred to Cady's. The two women were clinging to each other's arms for support.

Something crossed the wall mirror's surface, a stray reflection.

A reflection without a body.

A tremble in the air.

Cady split away from the witch's clutches. She followed the disturbance by its traces in the shivering strings and the turning sigils and by the discolourings in the flock wallpaper as the visitor made his way, yes, a *he*, for Cady had a good idea who it was; she had seen a similar figure yesterday on the river at the Grand Illumination.

The Trembling Man, as she called it.

And even as she watched the figure solidified a little, giving shape to itself, a shiver of form. The sigil directly above his head swung back and forth on the crackles of energy.

Cady rushed over to Lek, shaking him by the shoulders. "Lek, wake up! It's Pettifer, he's here for us. He's tracking us! Wake up!"

But the Thrawl was still out cold.

Cady went then to Brin, who was by now lost in her own world, eyes gently closed and her lips softly quivering, in expectation of the hest.

Queenie was standing at the television, her hand holding the glass tumbler over the myridi.

Time was slowing down. No, no, the music was slowing down, that was all, the radio losing its power. The strange presence walked the room. Chairs and tables lost their focus as he passed, and then regained their sharpness. He was a mirage of a man.

Now he stood directly in front of Brin.

If the girl knew of his presence, she took no account of it.

Cady felt sick. It was vile. She had to think: *in this form Pettifer cannot touch us, only keep vigil*. A spectator. Someone lonely, someone unable to grasp at reality. She had to pray this was true. Oh fuck. It gave pause to Cady's plans: if Pettifer should be this desperate to stop the hesting, surely then, could it be, that he was right? Had she made a mistake? If only she could… could *think*, just for a moment, a moment's peace. But there was no peace, only chaos and the urge to breed, to create, one desire fighting against the other.

Talk to me, Gods of the Deep Root, speak with me. What shall I do?

The gods were silent.

She was alone.

But the Trembling Man moved away from Brin. He was losing substance, Cady saw that now, becoming weaker, even less of a presence. Whatever messed-up science or magic gave him this power, it only lasted for a while. The ghostly figure was pulled away across the room to merge once more with the wallpaper. He vanished into the patterns. The sigils stopped their spinning.

Cady saw Jeb across the room and she hurried to him. "Help me."

"What do you need?"

"We need to pause the hesting." Even saying this, she felt her heart shrink. What in Lud's name would Lek say to her? The Thrawl was just now stirring from his slumbers.

Jeb was anxious. "But you've paid for it, you've paid! We've begun. You can't just–"

Cady screwed her entire being to the purpose. "And now we stop it!"

But Queenie was having none of this. She had already moved over to Brin, the insect trapped within her cupped hands, one on top of the other. She placed these against the girl's face.

It only took a moment.

The girl swallowed.

Cady stood in mute frozen attendance, helpless, hopeless, all the thousands of years of living and fighting and sailing, all adding up to nothing in the mad moments, when needed the most. The myridi was already on its way along the dark wet red pathways of the Alkhym body. A symbiotic creature, the scientists called it. Cady knew it by another name: parasite.

Brin opened her eyes wide, staring ahead.

She quivered under the witch's grasp, as though to escape.

There was a knocking at the front door, loud, insistent. Nobody paid it any mind.

The girl's body was glowing with a soft yellow light. Even Queenie moved away, dazzled. The witch had never seen anything like this, Cady knew. Great swathes of Xillithic energy rose from Brin's fingertips and hair, setting the sigils spinning like crazy, snapping the cotton threads, revolving the music box ballerinas on their endless travels. Light bulbs exploded and the wireless changed stations constantly, finding songs, static noise, the weather forecast. Sigils caught fire. Madness ruled the bungalow. Dogs were barking in the back garden, telephones ringing, and all the way down the street motor horns sounded one after another, all could be heard, all sensed in that moment, and the Xilliths were dancing, dancing on the walls and ceiling in blue and violet flashes. The semaphore beetle on Cady's arm was changing its colours a hundred shades a second and then gone, flickered away in the shower of light that suddenly flooded the room. Lek's brain was affected by all this noise and confusion, causing him to cover his ears and close his eyelids. Jeb was more used to it, but even he looked astonished by the severity of the events. Chaos ruled. And there was Brin at the centre of it all, Little Miss Brin, her temples shining bluer than any summer's sky ever did, her eyes sparkle-flecked, fixed on some heavenly expanse.

And that bloody ever-present knock-knock-knocking at the door.

Who was calling?

Cady fell to her knees, overwhelmed. Jeb's face was close. He was bending down, holding her hands, talking to her. But no words could be heard. Now he moved on, towards the door of the room. The knocking continued at a steadier rate, a regular rat-a-tat-tat.

Who was at the door? Who was calling?

It seemed important to know such a thing. Cady tried
to locate Brin. Where had she vanished to? The room
was filled with light, bright enough to blind an old lady.
But she saw Lek, suddenly looming close and then away,
stumbling on his wobbly legs. He looked dazed, his face a
picture of a picture of a picture of *Consternation*, each more
damaged than the last; the living machine was good and
fucked! Cady crawled on her hands and knees across the
carpet. She drooled. There was a great roaring in her ears,
like the sea at Cape Breakpoint on that long-ago voyage
when the storm had hit the galleon, Her Majesty's Ship
The Windlass. She had nearly drowned that day, the closest
ever, and the same was happening now, the same goddamn
feeling of being lost, powerless, rolling and tumbling in
the waves, dragged under! Yet this was dry land, she had
to remind herself. Ooh! And now she was falling, falling
upwards to land on the ceiling with a bump, next to the
hanging lamp. The room, the whole building had capsized.
She was looking down on the action below. It all seemed
perfectly normal to be suspended up here, to be gazing at
the people down below, going about their crazy business.
The room spun around once more, righting itself, and she
was deposited back onto the floor. *Focus! This is just Brin at
her play, messing with your mind. Be strong! Cling to the raft of
yourself and pull yourself ashore*. Yes, there was Queenie, the
Witch of Threadbare Street, busying herself at the drinks
cabinet, no doubt fortifying herself after the ordeal. Cady
licked her lips and wished for a wee dram or a tot or a full
keg or a yard of ale or a bathe in a barrel of rum. Then she
saw Brin. The girl had leapt onto the table, where she stood
with arms outstretched. She was laughing wildly, revelling
in her newfound powers.

Oh Lud, oh Lud, what have I done?

Is this for the good, or for the bad? Cady didn't know which of the city's many gods to call upon for advice and comfort. She found herself near the doorway of the room, looking down the short hallway to the front door of Queenie's bungalow, where the knocking continued apace, slowly now, *rap, rap, rap*. Jeb opened the door. It all seemed to take place in slow-motion, through the wrong end of a blurry eyeglass. Cady saw the newcomer entering. A man dressed in a dark blue suit and tie, a nice white shirt, but his face – oh Lord and Lady of the Flowers protect me! – his face was that of the Night Serpent himself, Gogmagog, a head of swirling smoke and dust and ashes and dung and rotten meat and two shining yellow eyes within the muck that burned into Cady's soul.

Jeb was talking to Mr Gogmagog, just chatting away, as carefree as you like.

Cady threw up. Black vomit mixed with lumps of earth. And was that a worm wriggling about in the dirt? Well, worms are good, good for the garden, and wasn't she a garden herself, yes, the richest loamiest dirtiest most flowerful garden in all of Ludwich and all of it contained within the body of a living breathing woman! That had to mean something, right? So why was she scrabbling about on the floor like a cabin boy hiding from the roar of battle? She managed to pull herself to her feet. Across the room, Lek was calling to Brin, urging her to get down from the table, this instant! But the girl took no notice. The crackle of her body formed into a crown of Xilliths; sudden arcs of violent energy shot out from her fingertips, connecting to the crystals on the wireless and telephone and television, to the light bulbs and plug sockets, to the beetle tank, and most importantly, to Lek's head. His crystal pulsed to the same wild irregular frequency. And then Brin clapped her hands.

I am myriad! We is people!

Her voice was electric.

The entire room vibrated into silence, a silence broken by a soft golden explosion like an overload of sunlight on a summer's day.

Cady was blinded.

And when the haze finally cleared, Brin was nowhere to be seen.

She had disappeared.

Lek howled. He ran about in vain, knocking over a chair in the process.

Cady felt her fingernails digging into the wallpaper. She sensed Jeb at her side and saw the blue-suited visitor with him. He was entirely average in appearance, a normal man.

Jeb was calling out, "Auntie, it's the man from the pools."

"The who? Is it the next-door neighbour?"

"No."

"Tell him to mind his own business."

Jeb raised his voice: "It's the man from the football pools. Have you got your coupon?"

"Oh yes, it's on the table by the door."

And so the strangeness of the day drained itself into the carpet, like Cady's vomit. Her vision of Gogmagog had flown away with Brin's leave-taking, perhaps delivered up by the girl, and removed by her, in evidence of her powers; or else dragged here like some monstrous ectoplasmic residue in the hesting's wake. Cady cursed and cursed, that she had not acted promptly enough to stop the ritual, that she had gone along with it, and never mind the warnings.

But the magic was not quite over. There was a tingle on her skin, warm and sensual.

She looked down at her hands, at her forearms, only now realising that the buds were opening, the calyxes falling away, the petals unfolding on the six sacred places of her body. She could feel them growing into life. *Oh sweet Luda! At last, I am flowering!*

Her body flooded with juices, full tide.

Incident In The Billards Room

"I saw the Great Valerio at Shrivings Fair one time, in the big top. He made a tiger vanish from its podium, mid-roar. Absolute fact. And now the girl, Brin, right, she did just the same, she vanished into thin air, poof! There one minute, gone the next. Saw it with my own eyes."

"You weren't even in room," Cady reminded him.

"I was there!"

"Jeb, you were standing in the hall at the time, talking to the pools man."

"I know that, but I… Well I…"

"Well, yes, what yes?"

"I know what my auntie told me, and she's a purveyor of truth, all our family the same, we never lie."

Cady guffawed. "You're making me piss my bloomers, you are."

"Very nice, I'm sure."

"Not one word of what you spew isn't tainted by untruth. Oh, I know your sort."

"There ain't no *sort* where I came from, they threw away

the master plan when they made me. I'm number one, I am, number one in a field of one."

"What, like a scarecrow."

"No. Like a–"

"Like a lonely scarecrow with a crow sitting on its head! And anyway, how come you're still playing the limpet? Got nowhere else to go?"

Jeb considered his response carefully for once. "After due consideration of the opportunities available to me upon this day I have deemed it best to throw my dice in with you lot, seeing as I was born for great adventures and not for grubbing about in the dirt of the gutter, and further, to this end I have left my municipal purification apparatus back at Queenie's place, no more of that, and further still I have taken rather a liking to you, you old bag of wrinkles, despite your rancid breath and your docker's tongue. And it seems to me, the *Juniper* might be in need of a good cabin boy, fair wages to be agreed as befits one of my station and expertise."

She glowered at him.

"I'm not afraid of hard work, if that's your worry."

Cady grunted. "I need someone to wipe my arse every time I take a dump, will that do you?"

"With a ten-foot pole and a greasy rag, happy to oblige."

That shut her up for the while. They were travelling on the upper deck of an omnibus through the streets of Lower Pelham and Maidensford, heading back to the hospital wharf and the *Juniper*. The bus journey had been Cady's idea on account of her knees and her feet, both playing her up like a knife fight on a foggy day. She was sitting next to Lek near the back of the bus, Jeb on the seat in front, twisting around to chat to them both, not that Lek did any chatting, no, the Thrawl was just sitting there, staring out the window at passing shops and the painted advertisements on the end terraces: *Burnstone's Gravy Browning. Hmmm! So tasty!* The May sun burned the rain away. The bus's other passengers kept their distance from this ragbag trio – the broken-down tinman, the old lady with the dirty unironed face and the knotted hair, and the young Ephreme scuttler with his mad chatter and his bird whistles and cat calls, obviously some kind of young hooligan out for a bit of bish-bosh.

But Cady hadn't finished with Jeb just yet. "Brin didn't vanish," she said. "It was a trick of the mind, that's all. Her hesting has given her special powers."

"You can say that again!" His sudden imitation of a dog howling in surprise made people turn their noses up in disgust.

Cady drew deep of the knowledge of years. "Myridi flies trigger the telepathic abilities of the Alkhym, we all know that."

"Granted."

"But in Brin's case, everything was supercharged and magnified. She reached into our minds and made us think she had vanished. Oh, she's a canny girl."

"And what happened then?"

"Why, she slipped away through the open door while you were poncing around with the man from the pools."

"She'll be waiting for us." These were Lek's first words of the journey. His eyes never left the passing street. "Miss Brin will make her way back to the *Juniper*. We will find her there."

It was a simple statement of desire. But Cady caught Jeb's eye, and they both passed the truth back and forth, no words necessary: the Thrawl was going to crash heavy and fall to bits. Cady thought of soothing him with a smidgeon of hope, but decided against it, and she kept her trap shut the rest of the way. They had searched Queenie's bungalow, and the corner shop next door, the back garden, all of Threadbare Street, and most of the brand spanking new Ibraxus Estate. But the girl was gone, good and gone, and Cady wondered when they might next meet, and what form the little terror would take when they did. She looked down at her forearms and saw the lovely flowers that had blossomed there, bright pink they were and flecked with gold. She saw them either as a parting gift from Brin, that surge of Xillithic energy that had opened her petals so nicely; or more likely as an invitation to a future fight. Well then, I will see you on the battlefield you little snot-nosed, hoity-toity, scallywagging, dragonising, gullyfluffing, good-for-nothing lump of vomit on a stick, Gogmagog or no Gogmagog!

Her fingers played gently with her new petals.

Next step of the journey: pollination.

Oh, she felt a tingle in her lower decks at the very thought of it.

The omnibus dropped them off a short walk from the wharf. Of course, there was no sign of Brin Halsegger. Lek went down into the hold straightaway, his face clicked to empty. Cady left him alone for a while, spending time with Jeb, showing him the engine, the dash, the binnacle, giving him a job of polishing the brass spokes of the wheel.

"I want to see my ugly mug in them, you hear!"

"Aye aye, captain."

Then she went below. Lek was sitting on the stool in front of Mr Carmichael's tank, staring into the brackish water, seeking a glimpse of the crystalback creature.

"What are you looking for?" she asked him.

"Miss Brin."

Oh Ludding heck, this was bad. "There's no hope of such a thing."

"Mr Carmichael will know where she is, he will scour the streets of Ludwich for her, he will travel in spirit from one crystal to the next, won't you, Mr C?"

He'd given the creature a nickname! Whatever next?

"He's asleep, poor thing," Cady said. "He's spent the whole day roaming the city, listening in on telephone conversations, peeping out from television screens, gliding the radio waves. Why, I'll bet he's even been rummaging around in the Crystal Archives beneath the Central Post Office."

This speech had no effect on Lek at all. Cady changed her tack.

"That Pok Pok is a lovely looking Lady Thrawl, isn't she?"

He gave a quick nod.

"Well then, do you think she's going to enjoy this face you're carrying, this *Self Pity No. 4*? Hm? How about something more stoical, a nice stiff upper lip, eh? Like in the war. And then put just a touch of quiver in it, ooh, she'll love that. Like you're holding in your emotions, but can't quite manage it. You know, like Elizabeth Lamore in that film she was in, oh, what was it called now, the one where she falls for that roustabout at the fair?"

"*Forbidden Desires*?"

"That's the one! Good to see your brain is still working."

Lek had placed both his palms flat against the glass tank and was concentrating his mind, as revealed by his face of furrowed brow and narrowed eyes.

"What are you up to, eh?"

"I need to find her. I need to."

Cady felt her heart melting, despite all the trouble this lump of spare parts had caused her over the last few days. She said to him, "I looked into Mr Carmichael's tank late last night, when we first arrived at the city's wall, and you'll never guess who I saw. Lord Pettifer himself, I swear."

Lek's brows furrowed even further, his fingers pressing at the glass as though he might break it and all the water flood out. Cady leaned in close and put her hand on his shoulder, feeling the pent-up energy coiled there like the main spring of the House of Witan clock just before midnight strikes on the last day of the year.

"Pettifer warned me about Brin, that she might, well, that she might actually be on the side of Gogmagog, that she might be working in tandem for him, paving the way, so to speak, opening the portals so that he can make his evil journey into the world."

A tiny crack appeared in the glass tank just beneath the Thrawl's right hand.

"For Ludding chuff's sake, Lek. Stop that! STOP IT!"

He did so, under the extraordinary power of Cady's raised voice, which sounded like an oak tree being split by a lightning bolt. His hands released their pressure. Cady checked the crack in the glass: it was alright, for now at least, but would need to be patched up at some point in the not too distant future. But Lek's attention was still firmly fixed on the contents of the tank, the black water where the crystalback lay at rest.

Cady went on, "I'm not saying I believe this Pettifer chap, not at all, but I would prefer... in my capacity as official watchwoman and Haegra of the realm... ah hum... at least to keep one half-open peeper on the off chance, of it being true, like."

Lek made no reply. His eyes were burning a lovely sapphire colour, sparkling at the edges. Then the two eye-beams emerged, but softly, diffusely, unlike Cady had ever seen him do before, and they just sort of *melted* through the glass and set up a sphere of blue light inside the tank. It was the size of a football and floated amid the darkness, bobbing gently rather like a bubble.

Mr Carmichael stirred in the depths; his crystal colours flashed and coruscated.

The Thrawl concentrated further, moving the twin beams back and forth. "I'm showing Mr C what Miss Brin looks like," he explained. "Then he can search for her."

Indeed, a small flickering black-and-white image of the Alkhym girl was forming inside the bubble of light, blurred to begin with but growing clearer as the seconds went by. It had the look of a home movie filmed at a garden party, but only a few seconds of it on view, looping back on itself over and over. Brin was wearing a fairy-style dress. She twirled and twirled and twirled and twirled and twirled: a moment of time captured forever. But the effect of this image wasn't quite what Lek was hoping for; instead of roaming the city in search of the missing girl, Mr Carmichael simply expanded the bubble of light. Now Cady could see where the moving image of Brin was actually stored in Lek's head, inside a large bell jar on a shelf. A tiny shard of crystal shone at the mouth of the vessel, projecting the moving image into the interior. It was an Alkhym memory jar, the kind of thing popular in the years between the wars. The bubble expanded further, under Mr Carmichael's control, until it filled more than half of the glass tank's volume. An entire room could now be seen, the jar on the shelf only one of many such items.

"Lek, what is this place?"

He was as surprised as she was. "It's my Reliquary, where I keep all my pictures and movies of Brin, and her storybooks, and old toys she's grown out of. Memories, so many of them." He sighed. "Mr C has joined himself with me. He's taking me on a tour of my own head."

"So this is part of your famous Crystal Palace?"

Lek nodded. Cady remembered that a similar connection had formed between the Thrawl and Mr Carmichael yesterday, during the river voyage. But this was different, a much clearer rendition, and she looked on in utter fascination as the storage room within Lek's palace formed around the little image of the girl. Cady saw the jars and toys and books as mentioned and the pictures on the walls and the boxes filled with trinkets and dolls and marbles and packs of collector cards. It was a treasure trove, but one imbued with melancholy. Then the viewing focus changed, roaming towards the door of the room and through, into a long curving corridor. The walls were made of crystals of many colours, not just the normal blue, but ruby and gold and silver, as well as gleams of bright emerald and sparkles of orange. It was beautiful, truly a sight to set your eyes upon. Lapis lazuli, turquoise, moonstone, fire opals, pink calcite, quartz, chalcedony, jasper, agates, aquamarine, and many more. Cady hardly knew how to gather all the loveliness for herself. They passed room after room: Gymnasium, Study, a Music Room with a grand piano whose keys were embedded with gemstones, the Central Index Chamber with its endless rows of filing cabinets. So many rooms, each one more vivid and scintillating than the last. There was even a small Chapel complete with an altarpiece depicting some kind of mechanical Son of God nailed to the crossbeams of a piece of machinery: Cady had never seen the like before, nor heard of such a religion. It was incredible! The stained-glass windows shone with a hundred shivers of multicoloured light.

"How many rooms are there altogether?" she asked.

"Cady, I told you, it changes all the time. But at the last count: one thousand, nine hundred and forty-seven." He blinked rapidly, adjusting his vision. "But I've never seen it this way before, from the outside."

Cady tapped at the glass. "Is that you?"

Lek peered closer. "Why yes, I believe it is."

A small animated image of Thrawl Lek was walking along a corridor, as seen inside the glass tank.

"So this is how you view yourself, is it? You're wearing a smoking jacket."

"One likes to relax after a hard day's butlering."

"Oh one does, one does. But I have to say…"

"Yes?"

"You're quite a bit more handsome in this version than in reality."

Lek shrugged this off. "They are both equally real." He watched the little model of himself walk into a large room filled with hundreds of paintings and photographs on the walls.

"I guess this is your Portrait Gallery?"

"That's right. I was given the Basic Set of Expressions on my Making Day – *Happy, Sad, Deferential*, and the like. But this is where I keep all the extra expressions I've learned from studying the human face over decades."

Cady read aloud some of the labels: "*Feigned Indifference. Bashful but Needy. A Desperate Desire. Remembering, Wistfully, a Long-Ago Fleeting Pleasure.*" She whistled. "Well kiss the arse of King Lud and call me a sinner, this is fuckin' incredible. I mean, I never realised."

But Little Lek had already left the gallery. He walked the corridors.

"What are you looking for?"

"Something's wrong. Something inside my head. A disturbance. This is why Mr C is showing me this. He wants to help."

Now they entered the Library, an extended room of glinting turquoise walls lined with shelves of books, magazines and pamphlets, floor to ceiling. Cady saw the bullet that was lodged in the Thrawl's skull. From the outside it was just a normal-sized projectile; but from the inside, it was massive, a huge missile that had halfway penetrated the Library wall, creating a nasty looking web of cracks in the crystal, splintering the shelves, charring books, and scattering torn pages everywhere.

Both Large and Little Lek looked pained. "I try to clean up, I make repairs constantly, but the wall always breaks open again."

"Perhaps we should find you a doctor, have the bullet removed?"

"No! No, no, no. That would destroy me, the whole edifice would come crumbling down."

And once again Cady's heart took a lurch into sadness. "This bullet must be the disturbance, I guess. Is that right?"

"No, this is an old wound. Mr C wants me to see something new, I'm sure of it."

"To do with the spell that the Witch of Threadbare Street cast upon you? I mean, I did warn you about that."

"Perhaps. But let us keep looking. It might help in finding Brin."

Cady made no comment on this.

The image in Mr Carmichael's tank twisted and turned, showing new corridors, new rooms. At one point it lingered on a shadowy figure hiding in a niche, perfectly still as though frozen in time. "That is my dream of Miss Jane Polter, my creator," Lek explained. "I told you that I dreamt of her? The only time in my life I have ever dreamed. And all Thrawls the same, dreaming the same thing at the exact same time."

Cady cursed freely. "And the next day you all went mad in the Frenzy, and that was that, the end of the line for you and your kin."

Little Lek moved quickly on. He entered the Billiards Room.

"I believe we have found the trouble."

They both bent as close as they could to the tank, their heads touching. Cady's eyes opened wide. "Well bugger me backwards, that is one ugly fucker."

It was, it truly was. A large cocoon lay on the billiards table, so massive the ends of it poked over the sides, port, starboard, bow and stern. Its crinkled dark brown body contrasted with the smooth green of the baize. Bits of it had fallen off, and were still falling off. The top of the cocoon pushed up at the light above the table, and red and white billiard balls were encrusted into its papery skin. A large fissure in the side of the thing showed where Brin's myridi fly had emerged, pushing its way free of confinement.

Cady tried to get the story clear: "So this is how your crystal mind pictures the cocoon in your head?"

Lek nodded. "In reality the cocoon is just a little bit of stuff in my skull, empty, dead, but the palace sees it very differently: enlarged, glorified, a symbolic object."

"I hate to inform you, me old tin can, but I don't think it's empty."

The cocoon was rocking back and forth, knocking a billiard cue to the floor, almost rolling off the table in its urgent, trembling motions. The fissure was widening. Something was poking out, a pair of long quivering antennae. Neither Cady nor Lek could speak a word. They watched in horror and wonder as the myridi fly crawled free of its casing. The wings expanded. Its abdomen was black and glossy, its bulbous thorax a bright iridescent greeny-yellow that glowed from within. The six legs worked feverishly to gain a purchase. Its multifaceted eyes captured the many colours of the crystal walls, reflecting them back as splinters of light, painful to look upon. Mucus dribbled from its mandibles, ruining the baize.

Little Lek disappeared from the Billiards Room in a blur and reappeared instantly.

"Where did you just go?" Cady asked.

"To my Library. I looked up *Lady Penniwick's Entomological Study of the Myridi, its Habits, Habitat, and Life Cycle*."

"Oh yes. And?"

"She states that on rare occasions a single cocoon might hold two pupae."

"Twins, you mean?"

"Yes. The myridi pupa breaks down into a liquid inside the silk wrapping, a biological soup, and then reforms itself into a winged body, its adult form. But sometimes it creates two adult myridi from the same soup, one of which might well be a mutated and malformed specimen–"

Lek suddenly put his hands to his head. He pressed at his skull while emitting a yowl of pain. Then he fell off the stool into the bilge, slopping about in the water and oil and muck. Cady bent down to help him. "What is it? Lek, speak to me!" But the Thrawl could only roll around, punching at his head with both fists as though to pound himself into unconsciousness. Cady clung to him as best she could, all the time calling out his name and adding her own fisticuffs to the struggle, hardly knowing what she was doing. And then, as suddenly as it began, the violent fit came to a halt. Lek sat up. His eyes were shining a soft pale opal colour, with a very peaceful look to them. His focus was set a long way off, and yet fixed with the utmost clarity on a distant object, whatever it might be.

"Lek, what are you seeing?"

"It's Brin," he answered in a whisper. "Miss Brin. I can sense her whereabouts."

"What do you mean, *sense*?"

Cady bent close, pressing her face directly against Lek's head to better see what was going on. There was a fly walking the curved interior wall of the skull; not huge as seen in the Crystal Palace projection, but small, the normal size for a myridi. This twin specimen had only now hatched itself from the remains of cocoon. Its green and gold thorax glimmered brightly as it went about its business: walking, trying to fly, disappearing momentarily, only to reappear on the inner wall to go on with its peregrinations. Lek was glad to have it there. He was smiling: his face full of *Happiness No. 1*, from the Basic Set of Expressions. His voice was tender.

"I will find you now, Brin. I am connected, my myridi to yours, my twin to your twin."

Mr Carmichael closed down his image of the Crystal Palace and the *Juniper*'s hold was dark once more. Only that tiny moving insect inside Lek's skull gave out any light.

"It might not be wise, Lek, to go on pursuing her."

The Thrawl got to his feet, bent over almost double to fit his height under the low roof. "I have my job to do. I promised Lady Halsegger I would look after her youngest daughter, at any and all costs, and I will continue to do so."

"You always do as the Halseggers bid, do you?"

"I made a promise."

"Always?"

"Yes, of course–"

"Always, always?"

"Nearly always, but–"

"But you've fulfilled your mission now, Lek, to get Brin to hest. All the effort you've put in! It's done. What are you, a loyal little doggie chasing after his mistress?"

The Thrawl's face was covered in shadows; no expression was visible, only the dull red glow of his eyes. His voice was deep and sonorous. "Without Miss Brin, my life is meaningless."

Cady blew a gasket. "Oh for fuck's sake, you're free, free, for the first time in your life! You big lump. Now is your chance. You can do anything you want, anything at all!"

Lek's voice changed, became almost maniacal: "I am the Thrawlkym. I have hested."

It scared Cady. She was all set to start unscrewing his head and let the fly loose, but then Jebediah appeared at the hatch, shouting down to her:

"Captain, there's a gentleman here to see you."

"Tell him I'm busy."

"He says he has urgent news. Awfully urgent, so he says."

"Keep him happy." Then she turned back to Lek. "Now don't you go doing anything stupid, just stay put, and we'll sort this out."

But the Thrawl's gaze had returned to that beloved faraway subject matter.

Cady climbed up to the deck, happy to be breathing clean air for once, for her thoughts were rattled and her heart a mess of worms. Then she stopped short, for Jeb had been speaking the truth: the visitor was indeed a gentleman, tall and well-built with a silvery goatee-style beard and hair of the same shade brushed back from an intelligent brow. His eyes were a sparkling green. Yet he was getting on in years, well into his sixties. Two ice-blue hesti shone at his temples. An Alkhym then, and a distinguished one. Cady wiped at the streaks of oil and dirt on her face, suddenly aware of just how untidy she must look.

"You are Arcadia Meade, I take it?" His voice was cultured.

"The one and only. What can I do you for?"

"Allow me to introduce myself. Mr Leopold Hill, here on a matter of some import."

"Well I only know one Leopold Hill, and that would be of Maguire & Hill."

He nodded assent. "I am that man."

"The mapmakers? Cartographers supreme?"

"How very kind of you to mention. Yes, we worked together, you and I, Arcadia, some fifty years ago."

"We did?"

"You helped Mr Maguire and myself with our first charting of the River Nysis."

"It's all a bit of a haze, I'm afraid."

"You were rather inebriated at the time, it must be said. But very useful, yes, your knowledge of the river's secret courses was unsurpassed."

She revelled in this and then asked, "What do you want of me? Not more mapping, I hope, because my brain is five fathoms deep these days."

"No, no." Mr Hill paused. "Quite a different matter, but strangely interjoined." Another pause. "Arcadia, I am here with an urgent message for you."

"Concerning?"

"Your blossoming as a Haegra. The search for the Lud Flower. Your subsequent pollination, and the possibilities thereof."

Cady felt suddenly light-headed, and quite taken over with desire.

The Mapmaker

Lek was standing in the cabin, transferring choice items from Brin's suitcase to his own. Cady sat watching him, getting her head back together after Mr Hill's arrival. She thought the Thrawl's behaviour rather sad; from what she suspected, Brin would no longer have any interest or need in these childish things. But Lek went about his task, choosing the glittery baubles and marbles and postage stamps depicting tropical birds with care, alongside a change of clothes for the girl. Every so often he would press a finger against his skull, knowing each time precisely where the internal myridi fly would be positioned; perhaps he could feel its little legs tickling at him. Then he returned to his task, this time showing Cady a set of collector cards.

"This was Miss Brin's favourite series, *The Haunted River*. She used to collect them from her father's cigarette packets. They show different places of weird and unusual interest along the Nysis, telling stories of their origins and development. Do you see?"

Cady took the offered card, taking in the image of a mansion house on the front, then reading aloud the words on the reverse:

"*Card No. 32. Blinnings Mansion. Jon Karak, the third Lord of Blinnings, built this riverside mansion on the site of an abandoned Azeel monastery. The residence was constructed with many priest holes in the walls and a secret temple whose altar featured an icon of the great god Naphet. Karak was credited with identifying the Earth's second Moon before his execution for heresy. The observatory he built in the grounds of the house is no longer in use.*"

Cady gave the card back. She knew how much Blinnings mansion meant to both Lek and to Brin. But the Thrawl changed the subject. He looked pensive. "The adult male myridi fly lives only a few days. So I don't have long, if I'm to find her."

"I would come with you, only…"

His fingers hesitated over the cards. "You and I, Cady, we are two forms of madness colliding, and repulsing each other, and flying off in different directions."

"Sometimes, my old tinplate begging bowl, I really do think you know me."

He looked at her as if for the first time. "Madam, I have, on balance, enjoyed our time together."

"Really?"

"Oh yes. Sixty-four per cent enjoyment, against thirty-six per cent utter despair."

Cady thought this an accurate assessment. But she added, "I'm still not sure about Brin. About her true intentions."

"I will face whatever comes to me."

With that he closed his suitcase and moved out onto the foredeck. Cady followed, watching as he deftly opened up the figurehead's skull to retrieve the crystal brain of Pok Pok. She was in mid-flow at the time:

"…tied to the wharf low haulage no tide *Juniper* and Pok Pok are waiting for a new job, a new destination, where are we going next, I wonder, perhaps we'll sail off into the sun... Oh... what is happening to me now–"

So cruelly cut off! A small cloud of Faynr mist was still in place around Pok Pok's crystal, but Lek blew at this, and scraped at it with his fingers, dislodging it. He placed the now bare crystal in a pocket of his jacket. Then he walked aft. He saluted the Dragon Ensign where it hung at rest on the mast. Mr Leopold Hill stood close by, leaning on a walking cane. Cady had taken notice of a slight limp in the mapmaker's left leg. Lek was ready to disembark, suitcase in hand. He gave Cady an amount of money in rolled-up notes.

"Wages for the boy," he explained. "And whatever you might need."

"Very kind."

"I hereby give you ownership of the *Juniper*."

"Right you are. I'll look after the old tub, don't you worry."

For a moment longer he hesitated. His eyes were blue and green, one of each colour, very lively and lovely to look upon.

Cady took this as a good sign. "Fair winds and following seas, Thrawl Lek."

He blinked. She suspected he was visiting his somewhat rundown library. Sure enough: "*A nautical blessing of good will before a voyage. First known usage: Captain Jacob Brownsville, the Year of Exploration.*"

"Oh be off with you, before I give you a clout round the ear."

And then he was gone, steeping onto the wharf and disappearing down an alleyway, heading west. Cady wasted no time, giving orders to Jeb to get the boat underway.

They sailed back down the tunnel towards the river, with the new cabin boy on boathook duties. Mr Hill was sitting alone in the cabin. Cady stood at the helm, handling the wheel in an easy manner; she had an innate skill, equal parts Haegra and old tar, to always remember a course once taken, even in reverse. Soon enough they entered the more concentrated outposts of Faynr's body. Shortly afterwards, the Nysis greeted them with a silvery dance of light and the rainbow sparkle of purification spray from a fire-brigade ship. The *Juniper* sailed upriver, against the tide. The first flush of the day's hesting was done, but the river's starboard course was filled with vessels coming down from the traditional Alkhym estates west of the city. The port side was relatively clear, however, and they made good time. She gave Jeb the chance to prove himself, handing control over to him, staying at his side, offering bits of advice and the occasional rebuke. The boy's story of helping his granddaddy on the western stretches of the river must have been true, for he quickly picked up the feel of it, keeping the boat slow and steady ahead. Cady went into the cabin and sat down opposite Mr Hill. She started on a luncheon meat and cheese sandwich from the picnic hamper her sister Nabs had made up for them that morning. She offered a bite to Hill, but he turned his finely pointed nose up at the prospect.

"So what can I expect," she asked, around a mouthful, "from Mr Maguire?"

Hill was examining Cady's set of original edition river charts. "Not a lot, I'm afraid. Henry isn't very lucid these days. Or rather, he moves in and out of lucidity. But I have learned to follow his thought processes, to a degree."

"When was he first put away?"

"He wasn't *put away*, Arcadia. He went to Medlock Island of his own volition. Eighteen years ago now."

"Well, I heard as such. But I never knew the real reason, only rumours."

"And what might those be?"

"That he was trying to draw up maps of non-existent places, or mythological realms. Is that true?"

Leopold Hill thought to himself for a moment. His hesti pinged quietly. Then he said, "We started working together as young men, Henry and myself. We made our first maps of the Alkhym manor gardens, including the secret river routes and Faynr pools that had long been hidden underground. The maps proved very popular among the higher families. We set up in business, and we made a lot of money. But over time..." He paused as his fingers traced the river's printed route. "Over time Henry became obsessed with other maps, things I could never comprehend. He made charts we could never publish; they were of no use to anyone."

Cady interrupted, "But they must have been of use to him, to Maguire, surely?"

"Well yes. But we were a cartography business, not an art gallery, or a psychology practice. And it just got worst. Eventually..."

Again he hesitated. Cady could see that he was pained. "Mr Hill?"

"Leopold... please."

"Leopold, I've lived for nearly one and a half thousand years. There isn't much I haven't seen, or heard about, or experienced."

He nodded at this, and searched through the river maps until he found the chart he wanted. He pointed to a bend in the Nysis. "This is the area known as the Withy. You know it well, I presume."

"That I do. A whirlpool down at Wayland Point." She opened a tin of prunes and ate them one by one, her fingers dripping with juice.

"You'll know that it's famous as a suicide spot. Especially for doomed lovers."

Cady's attention pricked. "So Maguire was in love?"

"No, no. In all my years I have never seen Henry in any kind of amorous company. He never married, had no children. He was a person who lived alone, and liked it that way."

"So what then? What was he doing at the Withy?"

"He wanted to map the patterns of the souls of the drowned as they made their way upriver to the Glimmie."

"You mean he tried to kill himself?"

Leopold nodded. "I'm not sure how far he wanted to go, to be honest. Or so I tell myself. But he weighted himself down and waded out, towards the whirlpool. Luckily, he was seen by a passing boat and pulled out of the river. Otherwise… Well, that final map would be complete, I suppose." He took a breath. "Instead, he ended up in Medlock Asylum, for his own good, his own protection. And he's been there ever since."

"But he's still drawing up his maps?"

"Oh yes, and many of them. The strangest maps I have ever witnessed. But one above all others, his *final chart*, he calls it. The one that points the way to the Lud flower's position."

"Can it be true? I really want it to be true!"

"He needs your help, to finish it."

Cady fell silent. Her fingers played at the flowers on her arms, and the one on her shoulder. Hill watched her with

interest. The agitation had vanished now that the buds had
opened. She was ready. If Henry Maguire really could point
the way to the Lud flower, well then... let it be.

The *Juniper* sailed on. Faynr lay upon the water as a thin
intangible mist of scattered particles that tickled at the nose
and fingertips. A large picador fish swam alongside the boat
for a while, its scales glittering. Half an hour later, Cady
stood at the prow, watching the Isle of Medlock approach. It
was a smallish island in the middle of the river, with a copse
of spike trees surrounding the only building, the asylum.
There were no purification vessels operating here, so Faynr's
sickness had taken good hold, wreathing fog around the
thin dark thorn-covered trees. Cady took over at the helm
to steer the boat to the landing dock. They stepped down
onto rocky ground.

"Jeb, stay with the boat, will you?"

"Glad to do so."

"And don't think about half-inching it."

"As if. Honest Jeb Yeomanson, that's me. Ask anyone."

Cady and Hill set off, taking a pathway up a slight rise,
passing through a gate in a wire fence into the grounds of the
asylum. The main building made for a stark silhouette, with
a domed tower rearing over a more recently built concrete
administration unit. Through the spike trees and the fog
she caught glimpses of the radiating detention blocks, older
structures with crumbling red-brick walls and once-ornate
carvings. The whole estate was laid out like a wheel, four
spokes from a central hub. They passed a vegetable plot,
a rusting pavilion and a tennis court: two inmates were
playing a game, mostly missing the ball on each stroke, and
laughing at their own bad efforts. Was there even a ball in
play? Cady could not rightly tell.

"There's been an influx since the war," Hill said as they walked along. "Lots of disturbed young men back from the fields of battle."

"Aye, I've met the same sad boys, and in more wars than I care to count."

A wretched soul circled a waterless fountain, around and around and around. Distant cries pierced the air and set the thin gaunt trunks of the spike trees quivering. These outgrowths were in fact saplings, only a dozen or so years old. They were bare of leaf and always would be, existing in a deathly condition all the year round. The trees were manifested this way, and not from a seed in the soil, but from a seed in one of the patient's heads.

"Is Myrtle still a resident?" Cady asked. "I know she liked to live in one of the greenhouses."

"She died last year, refusing this time to regrow herself."

"Oh that's a shame. We worked together on a number of never-never cases over the centuries. She was a fine watchwoman. If a little up herself."

"To be honest, Arcadia, I wonder how you didn't end up here, at least for a while. It can't be an easy life, being a Haegra."

Cady stopped to touch one of the spike trees, rubbing her hands over the bark, carefully and deliberately pricking her palm on one of the thorns. Myrtle Jones's spirit was in these trees, each one propagated from the intense overflowing of her damaged psyche, into the soil of the island. It felt good to commune with her, and she wished dearly that her former colleague was still alive to help her on this day of days.

A guard led them into the warren of the main block, where they were greeted by a doctor, the head psychiatrist. He chatted to Mr Hill, but Cady kept to herself, for she had never liked the idea of someone poking around in her thoughts and feelings; the Haegral mind was always finely balanced, never that far from tipping over into the abyss.

They took a staircase up to the second floor and then upwards once more to the roof, where the doctor left them. The tall central tower rose above Cady, making her feel dizzy.

"There's a lift, I hope? Or a bucket and a pulley?"

Hill shook his head sadly. They entered the tower and started to ascend a winding staircase. A little way up, Cady peered out of a slitted window, seeing that the asylum's small farmstead was also planted with Myrtle's spike trees. The patient's dreams of vegetable life had manifested on every spare bit of land. Perhaps it was a good job she died, otherwise by now the entire asylum would be overrun with spikes.

"Are we more than halfway yet?"

"Just about."

"Good, good, because I'm fuckin' knackered."

She sat herself down on a step. Hill leaned on his cane. He wiped sweat from his face with a handkerchief.

"You won't sit down?" she asked.

"I'll never get up again."

"There is that." She blew her nose loudly.

"I'm always asking Henry to move into a ground-floor ward, but he likes the view. Here we go, a wee nip might help us." He offered her a drink from a flask. "Whiskey, nineteen years old."

"Coo, yes please." Cady gulped at it and then spluttered. "Ruddy heck, that's not whiskey! What is it?"

Hill laughed. "A little concoction brewed from steeped myridi cocoons. After all, why let all those empty casings go to waste?"

A few more sips got her tongue accustomed. There was a
warmth in her throat. She found one of Queenie's custard
creams in her pocket, nicely purloined before the bungalow
hesting, and ate it in two bites. Another drink was needed
to wash it down. Now she was happier. A semaphore beetle
flew in through the window, its colours flashing madly as it
settled on her face and then flew off again, this time heading
up the stairs.

Hill said, "He'll know you're on your way now."

"He's been tracking me, has he, using the beetles?"

"He has. For the last few days actually, but especially
since you entered the city."

Cady tutted. "I knew a signal officer once, a paramour of
mine, he showed me how the beetles were manipulated, to
change the colours into the correct sequence for a message.
All those little gidgets and gadgets he had to work with!
They looked like a knife, fork and spoon set from a doll's
house. Too finicky for me."

"Just wait, Arcadia, until you see how Maguire controls
the insects." He put away his flask. "Shall we ascend?"

"Give us a pull up then. That's it. Oof."

Before they set off once more, he spoke with intent: "I do
hope Henry finds some peace from your visit."

"It's all down to me, is it?"

And so they trudged on until they reached the top floor
of the tower, where Hill rapped gently on a door. It was not
locked, and he opened it and went inside. Cady followed.
She was first struck by the smell of the place, a mixture of
sweat, wine and tobacco fumes, and a light underplay of
urine. Chalk dust covered the furniture, alongside many
flakes of charcoal; the single metal cot, the one wooden
chair and the simple desk were all victims of this smear

campaign. The room was circular, studded with four round open windows at the cardinal points, with a low ceiling and a bare floor. Every square inch of wall-space was covered in a hand-drawn map of some kind. They were layered over each other, in some places several inches thick: the work of years. The ceiling, Cady noted, absolutely crawled with semaphore beetles, a colourful if somewhat frightening canopy. One and two and three of the beetles descended to examine her flesh. She let them be for now. A young Azeelian man was pinning even more sheets of cartridge paper to the walls, each displaying yet another map. The cartographer himself, Mr Henry Maguire, was busy at work on a new creation, working on the floor, drawing freehand with a charcoal pencil. Mr Hill nodded to Cady, telling her it was alright to approach. She did so, bending over to examine the map, recognising the red-light district at Tolley Hoo. But Maguire worked quickly, scrubbing out sections and starting again, the paper becoming more and more disfigured, until with a soft moan of despair he scrunched the entire sheet up and threw it away under the cot, where it joined other such castaways. He called out and the beetles descended from above to cover his body completely. For a few seconds they crawled over his skin and clothes. It gave Cady quite a stir, but Maguire seemed to welcome the swarm to his person.

Hill whispered, not wanting to disturb the activity: "Henry has developed a unique way of communicating with the insects – the way they tickle his skin, the pattern of their bites, the subtle changing of the semaphore spectrum – gathering every last speck of knowledge."

Cady nodded, not quite believing it. But once the beetles had flown back to their nest on the ceiling, Maguire started on a fresh sheet of paper, working at a slower rate this time, carefully defining each street and alleyway, until the pencil's point broke. The mapmaker sighed. The young man came to his aid, sharpening the pencil with a small knife.

Cady unbent her back, feeling her tendrils tightening around her spine.

Mr Hill introduced the Azeelian to her. "This is Larkspur, another patient here. He's a mute. But Henry finds him very helpful."

Maguire himself had not yet looked up to inspect his visitors, being far too busy.

Hill tapped his partner on the shoulder. "Henry, I have brought Arcadia Meade to see you. The Haegra, as you requested."

The mapmaker's hands slowed to a stop. Then he looked up.

Cady saw his face for the first time, noting the bags under the eyes, the deep creases at each side of the mouth, and the furrows of the brow. Most of his hair had gone, but the remaining strands were long and greenish, entirely unbarbered, floating around in wisps on the liver-spotted skull. Larkspur was dressed in the standard blue trousers and buttonless tunic of the other patients she had seen, but Maguire wore brown corduroy trousers, a crumpled shirt and a purple cardigan two sizes too big for him. His feet were bare and smutted with dirt and charcoal. He stood up, a short stocky man, a physique typical of Wodwo men of his generation: built for factory work. His natural talents had released him from such drudgery, only to deliver him at the end to this place of confinement on an isle of spikes. Now he came up close to Cady and looked deeply into her eyes. She saw the city within his gaze, the streets, and the river through time, and the many routes taken and untaken by the people; it was quite the deepest and furthest Cady had ever voyaged without moving.

He spoke: "I have been following you." He took her by the hand and showed her a long line of blue paint on the floor, pushing aside sheets of paper to reveal its full extent. Cady knew it be the River Nysis, twisting and turning into a symbolic mapping. The Winding Way: it was truly named. She noted the sea and Pinchbeck Sound at the far end, and the source of the river at Chigley Tor on the other side of the room. A matchbox with a couple of spent matches stuck in it for masts and a tiny bit of rag for the ensign rested on the river at Medlock Island.

"This is the *Juniper*," she realised.

"My beetles have been chasing you everywhere, chasing and following and reporting back to me, every step of the way."

"And here's me thinking my sister Nabs was keeping her beady eyes on me. But no, it's you, you old madcap. Why, you're a nosy-arsed bugger, aren't you?"

He laughed, and took her on a tour of the room, showing off his collection of maps, lifting some of them up to reveal those underneath. Many were nicely drawn on rectangular sheets of cartridge, while others were more roughly sketched on large ragged pieces of paper. Some of the locations she could recognise, stretches of her beloved river and of the city, but others were more confusing. She asked about one and the mapmaker answered: "The flow of pollen from plants that grow alongside the river." Even a Haegra would have trouble tracking such a thing, but she left this unsaid, as Maguire explained some of the other charts to her: "Ley lines, the swarming patterns of the common skirl, the internal organs of Psephekarnidraxapor, the pathways of the Xilliths as they travel up and down Faynr's body, and this one here. Do you see! Gogmagog, his various inroads and points of access. Weak points in the ghost of Haakenur."

"So you know about the Night Serpent?"

Again he looked at her. "That's why you're here, isn't it?"

"I thought… Mr Hill said you might know the location of the Lud flower?"

"Both are long winding roads on the same chart, intersecting."

She looked around the room. "But how can you see all this, from up here?"

"Lie down with me."

"What?"

"Lie down with me, Cady Meade. I beg you."

He flopped down and lay full-length on the floor, shifting his supine body over the scattered papers and half-finished charts. She joined him and they both lay there, looking up at the ceiling. The mass of semaphore beetles crawled over every single spot, hundreds if not thousands of them, and every moment many more joining through the four windows, and others flying off in their place. It was an ever-changing display, a dance, a panorama. She felt Maguire's hand in hers, gently squeezing.

"Oh look!" he said. "Cady, it's yourself, can you see?"

"What's that? I can't see anything, Maguire. Only a bunch of beetles."

"It's yourself. At the effigy three days ago, trying to grow yourself. And not doing very well." He started to laugh.

"You find it funny, do you?"

"My beetles were watching you from the trees."

"By the sharp end of Lud's sword, I'll cut you up, I will!"

But Maguire's attention was fully on his beetle display. "Now they're showing me the House of Witan, and look, so many boats on the river, yourself aboard the *Juniper*. Just this morning. You, the Thrawl, the little girl. Oh, can't you see, dear lady, it's so beautiful. You're just emerging from Faynr's heart."

"No, I cannot see, not at all."

Hill and Larkspur were standing off to the side, both of them smiling.

"Leopold! I think your friend really is doolally. There isn't a biscuit in his barrel that isn't crumbly."

Maguire's hand gripped hers tightly.

"Ow. Do you mind!"

"Look, look deeply! I thought you were a Haegra?"

"Bloody fuckin' cheek of it."

Cady did her best, moving her head this way and that, squinting, making herself go cross-eyed until the room began to spin. But nothing good would form in her sight: the insects crawled around in their maddening games, all the colours of the spectrum flashing and changing. On occasion she did glimpse a vague shape of some half familiar object or event, but the image always dissolved, the more she looked at it directly. Maguire, however, was enjoying himself thoroughly. His hand relaxed its grip.

"There is your sister's house in Witherhithe. Number 29, Brickyard Lane, where you and your friends stayed last night. Isn't that correct?"

"You can see that? Really? What is Nabs up to?"

"This is from earlier today. They're throwing a street party for the bank holiday. I see bunting, children's games, and look… what is that? A band of musicians playing on a bomb site."

"That will be my cousin Oswyn and his group, the Eels of Ludwich."

"What jolly fun!"

"Oh yes, how splendid for them. And here's me, stuck in the room of a mad duffer, staring at creepy-crawlies."

Other beetles were arriving through all four windows, perhaps responding to Maguire's needs to witness more, to view the city in all its glory.

"Is there anything in particular you'd like to see?" he asked her.

Cady thought about it, going over various possibilities. And strangely, indeed very strangely, one desire came through stronger than all the others.

"Can you show me where Thrawl Lek is, right this minute?"

"Not right this minute, no. It takes time for the beetles to gather, to pass their messages from each to each, and then to fly home."

"Any time in the last hour, then. That would be nice."

Maguire concentrated. She turned her head to look at him, seeing that his eyes were clear, his body relaxed. There seemed not a speck of craziness in him. How could that be?

He spoke softly this time. "I see him. I see your mechanical friend, some half an hour ago. He is walking across a bridge, crossing the Nysis."

"Which one, which bridge?"

A moment's pause. Then: "Blackthorn Bridge."

"Heading north, or south?"

"South, I think, towards the Shrivings."

Cady eased her breath, holding herself as still as she could. She made no forcing movements of her eyes or head, but simply looked above at the ceiling, quite calmly. She wished only to see the beetles at their play, nothing more, nothing more…

Within the ever-shifting display she saw a bridge over the river. The beetles actually made the image appear, by arranging their bodies and their colours: the water below, the bridge, the figures walking across. One figure was taller than the others, an object of curiosity. People were avoiding him, or even cursing at him. But there was no sound. The edges of the vision were blurred, the centre at best equivalent to a television set on the blink, and yet there he was, Cady was sure of it, Mr Lek himself! By all accounts he was still on his search, following the directions given out by the myridi in Brin's head. He must be going to the funfair, knowing that she had visited there. But what was the girl's purpose at the Shrivings?

The image faded from Cady's sight as quickly as it had come, the semaphore beetles breaking up their ranks, the colours separating into fragments of red, blue, yellow, green.

Mr Hill asked, "Did you see anything, Arcadia?"

Cady sat up. "Well, yes. I think so."

"You are very privileged. I've never managed it, not in years and years of staring."

"I'm not sure. Maybe I imagined it?"

"Oh, I doubt that."

"I wanted desperately to see Lek, and Maguire here had already described the scene to me. So then, maybe I–"

"You saw it. You saw it!"

Obviously it was important to Hill that Cady shared the beetle vision: maybe to prove that his old colleague wasn't a lone raving madman.

Maguire sat up from his viewing position. He patted the strands of hair down across his scalp and said to her, "I have tracked your sexual reproductive pathways."

"I hope you're not flirting with me, Henry Maguire. Only, I'm promised to King Lud."

He pushed her sleeve up to reveal the flowers on her arms. "I am a Wodwo. I view the maps that Leopold and I create as the root system of the country." His fingers moved across the petals. "I would wish to make a map of the Deep Root one day. Could you imagine, Leopold?"

Hill smiled and nodded, happy to see his friend so engaged. "It would be a remarkable feat."

Maguire turned his attention back to his visitor. He spoke with reverence: "Only once every thousand years or so does a Haegra bear fruit. Are you ready, Cady, for a new becoming?"

"A new *becoming*?"

"Today, I believe, is the final day of Faynr's current life."

"No, no, that cannot be."

But Maguire insisted: "Tomorrow we begin again. Or else we drift into darkness. And let us hope the Council of Speculation, if and when they decide upon a name for this current year, they call it the *Year of Becoming*. I see a little way ahead, but the maps are unclear about which route the people might take."

"You can see through time?"

Leopold Hill helped her up, explaining, "It's one of Henry's delusions, I'm afraid, that he can map not only space, but time. He sees the river as a course not only from source to sea, but from day to night, to day again, ever onwards."

Maguire was not well pleased. He suddenly flared up, jumping to his feet. His knowledge broke into nonsense:

"I have viewed the living jewels of the Faynr running down the streets and lanes of Ludwich! Running down the streets as if abhorred!"

"Yes, yes, Henry, of course."

Hill tried to calm his old friend and business partner. But Maguire pushed him away. He tore at the charts on the walls, pulling them down. Larkspur the mute Azeel went after him, the triangle on his brow blinking with agitation as he tried to gather the sheets before they fell, doing his best to collect them all together. But Maguire was not to be stopped. At least now his ramblings started to make sense once more. "You, Cady, you are the city's warrior." He grabbed her by the shoulders. "You must act now! Only you can save us. You must bear fruit! Now! Today!"

At their master's cry of passion, the semaphore beetles fluttered into flight, every last one of them, their colours a glittering array that sparkled in Cady's eyes, bringing a broken mosaic to her vision, rather like the glittering interior of a kaleidoscope. When she could see clearly again, after the insects had settled, Maguire had finished in his destructive task.

Only a dozen or so maps remained in place on the walls. The floor was covered in the shreds of the others, torn into pieces. Hill was devastated. But Maguire seemed calmer than before. He stood at the room's centre, his arms outstretched.

"Choose, Cady. Choose!"

She walked from one remaining map to the next. Most were ragged in shape. Many showed places along the river, places the *Juniper* had visited during the last few days. Here was the ferry crossing at Anglestume, and here a fine rendition of Omega Point, where the never-never flowers had given out the riddle of the three clues – the bell, the gravestone, the unexploded bomb with its mist of green poison. And over near the east window, crudely drawn, the village of Ponperreth where Gogmagog had first showed himself. There were several other such places depicted, carrying memories of Cady's journey. But her hands lingered over four maps in particular, as each time a quivering took place in her belly, at the stigma's tip, that deeply held part of her that waited in hope of pollen. It was a new kind of feeling, a means of connecting herself to the Lud flower's location. Yes, she could feel it happening!

The first chosen map showed Rothermuse Wood, where her effigy stood, marked as a little figurine on the chart. Here the seven buds had been planted in her arms. The second map showed Maddenholt, where a bloodlark had explained to her about her need to propagate. The third was Ludforsakenland, where she had learned of the Lud flower, and its importance to her. And the final map diverted from the river, showing the new Ibraxus Estate, where the Witch of Threadbare Street lived and worked and where Brin had hested.

Cady pointed to each ill-shaped map in turn. Young Larkspur moved into action, carefully unpinning them and laying them out on the floor. Maguire and Hill worked together, nudging them into new positions. Connected in this way, the maps made for a bizarre sight, where the river flowed into new tributaries, joining up with city streets and flowing on; there was a strange dreamlike logic to it. Yet a gap remained at the centre; a blind spot. Leopold Hill was the first to move; he started to sift through the many discarded fragments, seeking a piece that would complete the jigsaw puzzle. The others joined in. Soon the room was filled with their grunts and groans of disappointment. But

Larkspur proved good in the end. He crawled under the cot and came back out with a piece of paper in his hand. It fitted perfectly, the four jagged edges lining up with the edges of the other pieces. The chart was complete. From these five very disparate pieces, a new map was created. It showed the wavy line of the Nysis in its lower portions and a pattern of streets to the north, the borough known as Little Pimlet. At the map's exact centre was an outline of a small building and a tiny area of accompanying land. Cady knew exactly where it was; in fact, she been there a few times before in her life.

"Here," Henry Maguire stated. "Here you shall find the Lud flower."

A Seeker Of Hidden Realms

They didn't have far to travel once they had sailed across the river to the north bank and found a mooring. Little Pimlet was a neat patchwork of tree-lined streets, a quiet secluded part of the city. But their destination – a small chapel – was a remnant from some earlier, untidier age. It was a crooked building, very old and mossy, with broken windows and a pallor of neglect about it. The lychgate in the wall creaked as Jeb pushed it open. Beyond lay the graveyard, which was covered in a layer of Faynr so thick as to appear pitch-black, more a semi-solid that any kind of spectral material.

Jeb said, "I wish I'd kept my purification gear now."

Cady didn't reply; the sight of the sickness only made her more determined.

"Still, I've got my mask with me."

He fished this out of a pocket and adjusted the mouthpiece and goggles over his face. Cady did without; she would breathe it in deep and care not a jot, if Maguire's map proved true.

"What are we looking for, exactly?" The lad's voice was slightly muffled.

She waved him into silence and set off. The rain had returned, but a tightly knotted canopy of trees kept the two visitors dry. Mutated elms cast weird shadows, vaguely human in shape, but twisted beyond any normal posture. Every grave and fencepost was knotted with briars and thorns; sharp-tongued needleweeds and bulbous mushrooms grew in profusion from the rich loamy earth. A streamlet from the Nysis snaked between the graves, giving the dragon's ghost access, and Faynr took full advantage, clinging to wood and stone and leaf alike, darkening the day.

"It's a sailor's cemetery," Cady told Jeb as they made their careful way forward.

"Aye, that will explain the hotchpotch."

He was referring to the non-denominational aspect of the chapel and its collection of graves: marble angels commemorating dead Ephreme; the wicker effigies of the Wodwo; the billowing silk shrouds of the Azeel with their ghostly occupants; and the simple stone slabs of the Alkhym. There were even a number of hanging lamps to represent those Nebulim who had finally passed over into death. A lone metal cross denoted the remains of a Thrawl, long run-down to zero. But everything was packed into the tiniest area, one religious marker jammed up next to another, and most of them damaged or leaning over at angles, wrapped in vines and creepers. Cady read some of the epitaphs, those that could be viewed amid the greenery: *Safe Harbour*; *Homeward Bound*; *His Final Voyage*. Typical nautical sentiments. The names of the dead told a similar story: Bold Jackie Brass, Harry One-Eye Cranshaw, Mary of the Marsh, Jakob Undersea. Could this really be the place where the Lud flower blossomed? It seemed unlikely ground for such an important plant. Mind, she had once seen a Penny Royal Blue – a rare but certain cure for syphilis – growing from a lump of shit in a pigsty.

"I've been here before," she explained now. "Burying shipmates."

Jeb pushed ahead and Cady was soon lost and alone in the ghost fog. Her vision faded to zero barely a foot or so in front of her. She pulled aside branches where she could, scratching herself on thorns. Swarms of gnats were stirred up by her boots. All that frenzy of discovery she had felt in Maguire's tower had vanished now, and her stigma had not a tingle to offer. Poor suffering Faynr touched at her everywhere, adding one shiver after another. But she kept on, compelled to find her true flowery love. A stirring breeze caught an Azeelian shroud and sent it billowing, knocking Cady off balance. Her foot caught on the jagged edge of a grave slab and down she went, falling heavily, landing on her side in the bare earth, which was soft and wet enough not to do her any great harm. But she was winded by the fall, and her ankle ached, and her mind blanked out momentarily. When her eyes reopened she found herself unable to move. Little creatures crept around her, worms and spiders and a church mouse and a grass snake. The fingers of one hand dipped into the waters of the Nysis, into the streamlet. This was comforting. But she felt also that something threatening was close by, some lingering presence of the dead perhaps. A winged angel loomed over her, deepening the gloom. She tried to call out for Jeb, but her voice was frozen, too cold, her mouth dry. The silk shroud rustled overhead, its ghostly silhouette dancing. There was a horrible slithering sound and the grass parted around a gravestone. Was that a shadow moving there?

Something remarkable happened then: Faynr lightened herself, just within this little pocket of the world where Cady was lying, knocked down and pretty much useless: the air lost some of its darkness, and she could breathe a little easier. A silvery light glinted over the waters of the stream. Goodness! And she thought, Old Faynr must be making an effort for me.

"Cady? Cady, where are you?"

"I'm here. Over here." Now she could speak, thank the Lud.

Jeb appeared among the tombs, his goggles gleaming like the eyes of a monster. "Oh, there you are, old dear. What are you doing lying down? Having a nice kip, are we?"

"I've done my ankle in, I think. Have a peek."

He did. "It's not too bad, sprained is all. Shall we get you up?"

"I've pissed my pants a little bit."

"It will dry up soon enough."

"I'll just lie here a while longer, I think."

He nodded and sat down on a slab. "It's nice here, I must say. Your own little bower. Like someone has come along and given the place a purification spray, and just for you."

"Faynr did it for me."

"Oh she did, did she?" He eyed his new captain suspiciously, and pulled down his mouthpiece the better to speak. "I need you to know, Cady sweet, that I was born within the sound of the Bells of Telltale. And you know what that means, right? It means I can read the closed book of others, and know what they really are, their true story, like."

"Oh aye, you reckon?"

"True enough. Course, I'm but an apprentice. My granddaddy, Jebediah Senior, the one of the western river route? Well he had the all-seeing eye real nice, he did. He could tell when anyone was bluffing at cards, or when his old lady was making fancy with another man, just by looking at her."

Cady grunted at this, wondering where the lad was going.

He soon let her know: "So when I take a gander at you, skipper, I'm thinking to myself all the time, what's her little secret, eh? What's that Cady Meade up to?"

"I really couldn't say."

"Something's not right with her, I says to myself. She's hiding something. Because otherwise what's the story with this gallivanting, here, there and roundabout, and me dragged along behind like a don't-know-what, not that I mind, because I likes an adventure, but Cady... Old dear..."

"Yes?" Her voice squeaked a little.

"What are we doing in a foggy graveyard on a bright sunny bank holiday?"

She lay there in silence.

"Tell the truth now, good captain, or I'm off out of here, back to the light of day."

He stood up and took a step away. The shadows and the sickness had almost swallowed him when her voice broke through: "Wait a while."

He did so, his back towards her. His wings ruffled themselves slightly.

"I'm very old," she said in a whisper.

"Well I know that. What are you, seventy-five?"

"Seventy-eight actually, in this life."

He turned to face her. "*In this life*? What other life is there?"

Slowly she answered: "Jeb... I am one thousand... four hundred... and eighty-six years old." She paused for breath. "There it is. Happy now?"

He stared at her. He tried to speak, and failed. Tried again. Failed again. Instead he gave out a long high whistle. It sounded eerie in this settlement of tombs and shrouds.

Cady went on with her story, speaking the truth. "I am a Haegra, seeded and born from a mix of plant and human substance, planted in the Year of Separation, when the Alkhym first went their own way, and the War of the Myridi began. I was released from my roots and set free to walk the earth as a protector of Ludwich and assorted boroughs, a watchwoman of the first degree."

"Crikey."

"Of the first degree, I tell you! And now look..."

"I'm looking."

"And now look at me, lying in a shallow grave with friggin' dog shit in my hair and pee in my knickers, and my back all crooked so that I can't even move!"

He knelt back down beside her. "A Haegra! Cor!" He shook his head in wonder. "And here's myself, a humble grubber in the presence of... well, bless the dirt on the bottom of my boots. A real-life vegetable woman! But I always suspected, of course, I happen to have good knowledge of such things, oh yes, green fingers I have, everyone says so, I can make a daisy grow from a rock. I think I must have some Wodwo in my blood, because we Yeomansons get around you know, why rumour has it there's even a drop or two of Alkhym swirling around in the kinship bowl, from way back when the family was landed gentry. Oh yes, we lost our fortune after the Holy Conflagration."

"Jeb?"

"Yes?"

"Shut up, will you."

"Right you are, Captain Cady, yes indeed, absolutely."

"I need you to find something for me."

"My peepers are peeled."

"A flower."

"This is Haegra business, is it?"

"Very much so. The Lud flower, they call it."

"Sounds like it might have some nice petals on it. And a royal aroma."

"There's only one in the world. It blossoms once every thousand years or so."

Again he whistled. "And it grows here, does it, among the graves?"

"Somewhere… yes. I'm certain of it."

"And what does it look like? Blood-coloured, I'll bet."

"I don't know. I've never seen one before, not even a drawing of one. But it will stand out, it will look like no other flower in the place. Perhaps kingly looking, or like a sword ready for battle, manly and upright and expectant. Packed with pollen."

"Blimey."

"Just have a good look for me, that's all I ask."

"You'll wait here, will you?"

She nodded. "I'm not going anywhere."

And he was gone, rushing off from the circle of Faynr's light into the black fog. She heard his footsteps fading, the brushing and snapping of branches and twigs; and then silence.

Cady lay still. Because of this bowl of cleansed Faynr a blue sky layered with clouds could be seen through a gap in the tree canopy, while all else was foggy and damp. Her eyes closed.

She was suddenly tired from the day's exertions. Her mind began to drift like a slow tide. She recalled a moment from her former days, when Queen Hilde had welcomed Dr John Dee and herself to the House of Worship at Templeton, to thank them both for their work in fighting against the Blight. Oh, such wonderful times! The Queen had said, "I know you have need of secrecy in your work, but on behalf of the people of Kethra I extend our gratitude." Cady remembered every word. Every single word! It was as though Faynr had entered her head with a clean bubble of time, and popped it in her brain – the Queen's gown, Dr Dee's finest black robe, the spaniel Her Majesty kept with at all times, yapping away.

Cady smiled to herself. Her eyes were still closed, dwelling on the memories. The little Nysis was gently lapping at her side and her hand sought out once more its cooling waters. But the stream felt different this time, like tar running across her fingers, sticky and hot.

Something was touching her face.

Her eyes popped open.

Darkness drifted above her body, a slowly billowing mass of it. At first she thought that Faynr had lost herself once more to the fog sickness, allowing it back into place. But it was different in texture, more smoke than fog. Cady could smell ashes and rancid pus and animal dung. The sky was totally obscured. Her limbs were frozen solid to the ground. Her heart raced.

Two yellow moons appeared through the smog.

Two moons? It didn't make sense. In the daytime? Was she seeing double? Or dreaming? The twin satellites blinked on and off, on and off, as they descended to hover just above her face. Now she smelled the rot of decay and imagined the graves were opening, spewing their inhabitants into a twitching shuddering life. But that notion was quickly dismissed as the truth came upon her.

The moons were the eyes of Gogmagog, and this was no dream.

The Night Serpent had found a new way through into the world and had squeezed a small thin portion of himself into the sailors' cemetery to gather Cady up, to bring an end to her and to sup on her remains. It was the dead bodies, the rot, the stench of them, that allowed him access, no doubt. Tendrils of smoke wrapped themselves around Cady's throat and started to tighten at her windpipe.

She could not breathe.

Lights were going out in her eyes, little dots extinguished one by one.

How cruel it seemed, that she had travelled so far and come so near to the Lud flower, only to be snuffed out at the last moment. If only she could move! Her fingers gripped at the soil, to seek nourishment and strength from the earth, her true mother. She pulled at a buried tree root with one hand and tore at submerged weeds with the other. Her limbs were straining to escape, in vain. The smoke had found its way into her mouth. She was choking. The outer fields of her palms opened up and the thin branches emerged like witch's fingers extending themselves on each side, the thorns at their ends sharp and cruel, designed by the first Wodwo witches for bloodletting; but she could not attack Gogmagog, it was impossible in this position. Instead she used the thorns to grab at whatever vegetation she could find nearby, pulling at it, wrapping herself in twigs and vines and leaves and the stalks of weeds and the great root systems of the elms, the branches and briars, the thorn bushes, everything, every bit of greenery she could feel and speak with, and touch, here where the outer fields met the inner fields. One plant above all others came to her call, fiery hexbane, its pungent odour a blessing, for it was employed in the First and Second Ages as a ward against evil. She took comfort from the press of the prickly leaves of the bane against her face and neck, and she increased her labours, pulling on every root mightily until her hands were almost breaking. The stone angels were leaning over at sharper angles as the soil beneath them was disturbed by the Haegra's efforts; the hanging shrouds of the Azeels whipped and clattered against the overhanging branches. A Wodwo effigy toppled over and was dragged along the ground by the root fibres of the flowers that entangled it. The dead were screaming in every taut creak of every tree and in the whining of the stretched vines that joined Cady to the graves.

Her field of vision was quickly darkening at the edges.

Her throat was burning.

But she was by now covered entirely in vegetation. A new wooden suit for a Lady Haegra.

The last blink of light vanished from her eyes.

Gogmagog's hold weakened.

She breathed again!

He tried to pierce her armour, stabbing at the tiniest cracks with his smoky fingers, but the branches bound themselves ever tighter around Cady's body.

There was brief hissing sound that held such anger and frustration.

And then silence once more.

Cady must have passed out for a few seconds. The next thing she heard was the creaking and cracking of the vegetation as it unwound itself from her body. She was free, and she sat up, taking in gulps of air. Her body was cut and scratched and bruised all over, and her coat and bell-bottoms were torn and dirty. Trails of blood covered her hands, and she knew her face must look the same, a frightful mess. At least her ankle and back felt stronger and she got to her feet, testing herself. The cleansed portion of Faynr had been expelled completely by Gogmagog's presence. The black mist clung to the graves and statues, but she was glad of it, and breathed happily within it, sickness or no sickness.

"Cady, come see!"

It was Jeb shouting to her. For a moment she hesitated, fearful of putting him in danger. She found the broken strands of the hexbane on the ground and pulled off a handful of the leaves: a few were still a deep russet in colour, but most of them had already turned back to green. A good sign. Following the sound of Jeb's voice she made her way through the rotting undergrowth, feeling her boots squelch in soft muck and taking careful steps unless she take another tumble. Creatures scurried away. A light flickered through the tombs and she headed towards it.

Jeb was kneeling down next to a big slab of granite once flat to the ground as a gravestone, but now angled upwards and cracked in the middle, broken in two by the powerful upthrust of a huge tree root. A small lantern lit the scene.

"Well then, have you found the Lud flower?"

"Not yet. But look."

Jeb held the lantern out so Cady could more easily read the name on the gravestone.

JOHN LUDLOW

"That's it, is it? The half word *Lud*?"

"It's better than nothing."

"Where did you get that lamp?"

"From a Nebulim grave. I'll put it back when we're done."
He held it high and saw her face properly. "Upon my wings,
what happened to you, Cady? You're bleeding."

"Oh that." She wiped at the cuts on her cheeks and brow.
"I got into a battle, and lost. I had to make a retreat, or more
likely a rearguard action."

"What?"

"The plants saved me."

Cady would say no more on the subject. But she took one
of the green hexbane leaves and placed it on the slab. "Keep
your eye on that, and let me know if it reddens."

"Why? What then?"

"It's a warning sign, that a demon approaches."

He stared at the leaf, eyes wide. "I have it in my sight."

"Good. Follow my orders, and no pissing about."

"Aye aye."

She looked around and felt on the pulse of the earth
and within the fungal pathways and along the tangled
roots, checking to see that the Night Serpent had truly
left the scene. The optic gland in her brow activated,
shining a lovely green light inside her head. All was good.
Satisfied, she rested herself on a tree stump. Jeb handed
her a bottle.

"I found this on a grave."

"Oh blessed Lud." It was navy rum. Jack Brimstone's, her
favourite tipple.

"It must have been put there by a mourner. In
remembrance for some old tar. Succour on the final voyage."

"The dead can go thirsty." She took a good long swig and
felt better by far.

Jeb went to work. He pulled a thick layer of moss from
the grave slab, sending spiders and centipedes hurrying

away from sudden exposure. John Ludlow's dates of birth and death were now on display, showing that he had passed away more than a hundred years ago. His profession was also listed: *BOTANIST AND SAILOR.*

"Oh there's a thing, eh?" Jeb said. "Botanist. That's a plant studier, isn't it?"

"That's right. I met his type in my olden days. Over-eager midshipmen and petty officers who thought themselves amateur scientists. They were always putting ashore on deserted islands to study the flora and fauna."

"Well maybe Mr Ludlow Botanist found the Lud flower in his foreign explorations?"

"I see the flower as native to Kethra, myself."

"He probably went botanising when he was home as well. Oh yes, I can see him, tramping the countryside in search of rare specimens, perhaps in the company of a young lady, his bride to be. He'll be an Alkhym, going off the grave slab. So quite high up in the ship's rankings?"

"I've known Alkhym down in the engine room, covered in coal dust. They're not all silver-spooners, you know."

"Okay, well then. Maybe he was kicked out of society because he wanted to marry a high-born girl, that will be it."

Cady nodded at this. "Aye, and the girl's family made sure he was sent away on a long naval voyage. He spent the years at sea pining for his true love back at home, and studying his books to pass the time."

"That's the ticket! And wandering the lonely islands, making note of the strange plants and the beautiful flowers, he thinks of her often, his lovely Alice."

"Alice Applegate-Smythely-Croquet-Budgerigar."

"That's her name."

"The first bits of it anyway, the rest would take us five minutes to state."

Jeb looked excited. "And once he's back home, they run away together, and live the life of merry wanderers."

Cady smiled. They were seated in a pocket of yellow lamplight under a roof of branches, with raindrops pattering the leaves above them, and the gurgle of a pond somewhere hidden. A bird sang a wistful tune from a thicket.

She steered the story in a different direction. "Maybe the girl's family accepted Mr Ludlow, finally, because he proved himself."

"Oh aye, that's better. And they go off on holiday together, maybe seeking the source of Faynr in the Tangle Wood."

"Many's been tempted that way, and all of them lost."

"They don't venture too far into the maze of trees, only the outskirts."

Cady asked quietly, "And that's where they find the Lud flower, is it?"

Jeb's eyes lit up. "I think so. Let's say so. Growing amid the roots of a tree, a specimen John Ludlow has never seen before, not on his travels and not in any book of flower drawings."

"He wants to name it after her, after Alice, his new wife."

"But she insists, it should take the name of the first king of Kethra."

Cady nodded. A gentle pleasure swept through her. She watched as Jeb pulled the last of the moss free from Ludlow's slab, revealing the rest of the grave's epitaph. He dusted away soil from the lettering and held the lantern over it.

"What does it say?"

Jeb read aloud: "*A Seeker of Hidden Realms.*"

"Let me see that."

She got up and peered at the stone. It seemed to waver in her eyes as though covered in water, but this was an illusion only, or more properly, a memory; a memory of the dream brought on by the never-never seeds. Her eyes blurred and she rubbed at them. She returned to the deep channels of the Nysis, swimming underwater, looking down at the gravestone lodged in the riverbed. In the dream the lettering had been unreadable, but now she understood what had been written there: *A Seeker of Hidden Realms*. Those five words stood out clearly, to join with those carved into the stone in the chapel graveyard. Dream and reality were overlaid, one on the other. The knowledge of such a joining was too much for her and she felt dizzy and would have fallen if Jeb hadn't reached out for her, offering a hand.

He broke into her reverie: "Is this it, Cady, are we near?"

It took a while for her to bring the lad's face into view. "Very near. Have a look underneath, will you."

He did so, placing the lantern down and then lying flat on the ground to peer under the angled stone. "There's something under here, it's twinkling." He reached in and pulled out an object. It was a pocket watch, very old and crusted with verdigris. It showed that time, for Mr Ludlow at least, had stopped at five minutes past four. Jeb went back to his search, discovering a Meerschaum pipe, definitely of nautical flavour, made of whalebone and carved in scrimshaw patterns.

"Keep going, lad."

He reached as far he could under the stone slab and this time brought back a silver locket on a chain. It was badly tarnished, but when opened up it showed the silhouette of a woman's face.

"That will be Alice," Cady said, hardly daring to breathe now.

"Ludlow's family must have buried a bunch of personal items with him, and the roots of the tree has disturbed the earth, bringing them to the surface."

Cady urged him on. "Keep looking, don't stop now."

Jeb almost disappeared under the slab, digging into the soil to gain further entrance. "Lift it up, will you?"

"Me? I've told you how old I am."

His voice was urgent. "Come on, show me what you're made of."

Thorns of ironwood emerged from her palms. Just two of them this time, hard and curved and powerful. She hooked them under the slab's rim and pulled upwards with all her might, drawing on the power of the vegetation all around, bonded by the rooted nourishment of the soil that joined one tree to another, and all of them to Cady.

"Well? Any sign of a flower growing under there?"

He didn't answer beyond a grunt. She held on tightly for fear of crushing the boy. The bower was silent, the rain having stopped. But the worms were active in the topsoil and soon the birds would arrive for their dinner. The slab was slipping from her grasp just as Jeb pulled himself free and sat up. His face and hands and clothes were now as dirty as hers.

"A right old filthy pair we make, eh?"

He held out his treasure.

It was a brass ornament in the shape of a semaphore beetle, its varicoloured back encrusted with bits of stained glass. A few inches in length, a little less in width, it fit perfectly within Jeb's palm. He cleaned off the dirt of years and blew on it, revealing the object's beauty. A pair of tiny blue jewels represented the insect's eyes.

"Sailors used to prize these," Cady explained. "*Beetle boxes*, they called them. They kept little trinkets inside, memories of home usually, or items discovered on the voyages."

Jeb ran a finger along the beetle's edge and found a little clasp. He clicked at it and the beetle popped open, the two halves of the wing-case folding back.

Within was a seed.

A large seed, about the size of a wren's egg.

As soon as Cady took hold of it the seed started to glow with a reddish light from within, seen through the casing, as through something alive was in there, something that had only this second been activated, and only by a Haegra's touch.

She stumbled back against a stone angel.

The light of the seed warmed her hand. Her belly fluttered.

The flames of the oil lantern flickered and died and the gloom of the Faynr fog seeped back into place, drifting through the leaves to cover the gravestone of John Ludlow and the two people standing around it. The Lud seed was now the only light, a shining red dot on the map of Cady's days.

PART TWO
Of Flesh And Flower

Card No. 19. Timmusk. Hidden beneath the River Nysis, Ludwich's underground cave system was originally a place of banishment for disgraced Ephremes. After the Winged Emancipation it was occupied by the Nebulim, who hid themselves in its crevices and balanced themselves on its rocky ledges. It was the Nebulim, with their inherent knowledge of alchemy, who perfected the mining of the blue crystals and other precious stones. It is said that at the centre of Timmusk there lies the crystallised skeleton of a great lizard, one of Haakenur's lesser cousins.

Monocle Cigarette Cards – The Haunted River

Elsewhere Elsewhere

They made their way through the tropical garden, where beds of flowers were giving up their rich perfumes. Cady revelled in the aromas; everything reminded her of her current state, of just how deep the channels and roots of her body were flowing with love. Insects clogged at her throat: let them! Her eyes blurred over and she could barely see where she was treading. Good! Plants and vines parted before her eagerly driven motion. Jeb followed close behind, treading carefully to not slip on the wet mulch. His wings were dew-covered and smeared with spores and pollen grains. He sneezed five times on the trot before he managed to speak.

"My nose is running fit to win the four-thirty at Steadwick Races."

"Oh wipe it up and stop blathering."

"What is that smell? It reeks like a glutton's privy."

"That my boy is the stinkpuff, a fungus." She took a deep gladdening breath. "It conjures up my early days, when I was first uprooted. Oh Jeb, I wish you could have been there! The Wold Gardens belonged to the people back then. No royal pavilions, no greenhouses, or regimented rows of flowers. But the wild marshlands and the witching gardens where new blossoms were created. And myself one of them, can you imagine?"

Jeb whistled. "I can imagine getting clear of this foliage."

Cady ignored his complaints. "The gardener priests intermingled three elements to create their planting grounds: the dark earth, the seepage from the Nysis, and dear old Faynr, who was lovely beyond compare in those days." She took another breath. "I feel myself back where I was, in my first self. Look! The petals are fluttering on my flowers. They seek the pollen of King Lud. Can't you see them dancing?"

From the look on Jeb's face, it was obvious that he could not.

She went on, "Dr John Dee once drew a picture for me of a fantastical bloom with little wings attached along its stem."

"An Ephreme plant? Surely, there's no such thing."

She nodded. "He told me that such a flower grew only in the imagination. He labelled it *Flora Non Flora*, the flower that does not exist." Her eyes twinkled in the greenery. "I feared the Lud flower of similar species. But now..." She gripped the brass beetle box tightly. "Now I have the seed in my hand. All I need do is get it germinated."

Jeb sneezed again, violently this time.

Cady wiped his snot from her face and carried on regardless. "Yes, to germinate. To sprout forth under the influence of sunlight and water and nutrients, and so on. But I need this to happen as quickly as possible, like today! Immediately!"

"Oh that's all, is it?"

She shushed him and moved swiftly on. They soon reached the exit of the tropical garden. A short path took them towards the grand central pavilion of the Royal Gardens at Wold. The River Nysis ran alongside, dotted with yachts and

pleasure schooners. The pavilion was a giant structure built
of glass and wood and metal, a testament to the engineering
skills of the last century. Instead of a flag, the upper branches
of a tree marked its apex. Cady and Jeb made their way
inside. The place was crammed with holidayers and revellers
of all kinds, all classes, all tribes. People scooted between the
rock gardens and the ornamental bushes and the decorative
water features. The most popular plants were on display
here, new hybrids cross-bred and grafted into bizarre shapes
and colours. One lily was so huge a child could sit within
its bowl of petals. Fluteflowers sang out their happy little
tunes. Snakelike fronds reached playfully for passers-by,
and striped cat-tulips prowled the edges of the flowerbeds.
Many Alkhym youths were running and prancing about,
enjoying their newly hested powers, their incessant high-
pitched pinging sounds giving Cady a headache. But she did
not care, not now that she was in sight of the first Great Tree
of Kethra. *Fotheringall*. Its massive trunk rose from a cloud
of mist at ground level to reach up high towards the ceiling,
and not stopping there but growing onwards through the
opening in the roof. This was Cady's present goal, perhaps
her only chance to accelerate the Lud seed's life cycle and
set the flower within free.

Her heart took a leap. "I need to have a chat with
Fotheringall," she said to Jeb.

"With the tree?"

"Aye. I seek knowledge of the Lud seed's growth patterns."

Jeb sneezed again and wiped his nose. But he seemed
overly happy. "I got up this morning expecting a hard day's
graft on the spray gang. Instead of which, I'm the assistant
to a Haegra! And which other wingboy can say as such.
None can! Not the one!"

"Well stay here and don't cause any trouble."

And with that she walked towards the mass of people clustered in the gazebos and pathways of the pavilion, bathed in light from the curved geodesic roof. The closer she got to Fotheringall, the more dazed and dizzy she became: the Great Trees always did this to her, one of the reasons why she tended to avoid them. Through hazy eyes she glimpsed a topiary sculpture of King Lud in his pomp, shield in one hand, Ibraxus in the other. She made a little bow to him and hurried on, snaking her way through the crowded spaces until she was brought up short by a solid wall of clothed flesh. People were gathered ten to twelve deep in a circle around Fotheringall, listening to a tour guide speaking; he was relating the history of the tree and its various fruits and flowers.

"The Great Tree has survived twenty-seven wars, four plagues, and countless icy winters and blighted summers. Its trunk measures…"

The guide stopped talking as Cady emerged sweating from the crush of spectators, causing a minor disturbance and much cursing and grumbling. Only a rope barrier stood between her and the goal. She stepped over the rope. The guide watched open-mouthed, not knowing what to say or do. Spectators looked over each other's shoulders the better to view the curious old lady who teetered on the edge of the cloud of Faynr mist. Cady realised she could not touch Fotheringall from this far away. She would have to step into the mist, to access the tree via the roots. But her progress was halted by the strong hand of a security guard.

"Here, madam, none of that."

Cady scowled. She spat a green lump of mucus onto the soil. There were murmurs from the onlookers; a larger audience was gathering to witness this event, whatever it might lead to. The guard and Cady squared up to each other.

"I need to make contact with Fotheringall."

"That isn't allowed."

"I don't need your permission."

The pavilion's tour guide added his own two-pennyworth: "This tree is over a thousand years old. It has a very delicate structure."

"Delicate my arse!"

"I say! There's really no need…"

Cady turned to view the crowd. So many eyes, all staring at her. She was still in a daze; the presence of the tree's spirit could be felt in her heart, and that overwhelmed all other senses.

The guard firmed up his voice. "Step away. Nice and easy." He had a hold of Cady's elbow and was wrenching her away from the mist cloud. Would she have to reveal her true self to these people? But then she heard Jeb's voice:

"Do you know who this lady is?" The lad pushed his way forward.

The guard glowered at the newcomer. "We can't have people interfering with exhibits."

"This here lady… This old dear…" His wings fluttered. Cady watched with interest as Jeb's story took flight. "This lady is my old gran, not long for this world. Seventy-eight she is, seventy-eight, I ask you! She lost brothers and a son in the First War, she lost grandsons in the second. Then, and then, and then she was bombed out of house and home. And what did the council do, in their wisdom, ladies and gentlemen?" He was playing to the crowd now. "They stuck her in a biddy's home, the cheeky blighters, they might as well have sent her to the knacker's yard."

Mighty Fotheringall was now crowded around by interested parties. Faynr swirled in her pool, perhaps stirred up by the noise and commotion. Cady could smell the dragon's ghost in her nose and throat, making her feel even woozier. Jeb's voice flowed on, a steady stream in her ears.

"And all she wants, my poor dear granny, her final wish in life is to view Fotheringall from up-close. It's her eyes, see, her peepers is terrible bad."

There were murmurs of disapproval from the spectators: *Oh, the cheek. These young ruffians. Dirty little scuttler, he doesn't know better. It's a pity he missed the war.* But there was also a swell of approval: *You tell 'em son! She's got as much right as anyone. Let the old duck have her fun.* And so on, the two factions raising their voices against each other. The guard let go of Cady to hold his hands out against a sudden forward surge of people, all trying to get a better view.

"Get back, go on, keep back!"

It was too late. Cady had already vanished into the mist. Immediately she felt she had entered a very different world; she could no longer hear the noise of the crowd, nor view a speck of light from the pavilion. Now she stood amid the knotted gnarled roots of the tree; they were extensive, these roots, sinking into the soil in every direction, taking nourishment from both the wet ground and from Faynr. The trunk was easily thrice her arms outstretched in width. The roots and bark were covered in fungal growths and patches of lichen rich in colour and stench, and squishy to the touch. Everything was eating everything else, and giving back as much as it took in sap and plant vomit. Cady's eyes focused, finding many insects at their work: ants, termites, woodworm.

Fotheringall fed them all. She tried to remember the last time she had visited here: it was long ago, back when the city was mud and straw and spilt blood. But she had never been this close, and never before attempted a direct communication.

She reached out with both hands. They touched first the layer of insects, and then the spongy fungal growth, then the tree's bark, then the inner pulp. Cady's flesh became the flesh of the tree, one with one. It was painful, as the tree's spirit bit back at her, sending its army of ants her way, and spilling acidic sap onto her skin. But this only made her stay the course with a stronger purpose.

"Allow me in, you motherfucker of the dark wet earth."

The inner bark would not part for her, not one inch.

"Grant me entrance. Open the Fotheringate!"

The way remained closed.

Now she was getting angry. "Come on, Fothers. Spread your tight-arsed, mushroom-mouthed wooden portal before I chop your branches into twigs and your twigs into splinters!"

Spiders crawled on her skin, testing her veins. But there was a softening of the bark, she was sure of it. She pushed a little harder, testing the doorway. Yes. Good. Forward we go! Her hands were lodged in the trunk up to the wrists and the wood had closed on them tightly. The tiny flowers of her blossoming nature quivered under the contact of the tree, and her stigma throbbed like the engine of the *Juniper* on a summer's night far out on the endless oceans of dream. The two sides of her nature – *water* and *earth* – were married in the lichen that painted Fotheringall's body. She was aware of the merged movement of algae and fungi in the pink and violet covering. Faynr billowed all around the

vast tree trunk, creating a kind of whirlpool effect. Cady
was battered this way and that, locked to the tree only by
her wrists, which might crack like twigs at any moment. Yet
she held on. Now she felt a pair of hands pressed up against
hers from within the tree, and for the first time ever she
felt thorns entering her outer fields, another person's set of
thorns digging into the earthy flesh of her palms. Oh Lud,
it hurt! And she cried out. Her eyes were screwed shut. The
thorns went in deep and pulled her forward, right through
the door of bark. Now she dared to look around. She was
standing in a green glade. A little stream trickled between
wafting grasses. It was very pleasant, and peaceful. She was
inside the Deep Root, in the region known as Colmacoombe,
or The Grove of the Everlasting.

A voice was formed: *I am Fotheringall. What do you want
of me?*

It was a man's voice, deep and gravelly, and very aged.
Cady looked around for the speaker but saw only the stirring
of branches and the rustle of leaves from the surrounding
copse.

"I am Haegra at root and stem, seeded in the Year of
Separation," she replied, trying to match his deepness and
failing, but nonetheless sounding quite the Madam of the
Green, even if she did think so herself. "I seek the spirit of
the Lud Flower."

For what purpose?

Her normal tone took charge: "That's my business.
Personal business, as it goes."

The leaves rustled angrily. *I cannot help you.*

"Oh I think you can, really. At least tell me where the
spirit lies."

In the walled garden. Do you have…

A breeze shook the voice into pieces and there was silence until the leaves settled back into their shapes and Fotheringall was heard once more.

Do you have payment?

"There's a fee, is there? See, no bugger told me that."

Do you have a key?

"Maybe I can climb over the wall. How about that?"

Not waiting for an answer she took the path alongside the stream, adopting her own lifelong rule: *always follow the flow of the water*. The stream curved its way into denser undergrowth. She had to step down into the brook when the going got too rough. It was a delightful silvery waterway dotted with lilies and stitched with flying insects. There was daylight, but no sun, no sky, only the glade reaching over to enfold itself in the constant green, and Cady the only traveller. Fotheringall was quiet now, perhaps offended by her attitude. But she had no time for the petty bureaucracies and hierarchies that often troubled the Deep Root. Today's mission was more important. As though to emphasise this, she came upon a clump of never-never flowers, grown overly large and luscious down here in the other world. They puffed out their seeds in clouds of little blue grains that formed the shapes of a man, a woman, a youth, a child, a baby, ever-shifting in their personification of the human body. And now, roused by the Haegra's presence, the seeds scattered and reformed, taking on three different shapes one after another: a bell, a gravestone, a flying bomb. These were the three objects revealed to Cady in her dream vision; a riddle whose meaning was slowly being unravelled. Emboldened by this message she walked on, excited, and nervous. Her body tingled in all its fibres. Yes, she was on the right track!

The stream disappeared into a hole in the rocky ground. She walked on a few more steps until the walled garden reared up suddenly from a green haze, as high as a two-storey house, its stones finely interlocked and pasted together by thick moss. There would be no climbing it, that was sure. She followed the curve of the wall until she reached a wooden door. It was locked. She banged on it, demanding to be let in. There was a small diamond-shaped peephole at eye-level. Cady gazed through, seeing a small part of a country garden complete with overflowing flowerbeds and a trellis wrapped in roses. She mused. Every plant in the wide world had a spirit living here in the Deep Root, each in its own location. And this walled garden was the home of the Lud Flower spirit. She had to gain entrance.

A blurry figure ran across the field of vision, laughing gleefully. Cady put her lips to the hole and shouted: "Let me in, dammit! I am a Haegra!" For a moment she thought her cries were in vain, but then she heard a reply from the other side of the door. It sounded like a little girl's voice. Cady stood on tiptoes but could still not see anybody.

"Who's that?" she called.

"Mildred."

"How old are you, Mildred?"

"In a week's time I'll be five and three quarters."

"Very good, a fine age. Can you reach the peephole?"

"No."

"Is there anything you can stand on?"

"I can climb up."

"Show me how you do that."

There was a pause and much scuffling before a little hand appeared in the diamond, holding on, and then Mildred's face took its place. She said, "You're very old, aren't you?"

"Oh I am. And awful careworn. Listen Mildred, I need to get inside the garden. I need to meet with the spirit of the Lud flower. Can you help me?"

Mildred stared at her through the peephole: blue eyes, a lock of blonde hair, a turned-up nose.

"Do you know who I mean?" Cady asked.

"The Flower King?"

"That's right. That will be him. Is there a key to this door?"

"Yes, it's hanging up here, on a nail."

"So why don't you open the door for me, there's a good girl–"

"This is a royal garden. It's private!"

Cady fumed, but tried her best to keep it in, and to hold off from swearing. Instead she smiled and nodded. "Let me guess, you're a maid of honour, am I right?"

"Of course."

"Running about on a summer's day, not a care in the world, eh?"

The girl grinned. "The King has many people in attendance. And you're not one of them, so there!"

"No, but see, I'm a Haegra. Half plant, half human."

"I don't care."

Angry little flashes of light popped in Cady's head until she remembered Fotheringall's talk of a fee being needed. She held up the ornamental beetle for the girl's inspection. "Look at this shiny little object, eh. See the colours on its back, and the wings, and its eyes made of two jewels, so sparkly. Here, I tell you what, you let me in and I'll give you this beetle box as a present, eh, what do you say?"

Mildred considered. "No."

"Why you little madam, you snivelling piece of…"

Cady stopped herself. The little girl stared at her, a playful grin on her lips. "What's inside the beetle box?"

"A seed. The Lud seed, actually. Have you heard of such a thing?"

The girl shook her head.

"Oh, it's very special."

"No it's not. You're just trying to fool me."

Cady looked away. She flattened a big fat bluebottle against her neck and licked the remains from her fingers. The girl laughed.

"You're funny."

"That's as maybe, but I'm telling you the truth about the Lud seed. I really do need to see the Flower King, it's very urgent."

"Why?"

Cady played her best card: "I am betrothed to him."

The little girl's eyes lit up. "Don't be silly. You're too old to marry the King."

"But see, here." She pressed her arm in front of the peephole, showing off the pink-and-gold petals. "See, my flowers are very young. Why, they only blossomed this day. This very day!"

Mildred was genuinely interested, Cady could see that.

"And anyway, age means little against the dreams we have, the King and I."

"What dreams?"

"We are to make a new bloom together. I need the Flower King to… to… to wave his magic wand over the Lud seed, to make it flower in an instant. Or something like that, to be honest, I'm not quite sure."

"And then what?"

"And then… and then we shall enter the bridal chamber together."

Mildred laughed again. "Can I watch?"

"Cheeky little tyke."

"Can I, can I, can I, can I, can I?"

"You might, you might."

The girl's head disappeared from the peephole. A full minute went by. Had the brat run off to find some more interesting pastime, chasing stupid butterflies for instance? But no: the sound of a key creaked in the lock and the door opened.

Cady entered the walled garden. In its growth patterns it had followed the eccentric nature of some olden God or Goddess, with deliberate irregularities and asymmetries among its beds and twisting pathways. Stone sculptures depicted creatures not of this earth, but of the Wodwo's home planet, Kharos. All this was new to Cady and she walked at first with careful steps following the maid of honour, who sometimes dashed off this way and that among the flowerbeds. Cady put on a sprint, but struggled to keep up. Other members of the royal household poked their heads over fences and from behind trellises, seeing who this visitor might be: the First and Second Ladies in Waiting, Master of the King's Hawks, Gentleman Ushers, Gilder of the Swans, Purse Bearers, Page of the Lower Chambers. And so on, and so forth. So many people conjured up here in the Deep Root, just to look after one single flower spirit. It was astonishing! Many of them appeared to be shy and retiring, while others gave Cady a keen stare, as though to scare her off. Meanwhile, little Mildred skipped and capered about, taking sudden turns, performing somersaults and cartwheels, only to turn up suddenly at Cady's back, crying out "BOO!" and making the old lady jump nearly out of her skin.

They came at last to a bank of moss around a still pool. A young man was sitting there, gazing into the water. He reached into the pool as though to grasp some submerged object, only to return with empty hands. He did this twice more as Cady watched. A shield lay propped against a tree stump, its face perfectly clean and undented. It had never seen battle. The man's hair was long and greenish blonde and well-combed, and his face was finely shaped, handsome, with the arrogance of youth in it. This was not the great regal warrior conjured up in many a crystal-show drama. No. In fact he displayed a leering smile as he once more reached into the pool. Cady knew this was not the real King Lud, and not even his ghost. It was the spirit of the Lud flower made into the semblance of Lud. And yet surely they were connected at some deep level, king and plant. There had to be a reason the flower was named after the first ruler of the land.

She approached warily, as her stigma gave a tremble and the petals on her arms and neck and thigh and stomach stood up like goosebumps. She cleared her throat.

"Your Majesty? Is that what I call you? Or plain Lud? Or King Lud?" There was no reply. "Or the Flower King? Perhaps you'd prefer that?" Still no response. "How about Mr Rude Bastard, eh?" She tried for a laugh; it came out as a weird gurgling sound. "Oh, I know! Ghost Lud. There you go, that's lovely that is."

Mildred was standing to one side, urging her on. Cady nodded. "Maybe I should shut the fuck up and sit my arse down, how about that?" She took her own advice, finding a place on the bank next to the young king. But he kept his eyes fixed on the water. Again his hand went searching, to come back as empty as ever. "What are you looking for?"

She bent over and was astonished to see a longsword lying on the bed of pebbles in the shallows. "Is that… Is that Ibraxus?"

He spoke for the first time: "You can see it?"

"Of course."

"No, no, it is a fancy of the mind. See." His hand reached down and closed on the sword, his fingers grasping at nothing but water.

"Let me try."

She reached in and felt for a moment the cold hard steel and then… and then nothing, only the water of the pool and a tadpole. "Ruddy heck. What a palaver." The pool settled back into stillness and Cady had her second astonishment, for she saw herself reflected as a young woman, the woman she would have been if her regrowth had worked this time. She was eighteen or nineteen, a couple of years younger than the kingly spirit at her side. My, what a handsome pair they made! Yet when she looked at her hands, her real hands, they were as wrinkled and as warty as ever, and a running of her fingers down her face only found the usual crinkles and potholes. Ah. How sad it was. But then she wondered, *If I can see Lud as a young swain, maybe he sees me in the same way, as a fair maiden?* It was a very pleasant thought and she kept it in mind as she clicked open the beetle box.

"I have brought the seed of your worldly flower to show you."

Lud touched the object on view with a fingertip.

Cady went on, "What I need to know, is this: can you make the seed germinate? I need it to push out a little shoot, right now, as quickly as you can, no hanging about, eh, a nice green shoot reaching up to become a flower, what do you say? Do your magic. Say a spell, or make a wish. Come on, Lud! Wouldn't you like your flower to bloom? It must be such a long time since you–"

His hand grabbed at her wrist with a sudden violence. Cady was taken aback. The King's eyes were icy and glittering, with a touch of cruelty in them. His gaze made her recoil, yet his grip remained tight, and she could not move.

"What use am I, without my sword? Without Ibraxus in my hand?"

"Well I don't know… I mean to say…"

Cady looked over to Mildred for help, only to see that the maid of honour had climbed up into the lower branches of a tree. But at last the King's hand released its grip. She turned back and was shocked to see Lud's head bowed in sadness. She thought to either show compassion or to tell him off for being such a big sop! Instead, and from no obvious part of her mind, she started to sing one of her favourite old ballads.

Come all you young sailors
And listen a while,
I'll tell of my true love
Though many a mile
Lies now between us
From Kethra so fair
To the land where he lingers,
The Isle of Elsewhere.

She took a breath, in preparation for the second verse. Her voice trembled.

I have travelled these oceans
For so many a day

Following a bearing
That turns oft astray,
And no matter my steerage
By compass or star
The Island of Elsewhere
Lies always afar.

Cady had never sung so well nor so beautifully, not in all of her lives. The King was looking at her with watery eyes. He stood up, saying, "My lady, would you walk with me?"

"Why, oh, of course, of course."

They moved away from the pool into another part of the garden. Mildred jumped down from her perch and skipped along behind, singing and giggling like a mischievous sprite. Other members of the royal entourage peeped at their progress from copses and pagodas: Gatherer of the Palace Insects, Lighter of the Torch, Cleaner of the King's Toilet. Eventually they came to a well. It was very old, the bucket missing, the rope severed, and the frame cracked. Lud had restored some of his royal bearing, or at least a likeness of it. He gestured to her. She leaned over the stone wall of the well and peered into the dark, seeing a level of water some three feet down, all scummy, and a place at its centre where a small mist of Faynr swirled. But something deeper moved below, a livelier shape. It curled about and then swam to the surface. It was a crystalback, much smaller than the one Cady kept in the hold of the *Juniper*, but just as bright and just as active. There was one difference to the crystalbacks of the real world: this one sported red crystals on its back, not blue. Cady could not take her eyes away from the sight, especially when the water began to colour and to form into a vision. The Oracle of the Well was revealing a truth to her. What would it be?

The Flower King spoke: "There is only one person in the city who can help you. Can you see his face?"

She could, for the scarlet crystalback produced a very clear image on the surface of the well water. It was the face of Dr John Dee, conjured here from the past, from life! Or rather, from death. "What is this?" she asked. "Is this crystalback joined to the underworld?"

The Lud spirit did not reply.

Cady continued to stare into the well, hoping for an answer there. Dr Dee's lips were moving, the words unheard, the well water already clouding over. "I don't understand." She looked to Lud for elaboration, only to find that he too was fading away. She spun about, making herself dizzy, and the garden spun with her. Mildred rushed up, laughing out loud and then shrieking at the top of her voice. It was so high-pitched a sound it set the leaves ringing like metal shards. Cady winced and shut her eyes, and when she opened them again she was back in the volume of mist surrounding Fotheringall, coughing and retching. Jeb's hands were reaching for her. She grabbed hold gratefully and was pulled into the light, into the Royal Pavilion at the Wold.

"How long was I away?" she asked.

"Five minutes, if that. Why?"

She held on tightly, unwilling to let go of the lad. He was her anchor. The crowd of spectators stood in their watching circle exactly as before, along with the tour guide, all gazing at her as she muttered and grumbled to herself.

Her hair was tangled with the burrs and spores of another world.

Gogmagoria

The *Juniper* bobbed at its mooring next to the Wold Gardens. Jeb stood at the figurehead, which was an old Thrawl torso modelled on the face and form of Queen Hilde. Following Cady's instructions he opened up the head of Hilde and carefully housed the Lud seed inside the skull, taking the place of Pok Pok's crystal. A ruby-red glow took over the figurehead's eyes.

"The Lud seed is now the spirit of the *Juniper*," Cady said.

"You mean the brain?"

"I know as much as you do, Jeb; everything from now on is unexplored territory."

Indeed it was. They cast off and headed upriver. She told Jeb of their next destination. Cady had only one plan in mind: to visit Tenebrae House, where Dr John Dee used to live. If Dee truly was the key, then Tenebrae was a good place to start.

They had been travelling on land and river since half ten that morning, when they had left Nabs' house in Witherhithe. Now the air was just beginning to darken, giving the river a soft violet hue. The water was calm; no sign of the rains of earlier in the day. Birds swarmed in darting formations,

seeking their evening meal. The buildings along the north
bank were burnished with gold, while the four towers of
the power station to the south were clouded at their upper
reaches with plumes of smoke.

The next bend in the river brought them in sight
of Blackthorn Bridge and beyond that the Shrivings,
its fairground rides and stalls already lit up in flashing
multicoloured lights. The sky was smudged in purple. A
little further on the strains of calliope music could be heard,
its forced jollity tinged with melancholy. Suddenly several
beams of light shot up into the sky, rather like the air-
defence spotlights of the war years. The beams converged
and brightened. Then they spilt apart once more and were
replaced by a monster in black with yellow eyes flashing at
its peak. Cady gasped. It was Gogmagog! Reaching as high as
the power station's towers, the Night Serpent writhed about,
his elongated body stealing gritty smoke from the chimneys.
It flew even higher, disappearing into the clouds and then
ducking down again, swooping towards the fairground,
only to pull up at the last moment to rise again and put on
an antic dance above the curves of the Big Dipper.

Cady pushed the engine to full ahead, forcing a path
between other boats and the Old Prison Ship at Longmoat.
The river churned under the propeller's strainings as they
sailed under the steel archway of the bridge. Cady's attention
moved from the river traffic to the monster in the sky, as
the yellow eyes of Gogmagog flashed and burned. It was by
now obvious that the monster was in fact a projection of
some kind, and she was reminded of the way young Brin
Halsegger had conjured the image of Haakenur into the sky
on the Night of the Dragon. Was this something similar?
Was the girl involved in some way? And then the smoke

monster suddenly dipped down to the river and reached for Cady, whirling about her head. She could smell him, and taste him on her tongue, and she knew then exactly what his true make-up was.

Once this message had been passed on, Gogmagog quickly vanished from sight, the smoke drifting away, his eyes blinking a few more times and then going dark. By the time the *Juniper* had moored at the Shrivings dock the twilit skies were painted only with clouds. "What was that?" Jeb asked as he disembarked to wind the hawser around a bollard. "Must be some new attraction, I guess."

"It was more than that, lad. Much more. It was Mr Lek himself, and I believe he needs our help." She offered no further explanation, allowing the various possibilities free play in her mind.

They walked the wooden walkways between the merry-go-rounds and the waltzers and the bumper cars. Teenage girls were shrieking in delight on the more violent rides, their beaus hanging on tight to them. Roustabouts clung one-handed to speeding spinning jolting cars, jumping from one to another, taking people's money and teasing the riders. Twilight changed the atmosphere of the Shrivings, giving it a darker, more dangerous, more glamorous edge. Courting couples kissed in the shadows of tents; the House of Horrors brought out its worst nightmares; the Hall of Mirrors reflected viewers back in more and more hideously malformed ways. Barkers called their wares from every Try-Your-Luck and Shooting Gallery stall, competing with each other to draw a crowd. A gang of scuttlers swaggered along, threatening trouble, their flick-knives on display. Every kind of music you could imagine clashed from crackly loudspeakers: Azeelian hit songs, calliope nursery rhymes, the wheezing polkas of the steam organs. Cady and Jeb dodged their way through the crowds until they came to the fair's main crystal show; and here they found the origin point of the Night Serpent's appearance.

The barker stood on a platform, shouting and cajoling. "Ladies and gentlemen, I give you a wonder of the world brought to life, a beast never before seen by modern eyes. Roll up, roll up! Are you brave enough to face the horrors of Gogmagog!"

The theatre was circular in shape with painted wooden walls depicting the dramas on offer: murder mysteries, bawdy comedies, titillating scandals, and "The strangest and most extraordinary people and places ever witnessed!" A queue had already formed for the next viewing. Cady chose some of her worst smells to send out from her pores. Jeb held his nose, as he had to suffer the most, while other people moved back, some of them even leaving the queue. Then she spat and swore, putting on a fine show of "mad old biddy". It worked, and they were soon at the entrance where an Ephreme woman took their fee. Inside was a large stage area carpeted with sawdust like a circus ring. Most of the fleapits Cady visited were traditional theatres with proscenium arches. But this was something different, a panorama effect. At the exact centre of the stage was a steel rod holding a blue crystal. Around this was a ring of sodium bulbs, which picked up images stored in the crystal, projecting them onto the canvas viewing screen which ran around the entire inner wall of the theatre. There were no seats, so the audience could promenade around the circle, watching different parts of the show at their leisure. Only the central dais was out of bounds. A show was under way as she entered, the usual mix of newsreels, advertisements for local businesses, and scenes of interest from around the Kethran Isles. Cady watched some of these for a moment and then looked up; the theatre would usually have a canvas roof, but this had been rolled back for the evening's entertainment. The sky was visible, still with traces of drifting smoke in it. She felt a tremor of fear.

The wall screen went dark and a couple of stagehands hurried to remove the central rod and crystal. The barker took up his position on the dais, walking around the ring of bulbs to address all sections of the audience. He was an Ephreme of some majesty, getting on a bit but his wings were very handsome and outspread, each feather dyed a different colour. He spoke into a microphone, his velvety voice bringing mysteries and dangers to vivid life.

"Often we have thought that only Faynr rules our city and our river, guarding us from danger. But what if some other creature exists, one not so protective, but wild of nature and ferocious and driven by evil intent! Good people, we now know such a beast exists in the world, hidden from us until this very day. His name is… Gogmagog!"

There was nervous laughter from the audience. Cady could see from Jeb's face that the boy was taking it all in with pleasure. But her own feelings were on edge, and bitterly so. She felt her thorns emerging to spike themselves into a wooden support. She would have to pry them loose with a claw-hammer at this rate!

The barker went on with his spiel: "Is Gogmagog an ancient creature transported through time? Is he a demon from another dimension, hungry for human flesh? Or is he an Enakor secret weapon only now unleashed upon us!"

People booed and jeered at the very idea of such a thing.

"But ladies and gentlemen, we give you many delights. Not only will Gogmagog make his appearance, but also…" He paused for effect. "Also we will give you a glimpse into the very depths of a Thrawl's mind. And no ordinary Thrawl, but a strange mutated being, part machine, part myridi fly!"

This announcement really got the audience going, they cheered, they chanted, they cried out for savage thrills. Their prayers were answered as a Thrawl was led onto the dais, his hands bound behind him, his head covered with a black hood. He looked docile, compliant to his captor's orders as they manoeuvred him inside the ring of bulbs at the pit's centre. Cady felt sick inside. Her fears were being realised.

A hush fell over the crowd as the Barker continued: "Many a year ago it was common to see Thrawls at fairs such as the Shrivings, performing tricks, and having their crystal brains projected into the walls of panoramas such as this one. But the events of the Frenzy…" A chorus of catcalls interrupted his flow. He let it die down before continuing: "Yes indeed, the terrible events of the Frenzy shall never be forgotten, when all the Thrawls in Kethra went crazy on the same day at the exact same time, damaging property, injuring people, killing people! O terrible days! Since then the mechanical men and women have been dismantled or else switched off and put in storage. But now, for your viewing pleasure we have a resurrected machine! Ladies and Gentlemen, I give you Thrawl 247LE54K, otherwise known as Lek, Master Magician of the Crystal World!"

At this the black hood was whipped away from the Thrawl's face. Lek was revealed to the audience's eager delight. He wore the same suit as before, all tattered and torn, and his head showed even more dents and scars than this morning. His crystal was dull and lifeless within the translucent skull. His eyes were two holes in a blank mask, for he wore no expression, none at all, and this upset Cady tremendously, for she had grown to love Lek's ever-changing moods and faces. Now he stood at rest, even when his hands were unbound.

Cady leaned over to ask Jeb, "What have they done to him?"

"I reckon the barker's throwing some kind of hex on him. You see the hand gestures he's making, right in front of Lek's face?"

"Aye."

"He's tracing binding sigils in the air. I know the old Ephremes used to control Thrawls that way, to give them new instructions. My granddaddy taught me a few when I was a kid, to make my pet dog do tricks."

Indeed, the barker treated Lek as some kind of performing automaton, going so far as to wipe down Lek's skull with a rag.

"The bastards!"

Cady called out in protest, but Jeb put a hand on her and shushed her into quiet. "Let it play on a while, my dear. Otherwise people will turn on us." Cady stamped her heels on the packed sawdust, but she saw the wisdom in Jeb's words and managed to hold her tongue.

All attention was now focused on Lek as his crystal brightened. He had taken the place of the theatre's usual store of images. The barker walked the circle. "Before we begin our demonstration, one more fact must be revealed. Thrawl Lek was the head butler for none other than the Halsegger family."

A beer bottle flew over the dais and bounced off Lek's chest. He paid it no matter at all, so dead was he to the world.

The barker played to the audience's base desires: "The Halseggers. High-ranking Alkhyms, revelling in power and position, but in reality… a family of traitors! Yes. Thrawl Lek was there and in all likelihood took part in the treason himself."

Cady was glad now that she had kept her restraint, for the crowd was baying like a pack of hounds for blood, or oil, or whatever flowed in the poor machine-man's inner passages. But it was Lek himself who quietened them by raising his hands to his head, one on each side. His face was still blank. His skull flickered and twin beams of blue light flashed out from his eyes to merge into a single focus of energy that was picked up by the sodium bulbs in the projection array. The bulbs glowed, each in turn. It only took a second for the images to travel from there to the circular wall screen. Lek's thoughts were now on full display.

Cady was instantly caught up in the wonder of it all. First to be seen was a pleasant memory of a garden party at the Halsegger mansion in honour of the eldest daughter's marriage. There were no sounds, only the sights of a croquet game on the lawn, the marquee where bright young things danced, and the Lord and Lady standing proudly on the terrace. King Herald was seen crossing the gardens with a pair of red setters leading the way. Tantalising the audience, Lek revealed some of the more intimate moments he had witnessed: family arguments, a stolen kiss, and most poignantly, Lady Halsegger at the end of a corridor, wiping tears from her eyes. Other memories followed, each travelling around the canvas screen, sepia-tinged but with dashes of colour: a leisurely boating trip on the river, a cricket match, the first hunt of the year. However, there were no glimpses of Brin, nor of the days at Blinnings nor the year or so on the run. The fact that Cady herself was also missing in action peeved her a little, but Lek was perhaps editing his memories, and there were some things he desired be kept secret. It was probably for the best.

But these glimpses of upper-class life soon palled, as evidenced by a shout of: "Where's the monster?" This was copied by other punters: "Give us the monster! Bring on Gogmagog!" Once again the barker waved his hands in front of Lek's face. The Thrawl responded instantly, replacing the memories with images of the corridors and rooms inside his own head. The whole circle of the wall was now filled with fragments of light as shards of blue, gold, orange and red danced around, enveloping the viewers in a kaleidoscopic display.

The barker enthused: "Before today no one has ever truly and fully seen inside a Thrawl's mind. Little did we know that such delights existed in such a dull container. Good people, I present for your delectation... the Crystal Palace!"

Lek took the whole audience on a whirlwind tour, darting from one room to the next, offering each for a few seconds of display before moving swiftly on. The rooms were cast directly onto the wall-screen and the audience equally, so that the spectators seemed to be standing within each room of the palace in turn: the Gallery, the Lounge Bar, the Conservatory, the Reliquary with its set of memory jars. Cady felt dizzy watching it and she held onto Jeb's arm for support. Her eyes blazed and blurred with dots of colour and her stomach lurched. Yet it was so thrilling! Far better than the earlier glimpses given to her via the medium of Mr Carmichael's tank. Lek was peeling images from the walls and casting them directly onto people's bodies, creating a sort of three-dimensional effect, rather like the stereoscope viewers popular before the First War. But this was far more real, because the audience itself was being used as a collection of mobile screens. More than one person tried to pick up objects from tabletops and bureaus, only to be disappointed. It was a superb performance on the Thrawl's part.

The journey settled into one room, the Library. The bullet in the Library's wall extended over the theatre's stage, looking for all the world like an Enakor flying missile that had failed to detonate. The bookshelves were cracked and broken, desk-lamps stuttered on and off, hundreds of books and almanacs and atlases were scattered about, their pages ripped to shreds. Bits of paper fluttered about like a snowstorm. Cady was appalled, for the Library looked a lot worse than her last viewing. She found the reason for this deterioration when a bookcase fell over and a huge creature crept forward on six spindly jointed legs, its hairy antennae twitching, its giant bulbous body glittering with shiny oily colours, green and gold, its eyes large and multifaceted. A viscous fluid dripped from its mandibles. It was turning a page from an encyclopedia into a filthy white pulp which it promptly ingested using its proboscis.

The crowd gasped, and cried out in both wonder and fright.

It was the myridi fly trapped in Lek's head, but magnified a thousandfold. It truly was the stuff of nightmares. Lek threw the image onto one person after another, transplanting the fly's head onto their shoulders. Now it was Jeb's turn to shiver and shake and he clung to Cady for comfort. The barker willingly accepted his turn as the myridi, adjusting his wings so they merged with those of the fly. His voice took on a sinister aspect: "We promised you monsters; monsters you shall have. A myridi fly has taken possession of the Thrawl's skull. It lives there, creeping and crawling about and slowly destroying all that is good and ordered in the Man Machine's inner world. Can you imagine the pain Lek must feel?"

No one could, not even Cady. It was beyond any kind of human understanding.

Throughout this display, Mr Lek remained in place at the centre of the circle, but his torso and limbs were shaking and his mask crackled with a sudden expression of anguish seen for a moment only before the blankness took over once more.

Cady couldn't help herself: "Let him go!" she shouted. "Set him free!"

Those around her did not agree. "No. Show us more, show us Gogmagog!" The chant was taken up all around. "Show us Gogmagog, Gogmagog! Show us Gogmagog!"

The barker hushed them and they settled into silence. Lek followed suit, dimming the lights on his Crystal Palace; he was still under the control of the hex spell. Ominous music played over the theatre's loudspeakers, lending further mystery to the showman's words.

"We are a city, a nation, and a people only now rising out of times of despair. The war is over, and we rejoice, but there are still dangers lurking, beyond the normal range of our senses. Chief among these is the Night Serpent, a dragon of smoke and poison. Ladies and Gentlemen, I present to you... GOGMAGORIA!"

His shout crackled the loudspeakers into a squawk of feedback.

The last fragments of the Crystal Palace vanished.

Cady turned her attentions to Lek.

His eyes were black, empty.

No beams of light, no images. Only his blue crystal pulsating.

His tremors had stopped, he stood rigidly in place.

Everyone in the theatre waited for him to act, to put on a show for them.

Not a person spoke or murmured, or even shuffled about.

Then the Thrawl's eyes clicked on again, becoming two intensely bright circles. But the blue beams, when they appeared, moved quite slowly through the air, reaching the first of the projection bulbs, then languidly passing on to the others in the ring.

Cady was held spellbound by the sight and by the atmosphere of the stage, the thrum of the music, and the twilight skies above, seen through the theatre's open roof. Everyone was breathing in step, not daring to break the mood. Jeb was shivering. Cady felt a sudden chill in her bones as the Thrawl's beams of light hit the canvas screen, which trembled and rippled along its curved length and then turned a dark smoky colour. There were as yet no recognisable images, only the illusion of smoke billowing around the room, taking over spectators' faces and bodies and then passing on, each person in turn shrouded for a few moments. It seemed to be taking flight from the walls as people moved under its influence, walking the outer ring of the arena. Drums pounded over the speakers. The smoke began to move more quickly, becoming a thick stream of grey fog lapping the circle at speed. A semblance only, yet it seemed to take on more substance with every circuit. First the head and tail of a terrible demon came into view, and then the long writhing body connecting the two extremes, all parts of it adopting a darker deeper presence. The creature was almost complete. Last to come were the eyes which suddenly burned into a fierce yellow light. The illusion was forceful enough that people were taken in by its spell.

A woman made a sort of gasping half scream.

A man ran for the exit door, taking his children with him.

Someone close to Cady reeled on his feet, threatening to faint.

Gogmagog wound his way around the stage, filling the space entirely. There was no bestial roar, no smell of decay; only the sight of him, which was enough to terrify the viewers. Lek was hidden from view amid the smoke; only a dot of glowing blue light showed where his crystal did its work. Cady suspected the Thrawl was simply drawing on his memories of the monster's appearance at the village of Ponperreth, and of his own temporary possession by the demon, but his powers were amplified by the theatre's apparatus. Cady's heart was pounding. The enemy was present and she was helpless to act as the people came under a kind of hypnotic control. *It's not real, it isn't real!* All of her watchwomanly spirit could not dispel the horror of the moment. *It's not fuckin' real!*

The climax came as Gogmagog rose from the crystal pit, up through the open ceiling, to be caught by the four powerful spotlights set on the outer edges of the theatre's roof. They must have been repurposed from their original anti-aircraft duties, fitted with larger, more powerful projection bulbs. The monster was cast onto the low cloud cover. The audience members cheered this, actually cheered! Cady fumed. Didn't they understand what they were witnessing? Whose bloody side were they on! People applauded loudly or punched the air in exaltation. Every eye in the place followed the Night Serpent in his progress through the heavens. He was gathering black smoke and soot from the nearby power station, the effluent from the four massive chimneys a perfect medium for the image's flight. Cheers and screams could be heard from outside the tent as the funfair's customers reacted to the sudden sight of Gogmagog. Lek stood on the stage, his arms raised high, the crystal shining in his skull at its brightest-ever blue. His face had taken on a single fixed expression, one of triumph. It scared Cady, and shook her to her core.

The show was soon over. Lek's face returned to its blank state and his hands fell to his sides. His shoulders slumped, puppet-like. At the same time Gogmagog vanished from the sky, becoming a cloud, a thin mist, without shape, without colour. The members of the audience looked exhausted as they trudged towards the exit doors. The whole performance had taken little over twenty minutes. Cady and Jeb remained behind. An usher tried to move them on, but instead Cady climbed the steps onto the central dais. She went up to Lek. The barker watched her carefully; he was smoking a cigar and drinking from a bottle of beer.

"You enjoyed the performance, madam?"

"Oh yes. Very enlightening. And by the way, this is my property." She tapped the now docile Lek on the chest.

The barker grinned, showing a gold tooth. "I know what you're up to."

"Oh you do?"

"You have to pay a second time, to watch it again."

"I told you plain, mister, this lump of machinery belongs to me."

"Funny, you don't look much like an Alkhym. Distant member of the family, are you?"

"What?"

"Some mad Halsegger granny kept in the attic for fifty years."

"I'm Wodwo born and seeded."

"Good for you." He raised his wings high on each side and gave them a good flutter. This close up you could see little gemstones stuck between the flights.

Cady wasn't impressed. "You like showing off, do you?"

He offered another flash of that gold incisor. It irritated her, and she gave him a good viewing of her own mouth in return, numerous missing teeth and all! "Oh, have pity on an old seafarer and a riverwoman of some years, yes, some good years. All I want is my Thrawl back." She waved her hand in front of Lek's face, hoping for a reaction. "Wake up, Mr Lek. Come on, old tin mug, show lively now, step to it!"

But the Thrawl's face remained empty, his eyes closed. The only activity was the myridi fly taking a stroll across the inside of the blank visage, its little legs jittering along.

Cady huffed. "Oh, the bother of it! What have you done to him?"

"I have returned him to a place of happiness."

"Lud's arse! You've mesmerised him."

"Perhaps you, madam, were the cause of his strife?"

Admittedly, this threw her a little. But she spoke a lie plain enough to make it real. "Mr Lek here is a crewman on my riverboat. He wandered off last night, absent without leave, following an altercation. And this my final voyage, and all. Isn't that right, Jeb? You tell him."

"Right she is, sir, ringmaster, sir. Chief Engineer Lek is much missed."

"And who might you be?"

"Midshipman Jebediah Yeomanson."

The barker looked at them, one to the other, then shook his head. "Sorry, but this here Thrawl is the best thing that's happened to me in a good long time."

Cady put her fists up. The barker just laughed at her. He was a big man, over six feet tall, with a chest in the shape of a barrel. He wore a striped coat with long tails, and he sported a gold top-hat. He took this off now, revealing a head as bald as the Thrawl's. "You should know," he announced, "I was the Shrivings' strong man before this present endeavour." He rubbed at his beer belly. "Fancy your chances in the ring? I'll knock your heads together. Clunk!"

Cady still had her fists in front of her. "You're a cup of dog piss. I'll have you keelhauled!"

Jeb calmed things down, asking, "How did you come across the Thrawl?"

Ever the showman, the barker was happy to tell his story. "He turned up earlier today looking lost, and helpless. In a daze he was, like his motor was running down, until suddenly he went a bit crazy in the head and started smashing up a coconut shy. Then he broke the bell on the Test Your Strength machine! I thought we were in for another Frenzy, I really did. But he calmed down a little and started gabbing on and on about, 'Brin, Brin, little Brin,' whomsoever that might be. A sorry sight, and many here wanted to get their hands on him. I punched my way into prime position. See, I have the bruises on my knuckles to prove it." His hands were two lumps of meat streaked with purple. "Imagine my surprise when I fixed him up in the old Thrawl way, crystal-show fashion. I got a look inside his head. My oh my, delights galore! And now, if you don't mind, I have the next show to prepare for. People are lining up already."

He gave rapid instructions to his workmates, who all looked to be of the same family: sisters, brothers, sons and daughters, all of them sporting wings that must have made Jeb envious. Even the old granddaddy had a better and more feathery pair that the young lad did. But Cady watched with interest as Jeb took advantage of the sudden activity to make a series of quick hand gestures in front of Lek's face. Sadly, it had no effect other than to make the Thrawl's eyes flicker a little. Jeb was pushed aside as one of the bigger sons came forward with a loop of rope, and another with the black hood. Lek stood there in slumped fashion, ready for the bonds to be applied. Cady couldn't stand it. She grabbed the hood for herself and tried to rip it in two, failed at this task, and so threw it to the floor of the stage and stamped on it. The whole family turned on her then. Jeb stood at her side, not knowing where to look for the best, but Cady was glad of his company.

"Don't you dare tie him up!" she cried.

For once, the barker showed some compassion. "It's only for show, riverwoman. We'll treat him nice and proper, don't worry."

Perhaps Jeb's reverse hexing had some effect, or maybe the Thrawl's mind had managed to find an exit door from the room marked *SLEEP*; whatever the case, he started to come round from his coma. His face took on a hundred expressions all at once, his entire repertoire, before settling into one: RAGE! His eyes burned red, as red as the world had ever seen. He rocked back and forth, his hands curved like claws at his side. The barker moved to his prize performer, family in tow; but they looked nervous of confronting the Thrawl. As well they might, for he was a machine on the edge of madness. Cady made her own endeavour, stepping forward. Was Mr

Lek glad to see her? She could not tell, but something in his manner told her to fall back, and quickly. She had seen him damage the decking of the boat only that morning. She made it just in time before his eye-beams shot out at full force to draw a bright red line along the curve of the wall screen. The canvas shrivelled and smouldered. For a moment there was silence as everyone stood in shock. Then with a soft *whoosh!* the canvas caught fire and started to burn.

The barker cried for mercy and tried to knock Lek off balance, but the ex-strongman was no match against the Thrawl. Indeed, Lek was not yet done: his beams continued on their journey around the entire circle of the screen, leaving in their wake a line of fire. Smoke billowed through the theatre. Soon the wooden support struts would catch aflame. Chaos hit as the family ran this way and that, some for the exits, others for the fire-fighting equipment.

Cady and Jeb slipped away in the melee, Lek in hand, leading him as fast as they could on a route between the rides and amusement arcades as the flames rose behind them and once more smoke gathered in the skies above the Shrivings. Other stallholders had seen them as the culprits and were raising a clamour. Jeb ran on ahead, towards where the *Juniper* was moored, but Lek had a different route in mind; he slipped away between two fairground rides. Cady was torn: to head for the *Juniper* with Jeb, or to follow Lek? The many shouts and cries added to her confusion, as crowds of people milled about, some of them aware of the fire, others lost in the merriment. The mad jollity of a roundabout's music was loud in her ears.

She made her choice.

The Crystal Wedding

There was a small brick hut on the far edge of the Shrivings land. Lek was there, his silhouette very distinctive against the trees. Cady went after him, crossing a set of railway lines as quickly as she could. She ducked beneath a broken wooden beam in the doorway of the hut and almost fell down a flight of stone steps, scraping her knee on the concrete wall. Lek's footsteps ran on ahead, echoing in the gloom. Three corridors led off this chamber. Which way did he go? The sound played tricks. But her optic gland glowed nice and green in her head and she followed its direction, letting instinct have its way. The left-hand route. It was a good decision; the Thrawl's footsteps grew louder.

This was no bomb shelter, but the entrance to a far larger underground structure. Moss on the walls, damp dripping down. Dare she call out Lek's name? No, not yet, in case the barker and his family were pursuing her. She stopped for a moment, listening. Silence now, fore and aft. Then a voice, and another. Yes, they were down here, seeking revenge. Lud's sword! Cady set off as quietly and as quickly as she could in the dark. The floor sloped downwards as the stone walls gave way to organic matter, which she recognised as the transparent flesh of Psephekarnidraxapor. No lamps, no signposts, only the diverging pathways of the burrowing creature's organs and veins. Old Seph was a damaged animal in these parts, with evidence of warts and cankers on the walls. Here and there were signs of human handiwork, a patching of the flesh; but the work had taken place a good while ago, and this area of the transport system was now abandoned and left in disrepair. Through the skin Cady saw only earth and roots and rocks. The air was thin, and difficult to breathe. She was now in the deeper darkness. But the corridor was widening a little. She was entering a different part of the creature's anatomy, where the skin was punctured by natural portals. Cady took another turning and she found Lek.

He was slumped down against the wall, his head lowered, his arms limp at his side.

She tapped on his shoulder. "Lek, it's me. It's Cady. Wake up."

But he wasn't sleeping. He looked at her with a weary raising of his head. His eyes were the only visible light: one blue, the other white, constantly blinking. His mouth moved rapidly but no words could be made out, only a series of guttural noises. The myridi in his head was doing its work. Cady brushed dirt away from the Thrawl's face. His expression was flickering between two extremes: *Determination* and *Resignation*.

She sat herself down at his side, leaning her aching back against the wall.

No sound of the followers, for now at least. That was good.

What was there to talk about? How could she rouse this lump of tin and resin?

She tried, "Did you know that when Haakenur finally met her end by Lud's sword, the great dragon fell to the ground at the foot of Red Moon Hill, and she crushed twelve sheep, three horses, nine of Lud's dead comrades, a whole flock of starlings, and one thousand and seventeen assorted insects."

She waited. Nothing. The Thrawl did not stir, not even to contradict her. And that was one of her best facts, as well! Now what? Her mind was emptying. She rambled on.

"I have done my work as paid for. I have guided you along the River Nysis to Ludwich. I have delivered Brin to the Hesting festival. That's it, job done." She grunted. "So why am I here? That is the question. I came after you. I didn't want to, believe me. I wanted to get back to the *Juniper*, with Jeb, and sail away upriver." She paused here, and looked at her companion. But there was still no reaction from him, so she went back to her ramble: "I have to get to Tenebrae House, see, the once-upon-a-time home of Dr Dee, in order get the Lud seed germinated. That's the plan anyway. At best, it's a leaky boat and a prayer. And as you know, tin mug, Old Hallows is a sealed community, tighter than a double sheet-bend tied in wet rope." She let another pause happen. Then: "Where are you going, by the way? Still chasing after Brin?"

Still no reply. But his eyes changed colour yet again, and his face clicked through at least a dozen expressions at random. He was losing control over himself.

Cady heard footsteps and the shouts of men, but distantly, and moving away. "I think we've lost them. Ha ha, there's one for the history books, Lek, me old darling. *Mad Thrawl sets Shrivings Fair on fire!*"

Lek nodded. A welcome response, if nothing else.

"Come on, get up." Cady got to her feet, by way of demonstration, but he remained where he was. She reached down and pulled at him. "Do I have to carry you? Because I will. Really."

She tried it, nearly breaking her neck in the process, and they fell to the ground together in a heap of metal and plant-like flesh. Their faces were pressed close. "Well this is very nice, I must say. Two old tubs in the dry dock, ready for scrap." But the Thrawl's head was alive with the blue light of his crystal, and the dancing shadow of his lodger, the fly. The beauty of the colour mixed with the nastiness of the insect maddened Cady. She disentangled herself from his limbs. Lek lay there in a heap, twitching and muttering.

She spat at the wall, giving Old Seph a bit of much-needed lubrication. "You really shouldn't bother with Brin anymore, I mean it." It was said in anger. "Are you listening to me, Lek? She's just a brat, a stupid, stupid fucked-up little posh madam. And perhaps more than that."

He murmured, close to speech. But nothing more.

Cady saw that he was still clutching his precious Pok Pok crystal, perhaps taking consolation from its low-level flicker. Then he mumbled something.

She leaned in closer. "What's that? What's on your mind?"

"I've lost… I've lost the suitcase."

"Suitcase? What?"

"It had Brin's favourite things in it. Her little playthings."

"Oh yes, I remember. You took it with you on your walkabout. Where did you get to, Lek, eh, on your travels?" She hoped a nice chat would help him reconstruct his patterns.

"Following… fly follow flutter… follow signal… ping, ping… streets and river."

"Yes, right. Very good. Well that makes total sense, I must say."

"Bridge crossing water."

"I saw you there, I saw you in a vision, Lek! You were crossing Blackthorn Bridge, weren't you, towards the Shrivings. What then?"

"Seeking Brin... ping ping ping... signal weakening... lost... lost..."

"And then the people at the funfair got hold of you, eh? Do you remember that? Come on. Put your story together for me."

He looked deeper into the surrounding darkness, his eyes set to night vision: bright green. His voice took on strength. "I was certain she had entered here, into these tunnels. I could hear the myridi in her head pinging at me. But gone now, gone. No more."

"Oh tell that myridi to fuck off! Nasty little sod."

"But I promised that I would look after Brin."

Cady shook her head in despair. "And that promise is killing you."

"While my crystal still shines, I shall keep to my promise."

"You're addicted, that's what this is. I've seen your type, on battlefields and around the poker tables, and in the brothels and the opium dens. It's not a promise, it's an obsession." The fibres were tightening around Cady's heart, and her stigma throbbed for attention. She was a garden in bloom. Yet here she was stuck in the dead organs of a giant underground monster, trapped in the dark with a broken-down Thrawl. "I just can't work out why I followed you. It doesn't make sense to me, not at all." Fuck it. She was exhausted, suddenly, and wanted only to rest and to sleep.

What was it old Granny Meade used to say: *Life is where you find it, until you lose it.* Well, she was good and lost! Her eyes closed. From the edge of a dreamworld Cady's words flowed like sap from a tropical plant.

"In war or in peace, I care not, give them both to me that I might drink of them equally. Glug glug! On land or sea, it's the same magic. In the beds of comrades or alone in the brig, in leg-irons, or even tied to the mast, lashed by the cat o' nine tails twenty times over till the blood runs under the hot sun of the equator, no matter, let it come. I will live. Because always there was a helping hand, someone who reached out and shook me back to life." Why, she hardly knew what she was saying, but she was saying it anyway. "There's this island I know, far off. It's called *Elsewhere*. You won't find it listed on any maps. Elsewhere Island. I went there once in a former life, or it might have been in a dream. Sometimes it's hard to keep track." She murmured the melody of the old ballad to herself, a reminder of days gone. Then a few words under her breath: "*I'll tell of my true love, though many a mile lies now between us.* La la la, and so on. You should never dribble your passions away. But I always do. I always have. I would like for once to not do such a thing."

Lek was stirring. He spoke quietly, with a croak: "I have a map of Psephekarnidraxapor in my Library. It might be damaged. But… Cady, it might help you in your quest."

"You mean there might be a way to get inside Old Hallows?"

He nodded. "Yes, perhaps. A secret way. We could find Tenebrae House together."

"We could! We could do that!"

There was joy in her heart. As though in celebration of

this moment, a voice called from the gloom and a lamp was seen, waving. "Who's there? Are you lost?" The lantern belonged to a Nebulim. The life-giving flame inside his clay head brightened into scarlet as he greeted them. The only sound was the vibrant clicking and tinkling of the Nebulim's ornaments.

"We're trying to get across the river," Cady said to him. "Towards Old Hallows."

The Nebulim's name was Sol Lanu. He told them that, and then he said, "That way is closed up."

"You think I don't know?"

"The best way under the river is via Timmusk village."

"Timmusk? I've been there a few times in my travels. In fact, I have a friend who might be there, name of Numi Tan. Do you know of her?"

Sol smiled. "Yes. She arrived with us last night." His voice was soft and fluttery. "This is her wedding day."

"Is it now, well there's a turn-up. Fast work!"

Ten minutes later they were making their way deeper into Psephekarnidraxapor's portals and pathways. Sol supported Lek for a while, until the Thrawl took over and walked on under his own steam. Cady felt her trusty sense of direction returning, giving her a glimmer of where they were. But the corridors kept splitting in two and three and four, and so on, a complex branching system rather like the bronchial structure of a lung. Eventually they reached a main avenue where the tube widened and the air was more breathable. The first dwellings were seen, pod-like structures that looked like growths on the flesh of the creature. The occupants watched them pass with low-level curiosity. It was certainly a very different atmosphere to the Nebulim village at Ponperreth which had given itself over to the worship of Gogmagog.

A series of hanging lamps hardly disturbed the shadowed gloom: the Nebulim preferred the semi-dark, being able to communicate with each other at ease as their flames changed colours rapidly. This was fire language.

An entrance led the party away from Psephekarnidraxapor, into a cave system. They came in sight of a waterfall, where an underground tributary of the Nysis dropped down to their level, forming a large pool in a crater, before going on its way to reach other streams. Faynr danced in the cascading water, her orange and pink sparkles caught within a purple spume. Tiny little birds barely the size of a penny flew about, scattering the butterflies and dragonflies that also lived in the pond's surroundings: each creature was electric pink or bright yellow in colouring, often dappled. Cady stood at the base of the Crystal Falls. She had been here a few times before, at different growths of her life, but the sight always surprised her with its beauty. This particular region of the waterfall was named Mother Lyra's Well, after one of the very first Nebulim matriarchs. The water's flow mixed with Faynr into a magical brew that reacted with objects placed in the downpour, most commonly the rocks and embedded pebbles of the wall, which turned over time into an abundance of crystals, some of which, the blue variety, could be used as communication and processing devices. But there were other colours on offer, with various decorative or ritualistic values. To this end, many small personal objects had been left in the flow of the waters, to become changed and bejewelled by the crystallisation process: teddy bears, bracelets, pocket watches, chess pieces, brass buttons. Hundreds of such items were collected here, gathering their new colours of green and yellow and orange. They were kept or sold as souvenirs, toys, memento mori.

Sol led Cady and Lek to another part of the Falls, a more secluded area. Here, a wedding was taking place, a Nebulim ritual that Cady had never before witnessed. Amid the colourful array of crystals, two figures stood hand in hand, perfectly still, at peace. A man and a woman. Shards of quartz were forming on their clay bodies, emerald green in colour. Attendants made sure the faceplates were kept clear of any encrustation. Cady recognised Numi Tan. The male form would be her "Romeo", Romi Omir, the person she had been searching for these past few years. It was a glad thing to see and Cady felt her heart unfurling its petals, and she waved to her friend.

Sol explained, "She is not aware of you. Bride and groom sleep through the ceremony. They are sharing their dreams."

"How long will it take?" Cady asked.

"Numi and Romi will remain here for three hours more before their nuptials are complete."

"And the green crystals? I've never seen them in use before."

"They act as psychic armour, to soak up any harmful or demonic thoughts and emotions in the atmosphere, filtering and dispelling them. Only good thoughts are allowed access."

"Ah well." Cady sighed. "I'm pleased to hear it. I fear I've brought some nastiness along with me, tangled in my hair, in my breath, in my odours. And most of all in the pains I drag along behind me like some blasted barge filled with night soil."

Sol looked at Cady with interest now, as though seeing her for the first time. "You are bitter."

"All four of my marriages failed, and failed miserably."

"That is sad to hear."

"Aye, here's to wedded bliss." She saluted the bride and groom.

Sol was pensive. "The crystals will be scraped away to make their dowry and their flames mingled to form two new faces, twins."

The old Haegra felt herself mellowing a little. "May their fires never be extinguished."

Sol nodded in acknowledgement of the traditional blessing.

Lek was standing close by Cady's side. He was silent during this viewing of the marriage ceremony, at least to begin with, subject perhaps to his own version of intoxication, an overload of signals. Cady could not imagine what it must feel like to be so close to so many crystals, giving out so many different messages. And then some kind of barrier was broken. He began to loudly moan. He stepped up to the waterfall with its two conjugal figures. The Thrawl's own crystal was now flashing in haphazard fashion. Cady went to him but then stopped as she saw his face with its mask of desperate scary intensity. He sent out a piercing howl. Little birds flew off in alarm.

"Sol, help me! Let's get him away from the Falls."

But Lek cried out, "No, no! Let me be!" This order was fierce enough to stop Cady in her tracks. "She is speaking to me."

"Who is, Lek? You mean Numi?"

"Yes. I am conversing with her. She is speaking through me, with a message for you, Cady Meade. I am the blue-green channel."

Cady looked to the bride with her gown of crystals. Numi's face of fire showed no emotion through the glass plate of her mask; any such conversation was taking place at a deeper level.

"Can't you hear?" Lek asked.

"Afraid not, old chum, too much wax in my ears."

Lek concentrated. Cady studied his face, taking in all of his little twitches and the redness of his eyes, then the yellowness. Even more strangely, she saw that the Thrawl's blue crystal was flecked with flashes of green light. He truly was linked to the Nebulim frequency. She whispered, "What's Numi saying, Lek. Tell me."

"She is responding to my thoughts about Dr Dee and Tenebrae House."

Cady was excited. "Does Numi know a way in, a secret door or something?"

Lek didn't answer straight away. His eyes were now tightly closed. Then he spoke: "There is an underground train station, closed down now."

"Does Numi have a name, or a location?"

"It's on the Shadow Line."

Cady had heard of this hidden line of the Tubular system, at least as a rumour: a network used during the war, connecting the War Office, the cellar of the House of Witan, the Palace at Wicker Hill, and various other places deemed important.

Lek turned away from Numi, to look at Cady. The crystal spell was broken. "The station is called Underhallow."

"And do you know how to get there? Did Numi tell you that?"

He nodded. "A branch line from Pollypeck."

Cady thanked Sol Lanu for his help. She gave Numi a wave and a bow and a final blessing for the future. Then they set off, walking down the tunnel, away from the Crystal Falls and back into Psephekarnidraxapor's body. Sometimes Lek chose the routes taken, and sometimes Cady, as her compass came back into operation and her optic gland

sought out the secrets of the dark and fetid world of the
burrowing creature's lesser-known organs. They turned this
way and that until the tunnel emerged from the rock wall
to travel along the bed of the River Nysis. The translucent
skin of the tube showed the dirty brown water, the strange
fishes, the bulbous billowing belly of Faynr, even a sunken
double-decker omnibus, another victim of the Enakor
bombing raids.

At last they came to the north bank of the river. She
followed Lek through a service door out onto a train
platform. This was Pollypeck underground station on the
first day of Hesting, so it was jam-packed with travellers.
Cady eyed the Tubular map on the wall and wondered
about all the lovely places she might be visiting right now
instead of this smoke-laden hellhole beset with sweaty
tourists, out-of-tune buskers, crying children, shrieking
tannoys. "Where now, tin cup? Where's this Shadow Line
of yours?" The Thrawl looked as lost as she did. Some of
the travellers decided it best to send a few choice curses
his way. Lek put on his best neutral expression. He walked
along the platform, forcing a passage through the crowd.
Cady followed, keeping hold of his hand in case they
got separated. A train came into the station and many
of the people got on board. The platform was a little less
crowded. As the train pulled out she saw that Lek was in
some discomfort. He reached out suddenly and took hold
of her, bringing her close. That blasted fly was buzzing
around inside his skull, fluttering madly from one perch
to another. Lek's face was coldly set, pure in its need. And
that need had nothing at all to do with Cady.

"I see her now," he said. "I see Brin clearly. Yes, I know
where she is."

"Lek, wait–"

"I am connected." His eyes blazed with desire. "We are connected. We is people."

He took no notice of the Exit signs, instead ducking into another service door further down the platform. They found themselves in a very dark, dirty and smelly organ. Cady dreaded to think which part of Psephekarnidraxapor's anatomy it might be. This was the Shadow Line. They were alone here, alone in a disused tunnel, where the train tracks had already been taken over by weeds and internal growths. Veins throbbed just behind the walls. It led straight and true through the earth, its walls covered in cancerous outbreaks of moss and dripping sores. The stench was strange, even to Cady's nostrils; the smell of an alien creature's stomach.

Lek forced open an iron door and they stepped through into an operation room of some kind. Here, the war had been planned, and followed, and strategized. The walls were filled with maps of Enakor and Saliscana and the Kethran Channel. A huge table held the remains of model aeroplanes and battleships. But Lek wasted no time on these marvels. He was already climbing up a metal ladder set in the wall. Cady did her best to keep up. Above was an access duct, which the Thrawl had already opened. She climbed through and rolled over onto blessed soil and lay there awhile, getting her breath back. She wiped dirt and flakes of rust from her eyes.

The sky above was decorated in night's early colours, light purple and violet, and ruby and yellow at the edges. A few clouds, the pale orb of the moon. Drops of rain, which she opened her mouth to, gratefully. Getting to her feet she looked around, seeing that they had emerged into a small private park, a wild place, but once of neater appearance.

A high wall lined with shards of broken glass kept out all intruders, so maybe the secret tunnel of the Shadow Line was the only way inside, without an invitation or a key.

This was high-level Alkhym territory. Old Hallows.

A line of elms blocked the view but Cady could sense the nearby river by its sounds and its smells. The outer reaches of Faynr moved through the branches, clinging to little rivulets among the plants, feeding them with phantom vapours. Lek was standing near a sundial, his head turning this way and that, as he waited for directions from the myridi. His face, Cady saw, was entirely his own. He spoke in an urgent whisper: "This way." They moved into an unkempt garden, keeping parallel to the river until they saw a large house abutting the elms. It was dark at every window, looking rundown and unloved. Really, Tenebrae House should be a national monument, seeing how Dr Dee, its first resident, had done so much for the country during Queen Hilde's reign. But many centuries had passed since Cady's last visit here and she had never approached the place from this direction before, only from the river. Even this garden was unknown to her, as Dee had been a very private, very circumspect person.

They came to a pagoda, its pillars wreathed in roses and vines, and its roof covered in leaves. Cady went inside, exploring. Within the structure, sitting on a raised platform, was a large fish tank. There were wooden chairs, four of them, arranged around this tank, presumably for some kind of viewing party. A creature swam in the murky water of the aquarium, a crystalback eel adorned with a pattern of blue shards. For the first time Cady wondered if Lord Pettifer was visited this location. He had communicated with the *Juniper* late last night via the crystalback spectrum. She imagined him sitting here in the pagoda, staring into the tank. If so, then the tank's occupant might well the sister of Mr Carmichael, as the species was very rare. There was one simple way to find out. Cady tapped on the glass. The crystals on the creature's back sparkled and the water coloured and formed into a moving image, showing the hold of Cady's boat. She was right; this was the channel of communication, joining brother and sister. Cady was looking out through Mr Carmichael's tank at the curved wall of the *Juniper*'s hull and the line of a bulkhead. She could see the propeller casing, her little three-legged stool, and the oily water in the bilge. And then a person appeared at the corner of her vision; Cady was happy to catch a glimpse of her new cabin boy.

"Jeb! Over here! Come and see."

He did so, looking with great surprise at Cady. She knew her face and upper body would now be filling Mr Carmichael's tank, her image carried along the wavelengths of the crystal world.

"Crikey. Good captain, you near knocked me for six."

"Where are you, Jeb?"

"I'm moored up at Keeley Hook. It's the closest landing stage to Tenebrae House."

"Well done, lad. I'm proud of you."

"Aye, I found the mooring on your river charts. I reckoned you might make your way there, after what you told me. Is Mr Lek with you?"

"He is, and as doolally as you might expect. He's been acting very strangely."

The water of the pond rippled as Miss Carmichael's crystals started to crackle. The image on the glass wavered. Cady knew she didn't have long to talk.

"Jeb, just stay where you are, with the boat. You got that?"

"Loud and clear, skipper."

But it wasn't; neither loud, nor clear. His voice stuttered and died and his image followed suit quickly thereafter; and the glass screen was greyed, all over.

Cady turned to Lek. "Any more signals from Brin?"

"Quiet, fading. But she has visited this house, and recently."

"Dr John Dee used to live here," Cady reminded him. "We met here a few times, myself and his other agents. But the house has been empty for years, I think."

"The signal still lingers."

They both stared at the rear of the dark house.

Cady said, "We're close, old chum."

Lek nodded. His crystal gleamed a very nice cornflower blue and his eyes took on the exact same colour. Cady led the way this time, finding the back door locked but a window partway open. She was thin enough to squeeze through, and then to open the door from the inside. They were in a kitchen, its sink piled with dishes and the worktop strewn with dirty cups and plates. Someone was living here, but not in any sort of capable way. Lek said in a hush, "Cady, do be careful. I'm not sure what we might find." She nodded in reply. They entered a hallway, passing a cellar door and a pantry, and then a parlour. A table lamp was on, giving the room a yellow glow. The silence was marred only by the muffled tick of a grandfather clock. Cady and Lek moved slowly, hardly daring to make a noise. Her optic gland tingled. The study was cleaner than the other rooms, and brighter. She was intrigued by a glass cabinet filled with nondescript objects, put on display as though they were great treasures:

bus and cinema tickets, cigarette cards, ration books, coins, picture postcards, a playbill, and so on. She eyed some of the items more closely, but none of the *Famous Landmarks* on the postcards were known to her, nor the *Great Actors of Movieland* on the cigarette cards. Betty Grable, Humphrey Bogart, Marilyn Monroe. Strangers, every one. Even the destinations on the bus tickets were a mystery: Clerkenwell, East Finchley, Kentish Town. Why had she never visited any of these places in her travels? And that certainly wasn't King Herald's silhouette on the half-a-crown! She picked up a cinema ticket for the Gaumont picture house on Kilburn High Street. The movie listed was *Brighton Rock*. She turned to Lek, who was examining a large framed print on the wall above the fireplace. "What have you got there?" The Thrawl did not answer. His beams, set to *gentle*, moved along the image, gathering knowledge. Cady saw it was a map, a knotted system of routes each printed in a different colour. "It looks a lot like the Tubular map," she said. "But it's not the same, the routes don't quite match. And the station names... Well, I've never heard of them." She read a few aloud, following the dark blue line: "Piccadilly, Leicester Square, Covent Garden, Holborn. What in Lud's wounds is this?"

"It's a London Tube map, if you must know."

The voice came from the open doorway. Cady turned to see Lord Olan Pettifer standing there. Despite the clue of the crystalback in the pagoda, she was surprised at his presence. Just what was he doing here? He looked tired and ragged, and there were streaks of ash and blood on his face.

"London?" she asked. "I've never heard of such a place."

"It's a city I dream about."

The Three Pages

His Lordship left the study without saying anything more. Cady and Lek went after him. She saw that the Thrawl was just about ready to explode. At the door of the dining room he grabbed Pettifer by the shoulders and yanked him back. Cady intervened: "Oh first let him speak. Then you can slug him into next Tuesday. Or knowing you… Wednesday week." As it was, this show of force had little or no effect upon Pettifer. He brushed down the front of his waistcoat and indicated the dining table with its plates of cold meats and cheeses. Then he dabbed at his leaking hesti with a napkin.

"Take a seat. I have sent my staff home, I'm afraid. But please, do help yourself."

Lek's fist came down at speed, smashing a dinner plate into fragments and making the teapot jump. There was a cracking sound as the wooden surface beneath the tablecloth splintered under the brute impact. The centrepiece, a silver candelabra, rattled.

"Where is she? Where is Brin?" Lek's voice was iron on iron. "Where are you keeping her?"

"She came to visit me, quite recently, yes, but–"

"Pettifer, I know you! I have knowledge of you. Don't you forget that."

"Of course." His voice was clipped, showing little emotion. But this calmness only served to further incite Lek's anger.

"I know how you treated Brin, at Blinnings. Forcing her to–"

"I can assure you, Mr Lek, everything that girl does, she does under her own command."

A sudden exhaustion came over Pettifer as he said this, and he sat down wearily at the head of the table. In turn Cady manoeuvred Lek into a seat opposite. Overly excited by anger, the Thrawl was now jabbering away at a low volume, producing a long string of random words and phrases: "Birdbath garden pond... island home... my mistress rings for me... silent bell..."

Cady sat down between the two men and assembled a meal for herself: cheese and crackers, boiled ham, piccalilli, a glass of wine. She spoke as any guest at a dinner party might: "Mr Lek here is picking up signals from Brin, via a myridi fly in her skull. When he does this, he's more or less fine, as fine as any poor ramshackle machine can be. But without that signal, he can fall to pieces, in body and words the same. It's a sorry state." She burped. "Well that's my theory anyway. What do you think of it?"

Pettifer was fascinated. "The signal keeps him sane. Like a god in the mind of a true believer. How very interesting. Of course, if only he'd trusted in me, none of this would have happened." He directed his words to Lek. "My friend, we could have worked together. I had such plans! For Brin and myself, and for you, Lek, you were part of the research team. Why, why did you run away?" He was genuinely upset. "And now, with Blinnings in ruins..." He wiped at his hesti vigorously. Cady could smell the oily ill-scented secretions. "I have given my all for the country's good. I was Wodwo born, but I adopted Alkhym ways for the sake of my advancement. But only to gain more influence, more funding, so that I could... I could work on my..." He sat up straight in his chair, putting all his effort into appearing sober and robust. The mask soon cracked however. "Have you any idea what it feels like, to take the hesting very late in life, against the wishes of your body?"

"You're an embittered soul, aren't you?" Cady said.

"I have some reason to be." He continued his pitiful wiping motions.

She took the chance to study Lord Pettifer. He looked nothing like he did last night, over the medium of the crystal spectrum. His elaborate costume and make-up were gone, as was his wig. Left behind was a slight, somewhat insignificant specimen of middling years, dressed in a plain blue waistcoat and an open-necked shirt, the silver loop of a pocket-watch chain the only decoration on his person. His hair was thinning, his belly was soft. His face showed signs of battle, not just the smeared ash, but also the bruise on his cheek and a bloodied cut just below his eye. These injuries were recently obtained. There was also about him, some quality of ... What was it... *Not-quite-thereness*. There was no other phrase that came close.

She fished a pickled onion from a jar on the table. "You've been in the wars, I see. And lost."

"I must admit, Miss Halsegger surprised me with her ferocity."

Hearing this, Lek lifted his gaze from the tabletop. But Cady jumped in before the Thrawl could react further. "Brin did that? Now there's a thing." The onion crunched between her teeth. "A ten year-old girl. I can hardly cotton it."

"I think by now, you know full well the young lady's powers." A smile came to Pettifer's lips. "She came to see me an hour or so ago. I must admit, I was glad to see her, despite everything, for she was always my favourite student, and my best hope for the future." He paused, looking inward for a moment. "I so wanted to reach the real Brin, to release her from captivity. But alas…"

"She has hested."

"Yes. I could not persuade her." His voice trembled, and the skin of his face seemed almost transparent, as though his grip on reality was slipping away. "I pleaded with you, Cady, did I not, to prevent the hesting from taking place."

"I tried. I really did. But you know, I was spilt in two, not knowing which way to turn. How could I know the truth?"

"I told you."

"Yes, yes, but could I believe you?"

"Anyway, it is too late now, the endgame proceeds."

Lek crawled with an effort out of the depths of his own despair. He asked a question: "What did Miss Brin want from you?"

Pettifer was glad to address this. "Certainly not to talk over old times. Instead, she wanted to see an item from my collection, a page from one of Dr Dee's notebooks."

"A single page?" Lek was puzzled.

He nodded. "It was a drawing of a map, in Dee's own hand. A chart of the Tangle Wood."

Cady felt her heart jump. "Brin's going there, that's her plan?"

"I fear so."

"But why? I mean, the maze has been closed off for centuries. Explorers get lost, and then wander out, looking dazed, lacking memories. If they wander out at all."

"Which is why she wanted the map."

"And you gave it to her?" Lek asked. His eyes glittered with intent, the need to know.

Pettifer lifted up the lid of the teapot and tilted it so that Lek and Cady could see the contents. Inside was a pile of ash, and flakes of paper. "I refused," he said.

Cady shook her head at this. "Ludding heck. You burned one of the Dee's precious papers? You must have been desperate."

He shrugged this off. "It was better, far better, than letting her know a route through the trees, to the place where Haakenur was killed, and where the dragon's bones still lie, hidden away."

"But you made a duplicate, am I right?" Lek asked.

Pettifer's eyes took on a strange look, darting here and there. His face spasmed. He reached into a drawer and pulled out several sheets of paper, which he threw onto the table. Cady looked at them. Each one showed a twisting criss-crossing pathway drawn in pencil.

"These are all different," the Thrawl observed.

"Quite so." Pettifer laughed at his own folly. "Whenever I try to copy the Tangle Wood maze, I always think I've got it right. But when I next look at the paper, it's never the same. Not the once. It's like something written down in a dream that makes no sense on waking." He relaxed a little. "The Tangle Wood keeps its secrets well." Then he took a harsh breath. "And for my pains, Brin attacked me. She smashed a wineglass, and used it to stab at me." He pointed to some fragments of glass next to his plate. "I am lucky to suffer so little, for she quickly enough fell into a reverie. She was close to tears, I believe, although I doubt such emotions truly exist anymore in her. And then she ran away. The worst has come to pass." He stared ahead. "Brin Halsegger has become a servant of Gogmagog."

Lek responded badly to this, his eyes flashing and his fingers scratching at the tablecloth, tearing into it. "He's lying... lying... he's lying, Cady! Brin would never..." He turned to her, his face full to the outer edges with *Urgent Desperate Pleading*. "You know her, Cady! Brin would never do such a thing!"

"Lek, you have to admit that–"

"No! No, never!"

The outburst triggered an equal and opposite response in his mechanisms, and he fell into a daydream, cradled perhaps by the remains of his Crystal Palace. Cady imagined him wandering lost and lonely, putting together his shattered dreams word by word, brushing up the fragments of his encyclopedias and road atlases.

Pettifer finished his wine and poured himself another. His eyes, so intensely blue, the only notable part of him, held traces of things unseen by any other person, even Cady. She leaned forward. Roughly she rubbed at the petals on her arm. "Last night in our crystal chat," she said, "you mentioned having studied the Haegra. Is that right?"

"All the existing texts, yes, what few there are."

"How about their sexual habits?"

Now he looked interested. "There is precious little on the subject, except... Well, it is a rare occurrence. Once every thousand years or so. But really, this is conjecture."

"Quit your pettifoggery."

He nodded. "Let us surmise, that when the country faces peril, worse even than the war..."

"Yes, come on!"

"Dee spoke of it. A Haegra will flower anew."

Cady felt delirious. "But I have flowered! Take a gander. Go on." She rolled up her sleeves to show off her blossoms. "Stick your nose in and sniff those aromas."

"I would rather not, thank you."

"Here's the trouble: I need next to be pollinated, and as soon as possible. And to do that I need to germinate the Lud seed."

"You have such a thing, do you?" Pettifer was genuinely intrigued by this.

"I do, in very safe keeping. And I have it on good authority that the secret of that process lies here, somewhere in this house. Or that it has something to do with Dr Dee."

"What makes you say that?"

"I was guided by an oracle, by Dee's ghost, as it happens."

They both looked at each other, neither wanting to give too much away. Cady felt that Pettifer was happy to keep his deeper knowledge safe, until needed.

"Well then, any ideas?" she demanded. "I'd like it to happen today. In fact, right this minute would be ideal."

It took him a moment to reply: "And if I were to help you, what then? Would you do battle against any such enemies that threaten our city."

"You mean Gogmagog, I take it?"

"I do. You are our last hope, Cady Meade."

Her green blood flowed strongly. "That is my task. I was born for it."

"Good." Pettifer nodded. "If the secret of the Lud seed lies anywhere, it lies within Dr Dee's books." He stood up and put a hand on Lek's shoulder. He spoke lightly: "Thrawl 247LE54K, Cady and I may be in need of assistance. Would you be willing?" This actually had some effect; Lek looked up, studying Lord Pettifer carefully, his eyes flickering with different colours. Cady could hear his mechanisms at work; he was a Clicking Man made of cogs and jewels and balancers and escapements and hairsprings.

Pettifer insisted: "Will you help me? The books of John Dee are really quite interesting."

The Thrawl stood up. "I would like to read them, yes."

He followed Pettifer from the room. Cady went with them. They descended the cellar steps. Pettifer said along the way, "You met with Dr Dee, I believe, Cady? I am envious, I must say."

"Quite a few times. He was a cantankerous snout, but we got on just fine. A man of secrets, though, he always kept his gob shut unless he had something to say."

"Luckily for us, he was not so reticent in his writings."

They entered a small room, bare, brick-walled, the floor made of stone. There was a single item of furniture, an antique writing bureau. Cady took in the smell of damp and the rot in the wooden beams, and the woodworm in the bureau. Delicious! The pickled onion on her breath added that final touch of magic; she had stepped into a charged space. Serious witchcraft had taken place here. That bloody Dee! He had never shown her this part of the house, always keeping everything and everyone in their separate compartments. Lek stood against the wall, passive for the moment. Pettifer went to the bureau, opened it with a key and showed Cady the contents, a number of books separately wrapped in vellum. Each one was very old, when revealed, their leather covers well-worn and crinkled, and their pages yellowing. A sweet musty scent rose from them, further exciting Cady. Her flowers made a stir and her stigma pulsed. Surely, a good sign!

Pettifer's hands rose to encompass the entire room in a gesture. "It is here that Dee prepared his spells. Some of his tricks were over in seconds, a flash of fire and powder, a stirring together of certain chemicals. But other effects would take many centuries to be completed, long after the magician was dead. He's like a man planting the seed of a tree for his great-grandchildren to sit beneath, enjoying the shade of the leaves." He stared at Cady. "I truly believe we are nearing the end of one such spell. All we need do now is discover its nature."

"You're not going turn me into a frog, are you? Because Dee tried that once, the bounder. And I bloodied his nose for him."

Pettifer laughed gently. "No indeed." He caressed one of the books, revelling in his beloved possessions. "Dr Dee wrote down every thought he deemed important, and other more frivolous things as well, his dreams and fancies. From his own record, we know he completed at least fifteen volumes. Three of these are under lock and key in the vaults of the Kethran Library, another one sits on permanent display in the Museum. Two were destroyed by his own hand; we can only guess at their contents. Beyond the five in my collection, there exist another four notebooks."

"Whereabouts unknown, eh?"

"Oh no, I suspect their location. I have searched for them there, many times, always with no luck. And now, I fear, I can no longer travel safely." He held out his hand to show the tremble in it, the thinness of the skin, the visible bones and veins. Cady was reminded of a book of anatomy she had once looked at, back when she was a young loblolly aboard HMS *Benbarrow*.

"I have made use of one of Dee's spells," Pettifer explained. "Using various substances taken from Faynr's body, he was able to transport himself over some distance, as an ethereal form. I used the technique yesterday, when I spied on you at the Grand Illumination. It very nearly finished me off. I passed through the closed entrance gate like a ghost." He took a weary breath. "Each time it is more difficult to reconnect with the flesh, my proper home."

"Aye, I saw you there. You looked like a smudge of ink."

He nodded, pulling on a pair of white gloves. "And today, at that dreadful bungalow. Where Brin hested."

Cady realised that Pettifer was more than halfway drunk. "The Ibraxus Estate, you mean?"

"Yes, yes. And for all my exertions, I could no nothing, nothing at all to stop the ritual! I could not even brush the girl's shoulder." He screwed up his eyes and then intoned, "Where will I end up, and in what state?" Then he pulled himself together. "Let us see if the books speak to us. Quickly Lek, assist me please." He picked up the first of the volumes and started to flick through the pages at speed. As he did so Lek scanned each one, looking for any words or images of interest. Pettifer guided him: "Anything that points to an experiment or a spell that might activate a dormant seed. Anything at all."

Cady craned her neck to get a look-in, but the pages were moving by at too fast a rate.

"Oh slow down you two, you're making me feel dizzy."

These orders were followed, and now the diagrams, graphs, words, and rows of mathematical symbols flowed by at a more pleasant speed. At the sight of this, Cady was tormented by memories of her times with Dee, when they worked on the witch bells together, battling against the

Blight. So many lives ago. Lud damn it! Time was eating at her. The pages blurred. Was Pettifer speeding up again? No, no, it was her own sight to blame. And out of the mist of the book the vision of Dr Dee came to her, as she had experienced in the field yesterday afternoon. He had been carrying a sheaf of papers with him then, pages from his notebooks, and they had slipped free one by one to float by in front of her. She tried to bring them to mind now.

"Stop!"

Pettifer did so. He and Lek had already moved onto the second volume.

"I think we're looking for three pages in particular."

They both looked at her, waiting for explanation. It came slowly, as she drew the pages from memory. She was there as before, in the field, the tall grasses, sunlight, birdsong, the ghost of Dee smiling at her, urging her to work out the riddle of her ways. The first page drifted by on a soft breeze and in her mind she grabbed for it. Then she could say confidently:

"The first shows the map of Faynr."

Pettifer found this quickly enough, explaining, "Dee was likely the first person to really study Faynr from an analytical point of view. He made various maps over the years, but this is perhaps the best of them, the most detailed."

Cady looked at the page on offer. "No, that's not it. The one I need shows the organs of Faynr only, each one labelled."

"Ah yes." Pettifer turned a few more pages. "This one perhaps?"

"That's it! That's what I saw."

"So then, the river is important to Dee's plans, especially the organs. Or perhaps one organ in particular?"

"Yes. Of course! The second page showed the dragon's womb alone. All marked over with lines and numbers and arrows and whatnot."

"I know the image."

Pettifer found the diagram: a large circle representing the womb of Haakenur with the young Luda sleeping within, the whole thing overlaid with Dee's mathematical equations.

Lek reminded them both, "The womb is dead, and has been for centuries."

Cady harrumphed. "I know, I know. And the fact pisses me off. Still, it makes me wonder: it has to mean something!"

Pettifer asked her, "And the final page shown to you?"

She tried to remember. The vision was hazy. But gradually it came into focus: a man, or at least a male figure, but exaggerated, taller, bulkier, more powerful than any human. That was it! She had it now, fully pictured.

"It was Dee's blueprint of the Thrawl, the very first model."

Pettifer reached for another of the notebooks. "Ah yes, it is a beautiful drawing. Dee labelled it *Thrawl One*." He located the page, which showed the blueprint for a mechanical man of crude aspect, his body made of iron, his head looking like a diving helmet.

Lek explained, drawing from his own History: "Some people claim he actually built Thrawl One, others that it remained a plan only. Until, that is, Miss Jane Polter took up the idea for herself, and so my kin were designed and manufactured."

All of the notebooks lay open for them to view. But a difficult question remained: *What did Faynr's dead cinder of a Womb, and the very first Thrawl, have to do with the Lud seed, and its germination and flowering?* Yes, it was a puzzle to Cady. The riddle of her task was still tightly knotted.

But Pettifer's eyes were alight. "I think I know where this is leading."

Goosebumps rose on Cady's arms and the petals of her newly blossomed flowers ruffled in some non-existent breeze. She had the feeling that Dr John Dee's phantom was pushing her forward from beyond the grave. Onwards. But towards what end?

Wombwood

Lord Pettifer came with them to the boat, only a short walk from Tenebrae House. He had donned a black overcoat and was carrying a briefcase. Except for the sequins sown onto the coat at lapel and pocket and cuff, he looked like a once well-to-do businessman on a night commute. Young Jebediah was waiting as promised on the deck of the *Juniper*. Pettifer climbed aboard, settling himself into the cabin. Cady let him be for now, and prepared for the voyage west. The boat was looking very spruced and lovely; Jeb had spent his time alone well, polishing and cleaning. She thanked him for this, but then said, "I believe it's time you scarpered off home, my lad."

"Home, captain? This is as good as any, and better than most."

"Your old ma and pa will be worrying, no doubt."

"If they do, I don't know of it."

"Where are they?"

"My pa, no one knows. Mother dearest? Lost in her cups by this hour. Well sozzled."

"And your Aunt Queenie?"

"She looks after me when needed, and I her, in turn, when the black mood overcomes her."

Cady had taken on board many a waif and stray in her life, but she was uncertain of this one, and what might lie behind his bravado. Her face must have betrayed her doubts.

"Honest to goodness, Cady dear, if you abandon me, I'll find new passage and come follow you, I swear that I will."

She shook her head at this.

He went on with a broken smile, "And anyway, how will you survive, without me?"

Cady puffed out her cheeks. "I won't have you come to harm."

"Haven't I lasted these years without a hand to help me? And now I have you, have I not?" His eyes gleamed in the spotlit dark. "I am bound to your care."

"Bloody fool."

"On a ship of fools."

Well there was no answer to that; it was a phrase Cady herself had used often enough. She went over to the prow to examine the figurehead. The Thrawl skull had sealed around the Lud seed so tightly that not even Lek himself could loosen it. It gave her hope to see this; seed and boat were joined. Lek came to stand with her. She asked him, "Are we ready?" He nodded. She couldn't help but feel he was keeping his first choice of expression hidden, replacing it with something more neutral. Perhaps he was scared of what lay ahead for them all. Matter-of-factly, she said, "Help the lad. We are heading upriver." Then she walked back to the cabin and took a seat opposite Pettifer. He had opened his briefcase to remove a single volume of Dr Dee's notes, which he studied. His hands were trembling, the veins on plain view through the skin. His face had the look of a death mask, thin and bony. His muscles twitched at cheek and temple. Cady felt some compassion for him: she knew well the delights and dangers of travel.

"Olan." It was the first time she'd used his given name. "I'm still half wondering if I can trust you."

He made no reply, not until the boat set off once more, gaining the current. The well-loved motion wove its pleasure through Cady's body. Now Pettifer revealed his thoughts: "I don't think you know, but I worked with Brin's father, Lord Halsegger, on various projects before the war. It was evident that conflict would break out between Enakor and Kethra, but James would not believe it. When it did, he made efforts to bring about appeasement."

Cady stared at him. "Which led to him becoming a traitor."

"He was a pacifist. That got lost in the scandal. Of course, we argued. I felt that he was hiding from the truth, and that the country would pay for such an attitude. He would not listen."

"Now he lives at peace in Enakor." There was coldness in her tone.

"We do not know that, not at all. He might be imprisoned, or he might be dead. We have heard nothing of him, nor of his family since their exile."

"What do you think?"

Pettifer sighed. "Knowing James as I do, I fear the worst. He could be easily fooled, I know that. If the Enakor persuaded him that his gifts might be put to good use… Well, he might not suspect the true intent of his new countrymen."

Cady thought about this for a moment. "So you took charge of the child?"

"Her mother requested it of me. And of course, I knew by then of Brin's gifts."

"And now?"

His eyes narrowed. "Now? Now I regret deeply not seeing the signs." Quickly he changed the subject, seeking safer ground: his beloved predecessor. "Dr Dee wrote of the Womb of Faynr in his final years, after the Blight had put paid to the womb's fire. He speculated that a certain array of crystals, crystal of a certain type and intensity, might be aligned to form a kind of giant lens. You see, here." He spun the notebook around to show Cady the diagram of Faynr's Womb. It showed the River Nysis as it passed through Wombwood Forest, the banks marked with tiny symbols depicting the crystals, hundreds of them, if not more. Identical symbols also crowded the water, perhaps to be fixed on poles, or carried on boats, a whole flotilla of them. Cady was excited. From each crystal a line had been drawn, to symbolise light, or heat, or some other energy. These lines converged at the exact centre of the red circle used to represent the Womb. Cady could imagine Dee at work, his hands shaking with palsy, his eyes screwed up in an attempt to remain in focus. The lines were crooked in places, and ink-splattered, but they did their job, they set out the mystical geometry.

Pettifer continued, "Such a device might produce enough heat and power to reignite the dead ghost-flesh. At least that was Dee's theory."

"It never went beyond that, an idea in a book?"

"No, not until…" His voice trailed off.

Cady wasn't putting up with this. "Is it still possible? Pettifer, speak plainly."

He hesitated. "I tried it once, and failed miserably."

"Why not again, then. Eh?"

"It caused such trouble last time."

"How do you mean?"

"When Jane Polter created the Thrawls, she used the

most potent vapours of Faynr in order to amplify the crystal's natural properties, thereby producing a new kind of consciousness. Imagine, the possible uses of such potency!" His eyes lit up. "So I considered, why not combine the two ideas? Combine Dee with Polter, and utilise the Thrawls as the separate parts of the lens array. If I could bring enough Thrawls together on the banks at Wombwood, I might well be able to replicate Dee's original device."

"You tried this?" Cady leaned over the table to grab at his hands.

"Yes, yes. I created an instruction in the form of Jane Polter's image, and a recording of an actress taking on her imagined voice. And I sent this out to as many Thrawls as I could, in radio range. I only meant them to…" Again, the worlds failed him.

"This was the Frenzy!"

He nodded. His hands struggled to escape her grip.

"Oh you fuckwit." She let him go. "People died because of your actions."

"You think I don't remember that? Cady, my life ever since has been in the country's service. I want only to make amends."

She gazed out of the cabin window, but there was nothing to be seen of the passing villages, only the night which clung tightly to the boat's hull, aided by Faynr's flesh which was gelatinous in the extreme at this reach of the river. Turning back to view Pettifer's face she noted a great yearning in his eyes, and in the way his fingers traced the page of the notebook.

"We have a Thrawl aboard," she said. "This is your plan, no doubt. We shall try again."

"Yes, that was my thinking. But now, having restudied the equations, I'm not so sure. One will hardly suffice. Not according to Dee's workings."

"Stuff the workings up your arse. We need the Womb to be lighted for a moment only! One moment! Then King Lud and myself, and the collected denizens of the Deep Root, will attempt the rest. Eh, what do you say, My Lordship?"

"But if it should fail? Imagine, what it might cause Mr Lek to do."

"But we have not *one*, but *two* Thrawl crystals aboard. Two! Do you see? Our chances have already doubled." With that she sprang up and hurried to the cabin door, shouting instructions to her crewmates as she went. And then back to her passenger: "And you, sir, work out your charts and your numbers, and work them good."

"Will Mr Lek submit to it?"

"I will throw him overboard, otherwise."

In the end, it took little such persuasion, for the Thrawl had descended once more into a state of internal disintegration; he was willing to try anything. Out of the tumult of his words he managed one phrase that grabbed Cady by the ears: "I will become fire." The stream of chaos carried on, until: "Luda womb blossom riverfold." This last was not as senseworthy as the first, but Cady took it in good heart. And now she stood near the forward hatch. The boat's spotlight split the darkness in two, before losing itself somewhere deep in the mists of Faynr's body. Beyond this beam, and the two navigation lights at port and starboard, it was full dark. Midnight was drawing near. There were homesteads on one bank, their windows unlit. The other bank, the southern, was already taken over by vegetation, by bushes and briars, and hedgerows lining fields. They were leaving the built-up and congested bulk of the capital behind them.

The twin ovaries of the dragon's ghost appeared, one on each side of the Nysis. They took the form of a pair of trees whose roots lay half in water, and half on land. Yet Cady knew well that the trees were not made of any vegetable matter, but rather of the haunted flesh of Faynr. They were formed to look like willows, with drooping branches, slender oval leaves, and yellow catkins. She had witnessed these ovaries before the Blight had struck, when the branches had been filled spring and summer long with birds of all kinds and colours and song. How beautiful it had looked, and sounded! And to imagine, the ghost's ova were actually formed from the songs of the birds. But now the trees were dead and silent, leafless, lifeless. Only the wail of the gillibray could be heard, a creature that dwelled in Faynr's most damaged regions. Throughout history, perhaps half a dozen people had witnessed it. Was it a bird, reptile, or mammal? Nobody knew. Did it tend to the last vestiges of the ova? Only the Blackthorn Road Balladeers made that claim, and they were famous for their drunkenness and their love of fantasy.

Cady went back to the cabin. Jeb held the course slow and steady from the helm; Lek was sitting on the afterdeck, half hidden in the shadows of the canopy; Pettifer sat with him, going over the details of the procedure. All was quiet. She turned on the wireless and listened to the twelve pips of midnight, and then to the Shipping Forecast. It used to be a regular and necessary practice, in her nautical days, and she still cocked an ear to it on occasion, as she lay abed, half asleep. *Fast Haven, Tallow, Mollusc, Thirties, Lun, North Eerie, South Eerie, Bannon, Penumbra, Pharaohs, Hogger, Palindrome, Solitude.* The names of the regions formed a wistful poem of the sea, recalling Cady back to times aboard steamers, colliers, tubs, and passenger ships. In full force gales, becalmed under sunlight, on a true heading, or lost in the Squalls; always that voice from home would find her, and console her with its coded messages. And for herself? Westerly, that was for sure. Moderate or rough, becoming very rough. Chances of a wreckage? Without a doubt. Or maybe, just maybe, if the gods played fair...

Pettifer joined her. "We are close, I think."

"Yes. Time to get ready."

They went forward, Lek with them. But there was nothing to see beyond the spotlight's reach, and only dark shadowy shapes on the banks where the first trees of the Wombwood crowded the water's edge, their branches knotted together.

"Dead slow ahead, Jeb, until we reach the Womb. Then cut the engine."

"Got it."

"And whatever you do, keep the rudder amidships. We mustn't drift off course."

Lek took up his position at the bow, Pok Pok in his hand. Pettifer stood just behind him, then Cady to one side, at the starboard beam. She was shaking with nerves. The ruins of the Temple of Luda hove into view, partly hidden by the petrified remains of the Wombwood. The fallen tower and broken pillars looked like a pile of huge fossilised bones from the Primordial Age. Within these tumbled walls the early Wodwo had forged a new religion in the decades after the Queen's passing. And shortly after this, the first of the Haegra had been grown. The Womb itself was invisible, until the *Juniper*'s spotlight picked out the dried skin that covered it, and gave it shape. The huge dark-blue sphere hung in the air, aligned with the temple on the starboard bank, and the even older stone circle on the port side. Little by little the sphere appeared to Cady's sight. Some sections had no skin on them, and they appeared as empty spaces, like pieces missing from a jigsaw puzzle. This protective layer had formed over the centuries, like a scab over a wound. The Nysis was about a mile across at this point, and the Womb was half this size at its diameter. The lowest point hovered thirty feet or so above the water. For Pettifer's scheme to work, the *Juniper* would have to sail exactly beneath that central lower point, the nadir. Cady could only hope that Lek's heat had melted and cracked the skin by then.

Pettifer put his hand on the Thrawl's shoulder, a signal.

Cady asked Jeb to switch off the spotlight.

Now darkness settled completely over the slowly moving boat.

Nothing could be seen.

The engine's noise fell away to a whisper.

Water lapped about the keel.

For a moment nothing happened.

And then Lek's skull brightened, the crystal within taking on extra power. Its blue radiance formed a halo around his head. He was hunched forward, rather like a bull ready to charge, his feet firmly planted on the deck, one forward, the other back. Slowly he brought up his right hand level to his eyes. There lay Pok Pok's crystal, safely clasped in his grip. A jewel beyond compare, at least to the Thrawl's mind. Cady moved forward a little, to view Lek's face. His eyes were wide open, glowing red. She might burn herself just by looking! But Cady kept herself steady, in place.

Lek's head shivered a little, and then he leaned back, before jabbing forward again with his upper body. The beams shot out from his eye sockets, left and right, both aimed perfectly at Pok Pok's centre. From there they spread out in the same manner a prism will separate light into a spectrum of colours. But this wider beam retained its original colour: fiery red.

It hit the skin encrusting Faynr's Womb in several places at once, sweeping expertly from bottom to top. It didn't take long before the skin cracked and crumbled, and then fell away in jagged sheets, small pieces to begin with, and then larger, until entire sections were dropping into the darkness. Their splashes were heard as the river took them. Only a few scattered patches of crust remained, and these were quickly aimed at, and destroyed. The Womb was revealed. Or rather, *not* revealed. For, once its defining skin had been removed, the shape vanished from sight entirely, leaving only the night air and Lek and Pok Pok's combined beams as they criss-crossed the now empty space, seeking a new target.

The boat drifted under the power of the tide, which was weak and slow this far from the sea. Jeb was doing a good job keeping a straight course. Pettifer had stepped back, no doubt to give the Thrawl room for the next and most difficult task. Lek moved Pok Pok a little closer to his face. This intensified the ray of light that pulsed and sizzled between them. And now, when it shot out on its journey, it was formed into a single intense beam the width of a surgeon's needle. Both Lek and Pok Pok were activated to their highest powers. In fact, the Pok Pok crystal was vibrating so much it became a blur of blue energy. The redness of the beam contrasted with it, both colours painting the night better than any human effort at illumination. Yet this beauty came at a price; Pok Pok was nearing the limits of her wholeness. She made a ringing noise, so high-pitched and dissonant Cady heard it only as a tingle at the back of her skull. She feared that Lek would desist, surely, to save his crystal love. But no. He carried on bravely, staunchly, and the needle of the beam found the centre of the invisible womb, the exact centre! With their combined brains, the two Thrawls had worked the geometrical formula correctly. Or at least Cady hoped so. According to Pettifer, one sixteenth of an inch off target would have no effect, or even a deleterious one.

The beam locked on, with pinpointed accuracy, to its chosen spot. All around the darkness gathered more thickly, as though in protest. By now Cady could feel the projected heat on her face. Lud knows how Lek or Pok Pok, or even the Womb itself, could survive this onslaught. Cady wanted to scream out, *Stop! Stop now! No more!* But another part of her, a greater part, forced her voice into silence. Her teeth were gritted together so hard she could taste blood on her gums and tongue. Her stigma quivered like a compass in her belly, seeking a direction beyond the four cardinal points. By all the power of Luda, she would journey there!

But the *Juniper* was by now nearing the lowest point of the imagined sphere, and there was still no sign of the Womb catching alight. Cady looked to the helm. Jeb, bless him, was using the Thrawls' beam as a heading, steering the boat along that line of light. Handsomely done, my lad. There was a smell of burning in the air. The Womb was now visible as a shivering in the sky over the river, a shivering that took on a little more form as Lek and Pok Pok kept up the pressure, on, and on. But Pok Pok was breaking up, fragmenting in Lek's hand. The screaming sound came either from inside the two crystals, or inside Cady's head; there was no way of knowing which. The *Juniper*'s hull was vibrating at the same intensity.

Now.

The flame caught.

A spark.

A single spark blossoming around the beam's point of contact.

Was it enough?

Cady found herself praying to all the gods from all the religions of Kethra. And most all to the Deep Root, and all who dwelled there, the many thousands of plant spirits, and over them all, the Lord and Lady of All Flowers. *Come on, come on, my beauties! Burn for me!* And they did, lending their support to the task.

The Womb flamed into life at its centre with a bright golden light that spread out quickly until it reached the sphere's circumference, where it flamed across the entire surface, making visible this ghostly organ, this Womb fully encompassed. The petrified trees and bushes along the banks were illuminated, as were the temple and the stones of the ancient circle. The waters of the Nysis boiled under the newly released energies. The heat was intense.

Cady stared ahead. She stepped forward to the prow. Above her, a figure was forming in the sky, nestled within the sphere of the Womb. It was a figure she had not seen for well over three hundred years. *Luda.* Queen Luda before she became so, a young girl of sixteen years, naked, and curled up in the shape of a baby in the belly of its mother. A ghost of a woman nurtured and protected by the ghost of a dragon. Cady had not seen this wondrous vision since the Womb of Faynr had darkened, and she delighted in it, heart and soul. The others aboard had similar reactions: she heard Jeb gasp, and Pettifer whimpering in awe.

But the Haegra had work to do, and urgently, for there was no way of knowing how long the Womb would stay alight. Even now Lek's beam was faltering. Cady laid her hand on the skull of the boat's figurehead, where the Lud seed rested. The metal was warm to the touch, not hot, but comforting. It glowed with a bright ruby-red light.

Queen Hilde's head was cracking under pressure from the powerful elemental forces now in play. The first shoots appeared through the cracks, growing more quickly than Cady had ever seen any flower form. Lud was germinating, blossoming, all in this one moment of grasped time. The stem appeared next, with leaves along it, and then the petals at its peak curled into a ball. But these opened immediately, feeling the warmth given to them by Luda and the Womb.

Cady stripped off – peacoat, smock, bell-bottoms, bloomers, the lot – following instructions so deep she was blind to them, fingers working the buttons and buckles on their own accord. Her body was part flesh, part tree bark, part a gallery of tattoos, the most impressive of which was the dragon Haakenur on her back, top of arse to curve of shoulder. Flesh and bark and ink all blended together to form a map of the life lived, and lived, and lived again, over and over in different eras and places. Thirty-seven times she had lived, died, and regrown herself as a young woman. Thirty-seven fucking times! *Hear me, you gods! I have been of service!* The wrinkles ran deeper with each resurgence of her spirit, joining with each other, making their own version of the waterways and sea channels that bound her, and set her free. Liver spots, moles, scars, abrasions, burn marks: these were the ports and towns of her progress. Her knotted hair, hanging halfway down her back, looked like it had been pickled in brine. She stank of salt and tar and wood and rum and sweat and, amid all this, the sweet aroma of flowers in the springtime. Lud knows what young Jeb made of the sight of her body, or Pettifer for that matter. She wasn't concerned; her whole attention was on the boat's figurehead where the Lud flower was now in full bloom, its scarlet petals fully opened to reveal the yellow-and-blue striped interior. The scent released was powerful and heady and almost animalistic, a pungent musk.

Lek's eye-beams faltered and went dark. The night closed in over the foredeck. Nobody dared to turn on the spotlight. But there was a warm glow still emanating from the Womb, enough to reveal the Lud flower growing from the head of Queen Hilde. A soft popping noise was heard only by Cady; the anther at the top of the flower's stamen had opened to release its cloud of pollen. They hovered around the figurehead, these yellow grains, forming a perfect globe, a tinier version of the sphere of the Womb. Cady stood ready, arms outstretched, waiting. The six living buds on her body opened their petals as wide as they could. She felt them! One thousand, eight hundred and forty-six years she had waited for this moment. The pollen grains shifted from their global pattern, drifting a little in the air until a magical breeze caught at them and blew them at speed towards Cady's body. They attached themselves to her at left shoulder, right thigh, belly, right forearm, and at two places on the left forearm, at wrist and elbow. Her eyes were closed. The pollen travelled within. She felt her stigma gathering and enclosing the gifts. *I am with flower, with seed.* The voice that spoke these words was Cady's own, and yet it belonged also to the Deep Root, uttered by some deeper wilder spirit that called to her.

A cloven-toed piper is playing in a field of lush green, blurred by sunlight. He calls the young lovers to the dance. Birds sing from the greenwood. King Lud takes Arcadia by the hand. They wade a brook to a clearing in the trees where a forest pool holds the sky and sun in its mirror. The piper plays on, hidden among the branches. The music maddens them both, a madness they willingly give themselves to. They dance around the pool's edge, king and maiden,

and then lie down in weeds and flowers, amid animal dung and
bird droppings, hard stones and soft grasses, alongside worms and
biting ants and slugs, and are themselves of equal nature entwined,
married one to the other. The piper stamps his feet. His wooden flute
makes a shrill note, their only wedding song.

Cady awoke suddenly, opening her eyes. She staggered and
fell to the foredeck of the *Juniper*. Pettifer came to her, covering
her nakedness with his overcoat. Looking up, she saw that the
Womb of Faynr had darkened completely, returning dear sweet
Luda to her realm of sleep. And when the boat's spotlight came
back on, every last element of the vision was undone.

The two men, Jeb and Pettifer, looked on. Their faces
were known to Cady, but not fully, not at first. Her hands on
the deck felt the *Juniper*'s engine throbbing, and that gave
her knowledge.

"Well, I'll be blown."

Pettifer asked, "What is it, Cady? Are we complete?"

"I am pregnant, six times over in six different places. Now
there's a turn-up."

She laughed wildly as she got to her feet. Walking over
to the helm, she asked. "How does the old girl go, Mr
Yeomanson?"

"Well, captain. Very well. Shipshape."

"Full ahead. The Thorn Gate approaches."

Then she found Lek. He was sitting in the cabin, the
remains of Pok Pok before him on the tabletop, in so many
tiny pieces. He did not speak, and Cady joined in his silence.
Pok Pok had given everything. Lek was arranging the
fragments into various shapes. She had the sense he was
working out a puzzle of some sort, but what the rules might
be, only he knew.

She stayed with him a while longer, as the boat sailed on.

At the Thorn Gate they moored at a landing stage. This barrier marked the far western edges of the city. There was a group of cottages clustered in the wall's shadow, one of them with a lighted window. The gatekeeper's home. Cady asked the son of the household if a girl had come this way, a young girl of ten years.

"An Alkhym lass?" he asked.

"That's right."

"Aye. We had one come through. A sprightly thing."

"Was she alone?"

"She had passage aboard a craft, a pleasure boat. A dingy looking vessel."

"Who was the captain?"

"Unknown to me. A single man of passing years."

"And they went on from here?"

"They did. Fretlands bound, according to the skipper. The girl paid him a pretty penny." He frowned. "Lud help them both. And yourself, if you follow them that far."

That was all Cady needed to know. She had been pollinated. Her next task lay ahead of her: protect Ludwich from Gogmagog, protect Kethra and her peoples. And that meant following Brin Halsegger. It had been a long day, but all sense of tiredness had left Cady. Seeds were forming within her body, many of them. But she had no idea how they would be scattered, nor what kind of new flowers would grow from them. That was to come.

But Pettifer drew her back into the cabin. "There is one more thing I must show you." He handed over a picture postcard. It showed a brightly coloured city scene: an ornamental fountain with many buildings all around it, each lit up with neon signs. Across the bottom was a printed caption: *Piccadilly Circus by night*. Cady gave it a good stare, but then shook her head.

"I've never seen such a place. Some foreign affair, is it? Far afield?"

He laughed gently. "In a way, yes. For this is the city called London."

"London? But you said that was a place you dreamed of. Now you're saying…"

"Yes, I have been there, a good few times, I have my souvenirs."

"And why haven't I heard of it?"

"It is a secret destination. Now turn the card over. There is a message for you."

She looked at the back of the card. It was addressed to *Arcadia Meade, care of Lord Pettifer*. Below that, in the same handwriting, someone had written: *I am looking forward to meeting you soon. It is very important, old girl! Wish you were here!* And then the signature of the sender, but this was scrawled so badly that Cady could not read it properly. In vain, she squinted her eyes.

Pettifer helped her out. "It was sent by Joyce Hicks."

"But there's no stamp on it."

"We have our own private postage service, Joyce and I."

"And who is she, exactly?"

"A fellow Haegra. She will help you, I'm sure."

"I've never heard of her."

"No, of course not. But in many ways, she has even more knowledge than you do."

"She sounds a bit snooty."

"Don't worry, she is not your rival."

"Only, I don't take kindly to being usurped. Just let her try it! What's her name again? Joyce What-the-Heck?"

"Hicks. She wants you to visit this other city, London. It must be important to your task."

"But why?"

"I don't know, not for sure. But I will take you there, or
at least show you the way."

They went out onto the foredeck. The boat rocked gently
at the mooring. Lek was standing at the port beam. He was
letting the fragments of Pok Pok's crystal fall into the river.
It gave Cady an idea, something she'd been putting off for a
while now. She went below into the hold. With Jeb's help
she lifted Mr Carmichael from his tank, and between them
they carried him onto the landing stage, and from there into
the waters of the Nysis. It had to be now, for these were
the final reaches of the salt water, his rightful habitat. He
took to the new home easily, swimming away downriver,
the river's surface around his body filmed with his favourite
crystal visions, one last picture show: the streets of Ludwich,
the gardens at the Wold, the spike trees of Medlock Island,
the sights and sounds of the Shrivings. And then the river
was dark once more.

Cady took control of the helm and steered the boat
through the opening in the city wall. The pillars and arches
of the gate were made from living trees whose giant thorns
were, in earlier times, used as protection from outside
invaders; now they acted as a deterrent for those within.
Jeb stood beside her, Lek also. Lord Pettifer stood apart, lost
in his own thoughts. They were moving away from those
parts of the river Cady Meade knew and loved so well, into
unknown territories.

PART THREE
A Child of the Dragon

No. 27. The Egg of Kharos. This giant vessel in the western reaches of the river holds secrets; the secrets of our original home, and otherworldly exploration, and returning to the cosmic source. No matter how much scientific research takes place, the structure remains a mystery. Over time it has changed its significance, and its inner properties, offering different generations of Kethrans different effects and delights, and dangers. Despite all restrictive notices and edicts, many still seek out this self-contained Realm of Fantasy.

Monocle cigarette cards – The Haunted River

The Thing in the Pit

In the daytime a market took place just outside the western wall, straddling both sides of the river. It did a healthy trade in black-market goods, bootleg medicines, love potions, in fact anything deemed illegal in the city. But the stalls were empty now, their awnings rolled down, the pathways between filled with litter and water rats. Only the colourful spices and residues of exotic dreaming powders remained as a kind of make-up for the skin of Faynr; she had put on her best costume. Beyond the market and the riverside lamps, the land was quickly taken over by darkness. The last vestiges of city life fell away. The *Juniper* moved slowly, her spotlight piecing the night together one arc at a time. Silence reigned. Pettifer directed them towards a riverside monastery, a place Cady had seen a few times before in her journeys west, but had never visited. She knew an order of Azeelian monks lived there, a small number of them she presumed, for the place was not large. It was stone-built, with a newer structure added to a much older building. Once the boat was tied up Pettifer led the way towards the heavy wooden door. He rapped on it and was answered from within by a gruff voice. Cady could not hear what was being said, but soon the doorway opened. A monk greeted them and allowed them entry. He was old, wearing a robe tied with a belt. He did not speak. Instead he led the way through the cold passageways towards the door of a central chamber, where he left them. Cady was suddenly nervous, and she did not know why. She felt sure some great event was about to happen, and herself the main actor.

Before they entered, Pettifer told the story of his first visit to the place. "Shortly after I moved into Tenebrae House, I began a serious study of Dee's writings, and his artefacts. His house held many secret compartments and boltholes. In them I found strange objects of unknown purpose. But after a time they gave up their secrets, at least some of them did. I felt I was taking on Dee's role in the city, as its resident spellcaster. It was of comfort to me, this practice, especially after the bombing of Blinnings Mansion and the closure of the research laboratories." He sought out Cady's eyes in the gloom of the corridor. "Then I found a reference to this monastery, the Qaladhura, an old Azeelian name for a zoo or animal pen, an enclosure usually reserved for creatures of a sacred or unusual nature."

"A funny name for a place of worship," Jeb noted.

Pettifer merely nodded. "Dee found this place through his own researches. The monks took to him readily it seems, as they have to me, after a time. Come."

He opened the door and went inside. The chamber's earthen floor surrounded an empty pit in the centre, some six feet across. The pit's circumference was lined with white pebbles. To one side a large silver bell hung on a wooden frame. A younger monk stood in attendance at the bell, holding a metal beater in his hands. As the party entered, he struck the bell to set it ringing. It made a loud and very deep tone. Cady felt the vibrations in her stomach. Then the monk bowed and left the chamber. They were alone. Lamps set around the walls gave off their flames, and shadows danced across the faces of the four visitors.

Pettifer spoke in a low voice. "This place gets under your skin. It changes you. I have been coming here for eleven years now, on and off. At first I merely stared into the pit. Dreams would come to me, dreams of the city. The *other* city. In sleep I walked along unknown streets: Petticoat Lane, Shaftesbury Avenue, Covent Garden. I strolled beside the mighty river that runs through the city, the *Thames* as they call it. And I thought at first that these might be the old dreams of Dr Dee, fused into the walls of the building." He paused, and his body trembled in that ghostly state that took him over every so often. "Now I know differently."

Cady took hold of Lek's hand and leaned out over the rim, to stare down into utter darkness. Something white and ghostlike was stirring, deep down. Was this another part of Faynr's body, something unseen until this moment? But the creature or whatever it was stayed in its hidey-hole. She came back upright to speak with Pettifer.

"You're telling me this... this pit is the way to the other city, as you call it. London?"

"Yes, in a way. Well, not the pit itself."

"I'm supposed to jump in, am I? Well sod that for a pile of pennies!"

Jeb giggled. But Pettifer's expression was stern. He did not answer the question. He simply went on, "When you get to London, Cady, seek out the woman who sent you the postcard. Do you remember her name?"

"Joyce? Joyce... Joyce..."

"Joyce Hicks."

"How will I find her, pray?"

"It will happen, no doubt. And when you meet, please, you must ask her about Gogmagog."

"Why?"

"She has conversed with him. Quite a few times, in fact. I can only think she has knowledge necessary to your further quest."

Cady whistled. "You're sure of all this, are you?"

"No, not at all." He hesitated. "Remember I told you last night of the Gogmagog Equations?"

"It's a bit of a blur."

"Dee worked out that Gogmagog and Faynr must be in balance, as Ludwich and London must be. But there's an anomaly in the workings: it cannot be iterated properly. This slight imbalance is connected to Gogmagog's rebirth; he will not remain in exile for ever. At some point the two sides of the equation might well collapse, and the portal will be opened. And then…"

His voice tailed off. By now, they all knew what he meant.

Pettifer finished by saying, "Dee stared into the future, saw this phenomenon, and put in place certain precautions."

Cady looked once more at the pit, and then over to the bell in its frame. "Is that a witch's bell, by any chance?" Even now she could hear the low vibrations deep in her gut.

"It is, and the finest known example." Pettifer's hand caressed the bell with a lover's touch. "According to Dee's notes it is partly made from the melted-down remains of Lud's sword, Ibraxus."

"The doctor did like a good fairy tale."

"The monks strike it once an hour. It will keep out intruders."

"Why am I getting the shivers, all of a sudden?"

"Stand back please. And watch carefully."

Jeb and Cady pressed themselves against the walls of the chamber. Lek had already picked up the beater of the bell in preparation for some imagined future battle. Jeb's face showed a mix of fear and fascination.

Pettifer bent down to select one of the white pebbles. He dropped this into the pit.

Then he waited.

There was a distant sound: the pebble had fallen into a substance, not water, but something slightly more solid. Cady could not make it out. Pettifer started to chant, emitting a guttural chain of phrases and glottal stops she could only compare to Dr Dee's own spells, which he always claimed were written and performed in a language of his own making. Perhaps Pettifer had learned this from the notebooks.

Now he stopped in his calling, his summoning, whatever it was.

The silence was intense.

Then a snuffling sound was heard from within the pit. A slithery sucking noise. No, not quite that, but a sucking sound in reverse, if that made any kind of sense. It certainly made Cady feel bilious. She stepped forward again, daring to peer over the pit's edge. A vast pile of yellowish-white, sludge-like flesh was rising up the funnel of the earth to emerge into the chamber. At first it had no form: it seemed both alive and unalive at the same time, a gelatinous mass of base material from which something new might be built. Then it took on shape, making for itself a head, a blunt snout, a pair of eyes set in the spectral body, eyes the exact same off-white as the head itself, so that only the black pinpoint of a pupil showed them to be capable of capturing light. The thing was more or less blind, a dweller in the deep earth.

Yet it gave off a sickly-sweet stench that made Cady feel woozy and a little drunk. The head was almost too big for the chamber's confines. It resembled in shape a giant worm, a worm whose long writhing body still lay hidden within the pit's confines. It appeared to have no mouth. A clump of short tentacles attached to the end of the snout acted as a sort of investigating tool. The head roamed about the chamber, its neck bending and extending and contracting as it explored the walls, the floor, and then the bodies of the four human occupants.

Cady felt her skin crawling desperately away from her bones.

The slather was warm and sticky.

Poor Jeb broke down. He vomited, and then lurched away, managing to find the door.

Even Lek was taken aback by the sight of the creature. His Library of Crystal Knowledge had no entry for the evidence of his eyes, and he was shaking. Cady was in awe of the sight before her, and in fright also. Pettifer had his hand on her arm, holding her in place.

"Stay, old lady!" His words sprayed out from between gritted teeth. "Stay!"

The creature was now apparent in all its hideous glory, and Cady understood its true nature. This was Psephekarnidraxapor, the furthest limit of him, usually concealed from human sight, as his body curled away under the city, extending for many miles in all directions, immeasurable. Cady tried to imagine the brain at work inside that soft translucent head: the organ of cognition was seen as a small lump of green matter. What in the world could he be thinking?

"Fuck!" It was the only suitable word in Cady's arsenal.

Pettifer took control of the creature, murmuring soft words in Dr Dee's magical language. Psephekarnidraxapor was calmed by this; his tentacles retreated back inside his head, vanishing completely. Cady wiped the spittle from her face, cursing, and thinking to herself: of all the lifeforms created within the body of Faynr, surely this was the most astonishing! And there were further secrets to uncover. She watched in a kind of sickening wonder as Pettifer placed his hands on the creature's face. He kept them there, left and right, each one placed just below those terrible pinpricked eyes. And then his hands melted into the skin, and were seen now as two wavering forms inside the creature's head. Then he pulled his hands back out and wiped them on a handkerchief. Both Cady and Lek were looking at him, each dumbfounded.

He said, speaking quite plainly, "The head acts as a membrane, semi-porous in nature. Can you imagine, my friends, a living creature that forms the borderline between two very distant cities? It really is remarkable."

"How distant?" Lek asked.

"You only need to step forward."

Cady tried to respond to this, but found herself speechless for once.

Pettifer went on, "The monks here have worshipped Psephekarnidraxapor for many centuries, as a minor god, one of Naphet's servants, although I view him as a part of nature. A nature we have not yet fully explored, or understood. He digs and digs and digs, feeding off moles and beetles and worms along the way, seeking a place as yet unknown, some final destination. The monks appease him with prayers, and weekly sacrifices, in order that his more normal passageways be kept open for human transport."

At last Cady managed to speak: "Sacrifice? I don't like the sound of that."

"Rats, mice, birds."

"Never a doddery old codger?"

"Never that. Although, I imagine accidents can happen."

Cady grumbled. "Now let me get this straight, you want me to… I mean to say… You want me to step inside…"

"I've done it many times, I can assure you."

She turned to her companion. "Mr Lek, you'll come with me, won't you, eh? Faithful retainer. And that's an order, by the way. Captain Cady has spoken!"

But Pettifer shook his head. "I doubt a Thrawl could make it. Too much inorganic material. No, you're on your own, I'm afraid."

Cady curled her lip. "I feel like Lud and Luda are pissing on me from on high, both streams combined." But to her surprise she had begun to trust Lord Pettifer.

She took a step closer. The creature stared at her, those two tiny black circles blinking. Cady thought to herself, *I am one of the few people in the world to have seen this, the head of Old Seph!* Then she reached out and let her hands touch the skin, caressing it gently, although every fibre of her being wanted to pull away, to follow Jeb out from the chamber and to keep on running! But her courage held fast.

Pettifer warned her, "Time can be fluid, between the realms. And they're usually two or three hours behind us."

"I understand, it's the same with the Deep Root. Hours can be minutes."

"Yes, but in this case, sometimes you come back before you leave."

"I'll be younger than I was, you mean?"

"Not quite."

"Well, that's a shame. Good Lek, are you prepared?"

The Thrawl was. He stood up tall and true by the witch's bell, the beater held in both hands to show he meant business. His eyes shone with a clear light; these last few moments had calmed him greatly. This gave Cady strength. *Right then. No more hesitations.* She pushed forward with her hands, copying the movement Pettifer had made. She stepped forward quickly, throwing all caution aside. The skin of the creature pulsed around her and then gave way and she was soon wrapped in its warm wet embrace, enclosed fully. Before her lay not the inner organs, the brain, the eyeballs, as expected, no, but a passageway of silvery light and at the end of it, a black doorway. The last words she heard came from Lord Pettifer, but they sounded like a distant echo, a call across a valley.

Find Joyce. Find Joyce Hicks.

And then silence.

The Other City

Something was sticking to her face, tickling at her, cold and clammy. She clawed at it, feeling it to be a spider's web, a lot of it. She blew the remains from her lips.

It was dark, pitch dark. Wherever she was.

Breathing harsh. Dust in her throat.

Keeping silent, scared of hearing some other presence close by.

But there was nothing.

Her optic gland glowed, but far too dimly. Something was wrong, and for now she could not work out what it was. Something missing.

Shifting about carefully, she turned to look the way she had come: darkly, a face stared back at her, her own face in the glass of a mirror. The maker of the web, a black spider with a large red dot on its back, was already hard at work spinning a new home across the surface. Cady tapped at the glass. Solid. No sign of Psephekarnidraxapor's so called porous membrane. Luddin' Nora! What was this, one-way traffic only? Panic flooded her. Was she trapped here? She tapped again at the glass, louder this time.

"Pettifer, you sodding twat, are you there, can you hear me?"

Nothing. Silence.

She turned again and knocked her shins against something hard, almost taking a tumble. Reaching down she felt the rim of a tea chest. She made her way around it and, walking with her hands held out in front of her, made it to the opposite wall. Her eyes adjusted a little. This room was not large and she quickly enough found a set of stone steps leading upwards. She was in a cellar, littered with a few items of old furniture and household goods. And that bloody mirror!

She climbed the steps and was relieved to find the door at the top unlocked. It took her out into a passageway, lit with a red glow. Music. A sleazy tune, bongos, double bass, saxophone. Voices from the half-open door of a room, which she snuck past and headed for the light at the end of the corridor. A doorway. A figure stood there, silhouetted, a woman of voluptuous outline. Cady had to squeeze past her, causing some consternation.

"Here duck, what were you doing in there? I never saw you come in."

"Me? Nothing. Just passing through."

"This isn't your kind of place, is it? Eh, you old tart!" She laughed uproariously.

Cady knew a molly when she saw one, lips and cheeks and eyes heavily painted, tight skirt, low-cut blouse, the works. She realised that she had just walked out of a bawdy house or a striptease parlour, or some such.

"I am here to see Joyce Hicks. Please direct me to her."

"Can't do that, can I."

"And why not?"

"Don't know her, that's why." Another dirty chuckle.

"Are you sure?"

But the woman had other things on her mind. She made a siren call to a trio of passing men: "Here, gents, this way. International models. Finest in Soho. They wear nothing but a smile." The men wisely moved on. Cady followed them down the alley, towards a blaze of light and noise and life, a main street. Lots of people, cars, street vendors. Neon signs shone brightly in every colour, advertising foods of all kinds, as well as books and films and other "artworks of erotic appeal". Raucous laughter, drunken caterwauling. More of those "international models" standing in doorways, even if most of them looked to be home-grown in nature. Public houses with crowds of people hanging around outside, drinking and smoking. Aye, it was a lively place all right, just like Tolly Hoo on a Friday night; why, she might even feel at home here. But the sights were wrong, the music was wrong, the smells were wrong. No, not *wrong* exactly, but knocked sideways. This was Ludwich at a different angle than she was used to. A nightclub with the name Gogmagogo only made her more confused. She was buffeted this way and that as she followed the general flow of the crowd and took refuge in an alleyway, only to see a man having a piss against the wall and beyond that the stage doorway of a club where two thuggish types were chatting with an off-duty dancer. The aroma of fried food was powerful and mouthwatering. A sudden blast on a whistle caused people to scatter as two policemen ran down the alley. Cady made a quick escape, back into the push and pull. A man at a stall was calling out, "Hot crumpets! Hot and buttered." Cady was starving; the journey had emptied her out, but when she tried to buy a tasty treat the vendor rejected her coins, with their profile of King Herald upon them, and the dragon on the reverse. "Here, what are these? Foreign? Go on with you! Cheek!" *Great Lud in the Battle of Bones! I am cast adrift.* She stumbled and fell into a gateway. From here she could see a sign above a coffee bar: Old Compton Street. At her back was a bombed-out church called St Anne's, according to the notice on the gate. Only the tower remained. So there had been a recent war in this world as well? The grounds of the church were accessible through the damaged wall. Here, amid a tumble of weed-covered stones, she placed her hand against the silvery bark of a tree and hoped to receive a quiver of movement from within.

Only coldness, darkness.

No Deep Root.

Loneliness closed upon her.

She wanted to scream.

And yet surely a flicker remained, something beyond her fingertips? She tried again, this time using the outer fields. The thorns pushed out of her palms and entered the wood. Blood flowed gently into sap, picking up the faintest of signals. Her powers were very weak in this place, this city. She was lost, that was the truth of it. Perhaps Pettifer had sent her here on purpose, perhaps to keep her away from Ludwich? Why had she trusted him, why?!

She went on her way, following her nose and nothing more, hoping at least to find the river. But there was no smell of the water anywhere near. Bewildered, she stepped out into a major road and was almost run over by a red double-decker. The driver beeped his horn at her and she skipped back in time, clattering her heels against the kerbstone. Even her internal compass was useless here: north, south, east and west, all were swapping places. Another sign told her she was now walking down Shaftesbury Avenue. She recalled that Pettifer had mentioned that name, as one of the places he had visited. Well if he could get back, then so could she! There must be other mirrors, other gateways back to Ludwich. But how to find them?

The noise increased, the colours of the neon signs burst open like red, blue, orange, golden flowers in the night, and people congregated in their groups and pairings. Or else alone, as she was. But no Azeels, no Ephreme. Nor Nebulim, and not even an Alkhym or two out for a stroll. No, but only the Wodwo in their various shadings. Or people that looked very much like the Wodwo. Then she stopped in surprise.

She had reached a roundabout, where pedestrians circled around a central fountain, the space surrounded by tall buildings, each of them holding a huge shining advert for *Bovril*, *Schweppes Tonic Water*, *Wrigley's*, *Guinness*. Cady had never heard of any of these things. She took out the picture postcard Lord Pettifer had given her. It was the same place, exactly the same. Piccadilly Circus. "Well then, here I am. Now what?" She sat down on the steps of the fountain, finding a space between a vicar and a man reading a newspaper. Taxi cabs and buses and delivery vans drove around the fountain, before heading off in different directions. It looked a little like Harlock Circle, back in Ludwich. But this was an actual place! Not like the Crystal Palace in a Thrawl's head, and not like the Deep Root, both of which were of insubstantial nature. No, this was *real*, flesh and blood and bricks and mortar and dust and grime. The concept was terrifying, and yet a wave of pleasure flowed along her channels, mingling with the panic and confusion.

I am here, I have travelled further than ever before!

Crowds of people wandered along in their Friday night finery, many hundreds of them in a never-ending stream. She watched a young couple kissing and felt a pang of loneliness. A one-man band was playing a lively dance tune, his knees knocking together to play the cymbals. People tossed pennies into a hat. Another man drew a crowd by being tied up in locks and chains; he struggled to escape his bonds, and finally made it, to much applause. *Maybe he knows a way out of my predicament*, Cady thought. She had nothing: no money, no drink, no food, no smokes, no way back.

Then the person to her side moved off and a young woman took his place.

"Hutch up, sweetheart. Let a girl have a sit down." She squeezed in tightly. "Oh, that's better. I've been waiting around all evening, I have, and nothing to show for it."

Cady looked at her neighbour. She was quite astonishingly beautiful, with flowing auburn hair kept in place with a decorative clip, and a face full of light and life. There was a glamour about her, akin to the leading lady of a crystal romance. She wore a matching jacket and skirt, not fancy, and often repaired, but they looked good on her. A brooch on one lapel and a bracelet around her wrist. She placed her handbag on the ground and took off one of her shoes, rubbing her foot and then adjusting her stocking until the seam was centred.

"I'll be glad when they put Eros back."

Cady could make neither head nor tail of this statement.

"Eros. On his plinth." The woman nodded towards the top of the fountain. "They're saying next year."

"Where did he go, this... What's his name?"

"Eros. Blimey, you've had your head under a stone. They took the statue down in the war, to make sure he wasn't damaged by a bomb."

"Oh."

"Because I could do with the God of Love looking out for me, I really could."

Cady just stared at her.

Luckily, the young women needed no encouragement. "I was supposed to meet a gent here, but he's stood me up. He told a nice tale, I must say. Claims his Spitfire was shot down over France and he had to find his own way back to Blighty. Which explains his gammy leg. But I'm wondering if he actually was a pilot now. Poppycock, I'll bet. What do you think?" Only silence greeted her. The woman frowned. "You're a chatterbox, aren't you?" She picked up the newspaper left behind by the departed neighbour and started to read. Then she tutted. "Renée Wiggins! Well I never. Have you seen this." She read aloud from an article: "*Rising movie star Richard Attenborough congratulates twenty-one year-old Renée Wiggins of Drum Lane, Marylebone, on being voted...* Now get this! *London's Prettiest Young Hopeful.* See, I know Renée, we both dance at the Jamboree Club, and she's pretty, I'll give her that, but *hopeful*? No. She's a misery-guts. Front page news, as well. And look at this. *Inset: A kiss for the winner.* Now I've seen everything."

"Where am I?"

"Piccadilly Circus, love."

"I know that. But otherwise... I'm lost, see."

"You poor old dear. Have you been drinking?"

"I bloody wish."

"Hm. New here, are you?"

"Very new."

"Is it the Tube you want? There's a station right here. Where do you want to get to?"

There was no easy answer to that question.

"Don't you know?"

Cady shook her head. But then: "Home."

"And where is that?"

"Ludwich."

"A long way away is it?"

"Miles. Ages. One step away."

"Are you sure you're not tipsy?"

"Let me have a look at your newspaper, will you?"

"Be my guest."

Cady took the paper. *The West London Chronicle*. She checked for the date. *Friday, 30 May 1947*. Her hands were shaking. "It's the same day, the same month. A different world, at the same time! Oh Sweet Luda, what does this mean?" She was mumbling to herself. Her eyes lost their focus. A lady carrying a banner walked by crying out, "Beware the Lord! His wrath will fall upon all sinners." The one-man band started on a waltz. The kissing couple danced to the melody, arm in arm. The escapologist was now rolling around on the pavement wrapped in a straitjacket. None of it made sense.

She asked of her new neighbour, "Can you tell me what this means?" She was pointing to the date on the newspaper. "This number here: 1947?"

"You don't know what that means?"

Cady shook her head. "I'm trying to work it out."

The young woman gave her a knowing smile. "Can I show you something?"

"What? Yes, if you like."

The woman was holding out a matchbox.

"You're having a ciggie, are you? Because I could do with–"

"No, sorry. Filthy habit."

She opened the matchbox. There was a spider inside, a black specimen with a red dot on its back. It crawled onto the woman's hand. She said, "I felt the web break, when you came through the mirror."

Cady froze. Her thorns emerged.

"All the webs are connected, you see, deep down." The woman smiled. "I had to check. I had to let you talk, to make sure. Pettifer got you through okay, then?"

"He did. But what a journey it was!"

"How is he? Still in one piece?"

"Barely. Fading away. He can walk through walls, apparently."

"I do feel for him. Last time he was here, he looked like an X-ray plate." She sighed. "I kept saying to him, Olan, I said, you need to stop all that palaver, that astral travelling, as he calls it. But would he listen? No."

"You're Joyce Hicks, are you?"

"Spot on. Singer, dancer, actress. Or if needs must, a waitress. And you'll be Arcadia Meade?"

"Cady is fine."

They shook hands. "Charmed to meet you."

"I got your postcard."

"Glad to hear it. It can be a bit haphazard, the mirror post."

"You're a Haegra are you, Joyce?"

"I wouldn't say that, no. I'm more of a Green Lady. That's what they call us here, in England. Green Men and Green Ladies. But these days, well it's sad, but we're pretty much just part of the folklore, and nothing much more."

"Only, I can't feel any... any connection to you, no quiver of the twigs."

"A different branch of the World Tree, my love."

"I see, yes. I think so."

"And this…" Joyce put a finger on the newspaper. "1947. That's the current year."

"You give the years numbers? How strange."

"Well, pardon me, but it makes more sense than giving them names."

"No, it doesn't. It's poetic. And poetry runs deep in the roots in the earth, flowing out from the private parts of the Lord and Lady of All Flowers."

Joyce was quite taken aback by this. "That's a bit rum, I must say. Right then!" She stood up and held out her hand to help Cady to her feet. "We need to get a move on."

"Where are we going?"

The younger woman made a little grin. "Why, to speak with Gogmagog, of course."

What a pair they made as they went along, the bright young woman of the flowing locks and the tailored suit, and the old woman behind, ragged and knotty and dirty and scowling. "Wait up, Joyce. Slow down!" They fell in step as they turned onto Haymarket. Joyce was happy to point out the sights for the visitor, especially when they skimmed the edge of Trafalgar Square. "The National Gallery, Admiral Nelson on his column, and that feller over there on his horse, that's Charles the First, long dead king. He got his head chopped off." Cady saw vague associations to some of these, linkages, mirror images of her own city. But some of the things on view had no equivalent at all in Ludwich. And everywhere there were signs of the war – World War Two, as her new companion called it – bomb damage, empty gaps in streets, half-repaired buildings.

Joyce picked up on this: "Our two worlds are joined in time and place, but separate. You have a war, we have a war.

England has a bus strike, Kethra has a train strike. And so it goes on. We run parallel to each other, see, but moving on slightly different courses. Now then, down this way, there are fewer people." They entered a street running alongside a large building. "Charing Cross train station. We're nearing the river now."

"Joyce, I'm puzzled."

"Of course you are, what else can you be?"

"What I mean is, I started off outside the city gates, and close to the river in Ludwich, but I came out here, in London, a long way away from the Nysis, sorry… What do you call it?"

"The Thames."

"A long way off. So that means, what, the doorways don't link up properly?"

"Like I said, slightly different worlds, twisting and turning."

That was the only explanation offered. The atmosphere of the street was changing, darkening. The smell of the river was in Cady's nostrils, and something more, also familiar. Grittier, dirtier, filthier. The way ahead was vanishing in a thick grey haze. The beams of torches moved here and there. A lantern swung lazily from someone's grip. The street lights burned in a series of blurred halos. The moon was clouded over. People were silhouettes, moving sluggishly, carefully. Cady and Joyce joined with them in the gloom, becoming part of the Realm of Night, folded in darkness twice over, three times, four, until it reigned supreme and London lost itself to another kingdom. Cady's eyes were smarting; she could see nothing at all in front of her, not even her own hand held a few inches away. But Joyce had a torch with her. She gave the handle a few turns and the beam flickered on. The dark ate it up greedily, but there was enough left over to provide a few steps of safety. In this way, they came to the riverside. Dots of light entered the darkness in a long straight line and then faded away over the water as the fog rolled and drifted along the river, billowing into every crevice, every socket, every orifice and pore.

"Hungerford Bridge," Joyce explained. "It brings the trains in and out of the station. There's a footpath along the side of the track. Come on. Stay close to me."

The bridge was crowded with pedestrians, crossing back and forth. Their faces looked ghostly under the walkway lights. Fog swirled about their forms, clothing them. Some wore masks, others wrapped their scarves about their mouths. But most went about unprotected. This was just another evening on the river.

Cady started to cough. Her eyes were running with tears of irritation.

"Ah. We're used to it by now," Joyce said. "You grow armour."

They stopped in the middle of the bridge. Cady looked out, sensing the greatness of the river beneath her, seeing the buildings on either side only by the dimly lighted windows of their upper storeys. And in-between, trapped on the water, the rolling bank of fog.

It was Gogmagog. Gogmagog everywhere. Gogmagog up the river, where it flowed among the boats and river cruisers. Gogmagog at her back, where it wreathed the passing steam engines in its shroud, hoping perhaps to be carried across the land, to other rivers, other cities. And yet the river held onto it tightly, and the wreaths of smoke snapped back as the trains thundered out of sight. The fog monster was held here, and reigned here. It defiled the wharves and landing stages and the waterside pubs and offices. Gogmagog prowled the riverbanks, it crept into the holds of ships as they passed under the bridge, their decks and cabins ablaze with light. It snuffled around the collier barges filled with coal, sucking up black dust for its supper. Gogmagog hovered in the rigging of ships, it befouled the flags at stern and bow. It drooped on gunwales like dirty rags and circled the buoys in midstream, trying to snuff out the warning lights. Gogmagog entered the eyes and throats of pensioners, it settled into the stems and bowls of pipes and snatched the smoke of cigarettes for its own. It combed through the hair of a wrathful skipper as he shook a fist from his forecastle. Gogmagog cruelly pinched at the toes and fingers of the shivering little apprentice boy on deck. Cady felt she was peering into a nether sky, with fog winding about her fingertips like the ten wedding rings of a demon. The air was heavy and dark, suffocating. The river laboured under Gogmagog's weight, its swirling eddies and currents pulsing, flooding, ebbing; the Thames was a sooty spectre, both visible and invisible, and so wholly neither. Boat lamps flickered with a haggard unblessed light, attracting the night-creatures that had no business abroad under sun or moon or the ten thousand stars, but lived only within this cloud of smothering cloggy gloom. Gogmagog caught every last speck of dirt, dust, ash, smoke, litter in its maw. His body was painted mustard yellow and snot-green at the edges where the city's lights made their grasp at its skin. At its midway section the darkness revealed itself in patches of dank purple and rusty brown and scabrous grey, until at the river's central channel it was black-hearted, a deep oily black. Birds flew about slowly within the murk, their feathers sooted and weighted down. Even the loftiest of the bankside buildings struggled to poke their heads above the massive all-enveloping body of Gogmagog, sending their lighted peaks into the night as little beacons of hope. The whole of the River Thames was a bed of vapour charged with the muffled sound of engines and flapping sails, the strain of oars and the twang and clang of wire rigging, and everything and all, the whole of the visible world upstream and down was enfolded in a gigantic slow moving flood of mucus spat up from the lungs of Gogmagog and gobbed out into the regions where the citizens walked even now, crossing the river in their droves, fiercely, proudly going about their business, joking and laughing and singing their homemade songs of spittle and joy. Cady joined with them, sending a huge glob of nasty green phlegm straight back into Gogmagog's imagined eye.

"Take that, you fuck!"

Joyce Hicks looked a little shocked at this language, but she came to laugh.

"Smog Monster. Peasouper. The Brume, the Hoar. Old Murky. Pogonip. He goes by many names, Cady, but to us, well, Gog is just a nuisance, that's all. Not evil or anything. We don't view him like that."

"I can feel that, he has less power here, far less than he does in Ludwich."

"And he's been here for thousands of years, ever since your lot banished him. As long as you don't spend too much time near the river, you're fine."

"How long is his reach?"

"About thirty miles, from Teddington Lock down to the Prime Meridian at Greenwich. But the mist gets a lot more diffuse the further out you go. No, it's Central London he calls his home." She pointed to a large yellow circle floating

in the sky amid Gogmagog's upper reaches. "Big Ben. The
clock tower of the Houses of Parliament."

Cady squinted, allowing the clock-face to rise out of
a blur. It was five minutes to eleven. She remembered
Pettifer's words, that London was a few hours behind
Ludwich. A queasy feeling came over her. The more she saw
of Gogmagog in his full powers, the more she realised just
how small and pitiful she herself was. How in Lud's name
could she truly battle a monster like this?

"Is this where you talk to Gogmagog?" she asked.

"No. We have to cross the bridge."

A train passed by, its carriages filled with passengers.
Faces at the windows. They looked out on Gogmagog with
tired eyes or more often ignored him, reading books and
magazines, smoking, chatting, and were soon gone into the
dark. The fog closed in again.

Joyce led the way across the river to the south bank and
then down a set of steps into a narrow lane. There was a
pub here called The North Star, well hidden on the edge
of the mist. Joyce tapped twice on the door, then three
times, then twice more. They were quickly pulled inside
and the door locked behind them. It was a select clientele,
the kind of people Cady knew from home: old tars and
retired stevedores, mixed in with more theatrical types,
blowsy madams and flamboyant swells, and a smattering of
businessmen in pinstripe suits and smart neckties. Joyce was
the youngest person there, but she was welcomed gladly by
the landlord. She bought her guest a Wood's Navy Rum and
herself a dry sherry. Then she placed some extra money on
the bar, a couple of half crowns. "Two please, Arthur." He
nodded at her. Cady wondered what was going on. They
took a seat near the fire. A man entered the public bar from

a side door, thanked the landlord, and left the pub. At this, a woman at the next table to Cady and Joyce stood up and walked out of the room via the same side door. Cady could see her ascending a staircase.

"It'll be our turn soon," Joyce said. "Come on, have a drink."

"What's going on upstairs?"

"You'll see. Now don't go causing any trouble, otherwise you'll get us thrown out."

The drink warmed Cady, easing her spirit and washing the remnants of Gogmagog away from her innards. The room took on a soft hazy glow. The clack of dominoes was good to hear, and she longed to play.

"Did you know, Joyce, I was around when the game of dominoes was first invented."

"Really?"

"In my world, oh yes. It was a man by the name of Ethelred the Dot Maker."

"I think you're making this up."

"See, he'd made too many dots this one time, and so…"

After their laughter had subsided, she asked of Joyce, "How old are you?"

"I'm twenty-three."

"No, I mean really."

"Twenty-three, Cady. What, don't you believe me?"

"But you must regrow yourself?"

Joyce smiled. She took a delicate sip of sherry. "I was twelve years old when the spirit took me over. This was down in Cornwall, where I was born. May Day, 1936. The Summoning Dance, when a man from the village plays the King of Thorns. He puts on a coat of leaves and a mask of bark." She smacked her lips, relishing the memory. She probably had very few people to tell it to. "This dancing figure tempts and conjures the spirit from the woods and it drops like an invisible cloak around the shoulders of a chosen one. The chosen one this time being myself. It seeps inside you, and with it comes the... the *knowledge* of what you are, and what you have been, through all the years preceding. It gets passed on, you see, from one person to the next. But what's funny, no one else knows, not these days, not even the fellow playing the King of Thorns. To them it's just a jolly good dance, an old tradition. But to me... Well, when I realised... When I woke up the next morning!" Her lovely eyes glittered in the firelight, holding Cady in their spell.

"But you have memories of those who came before you?"

"There's a few of us around in any given time, dotted about the country. But of my particular line, yes, I remember things, some more than others. Let's see now. I have faint recollections of the first of us, that was Ulric Greene. Then Edward Penhallick. I know a bit more about his life. Then, after Edward comes Freda Hayrick. I remember her very well. Then Alice Tiptree, Matthew of the Lost, Molly Metcalfe, Adam Dovecote. And then... oh, who's next?"

"I think that's probably enough," said Cady.

"Mistress Pennywort! She was taken for a witch, poor dear. Mind, she did get up to some rum doings. And then Piers Wyville. He was a right cocky knave. His memories make me blush! And then–"

"Jump to the end, please."

"If that's how you like it, eventually you get to me. Joyce of Penzance. More lately known as the Nightingale of Soho. That's what one impresario called me, by the way. Written on the poster it was, fourth from the top."

Cady was puzzled. "I wonder I haven't heard of your world before now."

"We didn't even know of Ludwich's existence, not until Dr Dee told us about it."

"Oh, so you knew John Dee, did you?"

"Not me directly, but yes. I see him as closely now as I did then, looking through the eyes of Adam Dovecote. I mentioned him, didn't I? Well, Adam was the Green Man of Dee's time."

"You can remember their conversations?"

"Bits and bats."

"Which means that Adam Dovecote visited Ludwich."

"No, no. John Dee was born here, in London, don't you know that?"

"I'm beginning to wonder if I know anything! Oh Joyce, I'm in a tangle."

"Don't worry, sweetheart. We all get a bit dizzy at times." She took out a powder compact and dabbed at her face, refreshing her cheeks. "Dee was a magician working in the court of Elizabeth the First. According to Olan, old Lizzie was a bit like your Queen Hilde."

Cady nodded, finishing off her rum. She noticed that the woman had come back down the stairs, smiling broadly, and straight away another person took her place.

"In truth, Dee was a charlatan," Joyce went on, "at least to begin with. But then he discovered Ludwich, and by all accounts became a bit lovestruck for the place. He couldn't stop travelling there. He was especially enamoured of Faynr, and he would bring tiny pieces of the dragon's ghost back with him, captured in jars, and those little flashes of energy that you have over there, what do they call them, those lightning bolts?"

"Xillith."

"That's it. And using those two things he created a new kind of magic, a real kind, I guess you might call it. And he became famous for it, all over England, Scotland, Wales, and Europe as well."

Cady was truly astonished. "He never said anything of this to me, nothing at all."

"Shall we have another drink?"

Cady eyed the clock over the mantelpiece. "I'll have to get back soon. I have people waiting for me, my crew. They're a sorry lot, without my help."

"Don't worry. There's an exit glass below Waterloo train station. It's not far from here."

Another of the customers came back down the stairs, and left the pub. Seeing this, Joyce stood up, saying, "It's our turn." They took the stairs to the top floor. Joyce stopped outside a closed bedroom door. She spoke in a hush.

"George Dunston worked the barges. He ferried coal up and down the Thames for more than fifty years, man and boy, so he's submitted himself to Gogmagog's domain far more than most. As I said, most Londoners grow used to the effects, but George, George was different. It happens to a few of us. He fell ill. Really ill. Bronchitis. At least that's what the doctors thought, at first. But they found these weird growths on his lungs, sooty growths."

"Gogmagog was inside his body?"

Joyce nodded. "But George never seems to get worse, that's the strange thing. He's retired now, and his son and daughter-in-law look after him."

"How long has he been like this?"

"Over five years. And one more thing you should know: the Dunstan family claim to be direct descendants of Dr Dee himself. How does that make you feel?"

"Like I'm about to meet a conman."

"Now listen, Cady. Best behaviour. I'll warm him up first, showing you how it works. Okay?"

The older woman nodded her agreement.

Joyce didn't bother to knock, she went straight in. It was a back bedroom, with a single bed, and a window looking out over the darkness of the river. A few personal odds and ends: a ship in a bottle, a copy of a London street atlas on the bedside table, a faded print on the wall of a galleon buffeted by storms. A woman was sitting in a chair near the window, knitting a shawl.

Joyce nodded to her. "Mary, are you well?"

"I am, thank you, Joyce."

"And your father-in-law? How is he this evening?"

"Talkative."

"That's good to hear."

The man in question was sitting up in bed, reading a book by the glow of a lamp. Cady saw the title: *The Secret Sharer and Other Stories.* The reader glanced up from the page, taking in the two visitors. Cady took him to be in his seventies, but he could have been much older, from the sallow hue of his skin and his shrunken cheeks and his rheumy eyes.

"George, it's Joyce here. Joyce Hicks, do you remember?"

He nodded.

She sat down on a chair next to the bed. "George, I've come to ask a question." She picked up the copy of the London atlas from the side table and opened it. Cady leaned in close to see what she was doing. The atlas was laid out flat on the bed. Joyce took George Dunston's hand and placed it on the chosen page, so that his index finger was pressing against a certain street. Cady saw it was in the Soho region of the city.

In a low voice, Joyce asked, "Gogmagog, are you listening?"

Again George nodded. He had not yet spoken.

"I ask knowledge of 37 Wardour Street, last Monday at two o'clock. I had an audition for a play called *Midnight Paradise*. Gogmagog, can you tell me, will I get that part?"

Cady said, "What is this? Some kind of parlour trick?"

Joyce shushed her. Mary Dunston looked up from her knitting.

For a moment there was silence. Then thin drifts of smoke came out of the old man's nostrils, as though he'd taken a drag on a cigarette or pipe. This done, he sat up straighter in bed and took a deep, deep breath. His lungs wheezed from the effort. When at last he exhaled, his breath was visible in thick strands, grey and black. Cady was both appalled and fascinated. The room took on a familiar rotten stench that lasted a few seconds only, until the smoke had merged into the lamplight. And then George spoke. Not with the voice of a man, but that of a ghost, weirdly disembodied. In fact, Cady could hardly see the man's lips moving at all.

"Success lies elsewhere for you."

Once emitted, the words drifted away in further strands of smoke, disappearing around the bulb of the bedside lamp. To herself, Joyce said, "Oh blast it! I was hoping for that job." Then to the room: "Ah well, he's been right more times than wrong." She stood up and offered the seat to Cady, explaining, "Gogmagog has lain upon the Thames for centuries. He recalls in his dust and smoke everything he has flowed through, overheard, seen, experienced. Everything. All you have to do is call up the knowledge."

"People use him as an oracle?"

"Well, it doesn't always work. But it gives comfort, at times." Then she took hold of George's hand and said, "I've brought someone new to see you."

Cady's face was now in the circle of lamplight. The old man looked at her for a long moment and then said, "You've got the river on you." His voice was surprisingly light and well-toned, his real voice this time, a human voice.

"That I have," Cady answered. "And the sea as well. You name it, I've sailed it."

"Not the Thames, though?"

"No, a river called the Nysis."

His eyes narrowed at this. They darkened. The night was in them. "The Nysis!" He spat the word out, causing his lips to dribble. Phlegm rattled in his throat. He started to shake, disturbing the covers. Mary stepped in quickly and calmed him, adjusting his pillow.

Joyce said, "There, there, don't get yourself upset. Cady's not here to harm you."

George settled down. His eyes were once again those of an old man. His breathing slowed. His daughter-in-law poured out a tumbler of water from a jug and allowed him to drink; then she wiped his lips with a cloth.

Joyce spoke gently: "Cady here would like a word with you, that's all."

The old man stared ahead. His thin nicotine-stained hair fell over his eyes. Cady wondered where to start; this old man had become a long-term refuge, a way, perhaps, for Gogmagog to inhabit humanity on a small scale. There had to be a way in. She picked up the street map, flipping through the pages. It was useless. Ludwich was her city, not London.

She said, "George, I know you're in touch with Gogmagog. Is that right?"

He nodded. "I speak with him. He speaks to me."

"Is he hurting you?"

"No, he keeps me alive."

Cady took out one of her coins, a Kethran shilling, and she gave it to George as an offering, or as a totem of her homeland. The old man's hand shook violently around the coin; he was obviously disturbed by it.

Mary said, "I don't like the way you're talking to him. Ask your question. And then leave."

Cady ignored her, putting some grit into her voice. "George, do you know what Gogmagog's up to, his plans, his thoughts, things like that?"

"He dreams inside me."

"What does he dream about?"

The darkness entered the old man's eyes again, momentarily.

"What does Gogmagog want? Why is he trying to get back into Ludwich? Do you understand what I'm saying? George?!"

The old man went into a spasm, his chest rising, straining against the sheets. His daughter-in-law closed in again, pressing him down. "Please, you must stop now–"

"No! He knows. He knows the truth. George, speak to me. I demand it!"

His voice became a growl. Smoke poured from his mouth. His words were muffled by it. Cady picked up the jug of water and threw the contents over his face. He spluttered and spat, and the smoke fell as soot on the bedsheets. Joyce was shocked. She couldn't speak.

Mary ran from the room. She was calling for her husband.

Cady said quickly, "Joyce, is there a bolt on the door?"

"Yes. But… I'm not sure about this–"

"Do it!"

Cady knew she didn't have long. She leaned in and grabbed George by the shoulders, saying with determination, "Gogmagog? Are you in there? Speak to me! Speak!"

The voice of the Night Serpent emerged fully, spewing from the mouth. He said, "Ludwich is my realm, my proper realm! I belong there. I will return to my rightful place and destroy Faynr. As a result I shall take her power, and make it my own!"

"Why? Are you too weak here, in London, is that it?"

Gogmagog howled at this suggestion. Cady knew she was getting to him.

"You're too weak. You need Faynr's power."

Someone was banging on the bedroom door. It was the landlord. "Open up! Joyce! What are you doing? Let me in!"

Joyce was backed up into a corner. "Cady, we should…"

But Cady ignored the call. She kept on at Gogmagog. "Where are you coming through? Tell me!"

"Ahhhh!" It was George's voice, crying out in sudden anguish. And then: "Tangle Wood." He had managed under his own power to spit these two words out, free of smog, free of darkness. Cady loved him for it! Then the poor bedridden man started to sing. It was a children's rhyme, perhaps something well known in England, or more likely something he'd made up for himself.

Where the bee sucks, there suck I.
In a cowslip's bell I lie.

Cady was about to ask what he meant by this, exactly, but George just carried on, his voice rising in anguish. His hands reached out to grab at her, pulling her close.

Where the flowers bloom, there bloom I.
Where the beetles wing, there wing I.
Where caterpillars crawl, there crawl I.
Where blackbirds peck, there peck I.

But this human presence was short-lived in the old man's face. Now Gogmagog's eyes bored into Cady's, stark yellow, infected with sickness and moonlight. The room stank of death. George's voice quickly turned into smoke, which hardened and took on body, becoming an elongated tongue, which raged and stabbed at the air like a snake drunk on its own venom, seeking a victim. Cady managed to pull herself away from the man's grip.

The banging on the door continued.

The wood was creaking around the hinges.

Cady gave the nod and Joyce unlocked the door. Arthur Dunston rushed in. "What the hell is going on here?"

His wife rushed over to the bed. "George, are you alright, dear? What did they do to you?"

But the old man simply lay there, as peaceful as when the Joyce and Cady had first arrived. The monster had retreated.

Arthur turned on Cady. "If you've hurt my father…" The intent didn't need to be stated. He turned to Joyce. "And you! I thought I knew you better."

Joyce looked apologetic.

But Cady wouldn't be intimidated. "Do you have any idea what you're dealing with?" Her voice held all her fierceness. "If Gogmagog finds his true power, then all the half crowns in the world won't count for a tuppenny shit from a sparrow."

The Dunstons stared at her. While in his bed, old George had picked up his storybook and was reading happily of distant lands, and of ships, and the boundless sea.

It was time to leave.

Joyce walked with Cady to Waterloo station, further along the Thames. The promised mirror was fixed to the wall of the Ladies' convenience. Joyce mollified the spider whose web covered the surface. Then she helped Cady to step over the lower edge of the frame. The last thing seen, looking back, was the Londoner smiling at her: *We are two of a kind, we work together.*

The sound of the witch's bell could be heard, calling, calling.

Cady walked along the silver corridor towards the sound and before she knew it, landed with a bump on the earth floor of the monastery's chamber. To her side the Ibraxus Bell was being struck with force by Lek, his face contorted into *Almighty Effort*, until Lord Pettifer called out, "Mr Lek, you can stop now." Cady was glad to see them both. Pettifer clicked open his pocket watch. "You were gone for sixteen minutes."

Cady could hardly believe it. "Sixteen. Is that all? It felt like…"

He pulled her to her feet and wiped at her face. There were traces of London on her clothes and skin; dirt and grime, droplets of water in her hair from the fog.

Psephekarnidraxapor plunged with haste back into his pit, happy to fall into darkness. Only then did Jeb come back into the room.

"How was it, Cady?" Pettifer asked. "I trust you met with Joyce?"

"I did." She got her breath back. "I know what Gogmagog is hoping for, and where he's heading." She explained about the Night Serpent's need to gain access to Faynr, in order to regain his full power, and his mission to come through at the Tangle Wood.

The crew made their way back to the boat. Pettifer was happy to walk back to the Thorn Gate from there; he would hire the gatekeeper's son to take him back downriver, home. Cady thanked him for his help. "Know the truth of Brin Halsegger," he said in reply. "And then act accordingly."

The darkness folded around him, a trembling figure, more bones than skin.

The Night Soil

The boat entered the bowels of the dragon's ghost, where the waters were dark and loathsome, and the countryside around the banks and a long way into the surrounding fields was squelchy and rank and filled with reeks and mucks and odiferous vapours. Fires caught alight spontaneously from these gases as they were released, only to burn quickly out in puffs of fetid smoke. The night was doubly dark, or so it appeared to Cady's eyes. Little of the moon was seen. Peculiar beasts prowled the mucklands, their fur and feathers the exact same hue as the faecal matter they lived among, shadows among shadows. They made slurping, dribbling, lapping, farting noises. Lud knows what they were eating. It made Cady half sick to think of it, and half hungry for something tastier than the drab remains of Nabs' picnic hamper. Jeb had wisely donned his mask, while Lek had no shame of bodily functions, at least that she knew of, and very little sense of smell. For herself, she went barefaced and open-nostrilled into this land, revelling in the stench, and yet also appalled at her own delight. There was no purification going on here, that was a fact. The people who used to live and work this side of the wall had left in droves as Faynr's sickness increased. And that sickness was only going to get worse the closer the *Juniper* came to Haakenur's final resting place in the Tangle Wood. For now, it had the effect of causing Faynr's guts to rumble and gurgle as they expelled gusts of effluence. Tapeworms, at least as long as the boat, made play in the clay-like water, more evidence of severe digestive problems. Bubbles popped on the surface of the river, adding their own contents to the bouquet of deliciously rancid aromas.

Jeb came to her. "You ever been this far west, Cady?"

"If a passenger called for it, and they paid enough. But not often."

"When I helped my granddaddy out, we had a closed boat, as did all the westering sailors. Keeps out the whiffs. I tell you though, Faynr smells far worse now."

Cady nodded in agreement.

"But do not worry, captain. It is not real, this muck, but phantom muck."

"Either way, lad, we are in the stink."

The tipping grounds on the south bank were cloaked in nasty yellow fogs. Here, the night-soil men of old used to deliver their collected loads of turds and piss and vomit from the outside loos and privy pots of Ludwich. In later times it was used as a council dump and a midden, and was still littered with old mattresses and mothy rugs and crumbling furniture. In the war years a lot of the metal items had been recovered to be made into weapons and boats and the like. The remaining items were covered in ordure and guano. In the near distance a sewage farm had recently been built, in some attempt to distil the tons of muck and convert it into fertiliser for the fields of wheat and barley that lay to the north and west. Reminded by this, Cady looked down at her arms. The flowers had lost their petals, and had sealed up, the skin showing only a series of faint scabs. Whatever was happening from now on, took place inside her body. The seeds were planted deep.

Handing the wheel into Jeb's care, she moved forward to the bow. She tried to look ahead, but the spotlight's beam was marbled with curls and strands of puce-coloured gases, making it next to useless. The way was dark. At least the river was straight enough in this reach, needing no tricky manoeuvres. But a sunken pleasure boat near the left bank gave lie to her confidence. It had been there for some time, this small neat craft, its cabin and deck entirely sealed in alternating sections of tarpaulin and glass. The river rippled and gurgled about the half-submerged hull like pigswill in a pen. As they moved on, Cady opened her mouth and nostrils wide and took a good deep whiff of the stench, testing the air for danger signs. Nothing. Nothing beyond the pong, which contained many, many smaller smells mixed in: dead rats, fungal growths, maggots at the meat, the breath of creatures that chomped on faecal matter for breakfast, dinner and tea. She listed them all, each separate aroma. And something else, perhaps, something as yet unidentified? Still, at least the bowels reached for only five miles along the river, according to the Maguire & Hill charts; they would soon have pleasanter climes.

Something caught her eye on the starboard bank, a movement. Was it animal, or vaporous in nature? She could not say, but it seemed to have some intent, some aim in its travels. Could it even be a person? If so, he or she quickly vanished, becoming part of the darksome clouds of methane and sulphur that billowed over the land to a height taller than a house. For a moment she thought of the girl, Brin

Halsegger, perhaps lying in wait for them, or even marooned here in the Nethering. Cady concentrated her eyes on the shifting miasma, hoping for another glimpse. Yes, there it was again! Not a girl, but a man, surely. Full grown. Yet he was clothed in excrement from head to foot, he had to be, for his form was perfectly camouflaged in the fug of the night air. The very idea was too obnoxious to think of, even for Cady's somewhat extreme tastes. Perhaps this man was a native of these lands: from muck we are born, to muck we sink.

Lek came to her. She asked of him, "Do you see that? A figure."

The Thrawl studied the bankside for a few moments, his eye beams glowing brightly. "I see nothing." His voice patterns had improved over the last hour. "Nothing seen."

"He's gone now anyway." But the vision continued to worry Cady.

The excretoplasmic fog clung to the water and the rank reeds, seeping and frothing from clefts and fissures in the ghost dragon's nether organs. The *Juniper* sailed on through the arse-end of the world – *slow ahead, slow ahead, dead slow* – parting the intestinal tracts of Faynr. It felt as though they were pushing their way through layers of thick mustardy syrup. There was nothing clean here, nothing of purity.

Cady heard Jeb coughing badly, even with the mask in place.

"Lek, you will take over from the boy."

He did so, and Jeb made his way into the cabin, closing the door behind him. With the cracks in the windows and the splintered boards, it would offer some little protection, better than nothing. Cady studied the muckfields, on the lookout for the mysterious figure. But the clouds of toxic gases were impenetrable, and heavy with flakes of dried sludge. It was a miracle that life could take hold here, but she saw a bird hopping at the bank, and a snake slithering into the water, both creatures with stool-stained colouring. The stench was worse than ever.

"Lud, I will be glad to be out of this–"

Her words clogged at her mouth. Something moved in the water, or rather, *upon* the water. It arrived at a swift pace out of the fog, taking on form, a man made of vapours only, his shape folding and unfolding as he moved, skimming across the Nysis, hovering, his stinking flesh held in place by some act of extreme will upon the gases that composed his body. His eyes were two lumps of yellow dung in his barely formed head. Smoke hung about him in a feculent mass of lank hair. He chewed upon excrement, his most joyful food. Cady was held spellbound by the sight, seeing him as a fellow of her own nature, a merrymaker in the stink. But then with a shock she came to her senses and spat out the dreaded word:

"Gogmagog!"

She turned to shout to Lek, to Jeb, to bring them to action. "Hard-a-port!"

It was too late. Before the words had left her mouth, Gogmagog dissolved into a scattered black mist and then reformed immediately into a long spike of soot and grit and turds, all tightly bound together into a spear-like implement. A lick of red fire played about the sharpened tip. There was a swift fierce movement. That was all. The blade penetrated Cady's flesh, scraping between bones, cutting at the heart. Blood and sap were set loose from their proper home. She had not yet registered the attack properly, but looking down at her reddened peacoat she thought to herself, *Dearie me, old girl, your attire is ruined.* Then the wound in her chest opened up fully and deeply. The spear's red flame was in her, and she felt both a terrible searing pain and a great and equally terrible love. She moaned loudly at the sweetness of the wound and stood in radiant ecstasy a few moments longer before dropping to her knees.

All signs of the Night Serpent had departed, as rapidly as he came. All that remained was the poor victim, who toppled from her kneeling position to the deck, her blood staining the wood both red and green, sinking into the cracks, greedily ingested by the *Juniper.* Cady was alive still, when Lek rushed to her. She heard his voice from afar.

No whisper… Cady slow… Breathe…

And then Jeb was also there, bending down. "Captain, captain! Are you alright?"

But all Cady could think was that the boat needed the boy, he needed to take the wheel. She tried to say this to him, but each word made her choke.

"Cady!" Jeb was crying now, weeping, she felt his tears warm on her face. "Mr Lek, help her please!"

If the Thrawl responded to this desperate order, Cady could not see: her eyes were blurring over, clouding. She felt hands on her, rolling her over, and then pressing on her chest, a forceful pressure at that: it must be Lek, doing his damnedest.

Jeb's voice again: "Look! Look, the wound! The fibres are tightening, pulling it closed."

Aye, she knew this, her plant nature doing its best to sew the torn flesh back together. But she knew also it was too little, too late: the green stitches were constantly pulled apart. She felt them, each one, pinging as they snapped.

There was too much loss. Jeb howled in despair. How she felt for the boy then, so little known, and yet so close to her. She made an effort, just for him, speaking a single word.

"What's she saying? Lek, can you hear?"

She said it again, that one utterance. So quiet. Then she felt Lek's cold hard cheek pressed against hers; he was listening.

"Lek, can you hear? Please, Mr Lek!"

"*Earth*."

"What? What did you say? Tell me."

"Cady… speaking *earth*."

"Earth, earth! Upon my sacred wings, yes! She needs to be on the land. Quickly!"

Jeb was gone from her side. Soon after, the boat was moving, veering to starboard; she felt the caress of the engine in her bones and was glad of that, for her final moments were upon her. If she could only reach the soil and dig deep, perhaps then…

Now she was lifted into the air by a strong pair of arms, the Thrawl at work. The boat slid into the bank, into the soft clutching mud, and came to a rest. Cady felt herself lifted further, only to fall again as Lek cleared the gunwale easily, landing in the shallows. She was jogged this way and that, but thankfully her pains receded as Lek laid her down on a crusted portion of muck.

She was in shock. Her eyes were closed.

The stink of the Nethering kindled the strangest visions in her. Here the coagulated waste-products of Faynr collected, as piss and dung and snot and vomit, the dragon's very own exorcism of its own internal nastiness. Why hadn't she realised that here Gogmagog would be able to make a sneak attack? Oh, he must have been angered greatly by her entry into London, and the confrontation in the room above the North Star pub. Useless, useless fuck of a Haegra! Maybe you deserve to finish your days in the fields of shit, a fitting end. But Thrawl Lek had other plans. He rubbed damp soil into her wound, thinking perhaps that would help her. "Cady soil... slather muck..." And was that Jeb as well, arrived from the boat? It was, it was! The two attendees at her passing. How odd, she had not known either of them until recently, one day, two days, more, how long ago, how near, how far... how far yet to travel...

The crusted earth split and bellied under her weight, dragging her down. She felt her hands digging in, fingers piercing the dung, pulping it, massing it into clumps that she might cling onto, to draw power from the rich manure, to rejuvenate herself; but always, every time, the muck slipped through her grasp. The sludge covered her, gurgling around her neck and mouth. Jeb's hands were holding on, as were Lek's, but they lost their grip, one by one, until only Lek's fingers remained, grasping at the lapel of her coat. And then they too fell away.

She was alone at the centre of the darkness of the wet earth that covered her. Planted deep in the primal ooze, her roots sunk as far as they could go, sprouting from the base of her spine. But her human side, that part of her that laughed and cried and loved and punched villains on the nose, that part was dying, the spirit falling off the stems and twigs that made her. Her back was bent at a cruel angle, her limbs were crooked like the roots of an old oak. Through these roots she felt a little of the soil's moisture entering her veins, a pitiful amount, hardly enough to feed a buttercup.

Now she wilted. Now she dried up in her vines.

Her mouth filled with night soil.

The flowers of her eyes darkened, losing their vigour.

Her body trembled.

Her mouth opened, closed. One last breath.

One last breath that took her under. She was carried far beneath, below the layers of flowers and bushes, below the level of ashes, oaks and elms, to where the World Tree was planted in the black heart of the Deep Root. She was at rest, and she felt content as such; at long last to be free of the struggle. What was it she had seen etched on the sunken church bell at the start of this quest? "Pray for us, now and in our days of need. At the time of planting, and in the autumn months, when the flowers fade and fall." So let that be. Fade and fall, and having fallen, to never again rise.

Lud, it was peaceful here, so peaceful. Bodiless, fleshless. She was a spirit in the soil, nothing more. Old Ludwich Town would have to look after itself, or have another Haegra take over her duties. Or perhaps the times of the Haegra were coming to an end.

Now they appeared to her, the Lord and Lady of All Flowers.

But she could not see them, only know of their presence. Every single flower in the world was gathered in their shapeless invisible form. Their voices were made from the rustle of the leaves and the petals. Their desires were simple.

"Haegra, the seeds will scatter."

Cady argued back, "No, no, I will stay here! I will stay here with you, my Lord and Lady."

And then the two gods of the Deep Root emerged from the darkness, one shade less dark, their forms entirely leaf-bound and flower-filled, dark blue petals on midnight green leaves, gleaming. Their eyes, and only their eyes, showed signs of distant sunlight. The Lord of Flowers held in his hands a living heart. It was Cady's heart, pulsing weakly and erratically, its proper colours fading. The Lady of Flowers breathed upon it. The Lord read aloud from the Book of Dark Eden, whose pages are written on the wind and the pollen: "None shall die that may not die, for we live as the Flowers live, pushing up through the soils of winter, seeking once more the light." And with each word spoken, the heart beat more powerfully, calling out to Cady.

"Rise up, rise up!"

She reached out despite her wishes, struggling, but the soil was packed in tight around her, pressing down on her from above, from below. There was no other escape but to crawl upwards towards the world, to push the soil aside. *Seed scatter, seed scatter.* Those damned voices, following her, whispering to her. *Rise up! Seed scatter.* From out of the earth she crawled, this dark spirit, finding her body of flesh and bones and twigs and branches sunk beneath the mud and muck of the Nethering. Her spirit broke into her own flesh, tearing the skin apart, inhabiting once more this broken carapace. First one hand and then the other clawed through the soil, these old woman's hands reaching back into life. Her first breath was more dung than air, it stank of rot and pestilence. Her limbs cracked as the bones fused with the wooden parts of her, as vines bound muscle to bone, as tendrils wrapped themselves around her damaged heart, holding it together, mopping up the blood, sewing it with little stitches of grass and fibrous creepers. She blossomed darkly. Mushrooms grew rampant in her brain pan, giving rise to one thought only:

Lud damn you, Gods of the Earth!

The pain was terrible, worse than any other she had ever felt. The world weighed her down, crushing her. One or two seconds she had been away, that was all, but everything was different, all was dank and mushy in her plant mind. Two people were with her, close by, one a boy, the other... the other a... the other not human, but metal and plastic, a machine man.

She could not remember them, their names, nor their faces.

But every last particle of grit in the air, every smell in her nostrils, every sight of moonlit sky and flying bird and gas cloud, all were known to her; every touch of worm and root, every sound: the boy's sobbing breaths, the machine man's workings, magnified; the nearness of the water, the river as loud as a tidal wave on the reedy shores of her own bodyscape.

"Cady, you're alive!"

The boy's eyes. She saw them clearly, every line and dot of colour.

She spewed up dung and half-chewed beetles and root tubers and pebbles. Her body was more plant than human, far more, as her vegetable being took control, growing the flesh into an approximate shape of her former self, like some monstrous ill-creation, one of nature's cast-offs. Her face was made equally of flesh and plaited leaves, dark green in colour. Her hands were tipped with sharp fingernails of bark. Her heart beat with a strange off-centre rhythm, dribbling blood from between the leaves that bound it, ever tighter, until the green flow was rerouted. She felt the flow of sap around the fleshy map of her stems and branches.

The boy was wiping at her face with a handkerchief, as though that snotty bit of rag would clean all the loathsome shit away, but she thanked him for it by clutching at his arm, squeezing, making contact with a fellow creature.

But even now she could not remember his name.

Jed, was it? Or Jem?

The machine man helped her to her feet. He was leading her away towards the river, a boat, the boy helping. But

her legs were weak, and every step was agonising. Most
of all she was angry, pissed off at being alive, back on this
stinking dung-heap. Until with a shock she became aware
of the tiny seed pods clustered around the green bulb of her
optic gland, like iron filings clinging to a magnet. They had
made their presence known to her, lying in wait between
her eyes, their shells almost ready to burst open, to scatter
their hoard upon the waiting world.

And then she grasped at life.

Katharine Hepburn

Cady stayed on the boat when they reached the depot, for she could not face people in her current state. Words would not yet obey her lips. She watched Lek and Jeb as they talked to the couple who ran this outpost; they were buying diesel oil and food, and asking for news of Brin. Lamps glowed along the jetty and above the entrance of the store, a few last curls of effluent gas haloed around them. But the river was cleaner this side of the Nethering, and sweeter smelling. They had left the salt and the tide behind and were now in fresh water. Memories crowded Cady's head: the world, the journey, her place in the riddle of life, and her past. The fibres of her body were binding themselves ever more tightly with every passing second. Thoughts would stray in from nowhere, surprising her, and then she would plant them where they belonged. But the skull garden was quickly overgrown, thick with weeds and nasty infestations of slugs and greenfly.

She could not yet walk properly for her legs were like two withered stalks, but with the use of a cane cut by Lek from a waterside tree, she managed to hobble to the cabin, where she stripped off her clothes and dressed herself in a

277

new pair of bell-bottoms and smock, her last such items. It was a painfully awkward business, but she was determined to show her best blossoms to the world, like a fine bouquet on display at a country fair.

Her two companions returned. Jeb knew the owners of the depot from his younger days, and so had readily gained information. Yes, Brin had passed this way some two hours previous, aboard a pleasure craft, the *Wayward*. Cady tried to work out what it all meant, these names, these people, this task. *I am Haegra, I am with seed.* That seemed plentiful for now, enough to get on with. But the image of Gogmagog kept intruding, his smoke wreathing through the garden, spreading poison; she dismissed the vision as well as she could.

The *Juniper* set off once more. Cady stood at the figurehead, happy to let the crew do the work. The Lud flower by now had wilted completely, already rotting away. But Cady was ready to burst, and she felt the clear strong moonlight warming her body; she was drinking in the light. The hamlets of Mickle St Mara, Half Colcliffe and Morton Brook passed by. Here the lawyers, bankers and insurance office managers of Ludwich had lived before the war. The houses and bungalows were still occupied in the outlying regions, but residents closer to the Nysis had moved away as Faynr's sickness quickened. Mournstead was the worst affected, its riverfront properties covered in frost and large colonies of glittering silverfish. The only true inhabitants were the once domestic cats now turned into silent predators of suburbia. Beyond the village, the Gardens of Arousal were deserted, their labial slopes no longer a playground for young lovers. The smooth marble curves of the Fertility Goddesses were crumbling, spattered in bird shit. The *Juniper* glided along under the permanent moonlight of this Organ of Procreation, where, in days gone by, Great Haakenur had pleasured her mates and given birth to her litters; until that final birth at the moment of death, when Queen Luda had exited the dragon's womb at sword-point. Now the place told only of loneliness and unrequited love, a mood enhanced by the ghostly radio signals the boat's wireless picked up:

I am waiting here for you…
Samantha, please, come back to me…
Let us meet by the kissing gate…

But there were no replies, only electrostatic dust. Where was Eros, indeed?

The long tail of the dragon's ghost began. There was very little river traffic, beyond the small boats belonging to those few hardy souls who had persisted in living in the area. They did meet the *Wayward*, the pleasure craft that had taken Brin on her journey upriver. Jeb shouted across to the lone sailor as the two boats passed each other. He had dropped the girl off where the River Herne branched off from the Nysis, and would say little beyond that.

"What about the Frets? How bad are they?"

The skipper made a sign indicating madness, and then went on his way.

Around the next bend the Egg of Kharos came into view. A congregation of Xilliths danced around the structure, brightening the sky with their sparkles and sudden flashes of violet energy. The crashed spaceship dominated the landscape, a huge egg-shaped object that had fallen to earth some four hundred years ago. Cady had seen it a few times in her travels west of the city, and every time it seemed to be perched at a more precarious angle. Wooden buttresses had been erected to hold it in position, but these were now rotting away. The spaceship's colour could not be described easily in any human language. At best people used the phrase "pearly luminescence", or that it was "pale green, but not green", while still others called it a "milky yellow". It changed over time, over very slow time. The outer surface was smooth, featureless. The bottom of the giant egg had smashed into the ground, so that the lower edges were torn and ragged, packed into the earth. It lay across the Nysis, covering the land on each side far into the neighbouring fields. But the river ran through it via a pair of openings at front and rear, initially made by the force of impact, and then enlarged and properly engineered by subsequent generations of workers. In height it far surpassed any known building. Cady had never worked out its exact dimensions, as a boat journey at full speed ahead through the interior might take as little as fifteen minutes, and then, on other days, an hour or even more.

The spectacle stirred her plant-made soul. She could feel every part of her body as a separate stalk and stem and twig and root, slowly but surely making her anew. She worked on her outer features, careful to create a good mask for herself, so as not to upset the boy too much, nor Lek for that matter. They needed her to be strong; and she needed them the same, equally. So, face and hands at first, as well as the heart. Yes, get that motherfucker bound and tight. And pump, you bastard, and keep on pumping! Keep me alive, until the battle is lost or won.

As they drew nearer to the crashed spaceship a roaring noise was heard, made by the engines of motorcycles, many of them, revving and backfiring. Some of them held sidecars.

Their headlamp beams criss-crossed each other as they raced across the fields bordering the spaceship. Fires burned in oil-drums, lighting the scene. Jeb was excited to see the bikers. He gave the wheel to Lek and went forward, standing next to Cady. She heard him gasping with delight. His wings fluttered. He waved to the nearest gang of Ephremes who stood on the bank, welcoming the new visitors. Some of them were sitting astride their bikes. The men wore leather jackets and blue jeans, scuffed with oil. Their hair was long and greasy, swept back from their brows. The young women sported ponytails or head scarfs, tight jeans and denim jackets decorated with silver studs. They held their protruding wings high on their shoulders, a form of salute. Jeb proudly responded with a similar movement of his own wings, miserably feathered as they were.

The mood changed as the *Juniper* entered the Egg's interior. Faynr settled peacefully on the Nysis, her illness curbed in some way by the alien structure. The vastness of the space gave Cady vertigo, as though she were about to fall a great distance, even from standing on the boat's deck. High above were fluffy white clouds, each occupied by its own family of Xilliths, and higher still glimpses of the hexagonal gridwork that gave the spacecraft its tensile strength. Apart from a circle of six tall columns, thought to be part of the ship's propulsion system, most of the internal structures and devices had been taken away over the centuries, either to be studied, or repurposed, or even sold on as scrap metal. Only the shell remained, and the singular atmosphere and gravity held within its confines. A soft glow of light illuminated every surface. The sleeping compartments of the Star Travellers had long been picked clean of every last bauble, bead and bugle; although nobody truly knew what these objects actually were. Of the seven occupants – all but one of them killed in the crash-landing – three of their bodies were on display in Ludwich Museum, while another two formed part of a tableau of "Life on the Planet of Our Ancestors" in the National Gallery. One more held pride of place in a private collection, to be seen only by a select few, strictly appointment only. And visitor number seven, the only one to escape the wreckage? People say he made his way to Old Ludwich Town, there to mingle himself with a resident. They say he lives on in that one particular strain, passed on from parent to child as the fancy takes him. Oh, they say a lot, the sayers do. Cady thought it so much cock and bull. The poor astronaut probably fell into the river and long-ago rotted away. Aye, Faynr's little creatures would make a meal of him. Tasty.

Looking up at the sights, Jeb cried out his joy in the old language, in words he could barely pronounce properly. Other voices were heard as the bikers shouted to each other from above, where they flew, their wings given the vital surge of energy needed to carry them aloft. This was the one place on the planet where their wings worked, this ship! But the Ephremes made short flights only, more of a hovering or floating, leaping from one propulsion column to the next. Cady studied Jeb's face. His eyes were bright but nervous, his wings quivering madly.

Her tongue of vines whipped out. "Have a go, lad. Go!"

"I've never… not before. I was too young." He climbed up onto the gunwale, balancing, his arms outstretched.

Cady urged him on. "Now. Take off! Go on, you great drip! Leap!"

But still he clung to the rail. In the end she had to give him a shove. He fell forward clumsily, skimming the surface of the water, his wings working overtime to gain purchase.

"There you go, Jeb, my boy! Keep flapping!"

And he did. Somehow or other he righted himself in mid-air and took off in an upward surge, banking this way and that, without any real control. He made it about halfway up a column, where he clung like a spider to a ridge. He was laughing. Or was he crying with delight? It was difficult to tell. Cady's shouted instructions were lost in the echoes. He took off again, more powerfully this time, with newfound confidence, floating towards the next column in the circle. He would never make it to the top, not with those pitiful wings, but he looked happy enough, even when he collided into a much larger Ephreme by accident and then bumped into the column awkwardly. But he bounced off it straight away, this time heading into a long swooping dive, skimming the *Juniper*'s foremast, and then merging with a Xillith, who raced alongside him, illuminating the boy with a thousand sparks of blue flame. Finally Jeb made a clumsy landing on the foredeck. He was exultant.

"I am the boy with wings. Did you see me, captain, did you?"

"With my own two peepers."

"I flew!"

"That you did."

"I flew high, I floated, I dived. I tangled with a biker, mid-air. What a dogfight that was, eh? Cady? Cady, did you see how we tangled up there? Did you?"

He was giving her a headache. She turned away, leaving him to his revels. They had reached the halfway point of their journey through the spaceship, marked by the giant pyramid of the Rune Engine with its incised scriptures and its little cloud of Faynr mist at the peak. Many a scholar had tried their hand at deciphering the message on the pyramid's sides, all of them failing in different ways. One such was still hard at the task, an old man, a Wodwo, with long tangles of greenish-white hair and a gaunt, cadaverous face. Cady remembered him from her previous visits to the spaceship. Tom Griggs. Tom the Bard, as he was known. He lived nearby in a rundown cottage by the river, and often spent time in the ship, especially when visitors arrived, like the Ephreme biker gang. But Cady couldn't believe he was still here; what was he now, sixty-five, seventy years old? His voice carried over the waters, amplified by Faynr, echoed by the weird geometry of the alien space. A lone Xillith danced about the bard's head, attending to his message.

"The Progenitors will return, as they did before. They will return for us!"

He hopped from one foot to the other like a maddened ecstatic preacher of old, awaiting the arrival of the ancient gods.

"Prepare yourselves, my fellow settlers. The Wise Ones of Kharos sent their seeds through the cosmos, landing here in their millions, fertilising our land with their Children. They came back centuries later, in this, their great Star Chariot, to look upon us, and to wonder at our progress, and to sing Praise Songs for the Young." He raised his hands high. "Disaster befell the Visitors, when their Chariot crashed. But they will come again, believe me. They will return!"

The bikers laughed at him, but good-naturedly, for Tom was as much a part of the crashed spaceship as the Xilliths and the propulsion columns and the mysterious Rune Engine. His voice followed the *Juniper* as it reached the west-side opening, only fading away as the boat exited and inky darkness returned to cloak the river. Once more the ghost's sickness cloyed at the lungs with its nastiness. Cady saw that a colony of aphids had landed on her skin and were busy sucking the sap from her veins; she wondered if an army of ants would march forward to protect her in exchange for the aphids' honeydew. Well then, all are welcome. *My body is yours, for however long it might yet exist upon this world.* This is how she felt. Her mind was slowly opening.

Soon, the Frets would arrive. Of all parts of the river this was the one Cady dreaded the most. Some old sailors claimed to be at home here, chortling amid adversity, and she would usually be the same, sporting many a scar to prove it, but something about the Fretlands really pissed her off. It was just so unpredictable. Faynr was changing, becoming darker, clammier, and more concentrated as the river narrowed. The propeller churned away as best it could in the glue-like consistency of the water, but even then, strangely, the engine and shaft could hardly be heard. The pistons moved in silence as though lubricated with oil secreted from the gland of a god. Cady realised that the Frets were already at work, muffling all sound. The beam of the spotlight faded away a yard beyond the figurehead as a black mouth opened up and swallowed the light whole. Another Fret effect? You could never tell for sure, that was the trouble. And of course the Frets were never seen, only known through their effects.

A noise startled her. Lights danced on the foredeck.

Cady turned to see that Jeb's wings had caught fire, the flames sizzling his precious feathers clean away. He was just standing there, the poor lad, startled, but incapable of moving. Cady looked on as though at a crystal show, a member of the audience enjoying someone else's pain. She took in Lek at the helm, his skull covered in a layer of thickened blood which dripped down, enveloping his

face in a close-fitting mask. His eye-beams broke through
the covering. His hands worked the wheel, steady, steady,
slow ahead. Cady saw it all. She looked down at her own
hands and saw them replaced with long crooked twigs,
whose buds opened into pink flowers even as she looked
on in wonder, attracting a swarm of moths for supper.
Each moth was decorated with a black skull design across
its wingspan. Jeb was dancing. His wings were no longer
aflame, but were fully feathered, and resplendent. They
were decorated with moths, with skulls, with a twisting
map of the Nysis. The *Juniper* was seen on the feather
map, moving along through the Fretlands. Jeb licked at
Cady's fingers, tasting the honeydew. He was starved for
sweetness, the poor lad. Greenflies crawled across his face,
laying their eggs on his skin. Lek stood alone, peeling the
dried blood from his face in a single flat sheet of dark red
material which he fashioned into a flag, the Bloody Ensign,
as it was called, the emblem of all those who sailed across
the Equator of Fire unafraid, battling for freedom. The
Thrawl draped the flag around Jeb's shoulders, a cape fit
for a hero. Now they were dancing a foxtrot, Jeb and Lek,
boy and machine moving arm in arm across the foredeck.
No one was at the helm. The boat drifted. The Frets had
taken over the crew, each and every one, feeding them
strange images. Cady knew she had to steer the boat. She
took up position in the wheelhouse. The wheel and her
hands were formed from the same piece of wood, a kind
of pale ash; there was no part of her that did not belong
to the vessel. She heard the *Juniper*'s voice. She had never
heard it before, not so clearly. What a lovely song the
vessel made:

Don't save your pleasures for later
But sate them now, all one by one,
Set true your course for love's adventure:
Sail on, sail on, sail on, sail on.

Cady laughed with joy, hearing this. The old tub was a romantic at heart, who would ever have guessed? She cried out, "Soppy git!" And then joined in, the same verse over and over. The two voices rang out sweetly, floating like dandelion clocks on the breeze.

And so the night went on.

And the river went on through the night.

And the land passed by the flowing river as the boat went on through the night.

The Frets danced around the deck, a glint of golden light here, and there, here and there. How many were there? Hundreds, Cady had no doubt. She saw that Jeb and Lek had disappeared. Where were they now? Useless sods! She left the helm. The *Juniper* carried on alone, guided by the song it was singing, dead centre of the channel. Sail on, sail on. Cady went into the cabin. Maguire & Hill's charts had turned into blue water and green earth so that the Nysis flowed in miniature across the tabletop, between little clumps of hills and tiny buildings, like a child's model.

Jeb and Lek were standing on the afterdeck. They had run the Bloody Ensign up the mast and were now proudly saluting it and chanting a pledge of allegiance. A Fret entered Cady's mouth. It tasted of greenfly, of maps, of feathers, of river water, of soil, of blood, of masks, of singing, of skulls, of moths, of flowers. There was no way she could resist the call of watchwomanly duty, and she fell to her knees before the flag and praised the boat for carrying her so far, and for so

many years. Lud bless you, sweet *Juniper*! Cady gave herself
up to the plant world. Her eyes were closed. She could feel
the seeds clinging to her optic gland, shifting about, tickling
her, all one hundred and twenty-four of them. Yes, she
could count them now, each one.

The seeds.

The Lord and Lady of All Flowers had spoken.

Scatter the seeds.

King Lud now stood before her, dressed in his silver
armour. "Red Moon Hill draws near," he said. "I must
make battle with Haakenur." He knelt down on one knee
and held the sword Ibraxus out to her, the blade flat, in
offering. Moonlight glinted on the metal. Cady saw in it all
the times of history past. Then the King drove the sword
point-first into the decking. He rose up, taking Cady with
him. They faced each other over the sword's hilt. His eyes
were very green; they shone with a depth and a vision,
dazzling her, holding her in a spell. What could it mean?
The Frets were about her, that was all, making play with
her senses.

And yet…

She took Lud in her arms, close, his face against hers.

Their lips met.

Lud's face melted away into that of Thrawl Lek. Sir Ludlek
of the Fretlands.

The kiss continued. Cady's lips of green pulp and flesh;
the Thrawl's projected from within, a crystal's version of a
lover's mouth. But they were warm, those lips; she could
feel the heat through the resin mask. She felt her mouth
give a little, opening. Just so. And they merged.

The moment was held in space and time, forever.

The night went on.

And the river flowed on through the lips of the night, softly.

And the land passed by as the boat dreamed its way along the night's endless river.

Set true your course for love's adventure:

Sail on, sail on, sail on…

When Cady awoke she was sitting in the cabin with her head flat against the table, a piece of river chart stuck to her cheek and dribble running down her chin. A nasty headache needled at her, just above the left eye. Jeb was sitting opposite. He was nibbling merrily on a slab of chocolate, purchased at the depot.

Cady raised her head and groaned. "What time is it?"

"Gone four."

"In the morning?"

Jeb laughed. "That's the one." He took her in. "Cady, you don't look too good, old gal."

"You're right for once. I feel like I've drunk the barrel dry, without actually drinking anything but my own spit. Which reminds me, is there anything on offer, by any chance?"

"Orange pop. Or I can brew a pot of tea."

"No alcohol?"

The boy just looked at her. She rubbed at her face, feeling it to be slimy with grease. Her eyes were crusted with sand from some far-off imaginary beach.

"Did you sleep?" she asked.

"I did. An hour. Lek took charge of the wheel."

"Good, good. Your wings are alright, I see."

"Why shouldn't they be?"

"Not on fire anyway." She groaned again. "Oh. What happened?"

"The Frets. They took us over. The usual rigmarole."

"Oh fuck. Fuck. I need a piss. And not only a piss."

"Madam, down below, please."

She went forward, passing Lek at the helm. How much of what she had seen and experienced in the last couple of hours had been real, and how much the effect of the Frets? There were certainly enough of the blighters dotting the deck and bulwark, visible now in death, dull yellowish creatures the size and shape of a squashed berry; they never lasted long after a night of spreading fancies.

She raised her voice: "Jeb, you good-for-nothing arsewipe!"

"Captain?" He appeared at the cabin door.

"Fetch the broom and clean these decks up, come on, snap to it!"

Cady smiled to see the boy jump into action. Then she went down into the hold and sat on the tin bucket to perform her business. *This might be the last proper shit I ever have.* Funny to think of such a thing, but there it was. It was lonely down there, without Mr Carmichael for company, and that got her to pondering on the warm friends and good lovers of her life, and before she knew it a memory came to her, of not so long ago, a very short time ago, actually.

A kiss?

Really? Had that happened? No, no. No! Surely not.

She climbed back up to the deck. The land was flat all around. Farmlands, mainly, from what she could see. Looking eastwards she noted a faint pink wash of light at the sky's edge. Nearly sunrise. Oh, she was looking forward to the sunshine. She would eat it up! Like a dawn flower she would transform light into fuel. That's the ticket! Mist swirled over the fields. Faynr lay sleeping on the river in the shape of a phosphorescent snake of blue and green stripes.

The boat moved slowly through this spectral body, careful not to wake her, lest her dreams overflow into the minds of those on board. The Frets were bad enough, those little fragments of ghostly nightmares; no more of that. Birds skimmed the surface of the water in perfect silence, their beaks capturing midges.

Cady walked over to Lek. His face was grey and blank, every expression hidden. As well they might be. Before speaking she looked to the afterdeck, where Jeb was hard at work with the broom, safely out of earshot. Although the lad had probably witnessed the scene, if scene there was.

She started off the chat nice and polite. "How's that Library of yours doing?"

"In tatters... But one word at a time... Put next to another... Building sentences... Making sense." His head vibrated. "They don't always make sense."

"I know the feeling." She blew out a breath that stank of rotting blooms. "Those blasted Frets, eh? They make people act in the strangest ways, don't they?"

"They do. Yes. Or so I have heard." His voice was measured, carefully constructed.

"Um. No effect on a Thrawl, then? None at all?"

"Oh no, we are affected as well. Our crystals go awry."

But that damned face was still blank. What was hiding behind there? Ah well, best to get it out in the open: "Tell me, old tin pot. Did we happen to kiss?"

"You and I?"

"That's right."

"I did kiss someone, but not you, Cady."

"Oh?"

His face found a smile. And suddenly his words flowed easily, and quickly. "I saw Miss Jane Polter, my creator, standing on the afterdeck. She was very kind to me, saying many pleasant things about my appearance, and my thought patterns. And then…"

"Yes?"

"We osculated."

"You did what?"

His face flushed red: *Extreme Embarrassment No. 8*. "To *osculate*. To touch at a… at a point where two… where two parts of a…" His lips twisted about as he sought the definition among his ruined books. "…where two parts of a curve… have a common tangent."

Cady laughed and shook her head. "Now here's the thing, see. I kissed King Lud. But no more had we touched, his face changed into yours."

"I don't understand."

"Well it's simple. We thought we were each of us kissing someone else, someone we adored, but really we were kissing each other." She paused to let this sink in. "You kissed me, I kissed you. What do you say about that? I mean, you must have realised."

He didn't answer. Not for a moment. Then he reached into a pocket of his jacket and pulled out a cigarette card. He handed it to her.

"What's this?"

"I found it at Lord Pettifer's house. Actually, I stole it."

"I see."

"I stole it for you."

Cady was taken aback. The card was number sixteen of the *Great Actors of Movieland* series. Yes, she remembered now: she had seen this collection in the glass cabinet devoted to souvenirs of that other world. The card's photograph showed a striking woman of proud expression, with waves of dark hair and angular cheekbones. Cady turned the card over and read aloud:

"*Katharine Hepburn. Born 1907, New England. In both her personal and professional life, Katharine is known for her courage, fierce independence, and for speaking her mind. She likes to play strong-minded, sophisticated women, and in many ways epitomises the 'modern spirit'.*"

There was a pause.

Then Lek said, "She reminded me of you, Cady."

"I'm not sure about the *sophisticated* bit."

"Apart from that."

"And the *modern spirit*? I'm centuries old."

"Shall I take it back?"

"No, no. I'll keep it. Thank you. Hmm. Cady Hepburn, well I never."

After a pause Lek said, "I thought I had lost you back there, in the Nethering."

She was all set to laugh it off with a quip, but instead: "Oh, I'm not finished yet."

A mansion house could now be seen on the south bank, standing alone in a field, its roof and walls badly damaged in several places, obviously from a bomb attack. The mists wreathed the house in a torn wedding veil of grey silk.

"Is that Blinnings?" she asked. "Where you and Brin worked with Lord Halsegger?"

The Thrawl nodded.

"Brin might be in residence, don't you think, Lek."

"No. Miss Halsegger is not interested in the past."

"Can you be so sure?"

"I have her signal again. The myridi calls to me, from the river ahead."

He turned the crystal lamp of his skull up high, revealing the fly crawling around the curved interior. It shone brightly, that little pest, pulsing with new colours.

"Very close now," Lek said in a low voice. "Very close."

Cady thought that Brin needed Lek in some way, for some final act of kindness, or one last promise to be fulfilled. Or else she was tempting the old Haegra herself, throwing down a challenge. Either way, Cady was happy to accept the invitation.

Half an hour later the *Juniper* took leave of the Nysis, as did Faynr, boat and ghost both taking a tributary flowing south-west, through open fields, through beds of reeds, through mist and swarms of insects. Red Moon Hill could now be seen, the only tor for miles around, its ruby peak softened by the grey and pink sky of dawn. At the slopes of the hill grew the Tangle Wood, where patches of fog beckoned from the branches. Their final destination.

The Red Crystal

The banks of the river narrowed as thorn bushes and briars took over the land. The *Juniper*'s hull was scraped at by overarching twigs, and submerged rocks scratched at the keel. Faynr clung to the water in a shape not unlike Cady's own knotted hair, innumerable strands of fog twisted together. It had the consistency of melted tar. The dawn air was warm, not unpleasant. A bunting sang from a reed bed, a lonely attempt at creating beauty. Cady had studied the charts. She knew that the River Herne flowed down through the hills of West Mondaine, entered the Tangle Wood as a series of streamlets, and exited as the reformed tributary they were now travelling along, until it merged with the Nysis. But what actually happened to the waterways inside the woods? Well not even Maguire & Hill could answer that question. The map of the wood was a patch of grey, a few dotted pathways entering, stopping after an inch or so, the rough outline known, but that was it: the interior was a mystery. Old Mother Meade would always say, "You must never take more than seven steps into the Tangle Woods." Her eyes would take pleasure in the fear of her grandchildren: "Or else you'll never come back out!" So many had found that to be the case.

Jeb stood in the bows, using the boathook to push away obstructions on each side. Lek was at the helm, carefully working the wheel. The boat moved slowly and then more slowly yet as Faynr tightened the tufts of fog that sprouted from this end section of her tail. The air was so thick at this point Cady could pluck chunks of it loose with her fingers, and hold them in her palm like a lump of black mercury mist. More birds sang from the reeds, invisible, accompanied now and then by the rude parp of a bullfrog. Sunlight slanted across the river and then disappeared as the boat entered the canopy of the outlying trees.

Cady checked the clock. It was half past five in the morning on the last day of May. She remembered Henry Maguire's prophecies: *Today is the final day of Faynr's life.* He then added: *Tomorrow we begin again, or else we drift into darkness. The maps are unclear.* Well, that tomorrow was here, and they had reached the Tangle Wood. And this old Haegra was in need of a good fight.

The *Juniper* settled in a small lagoon at the wood's edge, the prow disturbing the algae that patterned the surface. From here the Herne separated into twelve or more tinier streamlets, which spread out into the dark of the trees by different routes, with strands of Faynr bonded to each one. The boat could go no further. The crew disembarked. A deep silence took over, held in place by the repeated tapping of a woodpecker. The air was dusty. And then the woods came alive: bird calls, growls, the sound of little creatures slithering through the undergrowth.

Cady glimpsed Brin Halsegger standing within the woods, a good number of steps beyond the recommended seven. The leaves partially obscured her, but a constant flash and crackle of Xilliths among the twisted trunks and the web of branches gave her away. Lek wanted to go to her quickly, but Cady managed to hold him back.

"Steady on, old lump. You'll soon lose your way."

"We will keep the boat in sight." Lek wore his most anxious expression.

"I tried that myself, one half century ago. You take a glance rearwards, and nothing remains of where you were. I was lucky that day."

"We could mark the trees," Jeb suggested.

Cady shook her head sadly. "And then find no marks at all, or a hundred marks on a hundred different trees. Believe me, the old priests knew what they were about."

And then Brin called out, her voice taking a winding route through the woods. "Mr Lek, can you hear me? Mr Lek!"

The Thrawl responded, "I am here, my lady."

"I am in need of assistance. Pray, help me."

He so wanted to obey. His skull brightened into pure blue light and the little insect inside his head was seen flying around madly in the trapped Faynr mist. "I am connected. I see the pathway!" His voice was blissful. This time even Cady and Jeb working together could not keep him back, and he rushed away into the trees, flattening the undergrowth and snapping twigs in his progress. He would quickly be lost. Cady had to follow him.

"Jeb, stay here with the boat. You hear me! No moving. None!"

The boy nodded. He looked suddenly scared. That was good. Cady needed to keep him safe. But she also needed to face her task. She set off, hobbling on her cane, following the patterns of the broken twigs. A few steps brought her into a hushed realm. She could no longer see either Brin or Lek, and a glance back showed that the boat was no longer visible. Not one tree seemed to be in its previous position. Haze clouded her eyes. *Old girl, what are you getting into this time?* Nothing good, that was for sure. The ground was soft underfoot, a bed of moss and bracken, sometimes squishy as marsh water seeped through into the topsoil. Trails of Faynr mist drifted here and there, little reminders of the ghost's presence. At places it clumped together into a thick lilac-scented mist. A yellowish pink cloudless sky was intermittently seen through the woven canopy above. Branches scratched at Cady's face and hands in a constant communication: *this way, this way, now this way.* The mists surrounded her. She could only hope she was reading the instructions correctly. Brin's Xillith signs had disappeared. The only pathway was the quiver of a leaf, and a hovering of seeds in the air, making a vague arrow shape. But she trusted to these signs and followed them until she came to the edge of a clearing.

Brin and Lek were there. Between them stood a second Thrawl, a very old model, an antique construction made of curved plates of rusted iron held together with nuts and bolts. In places the metal skin had crumbled away, revealing the cogs and wheels and stalled pendulums of the interior. Cady recognised him from his shape and features. This was the so-called *Thrawl One*, as drawn up in Dr Dee's notebooks. The prototype for all later models. No one really believed Dee had actually had it built, and yet here it was, hidden away within the maze of the trees. How had Brin found it so easily? Whatever had happened to her at the hesting, it was powerful magic. The first-ever Thrawl was covered in vines and lichen and cobwebs. In the greeny-blue gloom it looked eerie and out of place, like a faithful servant awaiting its master's return, as one century passed, and another, and another. Lek was working within the open panel of the decaying breastplate.

Brin had not yet seen Cady. She looked older, more like a precocious young teenager than the nervous ten year-old who had turned up four days ago at Anglestume. From somewhere, most likely from the captain of the pleasure craft, she had picked up a sailor's jacket of blue cloth. It suited her. Her face was stretched, as though she had lost weight in the last few hours. A fierce determination had taken over her eyes. Her hair was a little neater than before, brushed back at the temples to proudly show off her hesti; Cady could hear the two raised nodules pinging as messages were sent out to the trees, perhaps scanning for intruders. A kind of echolocation. Thankfully, Cady's newly extended plant-nature kept her well hidden among the vegetation. Brin looked to be in control of herself, and the situation. Yes, a right little jumped up madam! Cady stepped closer to hear what she was saying to Lek, and this approach caused the girl to look round. Her eyes flashed with Xillith fire. She was angry. But the moment went by, and she put on her old innocence, or at least a good attempt at it.

"Mrs Meade! You've come to see me. How lovely of you!"

Cady did not reply.

"Do you see what I've found? It's Thrawl Number One. I just knew he'd be here, waiting for me. Isn't he handsome?"

"Aye, if you like old decrepit things."

A look of mischief came back to Brin's face. "You're far older than he is."

"Me? I'm younger that a sprig of a tree growing in a patch of cowshit."

The young girl and the old lady glared at each other, neither giving way.

"Child, do you know what you're doing?"

"Of course." Now Brin's eyes were filled with delight. Xilliths danced at her fingertips. "Mr Lek here is helping me to mend Thrawl One."

"You're too old for dolls."

"Thrawl One is not a doll. He has the way through the Tangle Wood hidden inside his head. Isn't that right, Mr Lek? Dr Dee placed a map of the maze there."

Lek slowly turned. He said in a drawl, "I cannot mend the old Thrawl, Miss Brin. I am sorry." His eyes were a dull insipid blue, barely flickering.

"What have you done to poor Lek?" Cady asked.

"Reminded him of his Oath of Fealty."

Yes, Lek was under Brin's spell, as ready as ever to follow the promise made to the girl's mother: *Look after my child, protect her, give her whatever she needs to survive.* His one true instruction. His face was pure *Devotion No. 10.*

Cady felt a pang of jealousy. She gathered knowledge. "Why do you want to go through the woods?"

"Don't you know by now?"

"You tell me. I would like to see you squirm when you say it."

"I will not squirm."

"Tell me then. Spit it out!"

Brin clapped her hands together, just the once, the report echoing through the woods. The brat was enjoying herself. But then her eyes darkened and the Xilliths crackled around her, making a harsh noise. When she spoke her voice was so deep and wretched that leaves trembled and withered on the nearby vines: "I am the herald of the Night Serpent,

Gogmagog." In that moment she was no longer an Alkhym youth at all, but something else, something not of this world. Cady was fearful, for herself and for so much more. She dropped her cane, willing herself to stay upright. She raised her hands in front of her, palms outward. Her thorns emerged: the teeth of a plant demon. But Brin only laughed at this display, and her voice now had a singsong lilt to it. "Old Hag, Old Hag, went in the woods to smoke a fag! Hitching her skirts upon a tree, she pissed on beetles, one, two, three!" Brin laughed at her own childish song. And then she *was* a girl again, younger even than her years. She kept disappearing, fading from view, becoming a stir among the branches, nothing more, and then reappearing in a different place, only her hesti showing her true pathway like a pair of fireflies in the gloom. "Now you see me, now you don't!" Cady knew this was an illusion only, caused by the girl's new powers, but that didn't make it any less real. Her mind was being taken over. Those damned pinging sounds were pitched so high they sounded like someone was stabbing at the inside of her skull with a tuning fork.

She bit down on her tongue to ground herself, loving the green sap that flowed onto her teeth. In this way she asked, "Why do you need to get to the maze's centre?"

"It all came to me, at the moment of my hesting. Oh, Mrs Meade, I wish you could live inside my head, even for a moment. It's an explosion of joy! So many colours and lights and sounds, all dancing about. Ever since I was little I've known I was special. Now I know for sure."

Her young face crinkled at the brow, and her lips puckered.

"When the myridi flies were married inside my body, they spoke to me in a sparkly voice: *Go to the centre of the Tangle Wood. Make your way.*"

"And then? Well?"

"To let Gogmagog through. It's the only spot in the entire world where he can come through completely. I just have to open the door for him."

"And if I stop you?"

"You won't. You won't, you won't!"

"You stupid little fucker."

Brin's face betrayed her: she was surprised at Cady's statement. "Mrs Meade, there's really no need to curse–"

"You dirty snot-faced turd."

"Please. Don't say such foul things–"

"Bitch toad!"

Brin looked indignant. "But I'm only trying to heal Faynr. Faynr needs her brother, you see. And then she'll be happy again."

"What are you, really? Can you answer?"

"I am a child of Gogmagog."

Lek was roused by this statement. He turned from his work to say, "That is incorrect, Miss Brin. You are a child of Faynr, not of Gogmagog. You have to believe that. It is in your blood, passed down through your family's line, all the way from Queen Luda herself, when she rested in the dragon's womb. That is who you are. I know your lineage very well."

She shook her head at this. "I used to think that, Lek. But not now."

"But Miss–"

"Oh do get back to work!"

Cady stumbled forward, but without her cane her legs were not at full strength. She willed the vines and tendrils to bind themselves more tightly, and they did so, inside and out. But a single Xillith was enough to stop her progress, shooting out from Brin's fingertips to dazzle the old lady with its colours. She tried to raise her hand but was too sluggish. Her thorns retreated in disgrace. She would have fallen to the ground without the support of the nearby branches.

"I do like you, Mrs Meade. But you're very poorly. You should be tucked up in bed, back on your little island, drinking your nasty rum." Brin turned to the two Thrawls, one old, one young. "Mr Lek, you know what to do next."

Lek started to unscrew the ring of bolts in Thrawl One's skull. They were rusted in and each one made a cracking sound as it was turned. Lek was shuddering with the effort, or from some inner desire to escape the girl's control. Cady could not even move from her nest in the trees. Brin was happy to tell a fairy story to her listeners. "In the Year of Conjuring there was Gogmagog, and there was Faynr. Twin ghosts of Dragon Haakenur, one a boy, the other a girl. They played together along the River Nysis, delighting in each other's company. But then the horrible Wodwo priests split them apart, and sent Gogmagog flying away to a distant land, there to live in exile." She paused, her eyes cold and sparkling. "They did the same to my father, you know, they sent him and my mother, and my brothers and sisters, they sent them all away!"

Lek had by now removed all but one of the bolts on his ancestor's headpiece.

Cady called out to him. "Lek! Stop this. Don't do it." But her voice was feeble and the words were lost in the tangle of trees.

Brin continued with her story. "Gogmagog only wants to come back home, that's all, to play with his sister once more, to race with her up and down the Nysis, and to cover Ludwich in his soothing embrace."

Cady tried again, this time addressing the girl. "Brin, you can't really believe that. You just can't! Gogmagog seeks to destroy all that is good."

Brin turned to the faithful servant. "You believe me, don't you, Mr Lek?"

Lek drew a smile from inside his head, so deeply buried it took a time to get there, to be put on show. It looked hideous.

Brin nodded gleefully. "Oh good. I'm so glad we're back together again."

"She's lying!"

But Lek took no notice of Cady's claim. The smile vanished, to be replaced with pages from his Library, projected onto his face: words, sentences, fragments of stories, torn and frayed, made into nonsense. Cady gave up on him: there would be no help from that quarter.

Thrawl One's head had now been opened. The crystal at the centre of the skull was on view, surrounded by its little cloud of Faynr. How patient that cluster of the dragon's ghost must be, to wait here for three and a half centuries. Crystal and cloud together cast a ruby glow into the shade of the woods. Only once before in any of her lives had Cady seen a red crystal of such size and beauty. Could this be the same one? She twisted her limbs this way and that, stretching her twigs, feeling the pain of each joint as it separated and then rejoined, stitched afresh by the fibres within. But she moved! She took strength from the surrounding vegetation, drawing sticky sap from stems, chewing on the petals of a bluebell, melting a fly on her tongue. She staggered forward on thin spindly legs, creaking at the knees, her elbows poking out sharply. Ragged and spiky and covered in leaf mulch and insects, she looked like a monster made of the

Green World. She plucked at thorns from the trees and swallowed them for strength. Then she hawked up a ball of phlegm, making it rattle loudly in her throat. Her eyes glared with the power of the Deep Root, a direct passage drawn from her recent near-death.

Brin panicked. She had never seen the Haegra in this fashion before. "Mrs Meade... I really don't want to hurt you–"

The gob of spit hit the little girl full in the face.

She was frozen in shock.

That shut her up!

The phlegm was the colour and texture of muck scraped from the bilge of the *Juniper*. Little fleas and worms jumped and slithered in it. Next up was one of the thorns from Cady's mouth, expertly kept on her tongue and spat out as a second attack. It shot out at speed and landed in the gob of phlegm, pricking at Brin's cheek.

At last the girl managed to move. She screamed.

The phlegm bubbled with noxious gases. The worms crawled at her nostrils.

The thorn dug deep.

Brin wiped the gunk away as best she could. It was horrible. She plucked at the thorn, failing to get a grip. Then she threw a fit, her whole body shaking with fury. She lashed out wildly at the nearest trees, snapping twigs and stamping on every flower she could find. Lek watched this, his face showing only a broken dictionary definition of the word *confusion*. His hands moved without purpose, as he tried to work out what to do for the best. Cady didn't give him a chance to decide; she closed in on the girl, moving in her truest form, a hideous plant-flesh Haegra whose body belonged to the woods, and whose passion was born deep in the soil. She blistered her own skin open with thorns and barbs, all over, giving herself a mask of spikes. Her hands were claws of oak. Lud, she could have torn a hole in the world ten feet wide and drawn blood down from the moon's face.

But Brin met her easily. And this time she did not hold back; the Xilliths wrapped themselves around Cady, head to foot, mummifying her in blinding light and cascades of fierce burning energy. They were added to by the girl's hesting powers, which sent its pinging spells into Cady's head. Brin was combining two very different magics.

Cady could not move.

She was rooted in mid-charge, tangled in the Tangle Wood. Cracked at bone and skin. Draped from the branches like a fall of vines, face drooping, arms splayed, her legs crooked beneath her. She lifted her head to see what Brin was doing next. It took such an effort, this single movement, it was painful. Her lips formed around words but her tongue was drugged. The Xilliths seeped into her, making her drowsy with their lullaby of sparks.

But she had to stay awake! To fight!

She tried to move her hands, a single finger even: hopeless, hopeless.

Brin was performing an operation, unscrewing the top portion of Lek's head. Once this was done the myridi fly made a quick escape, a flicker of movement in the air.

"How are you feeling, Mr Lek?" the girl asked.

In a monotone he replied, "I am missing myself. I have no sense. I am disembodied." Every word had the same flat delivery. He continued in this same manner as Brin removed the blue crystal from its housing, along with its cloud of accompanying Faynr mist. She threw this crystal away without a care. Lek could no longer speak. The final word disappeared from his face: *promise*. His mask was blank, a dead screen. No light shone in his head.

Cady was horrified by these events, yet she witnessed them in a daze. She was succumbing to the Xillith's song of sleep.

Brin took the red crystal from Thrawl One's skull and placed it in Lek's head, pressing firmly until it clicked into place. The red mist went with it, like a swarm of bees crowding around their queen. Brin closed Lek's head. The operation was now complete, and he started to speak once more, but with a different voice, one from Cady's distant past. The voice of Dr John Dee.

The sun was coming up, creeping through the trees.

Birds sang sweetly from their perches.

Cady's eyes were closing.

Her head was filled with cloudy skies and seas of black water and night-blossoming flowers of unknown origin. The last thing she saw before darkness took her over completely was Brin and Lek moving away deeper into the woods, the red crystal glowing in the Thrawl's skull, the old map of the maze guiding their steps. There was one last flicker of light, and then they were gone.

Omphalos

In her sleep among the trees Cady dreamed of John Dee, perhaps stirred by the voice that Lek had taken on. The vision moved in and out of focus. She was back in Tenebrae House on the riverside, centuries ago, watching as the doctor conducted his latest experiment. Perhaps this would be his final great work. Certainly he was old now, and very ill. His body was wasting away, becoming translucent. She could see his bones through his skin. Death was approaching. But he held himself erect, wearing the ceremonial robes he always donned for his magical spells.

The red crystal sat on the desk before him, mounted in a wooden housing. He spoke of the crystal's energy, how powerful it was compared to the common blue examples. Cady was only thirty-six years old in this particular lifetime, and she looked on with interest. His work had always intrigued her, especially as Dee often vanished from his house for days, weeks, even months at a time. She often suspected him of having two lives, but could not imagine where he went in these periods of disappearance. Perhaps he had a wife and a family somewhere, a more normal existence he kept secret for some reason? But no matter; he had called her here to witness this spell at work.

He spoke gravely: "I will give my whole self to this endeavour. Everything I know, all of the knowledge I have discovered. All shall be recorded and never lost. And perhaps people in future days will delve within. I shall live again!" He looked at Cady then. She saw the passion in his eyes, and the stirrings of madness also. He went on, "A tiny angel lives inside the red crystal. She will gather my soul to her."

This was his only explanation. Cady was reminded of insects trapped in amber. She had seen such things in the forests and jungles of distant lands.

Now he stood at the desk, his hands held over the crystal, moving them back and forth in the gestures of conjuring she had come to know so well. He swept his arms suddenly up to shoulder height and closed his eyes. Cady felt the temperature of the room rising. There was a faint humming sound, as of wind in the rigging of a galleon. She looked on, wondering what might happen next. Yet despite her attention the beam of light caught her unawares. A deep red in colour, it emerged from the depths of the crystal and travelled slowly through the air to touch Dee's head, at the very centre of his brow. They were now connected. The humming sound rose in pitch. There was a movement within the beam, rather like blood moving through a vein. This substance flowed out from Dee's mind, down the beam of light, into the crystal. She imagined the little angel collecting the good doctor's knowledge, securing it for some future use. Where would it end up, this crucible?

The red light grew brighter. It filled the room. Cady's head thrummed with the noise. She had to close her eyes against it; the insides of her eyelids were coloured in splashes of scarlet and yellow. Now she could hear a tapping sound, and feel herself bitten all over, at every exposed spot of skin. Her hands were caught in a series of ropes or loops. She could not move. *Where am I? What is happening to me?* Sunlight on her neck, a stir of a breeze. Ants and centipedes and spiders were crawling all over her face and hands, finding out her hidden places. She opened her eyes slowly and carefully and saw beneath her the mossy ground of the Tangle Woods.

She was hanging from the trees by her limbs, a sorry specimen. Raising her head she saw that Lek and Brin had long gone. The rusty iron remains of Thrawl One stood amid the grove, his head still open, the crystal removed. Cady was alone, with the creatures of the forest, the birds that tapped at her face with their beaks, the insects that bit at her, rousing her from slumber. *Yes, yes, I am awake! Leave off!* A moment's struggle bound her further in the vines, until she spoke directly to the plants themselves, demanding release. They obeyed the word of the Haegra. Cady fell to the ground, the moss making a soft landing for her. And there she lay for a few moments, listening to the plants moving and the animals creeping about. The sun had found a nice little pathway through the leaves. Her face was dappled. Revived, she got to her feet and brushed herself down. She tested her legs, hoping her knees were better now; yes, they seemed to be stronger, the bindings had done their job. She was a crooked bundle of twigs in the guise of a woman, but that would have to do. She set off in the direction she had seen Lek and Brin taking. How long had she been asleep, caught under Brin's lullaby spell? Certainly, the sun was higher in the sky. Any traces of the pair's journey were soon lost: broken twigs, bent flowers, trampled weed beds.

The Tangle Wood enclosed itself in its own maze.

Cady trusted to deeper sources, calling on the vegetable world to help her, to give her clues. The plants and trees answered, each in their own language: leaf-rustle, cracked seed pods, the drift of dandelion clocks and the trackways of pollen in the air. All combined into one way forward, between the trees which seemed to grow closer and closer together the further she went. Alongside the plant world, animals also helped her: the unseen trundling of moles through the soil, a sudden scurrying of red ants, a hummingbird with green wings flashing a GO symbol. Even a pile of maggots chewing on a dead rat were decoded, revealing a slight tendency in their choice of eating spots. Cady bristled with knowledge. She followed the scent trails of beetles, and the buzzing of bees in the undergrowth. Blink-a-blink flies lit the darker passages with their pulses of light. Every disturbance was registered and turned into a map, slowly unfolding. Forward, turn left, forward again, two steps back, now turn left, and keep on. Her optic gland picked up these messages; it was glowing brightly inside her skull, illuminated like a religious icon with its covering of seeds, more powerful than ever. In this way, Cady read the Book of the Woods.

Often she passed the remains of earlier travellers, the bones of long-ago maze explorers, each one lost in the tangle, unable to trace their pathways back to safety. And once she came upon the rusted carapace of a Hellblaster fighter plane in the broken branches of a mighty oak, its fuselage riddled with bullet holes, nose-cone and propeller hanging almost to the ground, the pilot in the cockpit rotting away within his fur-lined jacket and goggles. Cady shivered at the sight.

Little birds flittered around the cockpit, emblems of former flightpaths.

She was getting tired now, for there were no clear straight ways, and the ground was crooked and filled with potholes. Never-never flowers were seen in clumps, their spouts open to the skies; again Cady was reminded of the first seeding that had started this journey for her. The riddle played in her head: bell, grave, bomb. That last element was still to be found. What could it possibly mean? Exhausted, she sat on a tree stump. At her feet she spotted a cluster of fiery hexbane, the plant the first Wodwo priests had used as one of their guards against Gogmagog's return to Ludwich. They had planted this woodland maze around the point of his exile, and seeded it with every plant they could that might prevent the Night Serpent's return: spikes, nettles, bane and tanglevines.

Cady took the cigarette card that Lek had gifted her from her pocket. *Katharine Hepburn.* How lovely she looked, this star of another world. Cady took strength from the attributes listed on the reverse: *courageous, fiercely independent, strong-minded; the epitome of the modern spirit.* Yes, Lud dammit, that was her! She sprang to her feet, raising her fists and crying out loud to the trees, "I am Cady Meade, Queen of the Greenery! I was killed in action and buried in the fields of shit. But now I am risen from the dead for this task. I will keep on!" The birds encouraged her with their various songs: *tweet tweet, jug jug, wew, chur chur chur, woo it woo it, teerew, grig grig grig grig.* Yet only a few more yards took her into marshy ground and she was soon up to her ankles in the mire. Now every step was a struggle, as the sucking soil grabbed at her. It would take her days of travel at this rate, and she was worried that a deeper pit might be hidden amongst the moss, a trap from which she would not be able to escape. She came to a halt, breathing heavily, looking around for a pathway through the marsh. But there were no clues available, only the stunted trees and the knotted branches and the webs occupied by giant spiders as big as her fists. Sweet Luda, she would like to catch one of those beauties and bite into it for energy. But there was little chance of that, and no hope of a way forward.

Even the plant world had gone quiet on her.

The gods made no reply to her call.

King Lud's avatar spirit had retreated.

Only one little speck of colour was seen, flittering about in the marsh gas. It flew near to her face, showing itself off. She recognised it: the myridi fly that the Witch of Threadbare Street had trapped inside Lek's head. It had been released by Brin during the placing of the red crystal. And now it had returned to her, to Cady. But why? What was the attraction? She stood perfectly still as the insect landed on her hand. Its needle-like proboscis jabbed into her palm, and it sucked deep of the honeyed sap that came directly from the Deep Root. It was taking sustenance from her, and giving her something in return: a signal path. She felt the exchange taking place, back and forth. Now the fly took off once more and made its way from one resting place to another. The Haegra followed, taking careful steps wherever the insect led, and in this manner she made her way safely through the marshy ground.

A few more guided steps and the atmosphere changed, taking on a hush and a soft blue light that came from the trees themselves. The myridi flew off, leaving Cady to move on alone, pushing through the hanging vines and flowering creepers. As she went on the vegetation grew more unearthly: ghost-white lilies with animal tongues sticking up from their petals; flowers that sprayed blood at her as she passed; and a seed pod the size of a football, shaped and coloured like a human eyeball, weeping tears of ichor. Further on a stream of Faynr drifted into a small pool of water. The mist of the dragon ghost was a burnt orange in colour, and the texture of a woman's breath on a winter's day. Cady knelt down and moved her hand through the vapour, seeing how it joined with the water and where it moved on through the woods, clinging to a streamlet of the Herne. She must be very close now, to where Haakenur's body lay buried. Perhaps she was even standing over the deeply buried bones.

She noticed that a greeny-black liquid was dripping into the water at a steady rate, interfering with the Faynr mist, contaminating it. She looked up and got the shock of her life, seeing two eyes staring back at her from the trees above. Her first thought was of Gogmagog, but that quickly passed as she studied the head and body these oversized eyes belonged to. It was a Molokoi, one of the Enakor's fighting robots, designed for use in the war. Its gunmetal body was caught in the trees, so that it was hanging upside down, quite invisible except from this lower viewpoint. Its wings were broken, its eyes were dead. The carapace was scarred and broken in many places. Cady pictured a fierce dogfight in the sky between this flying machine and the Hellblaster she had seen earlier, a fight with no winner, and two losers. Was the dripping liquid some kind of oil from the machine? Yet it seemed too long a time for such a leak to continue, perhaps five years or more? She stood up and reached into the branches, finding the source of the leak. It was a grey canister, as long as her arm, shaped rather like a missile but with a blunted end. A nozzle poked out, from which the dark green liquid seeped. A single drop fell into Cady's mouth and she had a sudden and very intense vision as it touched her tongue.

It was terrifying. The River Nysis was polluted along its length by the dying Faynr, while the dragon's ghost writhed in agony. People were drowning, coughing, gasping. Buildings caught fire, collapsing into the river. The ghost whipped its length over the docklands and the crowded, terraced streets of Witherhithe and the markets and chapels of Templeton; richly populated or riddled with poverty, nowhere was safe from Faynr's death agonies. Ludwich was in ruins, the bell tower of the Witan crumbling, the great bridges cracked in two, motor vehicles falling to their doom. Faynr was turned into a poison that flowed into the city's veins, reaching far and wide, destroying everything it touched.

Cady fell back into the undergrowth, spitting out the toxin. Her heart was palpitating madly, threatening to split along the line of the green stitches. Her mouth was burning. Now she knew the truth, that the Enakor had sent this Molokoi on a mission, to infect the Faynr at its source, in the depths of the Tangle Wood. The desperate machine had held on in its final moments, trying to fulfil its given task. This must have been done in the early days of the war. This Enakor weapon would destroy Ludwich, the capital, by destroying Faynr, making her sick. And the people had been living with the sickness of the ghost ever since. Cady spat out the last of the poison. She cursed her old enemy, and she cursed the war that brought about such deeds.

Then she reached up and pulled on the canister, dragging it loose from the Molokoi's grip. It was marked along its length with Enakor symbols and appeared to be half full. Cady realised that this was the final item in the never-nevers' vision: the flying bomb marked *Gogmagog*. Perhaps the Night Serpent's attempted arrival was an accidental outcome of Faynr's weakness, as he exploited the sickened

portions along the river; or maybe the enemy had planned
this demonic intrusion all along? Who could tell? But Cady
did think of Brin's father, and wondered just what he had
worked on in his exile. Thankfully, the Deep Root had
worked out the problem, at least in part, and sent Cady on
her own mission into these dark and tangled woods. She
threw the metal canister away into the trees, where it could
no longer poison the ghost. This done, Cady performed
a little celebratory jig, as best she could on her crooked
legs. She soon collapsed against a tree trunk. But she did
feel pleased with herself. After all, she had just removed
Faynr's source of infection, at least that's what she hoped.
All three elements of the never-nevers' riddle had been
found, and interpreted. But she knew that her mission as
a watchwoman was not yet over. She remembered how
Gogmagog had gained partial entrance at the village of
Ponperreth yesterday, goaded by the worship of the cult
members. The Night Serpent was building in strength with
every minute, ready for the final push. The demon had
made his terrifying claim through the mouth of poor George
Dunstan in his London sickbed: "Ludwich is my realm! I
will return to my rightful place and destroy Faynr. I shall
take her power, and make it my own!" The Tangle Wood
would be the breach in the wall. Cady had to hold fast, as
both Lord Pettifer and Henry Maguire had asked of her,
demanded even. As she demanded of herself, the very same.
Her heart surged. Ahead lay the deadliest battle of her life,
of her many lives. Now she understood why the Deep Root
in its wisdom had not allowed her to regrow this time. The
cunning and experience of age was needed, more than any
youthful spirit. Finally, she wondered about her pollination
by the Lud flower. What strange hybrid would be born from

this union? Cady did not know. More than anything she felt an overwhelming urge to protect the seeds that lay within her body from Gogmagog's clutches.

She pushed on through a thick curtain of vines, following the stream. The air was filled with a fine off-white powder that collected on petals and in the boles of trees. Her eyes sparkled with a sudden glare from ahead, through the branches. One last step forward.

The skull of Haakenur lay before her.

It was lying half buried in the ground, with the whole right side of the head on view, the long snout, the mouth partly filled with earth, and the slope of the cheekbone leading up to a plateau where the eye socket must be. But it was too high for Cady to see that far; the revealed part of skull alone was bigger than a tugboat lying on its side. In view, high up above the cheekbone's slope, was the upper portion of a curved horn. Only the right-hand jaw was visible, but it was clearly part of an engine designed to crush enemies. The teeth were enormous, even those which were broken; piled alongside the giant crooked fang they looked like the ruins of a stone temple. Some of the teeth had worked loose or been knocked out in battle and now lay as boulders among the trees. She walked round to view the nasal cavity, which looked like a cave entrance or the burrow of a large animal. Vines and creepers had taken over the bottom of the skull, but the greater part was clean of all vegetation. Most incredible of all was the thin orange mist of Faynr that emerged from Haakenur's mouth in a slow steady stream of the purest hue winding between the teeth and creeping on over the moss to seek out the nearest rivulets and pools; from here it would flow onwards until it reached the Nysis, and there begin its sixty-mile journey downriver. Here it was, at last, the source of the ghost! Cady could not help herself; she fell to her knees in genuflection. She prayed to the Gods of the Woodlands that her seeds might find fertile ground.

Then she heard a noise behind her and got to her feet as fast as she could. It was Thrawl Lek. He came to a halt and watched her. There was no expression on his face. His eyes were dark, closed down. Only the red glow of the crystal inside his skull gave any indication of life.

"Lek! I'm so glad to see you."

But of course he didn't respond to Cady's call. For this was no longer Lek. It was John Dee. His spirit. Cady knew this, and she felt suddenly awkward. How should she act with her old mentor and fellow explorer of mysteries? She started with a simple question:

"Where is Brin?"

Thrawl Dee looked at her with his dead eyes.

"Brin. The girl. Where is she? Dr Dee, you led her here through the woods."

Still no answer, no response from the mechanism.

Cady went right up the Thrawl and tapped on its faceplate. "Old timer, it's me, Cady Meade. Haegra of this land. We worked together on the Blight problem, back when you were living inside flesh and blood. Remember?"

This got a reaction, of a kind. The Thrawl's face heated up and the red crystal glowed a little brighter.

"I need to find the girl, it's important. There is trouble in the realm, just like the old days. We can work together again, fighting the good fight, eh, what do you say?"

But this brought no further acknowledgement of Cady's presence.

"Fuck."

Maybe that evil child, Brin, had disabled him in some

way. But then an idea came to her. She reached up and gave a little twist to the bullet embedded in the skull; after all, it had worked when this big lump was called Lek. The response was instant.

"Arcadia?"

The voice was croaky, rusty, the sound of cogs grinding on sand. But yes, it was Dr Dee's tone, as remembered. Deeper, older, with a rasp to it.

"That's me! Spot on. Arcadia. Ha ha, and there you are, the mad scientist."

Thrawl Dee looked around, slowly turning his head this way and that as his eyes came alight to gather knowledge of his surroundings. He returned his attention to Cady. His face flickered. She imagined him searching through his Library, which must have been extensive, as it took a good while before an expression reached the surface.

It was John Dee's face taken from an oil painting.

Cady remembered the same painting hanging in Dee's study, all those years before.

"So long a time," he said now, "since last I saw you, Arcadia."

"It is that, you old pisspot. Three and half centuries and then some."

"I have been asleep. Asleep… and dreaming." He looked over to the skull of the dead dragon. "Haakenur. Haakenur!"

"The one and only. The first Great Ruler of this land."

Thrawl Dee collected some of his Histories and Memories. "To this place," he began, "I give the name Ludluda. Here the Battle of Red Moon Hill took place. Here the true Realm of Kethra began, with this act of war between rival species. Here Lud and Luda first encountered each other on a new world after their long journey across space. It marks the spot where

King Lud was midwife to the second birth of Luda, reuniting with his sister for a brief interval before his own death."

Thrawl Dee paused. Cady heard his mechanisms creaking. She pictured his rooms of crystal piled high with objects: encyclopedias, telescopes, astrolabes, star charts, maps of both Ludwich and London, tide tables, the number pi written out to a hundred digits.

His painted expression came into sharp focus. "Ludluda became sacred ground for the Wodwo priests. It is the place where death meets rebirth and the blood of enemies is spilled together. A place of great magic, a natural crossing-point between worlds."

His raised voice set the birds fluttering from the branches.

"It is here at Ludluda that the Wodwo priests conjured the ghost of Haakenur, separating the good from the bad, the placid from the turbulent, the lifeblood from the poison. Faynr from Gogmagog. They opened a window to another world and sent Gogmagog crashing through it. Then they sealed the portal." He calmed a little, his voice losing its rhetorical power. "Ever since, the portal has remained closed. Not even I, John Dee, Magus to Queen Elizabeth herself, and to Queen Hilde, would have the strength to open it, nor would I desire to do so. Instead, it will be opened by a child, as I predicted in volume fifteen of my books. Yes. A child!"

This last word was said in a howl. He was weakened by its utterance.

Cady was surprised. "A child? So you knew all along?"

Thrawl Dee looked her at. He quoted directly from his final notebook, a long-lost tome: "*A child shall be born, a worldling, through whose veins the blood of the dragon shall run. She will open a gate between worlds in her quest to free the Night Serpent and to take her rightful place at his side.*"

Cady grabbed him by the shoulders. "Now listen, Dee, where is the girl? You led her here, to Ludluda. But what happened to her then?"

"The child went on, further than I could ever go. Much further." His voice was slowing down, losing coherence.

"Deeper into the woods, you mean?"

"She looked into the eye of the dragon. And the dragon looked back at her."

This statement took such an effort that Thrawl Dee gave up on saying anything more. His face darkened into greyness and his eyes went out like two lamps extinguished.

Cady sighed. "You always were a bugger, never saying anything easy when you could make it difficult."

She turned to the skull, looking up the long slope of the cheekbone. She noted disturbances on the dirty white surface. A closer study revealed these to be the sudden skitters of miniscule lizards, or perhaps more likely newts. They were the exact same colour as the bone on which they dwelled, a perfect camouflage.

"Well then, best get to it, old girl."

Cady spat on her palms. She started to climb, at first using the creepers and vines for support, and then seeking little hand- and footholds in the bone itself. Her boots lodged in the crevices of the jaw and the ear socket, her fingers clung onto the tiniest cracks. Dust got in her eyes. Sweat covered her all over, making her hands lose their grip a few times. But she kept at it, and so, carefully, a few inches at a time, she ascended the skull of the fallen dragon.

The right eye socket was in view, and beyond it the horn rising from the curved plane of the head. The horn had received many gashes, no doubt from battles with other great creatures of ancient times. The left eye and the left-

hand horn were buried in the ground, along with the rest
of the creature's skeleton, the ribcage, the limbs, the spine,
the long tail. Cady had to wonder just how big Haakenur
had been in life, from snout to tail; nowhere near as long
as the ghost, obviously, but still it must have presented an
awesome and frightening sight to King Lud and his warriors.

Cady sat at the eye's edge, getting her breath back.

Down below in the clearing, Thrawl Dee was standing as
he was before, at rest. Above was the canopy of the trees
with a big enough gap in them to allow a little of the sunlight
through. There was a dark threat of rain. For a moment
Cady imagined the people of Ludwich getting up and going
about their early morning routines. Another world. She had
passed through a borderline of sorts, to get to this place. The
dragon's eye, she felt, was the exact centre of the known
world, the Alpha Point around which all things revolved. The
Omphalos. It was a slightly elongated circle, about five feet
across. Due to the head's final resting position, the socket lay
flat, perfectly horizontal. A silver liquid was held within the
eye's circumference, its surface undisturbed, a brilliant mirror.
Cady held her hand over the surface and saw its reflection,
exact in all details. She bent over and looked at herself. That
face. She supposed it must be her; who else could it be? But
the greasy hair, the sallow skin, the jowls, the wrinkles, the
moles, the missing teeth, the red eyes, the dry cracked lips:
a monster herself. There was nothing seen beyond her face,
as the silver liquid was opaque. She wondered how deep
the eye socket was and whether the liquid filled the entire
skull. Then she saw that a single never-never had managed to
creep up the other side of the skull, its open-mouthed flower
poking up at the far side of the eye. The little lizard creatures
ran here and there, suddenly stopping dead still. They were

impossible to see until they moved. And move they did, at least half a dozen of them suddenly running for the eye's edge and diving into the liquid, silently, without a single splash. So there was life in there, inside the skull.

So Brin had looked into the dragon's eyes?

Cady had done the same. Now what?

The girl had vanished, moved on into the woods, perhaps. But why?

Why come this far, and then move on?

Unless…

Oh fuck. It was madness to even think that…

No. Lud, no! Such a thing could not possibly happen!

Cady bent over again, to stare at herself. She dipped a hand into the liquid and felt the warmth of it, and the pressure on her skin. It had a thick, jelly-like consistency.

Did Brin drown herself?

Cady refused to believe that.

And then the never-never flower seeded into the shape of a woman, a very old woman from the look of it, the puff of tiny seeds hanging in the air for a few moments and then falling into the liquid, every last one of them. They sank beneath.

This was a sign, she knew it. The Deep Root had spoken.

Cady stood up and took a breath.

Then she stepped into the pool of the silver of the eye.

She sank down slowly until her waist, her shoulders, her head disappeared below the surface. Her knotted plait of hair took on the appearance of a strange, semi-mythical water creature. Then that too vanished and the mirror closed over, perfectly, unfathomable, sealing itself with the image of the reflected sky, the trees, and a passing bird.

The woods were quiet.

The Battle of the Skies

All she could see was the silver of the liquid through which she swam. There were no ledges or ridges of bone for her to cling to, no curving wall of the interior of the skull to act as a guide. The silver went on and on and she was lost inside it, spinning this way and that, panicking, scared that her breath would run out. She lunged around and tried to locate the eye socket of the dragon above her, so that she might swim up towards it. But the eye had vanished into the silver and the silver was all there was, and she was lost in it. But she had not been under for very long, less than a minute perhaps. She tried to calm herself, stopping her forward movement and just floating awhile. Her plant-like nature drank of the fluid in the Eye of Haakenur and she was refreshed by it, along her veins and vines. There was no sign of the girl, Brin. But now, staring upwards, Cady saw that a slight gleam played within the silvery expense. Was that the surface of the Eye? It had to be! She swam towards the light, feeling herself lifted up by the liquid, as though it were a living substance, a creature of some kind. Perhaps a relative of Psephekarnidraxapor? A shape could be seen, very like the outline of a small boat as viewed from below.

She moved towards it. Her breath started to run out but at last she broke the surface and bobbed there, quickly locating the vessel, a rowing boat afloat on a silver lake. There was a number 9 painted on the side, its only identifying mark.

She clambered over the side and fell into the well of the boat, her body sprawled across the boards. Only now did she realise just how tired she was. Her lungs worked at a rapid pace to gather air. It was clean air, no salt in it. No breeze, no sky above, only clouds the exact same colour as the lake: silver. All and everything was silver, except for the brown and cream paint of the rowing boat and her own clothes of navy blue and tartan. When she sat up she saw the surface of the lake spreading out in all directions until it reached a blurred horizon line. It was more of a sea than a lake, yet there was no tide pull. Hers was the only craft in sight. The only proper feature was a bank of fog to the port side, but this too bore the same silvery hue. No stars to steer by, no sun or moon. She took her place on the thwart and picked up the oars, placing them in the rowlocks. She pulled at a steady rate, not wanting to tire herself further, heading towards the mist, for she knew a coastal fog when she saw one. Her instincts were good. After a few minutes of rowing a smudge of land came into view. The fog closed around her, but she had a heading now and she kept on, praying that her old navigational skills would prove true.

Soon enough the keel of the boat ran aground on a pebbly shore. Cady climbed out. The fog had taken over the landscape completely so that only a short stretch of beach was visible and beyond that the hint of a grass verge. There was another rowing boat – number 5 – pulled up on the shingle with a sailor sitting in it, looking at Cady casually. She went over to him, making a greeting, but he could not answer for his

mouth was covered with a gag of cloth. He made no attempt
to remove this, but only stared at Cady with his dark eyes,
nodding. He was of middling years, neat of appearance, a
fine-looking oarsman. But he would not speak.

Cady asked, "Did you carry a young girl across?"

He nodded.

"Recently, was it?"

He shrugged.

"Minutes ago? An hour ago?"

He nodded at this.

"One hour ago, or thereabouts?"

Another nod.

"Good, good. I am on course. Tell me, where did she go
to, after disembarking?"

The sailor stood up in the beached rowing boat and pointed
over the grass. Cady squinted, for the fog was still hanging
low over the ground. But some buildings could be made out
in the near distance. When Cady turned back she saw that
the fog had left the water, which was now revealed not as a
vast lake of silver tears, but more like a boating pond.

She set off walking along a central pathway between
formal gardens. There were carefully shaped trees and edged
flowerbeds and immaculately striped lawns. Not exactly
Nature gone wild and Cady felt herself a voracious weed
among such dainty specimens. This was a public park of
some kind, but not one she had visited before in her travels.
She had no idea of the time but it was still early enough for
the place to be deserted. The sun shone down, and all was
peaceful. Before her was a regal palace, a massive house of
red and fawn bricks with many windows both rectangular
and circular and a host of decorative features. She looked
back one last time and saw that the boating lake was now

nothing more than a marble fountain with a small pond around it. The mist and the rowing boats and the mute oarsman had vanished.

Cady's journey through the Eye was complete.

But where was she?

She stopped to study a painted map at the end of the pathway. *Hampton Court Palace and Gardens.* No, she had never heard of such a place. But the blue ribbon of a waterway was shown at the map's edge and it was marked *The River Thames.* So she was back in London. A glance over the land to where the river lay showed the air was clear of Gogmagog's smog, so perhaps she had landed beyond the limits of the Night Serpent's reach. One particular feature on the map drew her attention and she noted the directions and set off again, taking the left-hand path along the side of the house until she reached a gateway in a hedge. This led to a garden named *The Wilderness,* according to the sign. Yes, a little more wild, but still firmly under control. She crossed this, taking a diagonal path between trees and flowering shrubs until she reached the location that interested her.

Hampton Court Garden Maze.

There was a motorcycle parked at the entrance, but no sign of any other visitors or gardeners. Why was the place so empty?

But Cady was feeling confident. Surely, after finding her way through the Tangle Wood, this had to be easy, right? But with her first step through the entranceway the air turned gloomy and cold. The tall hedges of yew closed in tightly. She took a right-hand turning and quickly reached a dead-end. As she knew already, the Deep Root was quiet in this world, so she would have to work with something other than instinct. Pissing hell, she would gleefully drink a whole bottle of Best Navy Rum right now, to get herself stoked up in belly and brain. Instead of which she pulled a few leaves off the hedge and chewed on them, seeking both sustenance and knowledge. A bit of the former, none of the latter. The left-hand way took her further into the maze, and she made good progress, turning this way and that, until she found herself in another cul-de-sac where her curses set the twigs trembling. On top of which she was now missing her walking cane, for the vines and stems holding her together were coming loose. This damn place! London, England. She had so little power here, only aches and pains, and rheumatism, and several cases of sooty mould, leaf rust and petal wilt. And never mind the dodgy ticker. Soon be time for the compost heap.

She retraced her steps and took another pathway, trying to construct a map in her head. She dearly wished that Messrs Maguire & Hill were with her right now, to guide the way. But then a voice called from within or beyond the hedge: "Cady, sweetheart? Is that you?"

"It might be. Who's asking?"

"Joyce Hicks. Green Lady of this parish."

"Joyce!" Cady bent down and tried to peer through. There was nothing to be seen but a patch of darkness, for the branches were too thickly bound. But the voice was clearly heard.

"That's right, Cady, it's me. How on earth did you get here?"

"In the blink of an eye."

"What?"

"It's a long story."

"Are you lost?"

Cady harrumphed. "Oh, I wouldn't go that far."

"Do you know which way to go?"

"Not as such. Haven't a clue, actually. Not till I get my compass cleaned."

"Okey-dokey. Let me think."

Cady waited. It didn't take long before the directions came through the hedge: "Walk back the way you came until you reach a three-way junction, then do a U-turn to the left, you got that?"

"A U-turn."

"Sharp as you can. Then keep going, and we'll bump into each other."

All proved good and within five minutes Cady and Joyce met and embraced within the maze. Joyce was dressed in suede jodhpurs and a tailored tweed jacket and sported a pair of motoring goggles hanging around her neck.

"Was that your motorcycle at the entrance?" Cady asked.

"She's a beauty, isn't she? I was a Flying Wren during the last years of the war."

"A what?"

"A dispatch rider. Women's Royal Naval Service. We carried messages from base to base, all over the land. You'll never guess, I had some orders for D-Day in my bag once. Of course, I wasn't to know that at the time. All hush-hush and mum's the word–"

"Joyce?"

"Yes?"

"What's going on?"

"A spot of bother, old duck. Heard it on the Green Way." She tried to keep up her bravado but there was a glint of fear in her eyes. "Gogmagog is gathering himself from the Thames. He's heading this way."

"And where are we, exactly?"

"Hampton Court. West of the city. This knot garden was built on the place where Smogface first arrived in England, yonks ago, before he drifted downstream and settled himself at his current limits. But now he's on the move again, coming back home."

"Back to the source. Right. Of course."

"This place has always been sacred," Joyce explained. "There was a stone circle here at one point, then a witch's coven, then a Roman temple, then the King's hunting grounds where the golden hart roamed. The maze is the latest marker. Come on, follow me."

The younger woman knew her way around the pathways, and put on quite a speed, so that Cady was both breathless and dizzy by the time they reached the final turnings. Suddenly Joyce stopped her with an arm across the chest.

"What is it?"

"Shush!"

Cady could hear very little but the morning breeze and the leaves rustling.

Joyce held up her hand. "There! A crackling sound. I've never heard anything like it."

But Cady knew. It was the noise of the Xilliths at play. She looked up into the morning light and saw them flashing and dancing over the hedgerows, hardly visible in this clean air and so far away from their beloved Faynr. It meant only one thing: Brin was here.

"How far is it now, to the centre?"

"Not long to go. This way."

But they were stopped at the very next turning by the sound of something heavy and powerful at their back, coming along to find them.

"He's here," Joyce whispered. "Gogmagog. He's moving through the pathways, following the maze. This must be important to him, you know, rather than just flying straight in."

"It's his nest," Cady suggested. "And his doorway. One maze to another. He has to do this just right, or else the magic won't work."

The thick black smoke of Gogmagog was now visible above the yew trees, and the hedgerows close by were shivering, their roots rattling in the soil. Joyce's face changed in an instant, taken over by leaves and little red flowers. A mask of green. Cady had no such protection. She turned at the last second to see the smog monster speeding around the previous turning, his body bending at weird angles as he drove forward. He was darker and smuttier than ever, packed to the limits with grime and muck, coagulated with oil, painted with soot, furred with ashes, glued together with slime and mould and germs and chunks of torn hair and shreds of rotten flesh, his entire body of thirty miles length crowded into this single garden maze. He had the strength now of a physical being. Rooks and crows and blowflies and beetles travelled with him, flying within the tightly packed smoke, dragged along by his sheer power. Onwards! Next came a wave of tiny pebbles drawn along in the forcefield, pummelling at Cady's face like hailstones. Onwards, onwards! It felt like she was being run over by a steam engine, but Gogmagog was paying no attention to her, nor to Joyce Hicks. The two figures meant nothing; mere shit scraped off his ghostly arse. He roared over them, around them, and through them. Onwards!

Joyce's leaves were blasted back against her skin, her flowers stripped away.

The grit in Cady's eyes felt like ground glass.

The rush of the wind almost knocked her off her feet.

She screamed but the scream was whipped away, caught in Gogmagog's slipstream.

The women clung to each other. Somehow or other Joyce managed to hand over the motoring goggles and Cady put these on. They were both bent double, pushed up against the hedges, feeling like a pair of butterflies caught in the turbine of a jet. Cady's knot of hair was almost torn out at the root; she could feel the skin stretching on the back of her skull and all down her back. Even her tattoos wanted to vacate her skin, and join the cavalcade.

The smokestorm went on for five minutes, unrelenting.

It stank of the charnel house.

And when at last it came to a halt the demon body of smoke settled itself into Hampton Court maze, occupying every twist and turn and dead-end, from entranceway to centre. Cady and Joyce dared to unbend themselves. The leaves and petals on the Green Lady's face were cut to ribbons, while the Haegra's face was bloody, lacerated all over. Cady smeared a little of this away. At least the goggles had protected her eyes. The smog was all around them, tightly packed between the hedgerows, and obscuring the sky. It was pitch black. Daylight had been sent into exile. The two women were coughing and groaning; they could barely speak. But Joyce took Cady's hand and led her by feel around the next two turnings.

They were now at the centre of the maze.

The Xilliths lighted the scene, their violet and blue flashes and crackle-sparks turning the scene into a bizarre theatre set, where Brin was the witch and Gogmagog the conjured demon. The girl stood at the centre, standing calmly to attention. The monster's form could not be made out, for it had no real shape as yet; a river's worth of smog had arrived here and been crammed between the walls of the maze. The air pressure was intense. Every part of Cady was being probed and pressed at. Her bones and branches creaked. Her tiniest twigs snapped in two, and her bindings came unravelled. Poor Joyce Hicks had it worse; her hair was pushed out of shape, her face looked like a fright mask. She had to hold onto the walls of the maze to stop herself from being knocked to the ground and squashed. Cady tried to move. It was hopeless. Her feet might as well have been sunk in glue. All she could do now was to watch in horror, as the Summoning spell began.

Brin raised her hands, moving them carefully in a crafted gesture. First of all she spoke aloud her full and true name: "I am Sabrina Clementine Far-Sight Abigail Maid-Of-The-Vale Xiomara Delphine Poppy-Moth Mina-Moth Marion Hollenbeck Halsegger the Third." Her voice was caught up in the Night Serpent's body of smoke and amplified. "While good Queen Luda slept within the womb of Haakenur, she was fed by the dragon's blood. From Luda that blood has flowed through time, in the veins of the Alkhym, affecting a select few boys and girls along the way."

Cady was amazed. The girl was speaking with a tongue part adult, and part childlike, saying things that no child should ever say.

"Yes, there have been children of the dragon before me. Pitiful squirts of piss! For I am not born of that blood. That blood bores me! Other fluids were taken into Luda's body in the womb. I am Sabrina Halsegger. I was born from the poison Haakenur used to paralyse her victims, and to defeat her enemies." Her little hands reached out within the smog.

She cried out: "I am poison!" She punched the air. She danced wildly about, as the spell took her over. Her two hesti were pinging and shining, drawn in the dark of the day as two curved lines of light. Cady was alarmed to see some of her own Way of the Willow movements in the mix of the dance; she had taught the girl too well, and was now paying for it, forced to watch this demonic ritual.

"I am your poison gland, Gogmagog. I have returned myself to you. I was born, and I arose to seek you out. To deliver your venom back to you, in its physical form. Once again, you will bite and spit and hiss and burn and tear asunder!"

The black smog whirled about the centre of the maze at speed. He was taking great delight in this litany of dread. Cady understood now the Night Serpent's incessant need to feed on muck and rottenness and dead things; he was desperately trying to return the missing poison to his body, his most essential fluid.

Now Brin came to a sudden halt, her arms raised, her voice quiet.

Language had come to an end, useless beyond this point. Instead she was groaning, moaning, wailing, howling.

Head back, she gazed up into the black sky of her master.

Then she vomited. Blood and bile, both of them as tarry as night.

It was horrible to witness.

This sweet girl of tender years who had turned up at Cady's door, hardly daring to speak at first, hiding herself, shivering and trembling. Now she retched madly, her whole body convulsing in a sudden movement of stomach, throat and mouth, overtaken by this one desire, to eject everything she had carried this far, from conception, from birth. Gogmagog drank it up. He adored it. He licked and snuffled at it. A ragged maw opened up in the fog of his face, enclosing the vomit. He choked on it, and enjoyed the choking.

Brin fell limp, her arms hanging down, her head bowed, knees slightly bent. Her attendant Xilliths lay in wilted strands dangling from her fingers. A puppet with its strings cut.

Gogmagog rose up. His body unwound itself from the length of the maze.

He roared. He spat out a rain of black ice, of rats and crows, of grey ashes from the burnings of all good things, of beetles and lice, of faeces and maggots and clumps of weed and engine oil and the matted fur of flea-bitten dogs and pus and infected blood. He stained innocence with his spittle. He painted the daylight sky with dark and darkened the dark further until the sun was blotted.

The land was eclipsed.

He was now an all-powerful being, the unholy incarnation.

Night Serpent Supreme.

Cady and Joyce quivered at the sight. But the monster was still here, still stuck in this world. How would he make the journey back to Kethra? At least by now the pressure had let up, and Cady could move a little. She saw Brin raising herself up to her full height. The girl's face was blank, her eyes pinpricks focused on the centre of nothingness. She held in her hand a small object.

Cady saw it. Even amid the thick smoke of Gogmagog, it sparkled.

It was a coin, the Ludluda coin.

Cady tried to reach Brin in time, not even knowing what the girl was up to, what the final part of the spell might entail, only that it must be stopped.

Brin flicked the coin into the air.

It went up high, spinning about, revealing each side in turn to Gogmagog's sight.

Lud, Luda, Lud, Luda, Lud, Luda, Lud, Luda.

Ludluda, Ludluda, Ludluda!

The Xilliths were roused. They flashed and struck at the coin as it reached its peak, hovered for a moment, an impossible moment, and then began to slowly fall. Too late, far too late, Cady banged into Brin, knocking the girl off balance. They ended up on the ground together. Cady could see the coin in the air above her, the Xilliths striking it repeatedly as lightning will strike at the spire of a church, over and over, in anger at the useless god or a wicked people.

It blurred and brightened, catching fire.

The air parted around the coin, expanded. A doorway was opening, a circular doorway, and through it Cady could see a giant eye staring back at her.

Not the silvery eye of the skull, but a real eye.

The eye of the living dragon, Haakenur, as it must have looked out over the primordial land during her lifetime. Cady had never been looked at so deeply, or so closely. Every last detail of her life was witnessed, and known, and stored away.

The eye blinked.

And blinked again.

And then opened wide, and stayed open this time.

Gogmagog dived into the centre of the dragon's eye, his entirety dragged along behind him. Cady and Brin were directly below this all-consuming force. The coin was falling towards Cady's face. The dragon's eye opened wide enough to engulf the Haegra, pulling her along. The last thing Cady saw of London was Joyce Hicks, that lovely face of flowers and leaves. And of sadness.

And then the eye closed.

Cady was aware of Brin's hand holding onto hers as they travelled. That one point of human contact kept her from going insane, a victim torn apart in a screaming surge of silvery light and smoke. But then the little hand was whipped away from her. Far below she glimpsed the lake of limitless silver, and then that too was gone. She was alone now.

The Ludluda coin fell to earth.

Cady saw it there, resting in the grass.

It was close to her face.

She too was lying on the ground. She tested herself bit by bit, bone by twig, happy to know that everything was still intact, at least to a degree. Her seeds were present, still clustered about her optic gland. Her head ached and her joints were numb. But she was alive, in both flesh and flower. Her eyes, wet with blood from her wounded face, did their best to take in her surroundings. She was resting in the undergrowth of the Tangle Wood near to the skull of Haakenur. Strangely, her shoes had disappeared, perhaps torn off in the explosion as the All-Seeing Eye had opened and closed. Her feet were filthy, gnarled with veins and studded with sores, all of them weeping pus. She sat up and looked around. Brin was curled up nearby in a position of repose, breathing gently. Thrawl Dee had disappeared from his waiting place near the dragon skull. Cady hoped he had set off on a return journey through the woods, heading back to the boat, and Jeb Yeomanson.

There was no sign of Gogmagog. *Dear sweet Lud, I have failed in my task. The Night Serpent has come through and is even now journeying towards Ludwich.* That was all she could think.

Brin was stirring. Cady was immediately on full alert. But the girl had an innocent look on her face; all evidence of the ceremony of darkness had vanished from her features. She was a girl once more, an Alkhym youngster, freshly hested and ready for the best that life could offer.

But Cady brought out her thorns nonetheless, from the skin of her palms.

Brin looked at her, blinking back tears.

"Can you remember what happened, Brin?"

The girl nodded.

"You know what you did?"

"Of course. But where's Gogmagog? Where is he?"

Cady didn't answer. She watched as Brin knelt up. They were sitting not too far from each other in the shadow of the skull.

"I don't feel too well, Mrs Meade."

"I see that. Your hesti are bleeding."

The girl touched at her temples, and then looked at her fingers, smeared with red. The blood darkened as it flowed from the tiny wounds that had opened in the skin. Brin looked frightened. She tried to speak, but could not manage a word. The lengths of blood now looked like two hideous tapeworms that had lived deep inside the girl's body. On and on they came, seeping out from her head, onto the grass, heavy with their own substance. They crawled away, one to the left, one to the right, through the undergrowth. The further they went, the darker they became. Now they took on the appearance of black smoke.

Brin laughed. What a delight this was!

Cady stood up quickly.

Gogmagog had become a stowaway for the final part of the journey. Brin was his vessel. Now he was escaping into the good air of Kethra, rising up, the two strands pulling free of the girl's hesti, meeting and twisting about, combining into one being. He grew tall and slender, a wavering form, a wraith, but nothing at all like he was in London, or as he had presented himself at Ponperreth. Not strong, not massive, but almost human in form, and frail. He was contained in some way, perhaps weakened by the journey through the Eye. But then Cady saw the truth: the Night Serpent was snarled in the neighbouring woodland plants and trees. The bindweeds were about his feet, and the prickle bushes were stabbing and hooking at his legs and torso, and the spike trees were a ligature around his neck, and the russet-toned hexbane flowers were shooting their peppery sprays at him. The old Wodwo priests were still at their game, down the long years. The Tangle Wood did its best to keep Gogmagog in his place. He struggled, howling in frustration, pouring his smoky tendrils every which way he could, only to be dragged back and caught afresh by the twigs of murkwood and knotted oak. He spat out poison, burning leaves and branches, but the plants quickly brought out new feelers and vines to wind about him tightly. Hope stirred in Cady's heart.

The gate was holding!

Brin had seen this as well. She made one of her little choked-off screams and then agitated her Xilliths into action. They spread out from her raised hands and she flung them through the air with great force, towards Gogmagog. He received them gladly. Girl and ghost were now joined, and she could easily tear him free from his woodland bindings. His body of smoke was shaped by the Xillith waves, and just as Brin had forged Faynr into Haakenur's shape on the Night of the Dragon, now she did the same for Faynr's brother. She gave him form, a monstrous form. The last bondage was broken, as twigs and thorns and roots snapped and broke apart. The trees shivered. Rain fell, hitting the half-buried skull of the dragon, hissing off Gogmagog's skin of oil and excrement. He rose higher into the air, smashing a way through the wood's canopy. Branches fell around Cady. She had to duck out of the way of them. Then she looked up and saw the Night Serpent in all his glory. Brin had shaped him into a dragon of her own imagination, a thing of the darkest part of her mind. Perhaps Gogmagog was feeding her his shape in some way, via the hesti. The girl's body was arched backwards, totally given over to the act of creation. She was ten years old and already a true artist of the dragon world, changing the shape of Gogmagog as she saw fit, making him now a creature of dark poison with black wings all tatty at their edges, and a breath of black fire; and next reforming him to a more nebulous shape, like the great cloud of gas left behind by the explosion of the Crystal Bomb at Yaniphar, the likes of which had ended the war. Quickly after this Gogmagog turned into the gigantic face of a man, a likeness of Brin's father, the traitor Lord Halsegger. Anger flared in the man's eyes. And then he became the Night Serpent personified: no wings, no fire, just the long writhing body of smog and soot and shit, curling about the clouds, eating birds and beetles and all manner of flying beasts, his eyes of yellow sickness driving him forward into the future he dreamed of. In this form he raged in the sky, his rightful domain.

Cady was dazed. She felt the weight of the years. She wished to stride forth in battle but her feet clung to the earth, old and tired. Only her seeds were young, and they glowed within her brow. They desired only to burst free and find fertile ground. Well, the Tangle Wood would do nicely, she guessed. If the woods still existed after Gogmagog had finished, that is, for the treetops were smouldering already, and were sooted and smutted all over, and the green leaves were dying on the branches as though autumn had come early.

With some last ounce of strength, Cady staggered towards Brin, only to be met with a blast of Xillithic power that scorched her and set her hair sizzling, throwing her back into a bush of spikes, where she fell. The Haegra screamed out in her pain and despair and scratched at her own face with her fingers and thorns, to drive herself into action. She dug deep enough to reach the bone. Words flooded her mouth along with blood: they had to be spoken. But to whom? She was alone here. Her only company was a never-never plant growing from the soil close to her face. She whispered into it, using the trumpet of petals like a microphone: "I have worked out your riddle. I've found the bell, the grave, and the bomb. I have done everything you asked, journeyed to this place."

The flower made no reply.

But Cady had an inkling of a new idea, a plan of attack. She leaned in even closer to the never-never: "Now I ask in return that you pass this message on for me."

And still, the flower did not respond. Cady's hopes fell. She was weakening.

Then she thought of Joyce Hicks, lovely Joyce, the Flying Wren of London. And that brought to mind George Dunstan in his sickbed above the pub, that old man taken over by Gogmagog, yet managing nonetheless to speak with his own voice, that poem, that rhyme, how he insisted that she heard it, his hands grabbing at her, not letting go.

There was a need, a need to speak!

Cady's lips pressed against the never-never, her tongue entering the petals. She didn't even have to recall the words, they came of their own accord, cast by spectral pathways.

"Where the bee sucks, there suck I. Where flowers bloom, there bloom I. Where beetles wing, there wing I. Where caterpillars crawl, there crawl I. Where blackbirds peck, there peck I." And then, after a pause: "Where the dragon roars, there roar I."

Her lips were dry, her voice croaky. Breath rasped in her throat.

"Come to me, Faynr, come!"

She could imagine the message being sent on from one root system to the next, from one leaf to the next, from one flower to the next, along the line of the Nysis until it reached the ghost's head far down the eastern reaches of the river at Woodwane Spar. It was here that Cady's message would be heard, or so she hoped. Her mouth was pressed tightly against the never-never's petals, as she repeated the summoning: "Come to me, good Faynr!"

Gogmagog did not hear this call, nor did Brin. The girl brought the Serpent down on her reins of Xillith and let him play among the trees, dancing about the skull of his mother, Haakenur. He licked at the skull and dipped a tongue of smoke into the Eye. He was stealing every last ounce of power that he could for his journey downriver.

Cady's voice rang out again, much louder, making the petals shiver: "Faynr! Ludwich needs you. Fly to me!"

Gogmagog rolled and tumbled. But he stopped suddenly. His yellow eyes flashed.

There was an answering sound to Cady's call.

The leaves rustled. A wind blew the rain slantwise, cold and heavy. The ground shook with fury. It felt like an earthquake. The dragon skull shuddered. The bone-white lizards leapt for safety. Brin turned to Cady, a sudden look of fear on her face. Xillith sparks filled the air. Gogmagog trembled. He crouched like a scared animal in the woods, or else like a predator in hiding for its chosen prey. Cady wished she could see along the Nysis right now, to witness Faynr in her travels. The waters would part in a twin wave before the speeding, gathering form, as the ghost returned home to the tangled woods.

The rain spat down, flattening the grass and stirring the branches into dark glitter. Cady's hair was soaking wet. There was an almighty creaking sound and then a young elm tree was uprooted, to be flung through the air, crashing into its partners.

Faynr arrived.

The ghost came in along the Herne tributary, tearing the sky open with her howling. In form she resembled images of herself depicted in illuminated manuscripts, shiny-scaled and striped red and gold along her length. Her head was that of a giant lizard, her jaws those of a big cat. Her fangs flashed with jewels and a wreath of flame shot out from the mouth. Her war paint was a blue stripe from top of brow to end of snout. All over her outer skin were the scabs and wounds of the sickness. She did not possess wings, but flew nonetheless, being lighter than air when she needed to be, a ghost merely; and as hard as iron when needed, made solid by the binding of the Xilliths that ran around her body. In this form, Faynr was as long, from head to spiked tail, as the Tangle Wood was across. The rain sparkled within her body in a cascade of silver. Her claws were hooked and badly damaged but still deadly, crusted with dried blood and the fragments of her victims from the ancient days. She passed overhead, whipping the treetops back and forth, and then turned back in a great swooping arc to hover above the hidden place known as Ludluda.

Xilliths poured out from Brin's fingertips and from the centre of her chest in flashing swathes of violet-blue fire, each one added to the mass of them all, in order that Gogmagog might keep his most powerful shape, that of the Night Serpent. He grew as long as a twelve-carriage locomotive, taking glorious power from his opponent's arrival. He had been waiting for this clash for centuries, and now his anger was fed by newfound malice. His body was a dart aimed at Faynr's heart.

The two dragon ghosts met over the Tangle Wood.

The Battle of the Skies had begun.

Gogmagog wasted no time. He spat out venom from his mouth.

The poison ravaged through his sister, burning into her exposed chest, entering the soft part of her neck where a sore of her sickness lay.

She screamed in pain.

The scream was unheard, but felt in the earth that trembled, and within Cady's skull.

Now Faynr lashed out wildly in retaliation, digging her claws into the body of her brother. But he turned his skin into smoke at the point of attack, and was scarcely harmed by the blow.

Cady looked on and despaired. Brin and Gogmagog working together were too powerful and the old Haegra had nothing to help Faynr with, her plant magic was useless here. Even if she could uproot every tree and turn them into clubs, it would have little effect.

The rain drove against her face.

Brin was seen as a blurred figure in the downpour, lit by the Xilliths that surrounded her and that streamed out of her. Blood was dribbling down from her hesti.

The two dragon ghosts whipped about, entangled with each other, leaping in acrobatic circles and loop-de-loops, hooking and scraping, sometimes fighting like two cats, at others like cockerels in a dirt pit, ducking and weaving and then attacking. Their claws struck each other in defensive postures. Locked so, they struggled for supremacy, each making the same claim: these are my woodlands, this is my land!

Cady heard them speaking thus, like rabid dogs fighting for territory.

Then they stopped suddenly to stare at each other.

Gogmagog's yellow moons of sickness ranged against Faynr's silver hot starlight in the orbs, starlight that had floated here from the home planet.

They each of them showed off their fangs. Their faces were scarred and bloody.

They snarled, they spat and hissed and stared each other down like two crystal-rays pointed at each other, each repelling the other equally.

And then they sprang into explosive action once more, stabbing and scratching. Faynr had no poison in her arsenal, but she had a long and powerful spiked tail which she used as a scorpion would, stabbing at her opponent's face, and then swinging it around like a boa constrictor, wrapping it about her brother's body, tightening, tightening.

Gogmagog fought back, with his claws and his burning spittle.

He threw clouds of noxious gas at Faynr, blinding her.

He wounded her at chest and neck and hind leg.

He tore her tail off at the spike and spat it out, with a cry of triumph.

Faynr, howling and writhing in pain, went for his jugular, hoping to catch him unawares, when his body was still in semi-solid form. But his smoke won out.

They both lost their physical forms. Now they fought as two ghosts of breath and shadows, making wounds of the spirit, and black blood flowed in the smoke of Gogmagog, and his yellow eyes blinked, running from the sting of his own poison. Faynr's blood was the colour of Cady's hair: grey, streaked with silver.

And where the two bloods fell, the leaves and branches smouldered, and melted.

Cady felt drops of it on her skin, and winced from the burn.

She screamed out to neuter the pain: "Go, Faynr! Kill, kill! Stab him!"

Faynr did strike, again and again, solidifying her body, fighting with tooth and claw, using her ragged stump of tail as a club, smashing it across Gogmagog's back, hoping to break him. But every blow she made in her opponent was easily met and returned in full.

The skies were lit with fire as the two rival Xillith systems clashed. A sorry old crow caught in the fight was sizzled into black feathers and scattered bones.

Brin was as much a combatant as the two mighty beasts. She devised a new tactic, using her hested powers to steal Xilliths from Faynr's body, stripping the ghost of her nervous system, her messengers, and her skeleton. Without the Xilliths she would be a mist of coloured vapours striped with ectoplasm, nothing more, easily dispersed by the Night Serpent's poisons.

The battle hung on this moment.

Cady wiped the rain from her eyes. She pricked herself with every spike she could find in bush and briar. She took up clumps of worms and stuffed them in her mouth. She chewed on them, taking all of their knowledge, of the soil and the roots. Then she stood up, pulling herself away from the thorn tree. Her hands and face were streaked with mud and sap and blood, a savage mask of war. Her eyes blazed from the Deep Root, staring forth with the vision of the Lord and Lady of All Flowers. She grabbed a branch from a fallen tree and brandished it as she roared out her battle cry.

"This branch of the yew tree, this is my Ibraxus!"

She had, only this morning, promised herself that she would kill the girl, if needs must. Yet now, at the moment of truth, Cady could not even move, for her feet were sunk ankle-deep in the sludge. Her wooden sword swung around. Brin laughed at this petty display, and went on with her warring. But Cady had not yet given up. In her mind she viewed the walled garden where the spirit of the Lud flower lived. She saw the King's hand dipping into the water of the pool. This time, he managed to grasp the hilt of the sword. He drew it from the water.

The vision lasted a few seconds only, but Cady was driven into power by it. She called out loudly: "Ibraxus! Forged in the Deep with the spirit of King Lud!" And this time when she waved the yew branch towards Brin, it gathered Xilliths for itself from the girl's body, a lightning rod. It glowed! This burst of Xilliths travelled down the branch and into Cady. Little Brin was too busy to even notice. The energy spread along the veins of the old Haegra, into the stems and shoots, rootlets and fibres. Every part of her was flowing with magic. The substitute Ibraxus fell from her hand, its part in the fight over. Now Arcadia Watchwoman Meade was illuminated, like a figure taken from an old Wodwo manuscript. Her optic gland burst into green flame in her skull. The seeds vibrated around it, and then they took flight, erupting from her skin, all of them at once. Her brow was pricked open in many places, but she felt no pain, only ecstasy.

The seeds were tiny, unseen in the rain and the smog and the Xillith storm.

Only Cady knew they were there.

She tracked each one of them, even through the blood that filled her eyes. What need did she have now for sight? None! She saw the world as the seeds did, as they spun through the air seeking their ground. But they did not fall in the earth, or in the trees, no, but they fell on the ghostly flesh of Faynr. The way was fertile and here the seeds took root, all one hundred and twenty-four of them, each in a different part of the ghost. They formed a constellation, sparkling brightly, attracting the Xilliths with their lights and their warmth. Many such made the journey across to Faynr, away from Gogmagog. The star paths formed between the two ghosts.

Brin raised her hands higher, she cried into the wind and the rain. Her eyes had rolled back, showing the whites only. Her body shivered in the trance of battle.

Cady sank to her knees in the mud. The earth welcomed her. She sensed each and every seed where it lay in Faynr's body. In her mind each pathway between each seed was a street of Ludwich, not the fancy shopping arcades and boulevards, but the places where pickpockets and drunkards and dollymops dwelled, where good people became lost, fallen in sin, cast adrift. The street names were a poem of the lower levels: Breakheart Lane,

Hanging Hill, East Woebegone, Old Lurch, Side of the Heel, Deadman's Court, West Wing of Crow, Whorehouse Walk, Black Shroud, The Grindstone, Pint of Blood Alley, Matilda's Axe, Pauper's Ditch, South Pennypinch, The Mocking Gate, Lower Hoodwink. Many more. This was Cady's world, here had she lived down the ages. And now she travelled them all in the dark of her eyes, criss-crossing the fields of Faynr, hoping to heal the war wounds of the ghost with this spell of the streets, shaping Faynr just as Brin shaped Gogmagog.

The two dragons met again and again in the sky.

Thunder sounded where they clashed.

Boom, boom!

Faynr took each flood of poison and spat it back, twice as deadly.

Xilliths locked together, striking sparks off each other.

The trees burned as far as the rain would allow.

But Gogmagog was weakening under the renewed strength of Faynr.

The seed armour bonded her body into a killing engine made of ghost flesh and the sparks of distant stars and the seeds of the Haegra. She went for her brother's eyes, tearing one of them out. Smoke poured free, littered with all the pestilential visions carried in the demon's head. He faltered under the fierce attack.

Now, Faynr, now!

Cady's voice was tiny, driven by wind and rain. But Faynr heard it nonetheless. She saw her chance, and took it, striking a fatal blow to the heart.

The Night Serpent plunged down towards the earth, shedding his black blood along the way.

The Xilliths left him, unravelling in the air.

Brin screamed at them to return to their task. The blood streamed down her face from where her hesti were torn: the sheer effort of the magic was breaking her, damaging her. And it was all to no avail. Gogmagog burst open into dust, ashes, grit and grime, into oil and grease, and bits of bone and patches of torn flesh. By the time he reached the ground his body was no more, but only made of a shrivelling stench that lost all hope of darkness. He fell as a sticky black ichor on the leaves and the grasses, and was quickly eaten up by bugs and flies and ants. Birds pecked at his remains. Oh, they supped heartily on him!

A silence took over the Tangle Wood.

Cady wiped the blood from her face. The woodlands were blurred and hazy in the aftermath of war. The dragon skull was trembling in the ground. A mist of dreams emerged from the Eye of Haakenur, drawn from the silvery pool by the death of Gogmagog, dreams the world had not known since Luda lay within the creature's womb all those years, adding her thoughts to those of the dragon, intermingling. The dreams of a mother transmitted to the incubating child. Now these same dreams appeared in the air, but only old Cady Meade saw them. She felt the bliss of them. They could not be described, only known for a moment before they faded.

It was done. Brin Halsegger had fallen against the lower slopes of the skull, half hidden by the flowers. Was she still alive, or dead? Cady could not tell. She would have gone over to check on the girl, to help her if necessary, but no movement was possible. Not now. Not now. Cady was sunk in the soil up to her knees. Her roots went deep, clutching. She could no longer see clearly. Her fingers were broken and crooked like the twigs of a blasted tree. Her body had cracked open in so many places, they could not be counted.

Her skin was more bark than anything that resembled flesh. Her hair was in tatters, the long knot untying itself, allowing leaves to sprout from her skull. Her back was bent. Her arms had already been colonised by lichen and aphids.

She was dying.

The years fell away, the regrowths, the struggles and temptations, the caresses, the wounds. The loves she had known, and the hatreds, they all fell away. The last of her was blood and sap, and even that sang on a little, staining the undergrowth, seeping in, wetting the tubers and mushrooms that grew all around. The last thought of her living mind was of those plants feeding off her, and she smiled. *That's right, you filthy fuckers, drink deep.* Her leaves sparkled with raindrops.

And then the slow, slow closing of the green.

But she was not taken down into the Garden of Dark Earth. She had other destinations. Her spirit was in the body of Faynr now, where those seeds had planted themselves.

The ghost of the dragon made its way back towards the River Nysis.

Cady went with her, distributed around the body. There was no one spot where she dwelled, but everywhere at once, more concentrated around the seeding points and spreading out from there. She saw the river below through these one hundred and twenty-four eyes. She saw the *Juniper* making its way downstream with young Jeb at the helm and Thrawl Dee lying stretched out on the foredeck. The ghost swooped down to bond with the water. Now the *Juniper* was witnessed from within and without by the many eyes. Jeb had one hand on the wheel, the other holding some object. It was a blue crystal. It was Lek. Lek's spirit, his Library, his many

rooms and corridors, his Gallery of Faces. Thrawl Dee must
have picked up the crystal on his way back to the boat. It
was good to see. But neither Jeb nor Dee nor Lek had any
inkling of her presence.

Cady flew onwards, as Faynr flew onwards, allowing her
body of light and colour to take on its accustomed shape.
They reached the outskirts of the city, passing over the Thorn
Gate, enjoying the river as it wound through the streets
and parks of Beltane Way. The Cady seeds were already
blossoming, each one a spirit flower. The ghost frolicked
madly as she rode the Nysis home. Her sickness was being
drawn out by the flowers, turning them a darker colour in
the petals. But these affected petals withered and fell away
immediately, and fresh blooms sprang up in their place.
Cady knew them as the Ludluda flowers. It would take a
while yet, this cleansing, perhaps weeks, months, years, but
she would make it happen. Helping her, the Xilliths flew
from one seeding point to another, weaving a frame for the
ghost's new form.

They reached the centre of the city. Crowds of people
were assembled along the banks of the Nysis. Cady
imagined they had been worried by Faynr's disappearance
from the river and were joyous at her return. They waved
as she passed. Wodwo, Azeel, Alkhym, Nebulim, Ephreme,
a scattering of Thrawls, and the Xillith, which Cady now
saw as a fellow tribe. All were kindred. Glimpsed among
them were many of the people of Cady's life as they went
about their Saturday pleasures: Lord Pettifer at the landing
stage near his house in Old Hallows; her sister Nabs among
the crowds at Steadwick market, all looking riverwards;
Yanish her former cabin boy sitting on an upturned boat,
among friends; Maguire and Hill at Medlock Isle poring

over their maps; and in a room above a waterside pub, her cousin Oswyn practising with his band, the Eels of Ludwich, no doubt already writing a song of the battle seen in the western skies.

Bound together in their shared body, Faynr and Cady reached the House of Witan, where the Old Bell of Bleary was striking the ninth hour of the morning. They saw the clusters of boats, crew and passengers alike looking up in wonder at the return of the dragon's ghost. Cady knew them all, these roughneck sailors, randy stevedores, rowdy riverwomen and drunken captains, each sharing the spirit of the water. The ghost skimmed the surface, sending up waves of greeting. Then they flew on through the docklands, visiting all the towns and villages that lined the river: Witherhithe, Grimley, Mallom, Nevernorton, East Trough, Hawkhampton, Islingword and beyond.

And further downriver they went, leaving the city by the Tithe Gate, travelling east, passing Ludforsakenland, the Glimmie, the ruins of the Thrawl Factory at Luhm, and Ponperreth. All of the places Cady had visited and sailed through so many times since her first seeding, now visited again in her final blossoming. And so at last they came to Woodwane Spar, where the ghost reached her natural limits. Here the Haegra rested, taking delight. Her thoughts were melding with those of Faynr; soon they would think not as two separate beings, but as one. The Ludluda flowers were by now all dressed in blue and yellow petals. Via root and stem and blossom, Cady became aware of the collected dreams of Ludwich – the heartfelt folk songs, ludic spells, the birthing cries in the tenements, the old tales of love and loss, the nightly arguments and reconciliations. The dreams joined with Faynr, and with Cady. They were drawn together as a current, taking a slow winding way back and forth along the river, through silver sun and moonlight, two ghosts carrying the city's lifeblood on each day's tide, at ebb and flood, ever renewing.

Card No. 46. The Tangle Wood. Every schoolchild knows that the first Wodwo priests created the Tangle Wood to protect the source of the Faynr. A host of surveyors and scientists have disappeared into its mysterious folds, never to be seen again. How many, though, know that the Tangle Wood was designed not just to keep trespassers out, but to trap demons within? Trolls and Snake People and Dung Eaters roam its endlessly twisting pathways, caught forever within a world of shadows.

Monocle Cigarette Cards – The Haunted River

Epilogue

The group consisted of twenty-one people. They moved along the fenced pathways, keeping to the permitted areas as requested by the tour guide. At each of the clearings he stopped the group to perform his spiel, telling stories of the magical woodland, delving into the history of the place. The punters were getting bored; they wanted to get to the centre of the woods. Even the guide's urgent warnings about not wandering off – for fear of getting lost, and never again found – even these failed to stir. They wanted more. Of course, the guide knew this and he played upon it, teasing them with mentions of the wonders to come. At last they moved on, walking the paths between the trees. They were a mixed bunch: Wodwo schoolkids, Azeelian pensioners, tourists from overseas, family groups, courting couples, a trio of Ephreme teenagers whose wings were decorated with sequins and glitter. Hawkers greeted them at each new turning: "Ludluda coins! Spin the faces of the King and Queen, historically accurate!" One or two of the party were tempted and bought the plastic coins and other items as souvenirs. But the guide pushed everyone on, as quickly as he could.

It was a warm and pleasant afternoon, a fine day for an outing in the countryside. A few other groups were making the rounds of the Tangle Wood, taking detours to the Iron Sentinel, the Pool of Glad Tidings, the Downed Fighter Plane, or the Fallen Sycamore Consumed by Spectral Rot. Strange noises were heard from the thickets, and shadows moved in the darkness of the trees, traces perhaps of the Dung Eaters and other bizarre creatures that were said to live there. Parents gathered their children to them, making sure they stuck to the paths.

The guide brought the group to a halt at a cordoned-off area containing the skeletal remains of a long-ago traveller. This was more like it! People shuffled about to get a better look. The guide told his audience, "For centuries these woodlands were unknowable, a maze of mystery, and of danger. Many explorers came here, very few returned from their wanderings." He gestured towards the poor unfortunate. "These days, because of the after-effects of the Battle of the Skies, we are able to walk the Tangle Wood, at least to a small degree. But there are still areas left to explore, and the further you wander from the path, the weirder the geography becomes. Trees shift position, areas change, the compass needle jumps about. The Darker Woods cannot be mapped." His voice dropped for effect, there was a slight look of disturbance in his eyes. "And people still go missing, half a dozen at least in the last decade."

The group moved on, taking the final turning that led to the centre of the woods. "Here, at the place known as Ludluda, the mighty beast Haakenur fell to earth, and died." He pointed to the giant dragon skull that lay embedded in the ground at the clearing's far edge. "Here also, a quarter of a century ago now, the dragon's two ghosts, Faynr and

Gogmagog, met in aerial combat. At stake was the fate of Ludwich and of the River Nysis. The defeat of the Night Serpent brought about the end of the first great era of our history, and ushered in the dawn of our current period, from the Year of Becoming onwards." People were keen to explore the skull, but the guide kept them back a little longer. He stood before a tree of curious aspect, ringed by a wrought-iron fence. The tree was bent almost double, its branches drooping, leaves coloured a dull green. It was a home to insects, more than any of the neighbouring trees. There were patches of diseased bark dripping with pus-coloured sap, and the twisted roots looked like a giant wooden spider trying to escape the earth.

The guide was pleased to reveal the tree's story: "The sacred Wodwo text, the Book of Dark Eden, tells of the five Great Trees of Kethra. Holiph Oak, Yallax of the Shadow Woods, Catholo, Fotheringall, and Bitterbark. These are known as sources of mystical energies. Now I can't say for certain that this specimen is also a Great Tree, but many followers deem it so." The tourists stared at the tree, but it was evident they thought little of it. The guide made one last attempt to interest them: "They say that the body of a great warrior rests here, beneath the–"

"It's ugly!"

A Wodwo kid made this claim, his spotty face covered in dirt and pollen. His mother told him off, but the mood was broken. People were already drifting away towards the Skull of Haakenur. Some of them gathered at the mouth of the beast, examining the complex array of pipes and tubes that captured the Faynr emitted from the broken jaws, carrying it away through the woods. Of more interest was a flight of steps leading up to the top of the skull. Some of the sightseers were already up there, throwing coins into the empty eye socket, hoping their wishes might come true. Sadly, the silver tears of the eye had been washed away, years ago: little of the magic remained.

Sighing heavily, the guide went over to join the group.

But one person stayed behind, a woman. She was thirty-five, a striking looking Alkhym with hesti of the brightest blue and layered, feather-cut hair. Her clothes were demure but stylish, a fitted jacket with wide lapels, flared trousers and a polka-dotted cravat. In contrast, her face told of a life well-lived, of struggle still unfulfilled: the first lines around the eyes, streaks of grey already in her hair, a far-away look in her gaze. The people in the group had avoided her, and she was happy to be apart from them. She went up to the stunted tree the guide had pointed out. Leaning over the fence, she parted the leaves and then smiled at what was revealed. It was a bulbous outcrop of bark, a burl of quite hideous proportions. From a certain angle it looked like an old woman's face. A very old woman's face. Pitted, scarred, crawling with beetles.

The visitor spoke quietly, addressing the crone of the tree. "There you are, Mrs Meade. What a state you're in."

The leaves rustled, the beetles hurried about their business.

"It's me. Sabrina. You probably don't remember. The commentators say you've moved on, but I can't believe you would leave the wooded world behind completely. No, you're still in there, part of you at least."

The tree made no reply. A bird sang nearby, its notes off-key.

Sabrina murmured to herself: "Twenty-five years." It sounded like a curse, or a warning of some kind. She leaned over further and touched the face of her former friend and enemy.

"Know this, tree hag. I am not done yet."

Then she turned and walked back along the woodland path, alone now, back to the lagoon of the River Herne, where the tourist boats were moored. There was a kiosk here, selling snacks and soft drinks. The captains were chatting to each other, enjoying cups of tea, and smoking. Cabin boys played cards on the afterdeck of the nearest vessel: *snap!* Sabrina had to smile. It took her back to her days aboard the *Juniper*, and that glorious adventure. And the battle. It had become a story in the history books, yet her own name was hardly remembered. She was unrecognised. Perhaps it was best that way, safer, but how she missed those times, when she held such power in her hands. And so every year Sabrina Halsegger returned to the Tangle Wood, on the anniversary, and waited for Cady to speak to her, to offer up a new challenge, or even to open up a door.

London awaited. If she could only find a way through.

She sat down at the river's edge and watched Faynr at her play in the stream. Midges flitted about in the trails of orange mist; fish swam among the pebbles. The water was very clean and clear. Pure. It disgusted her. She couldn't help but think of what might have been, if the battle had tipped the other way, if she had only kept her nerve. To magnify the feeling she took out a cigarette and lit it with a silver lighter, and then dragged deep and held the taste within.

The smoke was black on the exhale, and very slow and tarry. It stank of rot. The plume moved under its own control, forming into shapes.

ABOUT THE AUTHORS

JEFF NOON is an award-winning British novelist, short story writer and playwright. He won the Arthur C Clarke Award for Vurt, the Astounding Award for Best New Writer, and a Tinniswood Award for innovation in radio drama. He was trained in the visual arts, and was musically active on the Manchester punk scene before starting to write plays for the theatre. His Nyquist Mysteries series explores the interzone between crime fiction and SF.

STEVE BEARD is an experimental writer. He is the author of speculative novels and documentary fictions. He has contributed to various anthologies including Suspect Device: Hard-Edged Fiction, London: City of Disappearances, and The Big Book of Cyberpunk. His latest collection of theory fiction Pop Heresiarchs can be found at stevebeard999.substack.com.

We are Angry Robot, your favourite independent, genre-fluid publisher, bringing you the very best in sci-fi, fantasy, horror and everything in between!

Check out our website at www.angryrobotbooks.com to see our entire catalogue.

Follow us on social media:

Twitter @angryrobotbooks
Instagram @angryrobotbooks
TikTok @angryrobotbooks

Sign up to our mailing list now: